I0722139

PACIFIC NORTH WITCH

by

BETH GIBBS

Published in the United States by
Not a Pipe Publishing
www.NotAPipePublishing.com

Paperback Edition

ISBN-13: 978-1-956892-47-5

Cover Art by Michaela Thorn
Design by Benjamin Gorman

To all the would-be witches

searching for their magic:

I want to see you shine,

I want to see you storm,

I want to see you hit the world

like lightning.

Chapter 1

A dingy purple van pulled up to the sidewalk a few feet away from me, the motor rumbling unevenly. Moon phases were painted on the side in black. The driver waved cheerfully at me. I sighed and started toward my ride.

I'd spent the last days of 2017 hospitalized, feeling far older than my twenty-five years. Gray clouds hung low overhead as I walked toward the van. The first day of 2018 felt like a cold rain was on the way with the kind of January damp that seeps in everywhere, settling into the moods of the entire hungover city of Seattle.

I opened the passenger door and got in. My Aunt Sandra sat with her hands on the wheel, looking over at me with an expression full of pity and hope. We hadn't seen each other in seven years, until the call from the doctor had pulled her up from Oregon a few days ago. When she arrived, I wasn't in a space to notice anyone or anything, but now I took the time to notice her.

Sandra's salt and pepper hair was more salt than pepper now. The lines on her face had deepened, her cheeks more sunken and hollowed than before. Her brown eyes still sparkled with warmth and mischief. She smiled at me.

"Are you ready, Reva?" She leaned toward me, feeling me out for a hug. I stayed put. Sandra pulled back.

I nodded and put on my seat belt. Sandra put the van into gear and the car lurched forward. A pitiful yowl came from the backseat followed by a low growl. I turned and looked at the two carriers.

"Tuna hasn't been enjoying the car ride," Sandra said. I peered into the carrier doors, seeing my two gray cats peering back. They looked skinny as their big green eyes stared back at me. Guilt surged through me as I recognized how my episode had impacted them. In December, I hadn't gotten out of bed much. I was sure they hated me. I hated me for neglecting them.

"What about Kiz?" Both of them had nicknames — Tuna for Fortuna and Kiz for Kismet. I had gotten them on an impulse two years ago. Life was finally stable enough then for me to have pets, the cats I had always wanted. Their full names dropped away quickly to nicknames that Anthony had always teased me about, asking why I bothered with the full names at all.

Anthony. There was a name I was trying to forget.

"Kiz seemed sad to leave the apartment, but I think is hesitantly enjoying the car ride." My aunt smiled at me and patted my leg. I kept looking at the cats. I reached my fingers towards Tuna's cage. A gray paw shot out, claws drawn, just missing me. Okay, fair enough. I deserved that. I reached over toward Kiz's cage, putting a finger through the holes in the door. Kiz sniffed tentatively and gave my finger a lick. I pulled back before he decided to turn the lick into a bite. He meowed, accusatory and pitiful at the same time.

"They hate me." I turned around and settled into the seat as Sandra moved us through Seattle traffic, heading to the I-5 freeway.

"They don't hate you. They're just angry. Not an unusual state for a cat in a box," Sandra responded. When I didn't say anything, she continued. "I think they'll like their new home. I think you will, too."

I let the silence fill the car. Though I had agreed to leave Seattle and the crumpled remains of my life, I didn't think I was going to enjoy living with Sandra. There were reasons I hadn't spoken to her for so long; those weren't going to go away on their own.

Not that I had a choice. I had escaped being evicted only by leaving before the process was completed. I had been fired over a month ago from my job for not showing up, not calling. They had tried to reach me, finally calling my emergency contact. My emergency contact listed, though, was Anthony; I hadn't updated it. Not that it mattered.

"We'll see." I realized I sounded like a jerk to my aunt. The woman who had driven hours to help me even though I had barely talked to her for the last seven years. I added, "Thank you, Aunt Sandra."

She gripped the steering wheel tighter. "I know this hasn't been easy and I know we haven't spoken for a while. I'm glad to have you back in my life, though."

We drove on in silence until we were outside of Seattle and cruising down I-5, past billboards and trees. A deep-seated fatigue settled on me. The bandages on my left wrist felt itchy underneath the sleeves of my sweater. I pushed away the memory attached to those bandages. I'd always have the scar as a reminder. No need to dwell on it now.

"I called your mom," Sandra said after several silent miles. I looked out the window. "She was relieved to hear you're okay."

"God forbid she has to disrupt her life."

Sandra sucked in a sharp breath. "She doesn't have a lot of money or she would have come out."

"No, she wouldn't have. Ginny Quinn has no trouble finding money when she wants it. She didn't want to come."

Sandra sighed. "I wish she wasn't this way. She offered, but I told her not to. I didn't think she'd help."

"She never would have followed through anyway. And if she did, she would have made it all about her." My mother was my only other living relative I knew besides Sandra. I hadn't spoken to her much since I was fifteen. When she dropped me off with Sandra for the fourth and last time as she went with her newest lover. A surfer. Virginia Quinn often claimed to fall in love. It never lasted. She had long since left the surfer. I wasn't sure where she was currently as her infrequent email updates were too scattered to get concrete details, but I guessed it'd be somewhere with a large tourist population. Ginny, if she hadn't changed her name again, loved transient populations of easily charmed and scammed people who would soon be far away from her.

Sandra stayed quiet. I was right and she knew it. She had tried so hard to love her little sister, to be a second mother when they were orphaned and sent to live with relatives. None of it ever got Sandra anywhere with Ginny. Such is life being the sister of a narcissist. Better than being the daughter of one.

Sandra kept us driving, down into Oregon heading to her home where I would be living for the unknown future. I rested back, taking my cue from the cats who had quieted down, and let the car lull me into a fitful sleep.

Hours later with a few pit stops for restrooms and gas, we were driving along the Pacific Ocean on highway 101, heading south. I watched the sun set in between the pine trees, a few rays peeking out through parted clouds.

Sandra and the commune sisters she had lived with for decades had finally raised enough money to buy their dream property. Six years ago, they had left the outskirts of Eugene and settled onto several acres in the southern Oregon coast range. It had been a dream come true for Sandra. I had sent my congratulations when she wrote me the news. I knew it had broken her heart that I hadn't visited. She updated me every now and again, sending handmade cards depicting goddesses that included written letters about the progress of the commune: the vegetable beds churning out organic produce, the goats they were raising, the newcomers who were joining them. I responded a few times a year with a short email or phone call.

The light was almost completely faded as we drove through Coos Bay, the largest town close to the commune. We pulled up to a stop light where a group of people gathered on the corner. The group was composed of a handful of men of varying ages, holding signs. It seemed too early for political campaigning with a new presidential change happening in days. Under the yellow glow of the streetlight, I read one of the signs: "White Pride". Several of the men were chanting "Our place, our nation!"

One man in the group looked over and our eyes locked. He was scrawny with a patchy dark beard, probably in his early twenties. His chants faded as we looked at each other. It felt like minutes ticked by, but it was only a few seconds. His eyes were a dark abyss of hate.

"WITCH!" He screamed and pointed at me. "WITCH!"

The other men turned and looked at the van. They began yelling "witch" all together. Sandra cursed and hit the lock button for all the doors. The angry young man lunged toward the car. My whole body tensed. Hissing and growls rose from the cats in the back seat.

"WITCH!"

The light turned green, and Sandra gunned the van, shooting us forward and away from the group. Their chant faded as we moved down the street. We sat in silence but inside my head was a single thought ringing out over and over: not again.

Sandra turned us off the coast highway onto a small two-lane road heading inland. The town gave way to farmland interspersed with dense lush forest.

"Sorry you had to experience that today." Sandra's voice pulled me out of my increasingly dark thoughts.

"I guess my reputation has preceded me," I said.

"This nonsense started last summer. It's in the air, I guess. And in the White House. We can't be too surprised. Dismayed, yes. But not surprised."

I nodded in the dark. Sandra continued to prattle on.

"They recognize the van. We do have a reputation in the community. People don't like strong independent groups of women."

"He looked right at me." I shuddered.

"Well, he's not wrong," Sandra said quietly.

"About white power?" I was goading her, hoping to avoid this conversation.

Sandra made a disgusted face. "No, that's hateful and wrong. Don't try to distract me. You know what I mean. You're a witch, just like me. Just like your mom."

"I'm not. Let's not start this." I pulled closer to the door, an involuntary movement I didn't even notice until I felt the coolness of the night coming through the window glass.

"You haven't come into your powers, but you will. I think this episode of yours is what happens when you deny yourself. If you'd only —"

"STOP!" I shouted. "My depression is not because I deny my 'witch powers'. You have to stop this."

The van filled with a heavy silence. The same old argument. I hadn't expected Sandra to pounce on it so soon. I would have thought she'd know better. I felt a surge of anger and regret that I was here, in her car, headed to her home to be in her care.

"I'm sorry," she whispered. "I shouldn't have brought it up."

"No, you shouldn't have."

"You know you'll be living with witches, though. We're not hippies as you like to call us. Full Moon Farm is a community of witches."

"You are totally hippies. Come on."

Sandra laughed. "Okay, so a lot of us are old hippies. But we're also witches."

I sighed. If Sandra was explaining that they were pagans, Wiccans, normal everyday people who celebrated a few different holidays and called Christmas "Yule", I wouldn't have been bothered. But Sandra and her group took it further. They believed in magic. They practiced magic. And Sandra was sure I had magical talents, that we came from a line of witches. She was convinced the ongoing depression I had battled since I was fourteen was from denying my true magical self. An argument that had begun just like this had caused our seven-year rift.

We drove in silence in the dark. After a few minutes we approached a small town. The sign announced it as Silverdale, implying more luxurious intentions than reality. The town consisted of small white houses, many with peeling paint though carefully tended front yards. We drove slowly past a general store, flat fronted with a long awning like in a cartoon about the old West. The sign above it was hand painted in red: "Murphy's Merch".

"That's our store, post office and sometimes in summer and fall they have music out back. We can get basics there and we sell some of our goat cheese and produce with them. Also the jams," Sandra said proudly.

"So the town is friendly to you all?"

"Friendly enough. It took them a while but they're warming up." There was a note of caution in Sandra's voice.

We drove through the town in about two blinks. Right before the darkness of the road took over was a tavern with no name. A few trucks were parked in the small gravel lot, waiting in the purple glow of a neon beer sign. Then it was gone, the lights of the town fading behind us.

My exhaustion mingled with my dismay. After a large city of culture, restaurants, of energy, this was the closest civilization. How exactly was I going to "bounce back," as the troupe of medical professionals in the hospital kept saying, if I was in a drab little nowhere?

"Here we go," Sandra announced as she slowed the van and turned left onto a tiny road. A fence ran along each side, illuminated in the headlights. "This is the Kilgard's property. Nice folks, bit standoffish. This is an easement through their property to get to the farm. I think they were hoping to get a different set of neighbors than us."

Even in hippie Eugene, Sandra and her commune had been considered unusual. Welcome in town but as they moved out into the rural fringes, the mundane conservative streak of the state came out. I could only imagine how the locals felt about the newest community addition. Even at six years, I doubted they were as welcome as Sandra had suggested. And the incident with the awful men on the corner came roaring back in my head. What was I doing? Making a huge mistake. I should have thought about that before I imploded my own life. A pathetic sigh escaped my lips.

"It's going to be okay, Reva. I know you don't feel it now, but it will get better." Sandra spoke quietly.

I nodded in the dark. I didn't have it in me to respond.

The road turned to gravel about a half a mile in and the trees closed in around us. About a mile further, the trees opened up. The road forked, Sandra turning right.

"You'll be staying in the old farmhouse. We've built a few cob houses off closer to the fields where most of the original members prefer to live. Nothing beats living in a space you've built from the ground up. Sunray in particular loves it, you remember how much she had wanted to build a house out of earth."

My weariness was overcoming my wariness. I wanted a bed, to drift off into sleep. Though I had spent the last month practically nonstop in bed, the tiredness didn't abate. Hospitals don't help on that front. The last week had felt like a parade of insomnia enthusiasts rather than nurses and aides and doctors marching in right as I was drifting off.

"And here we are." Sandra pulled into a circular drive, and I saw my new temporary home. The house was two stories, windows glowing with light on every level, and would have been average but for the front being broken up by a triangle roofed section that rose from the front porch. It looked like a witch's hat on top of a rectangle. There was a round stained-glass window in the middle of the upstairs witch hat part.

"Welcome to your new home. Your room is up on the right, second story. Let's get the kitties and your overnight bag. The rest can wait until tomorrow." Sandra pulled up in front where a large, covered porch ran the length of the front. Up close I could see the faded blue and white paint. I opened the car door and stepped out.

The smell of the night hit me — cedar, dirt, wood smoke, and wet air. I breathed in, nostalgic for a place I'd never been before. It smelled like Oregon, the forest and the rain. For one second, everything felt right. I pulled out Tuna's carrier from the back seat and my ratty old duffel bag. Sandra was opening the back door on her side and pulling the other carrier out. The cats roused suddenly, as if they'd been in a deep sleep until we arrived. Tuna meowed pitifully and threw herself to the side of the carrier. She'd always had a flair for drama. Kiz was making a low meow-growl noise.

We climbed up the steps. I paused in front of the door, also set with an abstract stained-glass window in blues and purples. The door gleamed a bright violet, freshly painted where the rest of the house peeled. Sandra reached around me and opened the door.

"Go on. You're home now." The door swung open, and I walked in.

Inside was a large entrance hall filled with plants on side tables and stools. The stairs going up to the second story were at the end of the hall. Two doors lined each side of the hall, the ones to our immediate left and right closed. Sandra headed for the stairs with me following behind.

As we approached, the last door on the left opened and a small calico cat came prancing out along with the scent of vanilla, cinnamon, and butter. She flopped down in front of the stairs, perfectly in the middle of the pathway.

"Well hello, Midori," Sandra said, pulling the cat carrier in her hand further from the calico. "I can't pet you today, will you let us pass without paying the toll?"

Dangling in his carrier from Sandra's hand, Kiz growled at the cat. Tuna, catching the stranger cat scent, let out a furious meow and threw herself forward in the carrier. I put both hands on the carrier to try to steady it. The calico turned her big green eyes toward us and gave a slow blink. I'd always heard that was a cat's way of showing appreciation or welcome but in this case, I'd say it was closer to a "fuck you."

"Midori! Come here right now," a woman's voice called from the open door. I walked forward and looked in.

An Asian woman with a heart shaped face was striding toward us from what was clearly the kitchen, a vast room I barely could take in before she arrived in the door frame. She was wearing a red apron, and her hands and arms were covered in a dusting of flour. She looked my age, mid-twenties or maybe younger, with a messy black bun pulled up on top of her head also speckled with flour.

"You're here!" she said. Tuna's cat carrier rocked violently. The woman stood in the doorway and reached out a hand. "I'm Sora, one of your roommates. You must be Reva."

I looked at her outstretched hand and tried to shift the weight so I could accept the handshake. Tuna released a yowl like a hellcat.

"Oh, sorry! We'll make proper introductions later. Come down later if you want company! I prefer making snickerdoodles at midnight. They taste better that way." Sora retracted her hand with a smile and bent down to scoop up Midori, who went limp and stretched out even longer on the floor, foiling Sora's attempts to pick her up. "Come on, you, don't go into liquid state right now."

"You never should have taught her to open doors," Sandra said over the yells of my cats.

"I know. Good thing she doesn't have thumbs. Who knows what more mischief she'd get into." Sora laughed and finally gathered the calico up in her arms. She backed up into the kitchen and started to close the door with her feet. Midori stretched out and then turned like a dolphin doing a barrel roll in Sora's arms. She almost dropped the cat.

"You pest," she said fondly, quickly juggling the cat. Before the door shut, she looked out and added, "Welcome, Reva. We're happy to have you join us."

Sandra looked over at me and nodded up the stairs.

"Let's get these cats up and out in your room. Sora set up litter boxes, food, and water. And Keena set you up with a bed and sheets." Sandra started up the stairs.

"Who's Keena?" I followed up after her. I already missed the elevator in my building. Tuna and Kiz were going to miss being lords of their domain. They sometimes had trouble with each other; how were they going to handle another cat?

"Keena's our newest addition in the house, found us from clear across the country. She goes to bed pretty early, so you won't meet her tonight," Sandra replied.

We reached the top of the stairs where it opened out to a hall running both directions. Sandra turned right and kept going. The walls were painted lilac and lit with orange glass sconces. I glanced behind us and saw two doors facing each other in the hall, one blue and one black followed by a red one on the right. There was a green door at the end of the hall.

"That's the bathroom," Sandra said over her shoulder. "The green door,"

Great, sharing a bathroom with a bunch of women. What a regression. I turned and caught up as Sandra stopped in front of a gray door.

"This room is yours," she said as she opened the door and walked in.

The room was larger than I expected, cream-colored walls with a simple pine floor. A twin bed was shoved in a corner with a table lamp on a small overturned wooden box as a bed stand. The room was otherwise empty. Normally even empty rooms give off a sense of the past for me — lingering smells and a sort of energy from the people who inhabited it. This room lacked that even though it surely had a long history given the age of the house. A sense of relief flooded into my body. A blank canvas of a room felt like something I needed.

"We did a cleansing ritual just for you. I know how you are about the energy of a place. A lot of us witches are sensitive to that sort of thing," Sandra said as she briskly walked through the room, setting the cat carrier down. I closed the door behind me and set down Tuna's carrier. I let the "us witches" comment pass for now. I didn't have the energy to start the argument back up.

"These litter boxes will come in handy until the cats get used to going outside." Sandra flipped on the lamp, which emitted a warm yellow glow through its white shade. The blankets were white wool. Everything in the room was white, even the box the lamp sat on.

"They are indoor only cats." I opened the door to Tuna's cage. She sniffed cautiously out toward the room, looking like she was about to walk out. She sat down and refused to leave the carrier she had been so eager to get out of twenty seconds earlier. Cats.

"That'll change." Sandra sounded sure of herself.

"No, it won't. I don't want them to come to any harm." I paused. "Or to kill songbirds."

She clucked her tongue. "We can't keep living creatures confined to a single space without consequences. They'll be fine, you'll see."

I noticed she avoided the songbird reference. She opened the door for Kiz, who had put a single paw out of his carrier. He sniffed the ground before retreating into his cage as well.

"Well, I'll let you adjust. I know it's been a rough couple of weeks," Sandra said as she let herself out, carefully opening and shutting the door as if the cats were at her ankles instead of hiding in their carriers.

I sat on the bed and listened. Silence. No city noises, just the sound of wind through the trees. Alone with my thoughts, I couldn't help replaying the one thing I wanted most to block out. Anthony.

Tuna jumped up onto the bed beside me and gave a soft meow. She climbed up onto my lap, purring, driving the thoughts away. Kiz followed, settling in beside me since he knew his sister wouldn't share my lap. I let their purring pour over me; I hadn't realized how much I could miss them until that moment. We stayed like that until I yawned and kicked off my shoes. I lay back, the cats rearranging themselves to my new prone position. An aching tiredness consumed me, and I fell into a deep sleep.

Chapter 2

Morning light and cat breath woke me. Tuna was sitting on my chest, her blue eyes drilling into my forehead. She opened her mouth in a silent meow. I turned my head and then remembered where I was. The farmhouse with Sandra, in a mostly empty room. I was under the white wool blankets, still fully dressed.

My wrist ached, the bandages scratchy and damp. I sat up, sending Tuna skittering to the floor. My movement also roused Kiz, sleeping at the end of the bed. He lifted his head and glared at me.

"Sorry, sorry. God forbid I interrupt your twenty hours of sleep," I said to him. My mouth was fuzzy and dry. There was a light pounding in my head. I desperately needed water. And coffee. I needed coffee.

A knock came from the other side of the door. I paused, not awake enough to interact with anyone. The knock came again.

"Come in." I sighed and stood, wincing at the cold floor under my feet. I sat back down on the bed, pulling my feet up under me.

The door opened and Sora walked in holding a tray of dishes. She deftly closed the door with her foot just as the cats realized they had missed an escape opportunity.

"Good morning!" she trilled at me. "I thought you may not be ready yet for coming down for breakfast first thing, so I brought some up for you."

"I'm not hungry," I said as my stomach rumbled loudly.

"I'm sure you're thirsty." She placed the tray on the bed stand. The scent of coffee wafted up at me.

Seeing Sora in the light, I was struck by how pretty she was. Her hair was up in a messy bun again and she wore no makeup. She had large brown eyes under the fringe of bangs. She emitted an energy of all-encompassing warmth. I felt good around her as well as a tiny bit jealous. I wasn't the sort of person others would say the same about. Moody, stormy, unpredictable — that was more me. My natural hair color fell between the colors mousy and dishwater brown and was always a mess. I kept it shoulder length and dyed it dark brown to compensate. Mostly the effect ended up in my complexion being washed out. My face had been described as "distinctive" and "angular" but never pretty.

The tray contained a cup of steaming coffee, small containers of cream and sugar, a large glass of water, a plate with thick slices of buttered bread, a little jar of jelly, and another plate with three cookies. Snickerdoodles from the looks of it.

"I hope you don't have any food allergies or dietary restrictions. I'm usually pretty good at knowing that about a person and I didn't pick anything up from you. I wish that skill transferred to knowing how people like their coffee!" She smiled at me and stood by the tray.

"No restrictions. And black," I replied, reaching for the mug. My sleeves rode up and exposed the bandages. I hastily pulled my arms back and pushed the sleeves down. I shouldn't have been using both hands anyway, I remembered.

Sora picked up the mug and handed it to me. I was grateful she didn't mention the bandages. Of course she must know. They all must know. But I didn't want to talk about it.

"Thanks," I replied taking the mug from her with my right hand. I should have started with water, but the caffeine was calling. "Weren't you up baking cookies late? You said something about snickerdoodles at midnight."

"Just the dough. I baked them first thing this morning. That's how they taste best — dough at midnight, baked at sunrise."

"You were up at sunrise?"

She shrugged. "Well, maybe not right at sunrise but definitely morning."

"You're a morning person?" I sipped the coffee, relishing the rich bitterness. I had worried about finding good coffee outside Seattle, particularly out here in the sticks. This cup was a pleasant surprise.

"No. I think of myself as an afternoon person." Sora laughed. "But a lot of baking is done best in the morning."

"So you're into baking."

"Yes, it's what I do for the farm. I bake for caterers in the area and sell at the farmer's market in the warm months."

"I see," I said. There was a long pause between us.

"Don't you want to try the cookies?" Sora finally broke in. That's why she's still here, I thought.

"I'm not really into sweets in the morning." I watched her face fall for a second before she pulled it back up.

"Oh, okay." There was an awkward pause. "I'll get going then."

I watched her walk across the room, stopping to pet each cat, who had now figured out she offered a jail break opportunity. She managed to gracefully exit without having to kick either of them away from the door.

I looked at the cookies. They were beautiful, each the same exact size and sparkling with sugar and cinnamon. I pulled one off the plate and took a bite. Soft, chewy with a rich complex butter flavor — vanilla, cinnamon, and other warming spices all swirled together. Witches or not, those cookies were magic. I ate them all.

I found my overnight bag with the pain medication and the packet of clean bandages. I peeked out into the hallway to see if the bathroom was free. I was in luck. The bathroom was large and roomy with both a clawfoot tub and a small shower stall. The dark green square tiles underfoot were warm to the touch. Plants trailed up the pale blue walls from planters tucked into corners. This was someone's dream bathroom, probably Sandra's.

After a hot shower marred by the plastic I had to wrap around my wrist, I got dressed and changed out the bandages. The scar on my wrist was an angry pink with black thread. I made myself look at it. I waited for any sort of feeling about it, but the blankness remained. For months, exhaustion had been all I felt.

I looked out the window from the bathroom as I brushed my teeth. From this view in the house, pastures of cleared land ran uphill to a tall, dense pine forest. The trees swayed in the January wind, but the sky was remarkably blue and clear. It wouldn't last. I sensed more rain was on the way.

From the window I saw two covered structures, steep pitched roofs with no sides protecting two trailers underneath. There was a swatch of grass between the two. The trailer on the left was a two toned white and aqua sixteen footer. I guessed it was Sandra's, an upgrade from the one I had lived with her in years ago but still a Shasta, her favorite type of trailer. With a whole house and choice of rooms, she continued to live in her beloved camper. I spied her cat Magpie taking advantage of the sun on a wooden deck built around the trailer. A mass of pots filled with plants in various stages from green life to brown sticks were sprinkled around the deck. Wind chimes hung from the roof structure, metal glints catching the light in the breeze.

I looked over at the other structure. This must be one of her commune sisters. The construction was newer and the trailer underneath small and unassuming. There was no deck but rather a tall fence surrounding it. A large rust-colored dog walked around the side, catching my eye. The dog was fierce and strong looking, some sort of pit bull looking mix, with lean long legs and a white starred chest. The dog immediately looked up as if it sensed me watching it and let out a single deep bark. I backed away from the window. No way I was letting my cats outside with that creature wandering around.

I returned to the room, *my* room now I supposed, and dropped off my bag. The cats were asleep in a sun ray on the floor, curled up on each other. I needed to unpack and get them their kitty pillows. I looked at the bed with its rumpled white blankets and longed to be back there: unconsciousness. I grabbed my cell phone from the nightstand instead and tried to shake off the urges. That desire for permanent unconsciousness was what got me here, living with strangers and a bandaged wrist.

My phone showed the time at 11:45 am. Besides the usual spam emails, my phone had been silent. I had a social network in Seattle, but the friendships were lukewarm and shallow. I hadn't reached out to anyone in a while, so people had stopped trying to reach me.

I was walking down the hall toward the stairs when a door opened. A tall pale figure in black stepped out. She looked like she came out of an ad for Goths-R-Us with her long straight black hair, black lipstick, and a sweeping black dress. She raised a perfectly plucked and redrawn eyebrow at me before retreating silently and swiftly into her room.

"Hi to you, too," I muttered under my breath and walked down the stairs. So my new roommates were a bubbly baker and the Queen of the Night. What would be next?

I paused at the bottom of the stairs. Singing drifted from the room I knew was the kitchen. I remembered I had left the tray up in my room. Feeling guilty, I turned to the opposite door from the kitchen. I vaguely recalled Sandra saying the downstairs was all communal living so it seemed safe I wouldn't be walking into someone's bedroom. I pushed open the door and a blast of warm moist air hit me.

On the other side was a jungle, foliage in all shades of green. Bright light poured out into the hallway and a musky earth scent wafted toward me. I stood taking it all in when I heard a voice from within.

"Close the door, you'll let the heat out!"

I stepped in and hastily closed the door. The voice hadn't been unfriendly, so I assumed it was okay if I stayed. The room itself felt like an invitation to linger. I walked forward, ducking under a large leaf that looked tropical.

The room was so long and narrow, it looked never ending, an illusion from mirrored walls and the plants at all levels. I followed the path until it came to a fork. Off to the left was a large open space leading into another room with glass walls. I guessed it was a converted sun porch. The air was cooler in the glass room but still intensely humid and warm.

A small table with cushioned chairs stood in the middle of the glassed porch. A woman sat with her back to me, looking out to the pastures. The trailers I'd seen from upstairs were part of the view.

"Have a seat." Her voice was inviting with a hint of a Southern accent. A tea service in silver and blue sat on the table: one delicate cup in front of her, and one in front of an empty chair. I took that seat. I hoped for more coffee, but a cup of black tea would do.

"Hi there. I'm Reva," I said as I sat. She turned to me and picked up her cup of tea.

"Keena." She reached her hand across to me, which I took. Her hand was cool with a touch of roughness, the hands of someone who uses them daily in manual labor. "Welcome to Full Moon Farm."

She had long curly brown hair and warm brown skin and was in that nebulous female age of late twenties to forty. Her eyes were the most startling feature, an otherworldly light blue gray.

"Tea?" She picked up the tea pot and poured me a cup without waiting. "I know you're hoping for coffee, but I promise you'll like this."

"Thank you." I was used to presumption from the women of the commune from past visits to their Eugene farm. They called it premonition and intuition. I took a sip of the tea, letting the tannin flavor swirl over my tongue before swallowing. It needed sugar and cream.

Anticipating my need, Keena handed me a small pitcher and sugar bowl without speaking. I took it from her.

"Where's Sandra?" I asked. I needed to get my stuff out of her car, start setting up my space.

"She had a shift at the hospital and didn't want to wake you. She'll be back this afternoon."

I sighed out loud without meaning to.

"She took one of the smaller cars, don't worry. And Alex unloaded your stuff onto the front porch this morning." Keena smiled at me.

I stirred my tea, watching the tea leaves swirl. I waited a few seconds to drink so they could settle back down to the bottom.

"Sorry, I didn't mean ..." I trailed off.

Keena shook her head. "You want to unpack, settle in. Understandable. If you want help getting boxes upstairs, just say so. Any of us around can help."

We sat in silence a while longer. I looked out the windows at the land. The forest rose up in the background, calling out to me. The idea of a hike floated into my head. I paused mid-sip. I hadn't thought of hiking in what felt like forever. It seemed so small, but I recognized it as a significant shift. For months, I hadn't wanted to do anything much less hike.

Movement to the right caught my eye. A woman was coming out of the little trailer. Her red hair glinted in the sun, and she moved with a fierce swiftness. Much like the dog bounding at her side, the rust-colored pit bull mix who had barked at me earlier. Another dog came bounding out behind them, short and comical in comparison.

"That's my Bear." Keena pointed. "He likes to spend time with Alex and Flame, be part of a pack."

The smaller dog was dark brown with a golden face and perky ears. He ran as fast as his stubby legs would carry him to keep up with the striding woman and her long limbed regal dog.

"He's cute." I wasn't much of a dog person but her dog couldn't help but make you smile.

"Rottweiler-Corgi mix. He's still pretty young and I'm terrible at training him. So Alex said she'd help." Keena smiled out at the goofy dog who was loping along. When he got distracted and started to venture too far from her side, the red-haired woman would shout out a command that brought the dog back.

"So that's Alex?" I watched the woman and the dogs disappear toward the forest.

"Yes. She takes a while to warm up to." Keena spoke matter-of-factly.

"What about the other woman upstairs? The goth one?" I asked. If I was honest, the idea of some aloof roommates was fine. Wasn't that the best kind? Plus Sora and Keena had more than enough welcoming energy.

"Darcy? Long dark hair, tall?" Keena turned from the window. "Don't finish that last drop, I'll read your tea leaves."

I handed over my cup. I was used to tea leaf readings from Sandra. It had been a while since anyone had offered though. I returned to the topic of the mysterious roommate.

"She caught a glimpse of me and retreated back into her room."

"Oh, don't take it personally. A lot of us here don't do well with strangers. History leaves a mark," Keena said as she took my cup and turned it over on a plate, letting the last dregs of the tea water run out. As her last sentence landed in my ears, I unconsciously ran my hands around my wrist. The bandages crinkled ever so slightly.

Keena looked up at me. She rolled up her sleeves, showing a series of old scars crisscrossing the back of her forearms. They looked like they were born out of violence. A vision of a big knife slashing and blood filled my head. I shook my head, trying to banish it. Sometimes that happened — I would see things playing in my head like a short film.

A momentary startled expression crossed Keena's face before she pushed her sleeves down.

"You have visions." It was a statement.

"Anxiety. I've been told I can be overly sensitive and very imaginative." My voice held a hard note. I didn't know what my aunt had told all these women, but I didn't want to get into conversations of witchcraft and power. I could respect their quirks and their traditions, but I drew a line at magic and psychic abilities.

Keena looked at me carefully, reading me with her big gray eyes. I could see her wanting to press me further but deciding not to. She plucked the upside down teacup from the plate and studied the inside. Tension I didn't realize I was holding in my body released.

I watched Keena and waited. I'd had my tea leaves read many times. I found it mildly amusing, often trying to guess in my head what generalized platitudes the tea leaf reader would come up with.

"You're moving from an arrested place to one of reflection and receptivity. You'll come into a great deal of power in the next few months."

I snorted. To my surprise, Keena looked up and laughed. The others who had read my leaves before were always serious and then offended when I didn't take them seriously.

"I'm trying to learn new divination techniques. This one has a fascinating history but can sound so hokey." Keena winked at me and turned the cup, her smile fading.

"Is there a tall dark stranger in my future?" I joked.

"Yes." She responded with seriousness. "Maybe not all tall and dark but this suggests a group of men you should be wary of. A group of men led by an evil force."

I thought of the men on the street corner from yesterday. That seemed an accurate description of them. I opened my mouth to tell her about it, see if she'd run into them before, when something strange happened.

Keena dropped the cup and froze. It clattered down onto the plate. Her eyes stared past me from far away, her jaw slack. I understood the phrase "catatonic trance" watching her.

"Keena?" I said tentatively, reaching out my hand to try to touch her shoulder. Her hand shot up and grabbed onto my wrist. I cried out in pain, her hand gripping me on my bandages. The wounds underneath throbbed and everything went black.

I opened my eyes. I was standing in a white fog at night. It was bone chillingly cold. I looked around at the indistinct shapes of trees all around, the fog swirling through them. I tried to cry out, but no words came. I felt planted to the dark ground, unable to take a step in any direction. A wailing sound started to my right, off deep in the fog. It was the sound of heartbreak, of grief and unbearable loss. Another wail took up to my left. More voices joined in all around me. I tried to spin around but everything in me was frozen. The wailing grew louder.

Then I sensed it behind me, a feeling of dread magnified, of pure evil. Tingly pain radiated along my limbs like needles. My spine burned with piercing cold. I tried to turn. If I could see it, I could name it, the awfulness. But I couldn't, my body refused to work. The evil crept closer. The wailing became so loud my ears hurt.

I could feel myself giving up, a familiar weight pressing inward. My depression magnified a thousand times. My eyes closed, the fog getting thicker.

Give in.

The evil called to me.

Succumb.

Deep within me, a tiny spark kindled. As the chill wrapped around me tighter, I dove to that spark in my mind and touched it. A blinding flash like lightning ripped through the fog and I found my voice. But all I could do was scream.

Chapter 3

I came rushing back into my body. I was still sitting at the table, slumped in my chair. I had never left. Physically anyway.

As I came to, I became aware of voices and a dark figure crouched in front of me. Someone was holding my hand. I pulled away, worried about them touching my wrist.

"She's back." The person in front of me spoke. I focused my eyes on the dark goth woman from the hall, her pale angular face with precisely applied makeup. She was striking with deep brown eyes peering at me.

"Reva, I'm so sorry. I've never had anyone pulled into a vision with me like that." Keena sat on the ground beside my chair, wringing her hands. I turned toward her.

"What the hell was that?" I asked. My throat felt raw, like I really had been screaming.

"I don't know," Keena responded. "Your aunt mentioned you were strong but —"

"But she also said you don't believe." Darcy finished the sentence. She held a large black crystal in her hand. She saw me looking at it. "Black tourmaline. It helped pull you out."

Sora appeared behind Darcy, a big mug in her hand.

"Drink this." She thrust the mug at me. Her smile had been replaced with furrowed brow and worried pursed mouth. I took a tentative sip and almost choked on the bitterness.

"What is this? I can't drink this." I started to hand the mug back to her.

"Drink it." The command came from an unfamiliar voice. Appearing behind Sora was the red-haired woman, Alex. "You need it."

"The first sip is the only bitter one," Sora said. "It'll be better after that."

I looked at them, this circle of women peering down at me. I felt an overwhelming urge to be alone, to cry. Who the hell did they all think they were?

"Reva, you need to drink it. I promise you'll feel better," Keena said softly. Darcy nodded. Alex opened her mouth but closed it when Sora gave her head a sharp shake.

"Please," Sora said to me.

I sighed and took another sip. The second sip soothed my throat and as promised, was less bitter. A hint of sweetness came out with the deep herbal flavor. I took another sip. The women all around me seemed to let out a collective sigh.

I watched them bustle about, pulling up chairs around the table in the greenhouse, as I sipped the tea. Sora disappeared briefly and returned with a new tray of tea and cookies.

"Always with the cookies, Sora," Darcy said in her deep melodious voice I was beginning to recognize.

"When you stop eating them, I'll stop bringing them."

As they settled in around me, I looked closer at Alex, having only seen her from a distance. She had her red hair pulled back tightly into a ponytail, making her pale freckled face severe. Her eyes were narrowed, watching me. I estimated she was in her forties. She wore a tight sportswear pullover. Defined muscles in her arms stood out even through the fabric. She had the sort of body professional athletes and yoga instructors cultivate. Her pale mouth was set in a thin line of dispassion.

Her gaze unnerved me enough, I shifted focus over to Darcy, my other new roommate. Even sitting her height was impressive. She must have been around six feet tall. She was made of all sharp angles, but she wasn't gaunt or skinny. The edges of her bell sleeves were lined with black feathers. "Glamorous" was how I would describe her in one word. She gave me a small, close-lipped smile.

Sora poured cups of tea and passed a plate of cookies around. We all sat in silence for a bit, sipping tea and eating what turned out to be the best chocolate chip cookie I'd ever had.

"I thought it was snickerdoodle week," Keena said around a mouth full of cookie.

"I made those but threw in a batch of chocolate chip as well. It felt right," Sora replied.

I turned away from the table to look out the window. The humid air of the greenhouse began to quiet my racing heart. Until I started relaxing, I wasn't even aware I'd been breathing heavily, on the verge of a dissociative episode. Which, if I thought about it, was likely what had happened.

"What did you see?" Darcy asked. I turned back to see she was asking Keena.

"Is that a good idea?" Alex interjected.

"To talk about it?" Keena said softly.

Alex nodded at me. "She doesn't seem up for it."

"Hey, I'm sitting right here," I retorted.

"You don't seem up for it," Alex said pointedly. "And since you don't believe, it may just freak you out more."

"It was bad." Keena spoke in a whisper. "I think we have to go there. Even more important if Reva doesn't believe. It'll make her vulnerable."

"Again, I'm right here. What the hell are you talking about?" I had, for a few seconds, felt positive about my new roommates but this talk was what I feared would happen.

"Reva, I'm going to tell you what I saw in my vision. Can you confirm if you saw the same thing?" Keena turned to me, her eyes wide and serious.

I paused, not sure what to say. There was no way she could know what my dissociative episode looked like. Unless I was babbling about it while it was happening, a plausible explanation.

"She's not going to believe it either way," Alex said with a measure of disgust.

"Give her a shot." Sora came to my defense.

"Reva?" Keena asked again.

"Okay." I sighed.

"We were taken to a dark forest in fog. It was so cold, like deep to the marrow of your bones cold. All around were the sounds of wailing women," Keena began. Goosebumps rose on my skin.

"Wailing women?" Darcy perked up in alarm.

She nodded. "Keening like I've never heard, like their whole world was shattered."

Darcy, somehow, went even paler than her already snowy skin. "Banshees."

"How many did you hear?" Alex interrupted.

"Four, maybe five," Keena responded.

"Five," I said, surprising myself. I knew I heard five distinct wails.

"They were all around and then when the —" Keena broke off, taking a deep breath, "— when the evil arrived, they grew unbearably loud."

"What was the evil? Demon?" Alex barked out her questions like an army commander.

Keena shook her head. "I couldn't see it. It stayed shrouded in the mist. I felt it though. Very powerful."

We all sat quietly for a few seconds.

"What did it feel like?" Darcy broke the silence.

Keena's face crumpled and she wrapped her arms around herself. "Cold and misery. It approached Reva and forced me out before I knew what was happening. But not before it spoke."

"It spoke?" Alex's voice raised in alarm.

Keena nodded.

"What the fuck did it say?" Alex demanded.

"Give in. Succumb." A whisper from Keena but it rang in my ear. The exact words I heard.

"How the hell did you get away?" Alex had turned her hard eyes on me.

"I woke up," I replied. Keena's story sounded exactly like my vision. Mental health episode or not, I couldn't argue that I went into some sort of dream state. How Keena knew it all, I couldn't fully explain to myself. Even if I had been speaking out loud, she had captured how it felt as if she had also experienced it.

"Bullshit. You don't wake up from that. Did you hear Darcy calling you back?"

"I woke up," I repeated. Tears pooled in my eyes. I didn't know what to think, everything felt so overwhelming. I watched Sora lay a hand on Alex's tensed arm. Alex receded slightly.

"Reva, what happened right before you woke up?" Sora asked, her voice soft.

Suddenly short of breath, I took a gasp of air.

"I can't," I croaked out. Tears ran down my face.

Darcy and Keena both reached out and put a hand on my shoulders. I started to pull away, but the weight of their hands calmed me. My breath slowed. I took a deep breath in through my nose and out through my mouth.

Sora waited, watching me and encouraging me to relax. She gave me the slightest nod.

"I felt something inside, a spark? I tried to find it but then I just started screaming." I'm not sure why it was so hard to say the words. I felt stupid though. Here were the women I would be living with for a while, and we were having a serious conversation about demons and banshees in my hallucinations.

Darcy gave my shoulder a squeeze and released it. She sat back and looked at me.

"It sounds like you did find it. The tourmaline may have helped but that alone wouldn't have pulled you out of that sort of evil. I think your aunt is right. You do have a strong power."

Alex nodded and for the first time, her voice carried something other than hardness. "You need to protect yourself, get stronger. That sort of thing comes back."

I shuddered. I didn't believe in this shit. Maybe Keena drugged my tea earlier.

I knew better though. This wasn't the first time I'd had visions of otherworldly places. I'd banished them, pushed them out, explained them away, drugged them away even but they crept up now and again. Little things usually. I hadn't experienced anything this bad in a long time. Not for seven years.

I was a loner as a kid and even more so as a teenager. Between the constant moving and my mother, making friends was impossible. As soon as I settled into a town and tentatively started eating lunch with the other outcast kids, my mother would pull up our shallow roots and move us on. Usually after she had slept with someone who would cause me the most embarrassment: my fifth-grade teacher, my new friend's father, the mayor. Ginny Quinn relished leaving a path of emotional destruction wherever she went.

The visions first occurred when I hit puberty. I had no one to talk with about them. I'd be sitting in a desk at school, my mind drifting, and I would be in a forest, at a river, somewhere natural but otherworldly. In the beginning it was just the landscapes but as the visions grew longer, I started seeing ... creatures. I say creatures because they were usually in animal forms but felt like more. The animals always conveyed words or feelings to me. The first one I ever saw was a small blue chipmunk creature who made me feel like I was filled with warm light..

At first, I thought it was my imagination gone wild, but I began to see patterns to the words or emotions being conveyed, like puzzle pieces. If put together, I'd get a warning of situations and people to avoid or opportunities to take advantage of. Nothing life changing such as lottery numbers but useful things for a twelve-year-old, like which group of girls were planning on humiliating me at lunch.

The visions had been going on for a few months when my mother dumped me off with Aunt Sandra for the third time. Months spent with Aunt Sandra were my fondest childhood memories. My feelings were so complex whenever my mother came to pick me up, sadness at leaving Sandra and the stable life on the farm mixed with an intense urge for recognition and love from my mother, a hopefulness that this time would be different. Each time she picked me up again, it got worse.

I hadn't bothered to tell my mother, wary of a blooming jealousy in her that I sensed but couldn't name as I turned into a young woman. I didn't get that feeling with Sandra, and I confided in her about my "imaginings" as I had begun to call them. The relief from talking about it was immense, and Sandra immediately helped me with my powers, as she referred to them. She told me the visions were special, that I was gifted. The commune sisters joined in, and I began getting a crash course in witchcraft.

My mother returned swiftly, within a few weeks, almost as if she had sensed what was happening. She'd never returned for me that fast before. She promised to find a place to settle down with me and start fresh. I fell for it all, hook, line, and sinker. I asked if we could stay close to Sandra so I could continue my teachings. Feeling bold from the support I had, I finally told my mother about my visions.

She whisked me off to a psychiatrist. At first the psychiatrist was sure I was schizophrenic based on what my mother had told him. Ginny had filled my head with the same fear after I had shared, so I was certain as I mumbled my vague explanations to the doctor the first time that I was going to be locked away. I didn't have words to describe the visions well and was smart enough to not mention the witchcraft. Fortunately, he changed his tune upon listening to me talk about it all as "drifting off" or "imagination wanderings" and said it sounded like a potent cocktail of anxiety and depression with dissociative episodes. I got on medications and the vision episodes mostly retreated.

When I turned fifteen, Ginny was done pretending to be my mother and dropped me off with Sandra for good. There was no pretext of return. I wouldn't have believed it anyway, not after living with her for the last two years in misery. I knew my mother saw me as competition now that I was growing up, the final straw being a creepy boyfriend of hers hitting on me. My mother had dumped the boyfriend when I told her. The relief I felt at being believed was short lived, as then she dumped me.

Sandra and the commune sisters welcomed me back. I went off the medications and embraced the idea of being a witch. Until I started going to the local school, that is. The bullying and teasing were bad, the worst I'd ever experienced at any school. After a year of it, I fell into a depression, the darkest of places. Sandra tried to cure it all with witchcraft, giving me citrine jewelry charged with sunlight and other sweet gestures that didn't change anything. Finally, another commune member took me to the hospital. I remember her saying "not everything can be solved with witchcraft" as we drove. Sandra was beyond furious, but I got the help I needed.

The anti-depressants kept me numb but level, which only later I came to understand meant I was over-medicated. I can't recall much of my senior year; it was a blur of routine and loneliness. The teasing had tapered off but the damage to my reputation was done. I ditched the craft and focused on getting through school. I was done with the fantasy of magic. As I slowly came off the anti-depressants, Sandra pushed to have me return to the studies.

"You have so much power, Reva!" she would say. "There's so much you can do with it."

I caved and for one month, returned to the craft. That was when the last vision happened.

I had been meditating when it struck. I was plunged into a darkness. When I opened my eyes, I was standing on a dark street, empty unlit houses all around. A fog rolled in around the houses toward me. The cold came toward me. I turned around and a dark figure stood behind me at the end of the street, shrouded in the fog. It took a step toward me, evil oozing out like spilled blood.

Come to me.

I remember screaming and running. The street got colder and darker, but it never seemed to end, and the creature was always behind me.

I had woken up to find Sandra and her commune sisters gathered around me in a circle. I was drenched in sweat and shaking with cold. She claimed they'd pulled me out. I was sure I had a psychotic break, brought on by the witchcraft nonsense and going off my medication. I got back on the anti-depressants and gave up the witchcraft. Sandra and I had a huge fight over it all. She said she was scared I wouldn't be able to protect myself if I didn't learn. We parted on ugly terms, and I left to start a new life in Seattle. She reached out to apologize after a few months and after some time, I accepted. We talked by phone and video chat, email, staying in touch but always with distance in between. She knew only the surface of my life and seemed to accept with sadness that was all I was willing to give.

In Seattle, I worked retail and restaurant jobs while going to community college classes, then transferring to University of Washington. I tapered off the heavy anti-depressants to a low dose thanks to working with better doctors, all with no return of the visions. I had a decent life. Everything had been going well until Anthony came into my life. Then it all changed.

Chapter 4

I looked around the little table at the women, my new roommates. An awkward silence descended on the table, no one quite sure what to say next. After a few minutes, I excused myself to go to my room. The women all looked at each other, clearly not wanting to let me out of their sight.

"Do you want me to come up with you?" Sora asked, standing as I did.

"No, I need to be alone for a little bit," I said.

"That's not a good idea," Alex said. She wasn't shaping up to be my favorite person. I looked at her with my best back-off-bitch face.

"Reva, we're all worried about you. Would it be okay if we checked in on you later?" Keena asked, looking at me with a furrowed brow.

"We?" I imagined the lot of them standing huddled around my doorway.

"Just one of us," Darcy said.

Feeling stuck, I nodded and walked away from the table. I felt their eyes on me as I walked through the plants until I turned a corner out of their sight.

The rest of the house felt cold after being in the humid warm greenhouse for so long. Like exiting a sauna, a rushing coolness all over. It would have felt good if not for how it reminded me of the vision I'd just experienced.

I trudged up the stairs, again missing the convenience of an elevator. At least I didn't have to carry groceries up them. I walked down the hallway and opened the door to my room.

The tray I'd left on the bed stand was on the floor, the contents spilled everywhere. The little pitcher of cream was on its side, a faint smear of the liquid pooled on the floor. All that remained of the bread and butter were a few crusts. Buttery paw prints in cream circled the scene. The cats were placidly sleeping, yin-yanged together on my pillow.

"You two are assholes," I said as I cleaned up their mess. I gathered the dishes, which miraculously hadn't broken, and put them all on the tray. Fortunately, there was a cloth napkin which I used to clean up what remained of the cream.

"I thought you might keep off some of that apartment cat weight being out in the country but not at this rate," I scolded them as I set the tray by the door. I felt guilt as soon as the words left my mouth. They had already shed their plumpness from my month of neglect.

I looked at my cell phone. It was only 2 p.m. and already I was exhausted. I pushed the cats off my pillow, sending them scattering with vocalized complaints, and lay down on the bed. Kiz was the first to forgive, jumping up to curl up next to me. Tuna followed, snuggling up to Kiz with a pointed glance my way.

"You're the one who made the mess. I have nothing to apologize for," I told her and reached out to pet her. She purred, the best kind of apology. I closed my eyes and drifted off to sleep.

I woke in the darkness, under the weight of a heavy blanket. I turned over and reached out to find Anthony, but only cold air and space met me. Right. I was in a twin bed on Sandra's farm. Not at home in my apartment with my boyfriend. A boyfriend who no longer existed. I hated it when I thought about him. When I remembered his smell and ached to touch his shoulders again.

I heard the doorknob jiggling across the room. I sat up and fumbled to turn on the lamp by the bed. A low growl came from near the door. The hair on my neck stood up. Another higher pitched growl followed. The cats.

I found the lamp switch, turning it on in time to see both cats huddled in front of the bed facing the door in defense poses. The door handle turned again, unlatching. It swung open softly, light from the hallway pouring in. No one was standing behind the door. I swung my feet onto the cold floor.

The ungodly hissing of angry territorial cats broke out. I looked down at the calico Midori from the night before standing in the hallway. She meowed, a question mark at the end of it.

I sprang forward at the same time Tuna did, my hands extended like her claws. Midori fled like a hunted rabbit with Tuna right behind her. Kiz followed them out the door as well, galloping along like it was great fun rather than the fight to the death Tuna was gearing up for.

I ran out into the hallway behind them. Midori disappeared into a hidden cat door in one of the doors in the hallway. Tuna was right behind her, about to follow, when the door opposite opened. Darcy walked out as Tuna backed away from her, switching to stranger danger mode. A large black shape swooped around Darcy from her room and flew at me.

I screamed and ducked as the shape came at my head. Both cats froze for a millisecond before dashing back into my room, tails puffed up like squirrels. I stayed crouched and looked up as a big black bird flew back over and landed on Darcy's shoulder.

I pulled the door to my room shut for the cats who were hiding under the bed. Darcy took the bird off her shoulder and tossed it into her room. I could hear the flap of the wings.

Sora and Keena came up the stairs, one right behind the other.

"What in the heck was all that racket?" Sora asked.

Darcy and I looked at each other. Darcy opened her mouth to speak and giggled. I started to giggle as well and within seconds the two of us were laughing hysterically. It took a minute to be able to stop and tell them what had happened.

"Midori opened your door?" Sora's face flushed pink. "She's never tried to open anyone's bedroom door before!"

"There's never been a pair of cats living here before," Keena said.

"But you'd think she'd try to get into either of your rooms. Particularly yours, Darcy. Nevermore is a fascinating creature for her."

"Nevermore is a conundrum to her. A foe that looks like lunch," Darcy said. I guessed Nevermore was the bird. "Plus, I keep my door locked."

"Ah, that makes sense," Sora said.

"And my room smells like dog so no surprise there," Keena added.

There was an awkward pause. I could sense Sora gearing up to apologize which didn't seem fair. Women were always apologizing over things they couldn't control.

I broke the silence. "Well, that was exciting. Leave it to cats to make an introduction dramatic."

The other women chuckled.

"It's about dinner time. Why don't you both come down?" Sora swept her hand down the stairs in invitation. "Reva, you'll probably want to lock your door. I doubt Midori learned her lesson."

I'd heard of kitchens being referred to as the heart of a home but had never seen that in real life. The kitchens I had experienced often seemed shoe-horned into the space, narrow and functional. The kitchen at the farm was nothing like that. It embodied the heart concept so wholeheartedly, I expected to see embroidered tea towels proclaiming just that.

The kitchen was huge with a mix of old-fashioned charm and modern conveniences: a large brick hearth with a bread oven above in one wall; a full gas range and a modern wall oven on the other side; a dishwasher tucked discreetly under open cream-colored cabinets that ran up the tall ceiling. Large windows looked out over the pastures, same direction as the greenhouse windows. In the center of the room was a massive plank wood table with benches. It gleamed reddish in the light of the candles that ran along its center.

A fairy tale kitchen. I imagined a cauldron bubbling over the hearth and Sora offering up the food of my dreams, like all witches in fairy tales. Hopefully it would be the Turkish Delight of my imagination from Narnia rather than the actual rosewater gel candies of real-life Turkish Delight.

Darcy and Keena sat at the table, in opposite spots catty-corner from each other. It seemed like each of them had staked their claim on a specific seat. I hesitated, not knowing where to sit.

"Sit next to me, Reva." Keena patted the seat to her left. I sat, watching Sora pulling bread rolls out of the brick oven.

"Does Sora do all the cooking?" An image of Cinderella popped into my head. Did that make me an evil stepsister?

"We take turns weekly, but Sora is the best and enjoys it the most," Keena answered.

The backdoor off to the left of the span of windows opened. Sandra walked in, accompanied by Alex and the two dogs from earlier. Flame, the rust-colored dog, paused to give me a chilly look before trotting over to lie down on the hearth in front of the cheery fire that burned there. Bear bounded toward Keena, his tongue hanging out in joy.

"Bear!" Alex ordered sharply. The dog paused, looking back in confusion. He moved toward Keena again, his butt wiggling in excitement. "Hearth, now."

At the final command, Bear stopped and walked over to the hearth. He sat his butt down right near Flame's face and began to pant loudly.

"Can't have them begging at the table. Bad manners," Alex said as she sat opposite me on the other side of Darcy.

Sandra sat on the other side of Keena. I had expected her to take the head of the table, but no plates were set there. Sandra glanced my way with a worried look on her brow. The women must have told her what happened earlier that day.

The meal started in silence when Sora sat down with rolls and butter. A large soup tureen held a fragrant cream of chicken soup, and a large wooden bowl held a salad of winter greens, kale, chard and chicory tossed with an orange vinaigrette. The food was simple, filling, and delicious, a perfect winter meal.

The conversation warmed up with the retelling of Midori's break-in to my room. Sandra shared a few small stories about people she worked with at the hospital — the doctor who hated shoes and had to be reminded to wear them in exam rooms, the nurses in conflict with each other over birthday cake.

"Half of the nurses think we should be celebrating birthdays with cake each time they come around. The other half think it should be a set day each month for all. And half of those nurses think it shouldn't be cake since it wrecks their diets."

I looked around at the women chatting at the table and felt warm and cozy. I hadn't let myself have friends in Seattle. For the first time, I thought maybe this place was going to be good for me.

After dinner the other women were busy cleaning up with the exception of Sora. She sat at the table looking out at the dark landscape beyond the windows. She saw me watching her.

"This is why I like to cook. I get out of the cleanup." She laughed.

"Reva, I'd like to talk to you in the library." Sandra had finished clearing the table while Keena and Darcy started loading the dishwasher. Alex was dishing leftovers into glass jars and containers to go into the fridge.

"There's a library?" I hadn't explored much of the house outside of the greenhouse and my room.

"It's my favorite room in the house." Sandra smiled. She always was a book nerd. Like me.

"Lead the way." I stood and followed her. The kitchen's warmth made it hard to leave but I did want to see this library. Would it also be out of a fairy tale?

I followed Sandra into the hallway and through the first door on the right, one door down from the kitchen. The space was dark for a second before Sandra flipped on the light. A chandelier flared to life, old brass metal with blue-green glass tear drops. The room was long and narrow with floor to ceiling built-in bookshelves filled with books of all shapes and sizes. A fireplace sat on the far wall opposite the door with a series of small mirrors hanging above it. The two large windows that faced out to the porch were closed with heavy green velvet drapes.

"How did you get all these books?" I asked, walking into the room and gravitating right to the shelves, bypassing the antique side tables and the wingback chairs re-upholstered in denim.

"We've been collecting them for years. We all pooled our collections together and just keep adding. There's still space." Sandra gestured to the upper shelves. The shelves further up weren't as full. I looked to see if there was a library ladder hanging but was disappointed.

"How do you get to the books up there?"

"We get the ladder off the porch. Not the best system but it works. Fortunately, we rarely need those books. You can find so much on the internet these days, even on witchcraft." Sandra walked to the fireplace and began crumpling up old newspaper from a metal basket next to it.

I sat on the leather couch that faced the fireplace. It was old and sagged a bit, the leather worn out on the edge of the seat cushions, but it was comfortable.

"How did you get all this stuff, the furniture?"

"It's a mishmash of stuff from the sisters or we picked it up in thrift stores, antiques stores, as we came across it," Sandra said as she laid small pieces of wood in the fireplace, layered with the paper.

"How come the sisters don't live here? This seems like the prime spot." I gazed around. Why would the women who founded the place choose to live in the tiny hobbit-looking cob houses across the way when they could be in this space? The old commune had been lovely, but since it was rented land, they'd been more reserved with putting down roots. The farm felt different, like they'd been there sixteen years instead of six.

"They do come and use this space, borrow books and that sort of thing. But they're getting older and a lot of them want privacy. A lot of them are stuck in their ways." Sandra blew and the paper caught fire. Had she lit a match? I didn't think so. I sniffed for the sulfurous smell of a lit match but caught only the smell of woody smoke. Maybe there had been coals in the fire.

"What do you mean stuck in their ways?" I caught an undertone there in Sandra's voice.

"And you remember Lily and Sunray? They'd wanted to build a cob house for decades." Sandra watched the flame, making sure the wood caught. She was pointedly ignoring my question. I did remember Lily and Sunray, a sweet lesbian couple a few years older than Sandra; they used to work on their cob house drawings in the evenings at the old commune. I could see their drawings of round windows and thatched roofs in my mind.

"I remember them. They used to give me raspberries threaded onto a piece of green hay in the summer. A Swedish tradition?" Sunray was originally from a Northern European country.

"Norwegian," Sandra corrected. "We all agreed when we moved here that the place couldn't die out with us, that we needed to widen our circle."

"A bit morbid."

"Realistic. Our dream for this land wasn't just for ourselves. We wanted to establish a place that lived on, a safe community for fellow witches."

"So this is like the witch sorority house then?" I couldn't help dropping in a little snark.

Sandra laughed. "Not far off. I never really thought of this as a witch college, though."

"Too bad, I was hoping to transfer my college credits." I meant it to sound light, but the bitterness seeped into my voice. I had worked hard on my undergrad and had been gearing up for a master's in history when my life went sideways. I wasn't sure I'd ever get back to it.

Sandra got up from the floor and sat next to me. The fire was crackling and dancing in the hearth.

"Reva, I'm sorry this has all happened," she said, putting her hand over mine. I tensed, waiting for more from her, the I-told-you-so. She stayed quiet.

"I know. I'm sorry too," I finally responded when I was confident I wouldn't cry. My voice still cracked a little.

"I wish I could make it all better. I know this isn't your first choice to be here."

I chuckled softly. "Sandra, it's my only choice. And I'm the only one to blame."

"The only one?" Sandra looked at me thoughtfully. I hated it when she did that, searching me for another level of truth like a human lie detector.

"Yes." I didn't want to tell her about Anthony. I had never told her about him, as if deep down I knew it was never going to last. And even everything that had happened with him was my fault. I looked away.

We sat in silence for a while, watching the fire. I remembered spending nights like this with her and the commune sisters in the past. Watching the fire, telling stories, but mostly just sitting with our thoughts. I had enjoyed my thoughts more back then.

"I'd like to ask you about what happened this afternoon," Sandra said in a quiet voice. She kept her eyes trained on the fire.

I sighed. "I guess the others told you. What more is there to say?"

"I would like to hear it from you." Sandra paused, as if she was searching for the right words. "I know you left the craft behind years ago. But we need to talk about this. It sounded like a pretty intense vision."

"Or hallucination. Or a psychotic breakdown."

"Whatever you want to call it. We don't need to fight over the words. Or even what it means. You were dead asleep when I came into your room, and you were cold. That took a lot out of you. A lot you don't have to give right now."

I couldn't argue with her about that. Whatever it was, it had left me drained. I was already exhausted, though I had slept most of the day.

"I want to help you heal, Reva. Will you let me?" Sandra turned to me with beseeching eyes.

I sat back on the couch. I was here to heal. And I really didn't want to have any more visions or whatever that was.

"Let me think about it."

I spent the next few days unpacking. Alex carried all the boxes up for me, waving away help from me.

"Your wrist is still healing," she said as she stacked my possessions in the corner.

I felt a weird mix of relief and irritation that she so blatantly talked about my injury, like she was treading on something private but also not tiptoeing around it like so many others might.

In the hospital, they had told me my injuries were a cry for help, the wounds were superficial and fortunately not deep enough to have left permanent damage. After an evaluation and being held for seventy-two hours, I was released. One week later, I tried a different method. That one almost worked.

I unpacked slowly with one hand. Keena helped me with a few of the items. A dresser and a blue armchair materialized one day from the back of Sandra's van. She and Alex moved the furniture up for me. Within a few days, I had a private space that was mine. Nothing hung on the walls, but I had clothes in drawers and a chair to sit and read in by the window. Spare and clean, a new start.

I stopped by the cobb house and circle of trailers on the other side of the farm, trying to catch up with the women I had known years before. It was shocking to see how much they had aged and how many of them had become reclusive, their warmth I remembered from my youth replaced with the tepid conversation one has with a stranger. Which, I realized, I was to them. I was no longer the child they remembered so I supposed it was fair that they were no longer the aunties I recalled.

Sunray and Lily were still welcoming. They had always been my favorite of the commune members. We sat around their kitchen table in their cobb house chatting over tea and catching up.

"Sandra told us she was going to get you from Seattle, I was shocked it was out of a hospital!" Lily eventually couldn't stop herself from going to the topic I wasn't ready to discuss. "What happened?"

Sunray remained quiet while Lily kept going after an awkward pause where I sat frozen. Lily started a story about a friend struggling with depression, trying to relate to me. She meant well but I wasn't ready to face my own thoughts about what had happened, let alone with women I didn't know anymore. I wrapped up the visit and promised myself I'd go see them later, when I felt stronger.

Mostly I stuck around the house. The weather was gray and rainy with damp chill. In between setting up the room and sleeping a lot, I found myself in the library. I wanted to be able to visit the greenhouse room, to sit in the warmth and greenery, but the memories of the vision kept me away. I had explored the altar room briefly but found it a little creepy. It consisted of large open shelves running the walls like the library but instead of being filled with books, they were crammed full of a weird assortment of candles, rocks, animal skulls, and figurines. Each shelf was reserved for a different deity. A large antique mirror hung over the mantle of another large fireplace. There was no furniture aside from pillows and low tuffets.

In the library, I found a denim-covered wingback chair by a window where I took to sitting each day and reading. I had found a shelf of books I remembered reading when I was a teenager. Revisiting the collection was comforting but after a while I branched out and looked at the other shelves. The subjects ranged from herbs and astrology as I expected to serious biology and physics books. There was a history section I found one day and spent hours in, finding small booklets on the local area history of logging and Native tribes interspersed with books on the history of the Salem witch trials. I would have stayed there, immersed in my favorite subject of history, but one afternoon something strange happened.

I was flipping through a slender volume on the founding and rivalry of the towns of Coos Bay and North Bend when suddenly a warm sensation ran up my spine, nerves activating. Then I heard whispering, the sound of unintelligible voices in the wind or hidden in the white noise of a river. The sound was coming from a corner of the room, down low.

I froze, worried I was about to go into a vision. Minutes ticked by, the whispering continued at the same level. I got up, putting the book on a side table. I walked toward the door, ready to run, but paused. This was the one room I had felt comfortable in. I didn't want to be run out of it.

Turning back to the room, I walked toward where the whispering was coming from. In the corner of the room by the fireplace was a low set of shelves with closed glass-front doors.

Crouching down, I peered in through the wavy and bubbled glass. It looked like more books, nothing more. I lifted the small latch keeping the doors shut and pulled open the cabinet.

The whispering became louder and faster. There were a few books, leather bound with no titles. I tentatively flipped through them. They looked like journals, which normally would have intrigued me but something behind them caught my eye. The shelf was deep, the journals in front blocking how deep. I took a few of the journals out and stacked them on the floor. Behind the books was another one, lying flat. I put my hands on it and pulled it out in a cloud of dust. The whispering stopped.

The book was about twelve inches wide and sixteen inches tall and thick with rippled pages. It was bound in cloth, faded and tattered navy with a faint silver star pattern embossed all over. The spine and edges had little scraps of equally faded multicolored fabric over the navy cloth, attempts to keep the whole thing together. A handmade book and likely another journal.

There were no words on the cover. It smelled musty, like fall leaves late in the season. A simple brass clasp held it closed. I carefully tugged at the clasp, cautious to not damage it. At one point there had probably been a small lock on the clasp, but it was missing.

I opened the front cover, feeling the need for white cotton gloves like libraries use for looking at rare and old books. The title page was pale brown around the edges, the sign of aging paper. In the middle of the page someone had written in cursive with brown ink:

Book of Shadows

Quinn

I'd heard of books of shadows, or grimoires as they sometimes were called. They were personal books of spells, recipes, healing techniques, often handed down over generations of witches. Sandra kept one; she had promised to pass it on to me one day. Despite my reluctance around witchcraft, books of shadows were intriguing to me and my history bent. Seeing my own last name on the page was particularly interesting ... and disconcerting. I would have thought Sandra would mention such a book to me.

I turned the page. There began writing in small loopy cursive. It was hard to read. I picked myself off the floor and walked back to the chair so I could look more closely at the book with the light of a lamp. With focus, I was able to decipher the following:

Here begins our craft in America for the two Quinn sisters. A new beginning meant for a new book as the fire deprived us of our history. We left much behind: a grave of an innocent for Mary, and for me, Helen, a secret too dangerous to share. We arrived on the shores of New York on a July night, carrying with us three items that survived from the old country: the last surviving teacup from the Quinn china, Mother's ruby ring, and the knife. Our overseas journey is finished but there is more to come.

The next pages contained a recipe for an herbal compress for fever, a spell for finding decent employment and an invocation for good luck. I flipped through looking for more writing from Helen Quinn. After about five pages, I came to one page that read:

Mary took her own life on Saturday. By the time I knew of the demon sitting on her chest, it was too late. Forgiveness is the hardest part. The anger I feel at Mary for leaving me is eclipsed only by the anger at myself. The visions had told her that death would greet her in America. I didn't listen, choosing to believe that would be years in the future as aged ladies. Fools we all be.

The next pages were more spells. As I flipped through, they shifted. What had started as almost a recipe book was now becoming much darker. There were pages devoted to descriptions of summoning spirits and talking with the dead. It made sense to me, the death of her sister and Helen wanting to communicate with the dead. Pages later was another passage:

I am with child. Mary tells me in dreams that the child will be a girl. He makes promises to take care of us, to protect us, but I know they are hollow. I don't need the ghost of my sister telling me so. He was never meant to be more than a passing fancy, but I was a fool and fell in love. Mary also told me to leave this state, head West. I have waited, thinking my dreams could come true. That he could leave his wife and be with me. More foolishness on my part. I have bought passage to San Francisco, a rough long journey that I worry I may not survive. Of him, I will say my goodbye and not look back.

The next update came up quickly, a page or two later.

She has arrived. Oona Mary Quinn was born on a Friday on the twelfth day of April in the year of 1861. She arrives into a battle-torn country, a child born into war. We left not a moment too soon for the West. The next years will be difficult in more than one way, but we are out of the heat of Savannah.

More pages of healing recipes and spells followed with a focus on children.

I have left the maiden behind and am now the mother. Oona is a joy and a curse in the same breath. She holds a power down deep that is chaotic and strong. I worry that she will have a difficult life for all the strength she keeps. She took to my marriage poorly. I have not been able to keep much in this book for fear of my husband finding it. He is a good man but not my equal. Needs must, we couldn't have gotten through another winter on our own. A hard life it is for us women.

I flipped forward and found blank pages. That seemed to be the last of Helen's writing. I was about to close the book with the assumption that was the end of the story when I found a page with writing different from Helen's, looser and larger with a significant slant. I found it easier to read though.

Mother has passed from this realm as well as my last brother she tried to bear. She left me this book in secret, telling me in her 8th month as if she foresaw the outcome. If only she had never married that pig. Four children in and still he demanded more. Here ends the shadow of Helen Quinn. Here begins the shadow of Oona Quinn.

I flipped the pages and found only blankness again all the way to the end. Disappointed, I went to close the book when my hand came across a strange bump on the inside of the back cover. The whispering started again. I carefully opened to the back cover and found a small round protrusion there. A circular piece of faded gray velvet had been stitched with red string into the book. The stitching looked tight, as if it had been done yesterday.

I touched the tip of my index finger onto the circle of fabric. The whispering doubled in volume and speed. I could feel a small hard object underneath the velvet. I pushed my finger against it. The thread loosened and unraveled as if an invisible force was unthreading it.

I gasped and pulled my hand back. The unravel continued and the thread floated to the floor. My curiosity got the better of me. I reached back and touched the velvet, watching it crumble into little pieces under my touch. Under it sat a small gold ring set with a gemstone.

I pulled the ring out and the whispering stopped. The metal was dull from years of being enclosed in the book and embossed with tiny stars, much like the book's outside cover. The stone was set in the band, a modest small stone in a deep reddish purple. It was not faceted but rather was round and smooth. When turned in the light, a star pattern appeared in the middle of the stone.

I slipped it onto my ring finger on my left hand, the injured one. The ring slid on as if it was meant for the finger. As I positioned it, a strange but pleasant sensation came over me. Nerves on my hand tingled up my arm, running down my spine. A warmth and calm came over me. A thought came into my head: this ring had been waiting for me. It was ridiculous but I felt certain of it. We belonged to each other.

Chapter 5

We were all seated at dinner the next day, the shared meals being a routine I enjoyed already. Some nights there may have been one or two people missing due to a work schedule or various other reasons, but breaking bread together was the norm. Keena had cooked this time, a vegan take on Southern cooking that was surprisingly delicious to non-vegan me: fried tofu with hot sauce, collard greens stuffed with rice, a pecan and apple salad, cornbread.

Keena was in the middle of explaining that she grew up in the South when Darcy interrupted and pointed to my left hand resting on the table.

"Where did you get that?" she asked.

"What?" I replied. I put my left hand on my lap.

Given the jewelry Darcy wore, elaborate large stones set in silver that twisted like tree roots, I should have anticipated she would be the first to notice. I didn't want to talk about the ring. It felt private, my own secret. I wanted it to be mine as much as it felt like it already was. I didn't know who it belonged to originally or who the book of shadows belonged to now.

"You know what. That stunning ring on your left hand. Is it what I think it is?"

"Don't know what you're talking about."

Keena and Sora were watching with interest. Alex was out that evening and Sandra had a shift at the hospital. Bear, sensing a distraction, came over from the hearth where he had been relegated along with Flame. He sat and looked at me as expectantly as the other three women at the table. Only they wanted me to spill my guts, not my cornbread.

"I found it." I watched Darcy's eyebrows go up to her scalp.

"Let me take a look at it." She held her hands out across the table. I reluctantly placed my left hand out to her. She peered closely at the ring, spinning it a few ways on my finger. I was grateful she didn't ask me to take it off.

Darcy scrutinized the ring. "That's a star ruby. And the band looks antique. Victorian maybe. The star pattern is unusual." I gently pulled back my hand and was grateful she let it go.

Sora and Keena insisted on seeing it though, exclaiming at the beauty.

"I love the stars going around it," Sora said.

"Where did you get it again?" Darcy broke in.

"I ..." Unsure what to say, I paused. I didn't want to explain I had found it stashed in their library, afraid it would be lost to me. It also felt wrong to keep it under lies. The ring felt like a force of good, if that made any sense, given it was inanimate. If it wasn't mine, it was better to deal with that before I got more attached to it.

I told them about the book of shadows in the library, tucked behind other books. I hesitated to mention the whispering. It sounded so crazy to say out loud. Keena and Darcy took my explanation as is, with the whispering omitted.

"Let's check it out after dinner," Keena said with excitement in her voice.

Sora looked at me thoughtfully. "What made you look in that cupboard? You described it as hidden."

"I was just digging through books and came upon it," I said nonchalantly. Sora gazed at me, like she could smell the omission but didn't say anything.

After dinner, washing up, and putting away leftovers for our missing members, we all trooped into the library. There were hot coals in the fireplace from earlier when I'd made a fire. Keena added smaller pieces of wood to get the flame up.

"Too bad Alex or Sandra isn't here," Darcy remarked. "They both have a way with the flames," she added for my benefit.

Keena smiled at me. "We each have our elements we're best in."

Sora turned to me. "Where's the book?"

I had put the book back on another shelf, tucked between a book about bat species and another about the Northern Lights.

Sora held out her hand. "May I?"

"Sora loves books of shadows," Darcy said. She and Keena walked over.

"They have some of the best recipes in them," Sora said as I reluctantly placed the book in her hand. "Not just for food but for healing techniques as well."

The other two women stood next to Sora as she turned the book over in her hands.

"This is really old, Reva."

"I'd estimate it's from the 1850s, right before the Civil War," I said, my enthusiasm for history overriding my protectiveness of it.

Sora handed the book over to Darcy who brought it up close to her face.

"The stitching on the spine with all these patches is amazing. Whoever owned it had a special technique with their needle skills. You can feel the magic sewn in with the threads." She ran her black pointed nails over the patches of fabric.

"The drawings inside are very intricate as well," I said. All three women turned to me, puzzled looks on their faces.

"How did you open it?" Sora asked.

I stared back at them in puzzlement. "What do you mean how? I opened up the cover and started reading."

Darcy, Sora, and Keena looked at each other. Darcy turned the cover toward me and tapped on the clasp. A small but sturdy lock in a teardrop shape adorned the clasp. It looked tarnished and rusty, at that stage of disuse where even the key wouldn't open it.

I looked at it in astonishment. "It was open this morning. There was no lock on it. I swear!"

"No need to swear. We believe you," Sora said. "How did you find it again?

I felt her eyes on me. I felt all their eyes on me.

"I heard whispering," I said in a low voice. "Coming from this cupboard here."

I walked them over to the spot where I'd found the book. Darcy crouched down and peered through the glass before opening it. The journals were stacked back where I had put them.

"Behind those journals, this was laying there." I pointed to the shelf.

"Interesting. What did the whispering sound like?" Darcy asked.

"Like — oh, it's hard to describe. It was creepy but not bad, if that makes sense." Darcy nodded, though Keena and Sora looked at me as if it did not resonate with them. "It sounded like when you're out in the woods and hear a stream in the distance or the wind through the trees. The underlay of not quite words."

"Le Mer Murmure," Darcy said. She must have read the bafflement on my face, and clarified, "It's a French witch term for whispers of the sea. It's a magical calling technique. Only if the message is meant for you do you hear it. It was a common practice on the Breton coast."

"How do you know about that?" Sora asked, stealing the question from me.

"I read things, I've been around," Darcy said cryptically. She handed the book to me. "Where was the ring? You said it was inside the book?"

I nodded and took the book. As soon as my hands touched it, the lock disappeared. We all gasped. I looked at each of the women.

"Did you see that?" Sora asked excitedly. "That's strong magic!"

"Very strong," Darcy agreed. "The ring was inside?"

"Yes." I opened to the back of the book and showed them the pocket, reluctantly adding that it was sewn shut. "Then I touched it and it sort of unraveled."

"Unraveled how?" Keena asked.

I looked at her. I didn't know how to explain it.

"Unraveled like it was opening for you?" Darcy said, waiting for a nod from me before continuing. "I've read about such spells. They're a combination of a powerful binding with a calling spell. Rare and require a lot of knowledge and power to pull off. This was one powerful witch who put that together."

"Why would it call Reva?" Keena mused.

A small part of myself wanted to take offense at the question but I also knew Keena wasn't coming from a place of jealousy, only curiosity. And it was a question I asked myself, though I knew one thing more than they did.

"The book and the witches referenced in it share my last name, Quinn."

"Well, that makes sense. A book of shadows often is handed down over generations," Sora said.

"If that's the case, why wouldn't it have called Sandra?" Darcy asked, almost to herself.

"Why wouldn't what have called me?" Sandra appeared in the doorway behind us, eating a piece of cornbread.

The women proceeded to animatedly tell her what I had shared. Sandra walked over and looked at the book in my hands. Her face registered shock when Darcy said the book had unlocked for me.

"Really? The Quinn Book of Shadows opened for you?" Sandra asked me.

"You know about this book? That it belongs to the Quinns?" I had never heard of it before. Usually anything related to the family Sandra shared with me. She and my mother had lost their single mother in a car accident and had been raised by a taciturn uncle and aunt I had never met.

"It was passed down to us in our inheritance, but I only found it a few years ago, after Aunt Margret died. It was in a box of items in her attic. I have vague memories of my mother using it so yes, Quinn. We're lucky Aunt Margaret kept it; she was an unsentimental woman. I tried figuring out how to unlock it but with no luck."

"It was bound with a pretty complicated spell. Here — watch this." Darcy grabbed the book from my hands and handed it to Sandra. The lock reappeared. "Hand it back to Reva."

Sandra passed it back to me. Her mouth opened in surprise as the lock disappeared.

"What's inside?" she asked eagerly.

"Here, I'll show you." I opened the book to the first page. It was blank. I turned the page. Blank. I flipped through frantically. Every single page was blank. I looked up in horror. I must be going crazy. Magic unlocking book or not, had I spent the afternoon in some sort of hallucination?

"What's wrong?" Sandra was watching me carefully.

"It's blank! I swear, there was writing, recipes, spells. A journal of Helen Quinn." Panic seeped out in my voice.

"I believe you," Sandra said. "Helen Quinn is a direct ancestor of ours from what I've found in ancestry research."

"Maybe the book is shy around others," Sora spoke up. "I have a book of shadows that was passed on to me from my mother. It looks like it's all gibberish to others, but I understand it perfectly."

The panic receded. If I was crazy, I was in good company at least.

"Oh, show Sandra the ring," Darcy broke in.

"The ring?" Sandra asked.

I held out my hand and showed her the star ruby on my left hand. Sandra took a sharp breath in as she looked at it.

"You better tell me everything, from the top." She led us all over to the couch and chairs by the fire.

Later, after the retelling and sharing Helen's stories I'd read in the journal, we were sitting around the fire drinking tea that Keena and Sora had brought in. Each woman mused on private thoughts. Sandra finally broke the quiet.

"Thanks for sharing all of that. I'll admit I'm a little jealous it never opened for me." She looked down sheepishly. "But I'm glad it opened for you."

"It's all blank now. What if that was the only chance I had to take it all in?" I was feeling low after the high and attention from earlier.

"I'd be surprised. But if that's what the book wants, then so be it," Sandra said in her usual fatalistic way. "What does make me wonder, though, is why the pages Oona Quinn wrote were blank."

"How do you know Oona wrote in the book, besides that one page?" I asked.

"Oona Quinn was a powerful witch, probably the most powerful in our known family history. She had the skills to create that sort of binding magic. It's old and strong. She had the skill to make the book behave like this."

"I felt how old it was when I held it in my hands," Darcy said. She looked wistfully at the book as it lay in my lap. Sandra reached over and gave her hand a pat, the sort of simple gesture that conveys understanding in a whole complicated emotional history.

"Hopefully it will reveal more to you, Reva," Keena chimed in softly. "Probably you need to work on your craft and more will come."

I looked at Keena, wondering if she was campaigning on behalf of Sandra to start the witchcraft back up. She looked back at me with an open face. If anyone was campaigning on behalf of Sandra, it was apparently a long-dead ancestor of mine. A lot had happened in the course of the day, things I could only explain with magic. I had guessed the whole thing could be an elaborate set up — switching of the book I read for an identical blank one, a recording of whispering noises. But it didn't explain the solid lock that had disappeared and reappeared in front of me more than once. Or the way the ring made me feel, the healing and protective energy it emanated. After years of turning my back on magic, I wanted to believe again.

I ended up agreeing to study the craft again, hesitantly letting Sandra know after a day mulling it over. I was feeling restless and I needed something to do. I had one caveat with the studying. I wanted to know more about our family.

"I've never known much about them. There's a whole history that's also part of my own history," I told Sandra.

"Your mother felt differently," Sandra replied. "She all but forbade me from telling you about the history. She wanted a clean slate for both of you."

"Ginny does love clean slates. She's like a whiteboard, sketch a life out with some marker and then wipe it all away. Never really gets fully clean though, all the past sketches linger like ghosts." A bitter note crept into my voice.

Sandra chuckled. "That's a very apt description of her."

"I just hate that she made the decision for me." I held many of my mother's decisions for me against her. She never seemed to be operating out of my best interests.

"Well, that's only partly fair. When you were little and visited me, she made the decision on what I could and could not tell you. But once you were on your own, I would have told you. I had planned to." Sandra let the unspoken lie between us. If I hadn't left, if we hadn't fought, I might know more now. I felt a flash of anger before taking a breath and reminding myself I had to own my actions. It was easy to assume Sandra was laying blame with her words, but I didn't think so. Sandra was taking more blame than she was responsible for, and I was claiming the opposite out of guilt. I had left and pushed her away for so many years.

At least I was back and working toward rebuilding with her now. And agreeing to get back to the craft was a huge leap forward with us. I was still wary, but Sandra was beside herself with excitement.

"You have so much potential. I've always been a mediocre witch —" She waved off Keena's attempt to interrupt in protest at the last sentence. "No, it's true. I've learned a lot and I can hold my own, but I think my real power has always been in skills that don't need magic. Like community building."

I smiled. Community building was exactly the type of skill that Sandra, a West Coast hippie to the core, would own over being able to produce fire at her fingertips.

"There are many other witches here you can learn from, here in this house. I'll start setting you up with them."

"But you'll be on the history lesson duty," I replied.

Sandra grinned. "I suppose I'll be the best one for that."

Chapter 6

The first day of lessons began with Sora. I wasn't sure what to expect, what I'd be learning. I came downstairs with Tuna and Kiz following me. After the excitement that first day with Midori opening the door and the cat fight, I had been careful to lock my door. One afternoon it slipped my mind and I returned to find the pile of cats I had left on my bed had increased in size. Midori lay curled up next to Kiz and Tuna, all a happy purr fest. A truce seemed to have happened between the cats and now I could let Tuna and Kiz roam through a large part of the house. The kitchen was off limits at dinner when the dogs were in at the hearth, and the greenhouse was off limits to all the animals. Which made sense to me; my cats would only see a vast area of toilet options or plants to destroy.

Tuna had taken to following me down for breakfast each morning to sleep on the hearth. Kiz came in hope of treats. Sora greeted us as we entered the kitchen together. She was sitting at the table waiting for me with a plate of scrambled eggs, sausages, and fruit. Breakfast was the opposite of dinner, every woman to herself and on every different schedule. I normally cooked a soft-boiled egg on toast for myself unless someone had made something to share.

Sora knew everyone's schedule by heart. "Alex is the first to rise, getting up at some dark hour to make herself a protein shake before exercising. Then I'm up, often baking first thing. Morning baking produces better quick breads, and if you're going to make yeast bread, you have to start early. Sandra follows with granola and whatever fruit we have on hand. Keena is next, taking a leisurely tea and toast in the green room. And then you."

"What about Darcy?"

"Darcy doesn't eat breakfast. She's still asleep. Total night owl."

Kiz gave a hopeful meow and jumped up on the bench, heading to the plate. I shooed him off and sat. A large steaming cup of coffee waited for me.

"Thanks for all this, Sora. You didn't need to go through this much trouble." I immediately took a sip of coffee.

"You'll need a good breakfast today for what I have planned." Sora smiled at me. She was wearing a green wool sweater, probably hand knit by one of the older women in the community. I looked at it with a bit of jealousy. I loved hand knitted items. They had more soul than manufactured clothes, as if the knitter included a bit of themselves in each item.

"What do we have planned? Magical baking?" I asked as I shoveled eggs in my mouth. Kiz looked at me with his big green eyes and jumped up next to me on the bench. It was useless to push him off.

"Magical baking?" Sora asked with a hint of irritation. I looked up at her slight frown. I had offended her though I wasn't sure how.

"Sorry, I didn't mean ..." I paused. "If I offended you, I didn't mean to."

She softened. "I didn't mean to jump on you. I'm not always taken seriously as a witch because I do a lot of kitchen witchery."

"Kitchen witchery?"

"It's a type of witchcraft. It's not exactly as it sounds, all focused on the kitchen. It encompasses much more. It's the magic of hearth and home. I'm studying other types." She had an edge of defensiveness in her voice.

"Well, I don't know a lot about different types of magic," I said cautiously.

"But the judgment on the domestic side of it was still there," she pointed out, taking me aback. I hadn't seen this side of Sora before. It was refreshing.

I laughed. "Touche. There was bias there I didn't even know."

"Exactly how bias works." Sora smiled back. I saw relief in her eyes. I was beginning to understand she had this deep seated need to please that was maybe at odds with other parts of her. "Eat up, we're going for a walk after this."

"A walk? It's raining." I picked up a sausage and ate half. Kiz murmured beside me, a reminder that he was still there, waiting. He was practically on my lap. If I wasn't careful, he'd reach out and snatch the meat right out of my hand. I gave him a pet on the head, which he dodged to sniff my fingers.

"Rain is rather constant this time of year. You'll get used to it. Besides, it's the best way to see the forest."

I sighed dramatically. A drop of drool hit my lap from Kiz. I gave up and threw a piece of sausage on the floor. He dove after it with a small warning growl to Tuna who was curled up in front of the fire with not a sausage concern in the world.

"You lived in Seattle, Reva. You can handle a little rain," Sora said. "I have rain pants you can borrow. They'll be short but with boots, you'll be right as rain."

I couldn't help but smile at her. She had an odd way of being young and old at the same time but in a welcoming way. After finishing breakfast, I put on the rain pants, which weren't as snug as I expected them to be, and some old hiking boots with a raincoat. I moved stiffly from the fabric on the pants, a waxed duck cotton rather than artificial poly, but after the pants warmed up to my body, I was fine.

Sora put on a ratty old gray wool sweater and a wide brimmed felted hat. She seemed to be all in wool. We left the cats sleeping on the hearth with a few extra logs to get them through the next few hours and headed outside.

The cold air shocked me. I hadn't been outside much in the last few weeks, choosing to stay inside holed up for weeks as January ran by. In a few days, it would be February. My wrist was healing at an accelerated rate, about a week faster than predicted. Several of the witches were sure it was due to the ruby ring I wore all the time. The skeptic in me thought it was hooey but a bigger part of me agreed despite the fact I had only been wearing the ring for a few days. It was a strange thing to see the witchcraft skeptic receding so quickly and the witchcraft believer taking over.

Sora walked ahead of me with a thin wooden walking stick, the top of it carved into something I couldn't make out. It seemed like it had materialized out of thin air, but she must have picked it off the back porch or something while I had been lost in thought about the weeks and the cold air on my cheeks.

I felt good being outside, my breathing a little labored as I tried to keep up with Sora. She kept a quick pace following a narrow path in the dead grass towards the forest behind the house. As we got closer, I could see the pines and leafless branches towering above the dense understory of ferns.

Two towering cedars flanked each side of the path at the entrance to the forest. Sora paused there, waiting for me to catch up.

"Are you ready?" she asked me, more behind her question than just asking if I was ready for more walking in the woods. I nodded, looking up at the cedars.

"Our sentinel trees," Sora said, awe and pride in her voice as she followed my gaze up.

"Tree guards?" I liked the idea.

"They've been standing watch for hundreds of years. These two are probably getting close to five hundred years old." Sora reached out and fondly patted the trunk of the cedar on her left. "Come on, more to explore."

I followed her into the forest, passing the two cedars as if going through a gate. I wondered idly if it would feel different approaching the sentinel trees on my own, without Sora as my guide. As we walked, the sound changed. Everything was quieter and calmer. I breathed out and felt a type of relaxation I hadn't experienced in years. I had forgotten how wonderful it was to take a walk in the forest.

"It's quiet today. It often is in winter. The season of the moss." As soon as she said it, I noticed the green moss hanging off the limbs of the trees, rich golden greens that glowed in the gray light of the day.

I looked over and found Sora watching me. She smiled, clearly pleased to see me taking in what she was pointing out.

"Today we're going to look for mushrooms."

"Oh." I felt a twinge of disappointment. I had told myself we were just going on a walk but deep down I was hoping for my first day with the craft to be more dramatic than looking for a food I wasn't even fond of. Sandra had taken me mushroom hunting before, for chanterelles, but I had never gotten the appeal.

Sora looked at me for a second, pushing a few strands of her long dark hair out of her face. "This is part of the craft, I promise. You won't be disappointed."

"Looking for waterlogged, tasteless sponges for dinner? No, I'm sure it'll be great." I felt like an asshole as soon as the words left my mouth.

Sora, to her credit and my relief, laughed. I understood why Sandra had started me with her; my bitter humor didn't faze her. "Not a mushroom fan, I see. We're out of the season for edible mushrooms. And there are ways to make them not so soggy. That's not what we're doing, though."

She turned and veered off the trail, sidestepping a big fern that looked worse for the wear from the winter. I followed her less gracefully and ended up brushing up against the fern, a slap of moisture hitting my shins. I was glad I had put on the waxed pants.

"What are we doing then?"

"We're getting our mushroom eyes on. It's the first step in seeing the rest of the hidden forest," Sora said matter-of-factly.

"Mushroom eyes?"

She nodded. "You have to train your eyes to look for what's hidden. There's a whole world you can't see with your regular vision. Fungi are a part of that world, blooming into the in-between."

"Okay, I'll take your word for it." My skeptical self clicked in, not wanting to believe in some "hidden" world. "Are we looking for fairies next?"

"You're not ready for fairies," Sora said in a serious tone. She stopped in front of me and bent down. "See, look at this."

I bent down stiffly in the wax pants and looked where she was pointing. At first, I saw moss and dead leaves. Then slowly, I saw tiny mushrooms, sticking up from the ground. They were scarcely bigger than a pin, their rounded caps a bright orange. Once I saw them, I couldn't help but wonder how I'd missed them.

"Those are cute."

Sora nodded. "They're good indicators of what may be close by. Imagine the network of mycelium connecting them all under the forest. The internet of the plant world."

"I didn't know you were such a plant geek, Sora."

"Guilty. I get it from my dad."

"Oh, is he a plant guy?"

"He was." She said it with a finality that told me he was dead.

"I'm sorry," I said.

"It's okay." Sora looked sad, like a lost little girl for a moment, younger than her already young age. "It was a few years ago. Car crash. I miss them every day."

I tentatively reached out and put my hand on her arm. She smiled weakly at me before standing up abruptly.

"Let's look for more," she said, leading us deeper into the woods.

We continued to tromp through the woods, eyes downcast on the forest floor. A tiny little world unfolded, not just of mushrooms. The floor was covered with clumps of moss, rotting logs with lichen. Sora walked ahead of me, sometimes pointing out different flora and briefly describing different medicinal or ritual use of them.

After a while, we both became quiet and focused, the little bits of conversation ceasing. Sora was about a yard in front of me when I caught movement out of the corner of my right eye. I turned my head as a fawn bounded away. As it leapt into the brush, I noticed it had horns. Without a thought, I veered after it. It seemed early for baby deer, and horns seemed unusual. Did I imagine the horns? The size?

I followed the direction of the deer, ducking under leafless branches and pine boughs. As I climbed over a fallen log, the damp wood crumbled underfoot. I fell forward onto the other side of the log. I managed to catch myself before I fell flat on my face. I still went down on my hands and knees, my damaged wrist twinging in pain. Fortunately, the ground was soft with moss, which minimized the impact.

My breath was coming out a little ragged. I hadn't even realized I had been running but my lungs were telling me a different story. I paused, looking up from the ground. I was in a little clearing, dead clumps of grass and foliage suggesting a meadow area. Across the clearing about five yards away stood the deer, watching me.

The deer was small, as I thought, but bigger than a fawn. It had white spots at the rear, its coat turning from a golden brown to a pale tan as it neared the neck and head. One of the deer's eyes was a pale blue while the other was a golden brown. The horns were full antlers, reaching out like tree branches, and mottled with patches of pale green.

We continued to look at each other as seconds ticked by. My breathing returned to normal and a calmness spread through me as the deer watched me. I felt a strange deja vu of familiarity with the deer before remembering my visions as a child. Maybe I hadn't met this deer, but I had met his kind before. Just not in real life.

The deer watched me, motionless as a statue. I waited and tried to recall what I had felt as a child. The word "open" came to me. Be open, I told myself. The deer waited.

"Reva!"

A voice called out in the distance. I looked over my shoulder toward the sound. Sora must be looking for me. When I glanced back, the deer had vanished. The clearing was still but for a slight trembling of a low branch.

I pulled myself up and walked back the way I came. Sora called my name again, a note of concern in the sound. I called back to her and walked over the forest floor in her direction. I climbed over a log and around a tree to see her scrambling quickly toward me.

"Reva! Where'd you go?" Her brow was furrowed in worry, and she was breathing heavily. I immediately felt guilty. How could I ditch her like that?

"I ..." I paused, not sure what to say. "I'm sorry. I saw something and took off after it."

"It's so easy to get lost out here!" A cloud of anger passed over Sora's face. "What were you thinking?"

"I wasn't thinking. I'm so sorry. I didn't mean to worry you."

Her face softened. "It's okay. I should have said we needed to stay together and warned you about getting lost. Until you get to know these woods, it's better if you're with someone, particularly when hunting like this. So easy to get turned around."

"Don't apologize! It's my fault." I cringed inwardly as she took on the blame. "I know better, and you didn't need to spell it out to stay with you."

"Let's go back and warm up with some hot chocolate." Sora turned away and led us back to the trail.

We walked single file along the trail in silence.

"What did you see that you were following?" she finally asked.

"A tiny deer." I felt stupid as it rolled off my tongue. I didn't know how else to describe it. Sora stopped so suddenly I almost ran into her. She spun around.

"A tiny deer?" Her voice held excitement.

"It sounds silly now. I saw what looked like a fawn and bolted after it. You'd think I'm part Labrador or something."

"Did you see it? Or just get a glimpse?"

"I followed it into a clearing. Tan and white spotted miniature deer. With big weird colored horns —"

"Horns? It had horns?" Her excitement level had reached a new peak.

"Yeah."

Sora looked at me with wide eyes. "That's amazing."

"It was weird. I've never seen a deer like that before. I thought maybe it was a hallucination."

"No, it was real. I've never seen one of the Evernia deer before, but I've read about them. And you saw one on your first visit." Sora turned, walking fast toward home. "You have to tell me everything. I'm so jealous."

"The Evernia deer?" I scrambled to keep up with her.

"They're a rare subspecies of deer that live in the in-between. You have to be in the right space to see them unless they're passing on a message. To see a horned one, even more rare. You're sure it had horns?"

"Yes. Pale green horns."

"Definitely Evernia. Come on, let's get back!"

The light through the trees increased as we got closer to the end of the forest. We walked out between the two cedar sentinels into the fields above the commune. I felt a pang of regret leaving the forest even as I looked forward to the hot chocolate. There was so much more there to learn.

Back at the house, I changed into warm, dry jeans and joined Sora in the kitchen. Keena had flatbread and a big pot of potato soup for lunch. Sora whipped up a rich and milky hot chocolate as easily as a normal person would make instant coffee. I sat at the table and took a sip. Chocolate, ginger, cinnamon, and something else swirled on my tongue.

"Is that rose?" I asked, trying to decipher the floral hint.

"It is!" Sora said. "Brings good luck."

Keena and Darcy were sitting at the table, Keena finishing up the last of her soup and Darcy nursing a cup of coffee. Sora excitedly told them about our hunt, as she kept calling it, and my run-in with the Evernia stag.

"The green on the horns, that's lichen growing on them. Hence the name, Evernia, beard lichen," Darcy said, perking up either due to the caffeine hitting her blood or the excitement of the deer.

"How long did you say you watched it?" Keena asked.

"A few seconds," I said.

"Reva, I lost you for about twenty minutes," Sora said. "You make it sound like you were gone for a few minutes."

"That's what it felt like to me," I said. "I saw the deer out of the corner of my eye, ran after it, and saw it in the clearing where I tumbled over a log." I hadn't wanted to mention my clumsiness, but my wrist was aching since the event. I would need to let Sandra know anyway so she could examine it and make sure I hadn't caused any damage.

"Cryptids like that live in another time boundary, the Other Realm. It's not surprising there's a disconnect in how long you were away and how long you perceived you were." Keena looked out the window thoughtfully. "I'm glad it was an auspicious cryptid. It sounds like the stag respected your time.

There are stories of people having an interaction that lasts minutes to them, but they come back days later."

"The Evernia are benign but I'm not sure it was a good luck encounter. It sounds like there was a message for you, Reva. It wouldn't have shown itself otherwise. Particularly not a stag of substantial age, based on the horns," Darcy said.

"Did I mention the eyes?" I said after reflecting on the encounter. "It had one blue and one gold."

The women became silent for a second.

"Those are known as ghost eyes," Darcy said softly.

"Or witch eyes," Keena replied. "Seeing an animal with them is an omen."

"A good one?" I said hopefully.

"Omens can be more complicated than good or bad. And ghost eyes even more so."

I didn't like the sound of that. "What does it mean?"

"It's not something we can interpret for you. We can guess but it really is between you and the spirits," Darcy said, setting her coffee cup down and standing.

"You'll figure it out," Sora said confidently.

"Let's just hope it's in time," Darcy said before walking out of the room.

The other two busied themselves with dishes and prepping for dinner. I sat for a few minutes staring at the fire. What a turn this year was taking for me. Months ago, I couldn't have imagined my life like this: living with witches in rural Oregon, discovering ancestor journals with family rings, and having secret deer creatures sending me cryptic messages. Oh, and crazy visions of demons. Let's not forget that, I thought.

I sighed and rose to help my housemates. I wasn't ready to call them my coven yet. One step at a time. I started drying dishes.

Chapter 7

I spent the next few days working with Sora and Keena on different parts of the craft. I got to know them both better each time and learned my own limitations even more.

"I would have thought you'd be good at divination, what with your visions," Keena said as I struggled with a tarot reading. We sat at a table in the library, books scattered around us.

"Well, it doesn't seem to be my cup of tea."

"What about ..." Keena started.

"I'd be worse at tea readings, Keena. I just told you the Queen of Swords meant a cold, bitter woman who will try unsuccessfully to read your future." I looked at the cards laid out in front of me. I didn't see any special meaning in them despite all the history and information Keena had spent the morning describing to me.

"I don't think of you as cold," Keena replied, smiling.

"I guess I got fifty percent of that right then. You didn't even laugh when I said it."

"I'm trying to take you seriously. More than you're doing for yourself." Keena scooped the cards up from me, wrapping them back in a silk cloth to be stored away. "It's okay, the tarot takes years of study to understand and get good at. I just wanted to see if there were any special gifts in this area."

"Nothing discovered this morning. Or yesterday with Sora in the kitchen." I had never been a strong cook. I could count on one hand the dishes I prepared well: fried eggs, boxed macaroni, spaghetti, and the best ham sandwich you'd ever have. I wasn't sure if the macaroni qualified, though surely my addition of green beans and basil counted for something. Anthony had always laughed at my ineptitude in the kitchen. I hadn't thought of him in days. My mood plummeted.

Keena must have sensed my change in mood.

"Let's take the afternoon off," she said, stacking up some of the books.

"I'm already behind. We should probably soldier on." I pulled a book off the stack and flipped it open morosely. Keena took it out of my hands.

"Have you left the farm since you got here?"

"No." I looked up at her. "Well, I went into the forest with Sora."

"That's our land. I mean, have you gone into town or driven to the ocean since you've been here?"

I shook my head. I had forgotten the ocean was close by. Saltwater had always been a presence in Seattle that I enjoyed. Up until those last few months, it had grounded me.

"Let's go for a drive, then. Get out of here." Keena pulled open the door to the hallway, looking at me expectantly. I sighed theatrically and followed her.

Keena drove a two door Honda Civic hatchback in a faded blue. I slid into the front seat next to her clutching the list of groceries Sora had pressed into our hands upon the news of our excursion.

"We're celebrating Imbolc tomorrow. This is great timing! I was dreading going in," Sora had said cheerfully while drawing up her list. "Do you think you can find white truffle oil?"

"We're going to Coos Bay, Sora," Keena had responded.

"Okay, so no. Oh, but you can get cream cheese." We waited another ten minutes while Sora's list grew before being allowed to escape.

I sat in the front seat reading the list while Keena tried to start the car.

"It takes a few turns, but it always catches." She smiled. "It drives like a tin can. A reliable tin can, though. And high gas mileage."

I nodded. "This is a long list. I thought we were taking a break. Looks like errand running. Where's the Wilson Dairy?"

Keena laughed. "We'll stop at one store for Sora and collect the items she actually needs. Most of this is aspirational. She always has grand plans for our celebrations but can usually only make half of what she dreams up."

I felt a wave of relief. I was excited to get out, but grocery shopping wasn't appealing.

The engine caught and Keena put the little car in gear. We shot forward, heading out of the driveway by the house toward the road, toward town. I felt myself lighten.

We came out of the trees that stood at the edge of the farm and into pastureland where cows and sheep grazed. I had forgotten I had arrived in the dark. The farm was tucked up in the foothills of a small valley which spread out before me. We came to the end of the gravel road and turned right onto the small highway.

"Where does this road go the other way?" I asked, craning to look back.

"It goes up into the forest and ends at twin waterfalls, Golden Falls and Silver Falls."

"That sounds pretty."

"It is. We'll go next time we need a break. The hike in is fairly short."

I nodded and looked out the window. We were approaching the small town I remembered from the first night. I was searching for the name of it when a small sign declared it: Silverdale. Unlike when Sandra and I had driven through at night, there were signs of life now. I watched a man in a camo jacket walk into the tavern.

Keena slowed and pulled in front of the store Sandra has pointed out on the way in so many weeks ago. A long, covered porch ran the length of the front and was dotted with a few chairs and tables. The windows were filled with various signs ranging from advertisements of beer to promises by local hopeful politicians.

Keena turned to me. "Do you mind? I want to check the PO boxes, see if we have any mail."

"I don't mind but they look like they do." I nodded toward an elderly couple coming out the door. They looked at us suspiciously as they walked in front of the car toward their own.

"Oh, don't mind the Graftons. They're always like that." Keena waved her hand and hopped out of the car. "You want to come in?"

"Yes." I didn't want to stay and be subject to the evil eye by the Graftons, who were peering out of their SUV's windows at us. Plus, this was my new home. I should see what it offered. I followed Keena up onto the long porch and through the doors.

The store was surprisingly large inside, longer and wider than I had expected. Off to the left was the store portion, aisles of canned goods interspersed with boxes and candy, a wall of coolers filled with beer at the end.

Off to the right was a separate room that Keena headed into. I followed her into a warm space I took an immediate liking to. The floors were old wood patched with metal here and there and the walls were lined with shallow wooden shelves that held produce, bread in paper bags and an array of bottles and jars. An assortment of chairs and tables were spread around.

"Hello there! I haven't seen you here before." A jovial voice distracted me, and I turned to my right. A tall woman with short curly hair stood behind a wooden counter. She reminded me of Bea Arthur from the Golden Girls. She smiled at me, and I shyly smiled back.

"Good morning, Lonnie," Keena said, walking up to the counter. "This is Sandra's niece."

"Reva," I introduced myself as I walked up.

Lonnie's hand shot out across the counter, an offer I couldn't refuse. I reached out and met her in a firm handshake. Her hand was dry and warm. I caught a quick flash of a vision — a tall young woman with blond curls, bleeding from a head wound next to a crashed car. I looked into Lonnie's eyes momentarily, recognizing the young woman in the vision was her, years ago. I dropped Lonnie's hand like she had burned me. What was wrong with me? Lonnie's smile wavered slightly in confusion before she recovered, pulling her hand back.

"Pleased to meet you and welcome, Reva. Sandra was just thrilled you were coming to stay here in Silverdale." Her voice was light and welcoming. I forced myself to return her smile.

"Nice to meet you," I replied, curious what all Sandra had told this woman. Hopefully no details. I was suddenly aware of the bandage around my wrist. It was healing so quickly I rarely thought about it. Soon I'd have to get the stitches out.

"Is there any mail today?" Keena asked. As Lonnie turned to check, Keena gave me a quizzical look. Either she sensed something witchy had occurred or she was wondering why I was weird. Same difference in my mind.

Lonnie returned with a stack of mail. "I assume you're picking up that Darcy person's mail as well?"

Keena radiated frostiness. "You know the drill, Lonnie. Any of us can pick up Darcy's mail."

Lonnie gave a small curt nod my way. "Her, too?"

"Me, too what?" I asked.

"Yes, we trust her to get Darcy's mail as well," Keena replied tightly.

"Federal crime to open another person's mail," Lonnie said.

"No one is opening anyone's mail. We're just saving ourselves multiple trips."

Lonnie nodded again but her disapproval was apparent on her face.

"Well, better get going. Have a good day," Keena said. I could hear her trying to summon up warmth in the salutation and failing.

"Nice to meet you, Lonnie," I said and followed Keena as we exited.

We got into the car in silence. Keena threw the mail in the back seat and started the car. We pulled out from the lot and back onto the road. We'd driven about a half mile when Keena slammed her hand on the steering wheel.

"Bitch!" she exclaimed.

I sat in surprise for a moment.

"Who?"

"What?" Keena looked over at me.

"Who's the bitch?"

"Oh. Sorry." She looked contrite, as if my presence had been momentarily forgotten. "Lonnie. Not you."

"I didn't really think you were referring to me," I replied.

"Lonnie means well, most of the time. And generally, I like her. She is actually one of the few people who support a bunch of women farming out here," Keena said. I waited.

"But ...?" I supplied.

"But Lonnie is such a dinosaur when it comes to Darcy. Darcy isn't really welcome in town, and she knows it. So we get her mail for her so she doesn't have to deal with the stares and the whispers and the rudeness. Lonnie always brings it up."

I pondered a moment. "Is the town that weird about her being goth?"

"The goth doesn't help but being trans really freaks them out."

"Wait, what?" I looked over at Keena. Of course it all made sense now that I thought about it. Darcy's tallness, her deep voice.

"You didn't know?" Keena looked over at me. "I thought Sandra would have told you."

"Sandra didn't even tell me your names." I felt guilty. It was entirely possible Sandra had at least told me names on the drive up and I had forgotten. That would be like me. But this I would have remembered.

"That surprises me," Keena said. "Well, not the names part. That sounds like her. But her and Darcy are pretty close. She basically saved Darcy's life. I thought you would have heard about Darcy over the past few years."

"Sandra and I didn't get past the surface when we talked these last few years."

"Kept each other at arms' length?"

I shook my head. "It was all on me. I kept Sandra out and she matched it when she realized it was the only way to stay in touch. I was pretty shitty to her."

We both went quiet. I watched the farm fields rolling past, the pine forest hills behind them.

"Does it bother you?" Keena asked.

"Does what bother me?" I asked, my mind on my relationship with Sandra the past few years.

"That Darcy is transgender? I feel bad outing her. I really thought you knew."

"Oh." I shook my head after a few seconds. "No, not at all. I have a lot of questions that are probably inappropriate to ask, but no."

"Good," Keena said. "It bothers some of the other witches in Sandra's crew. That's one of the reasons we don't see them much."

"It'd be a real shit show if it did bother me, wouldn't it?" I laughed awkwardly as a few things Sandra referenced fell into place. I'd heard of women freezing out transwomen before, particularly older generations of lesbians. Which exactly described most of Sandra's old crew.

Keena looked over at me. "I'm not sure Sandra would have brought you back here if she thought you would have a problem with it. Like I said, she's very close to Darcy. Very mother-daughter, really."

A twinge of jealousy passed quickly into regret. I had once been that close with Sandra, and it was my own fault for letting that lapse. Neither emotion would change that. Only time would.

We fell quiet again as we drove through Coos Bay. I took in the little town, noting the crumbling art deco buildings and empty storefronts in the downtown. We kept driving through, passing normal looking houses and little strip malls of stores. I was surprised it kept going before remembering from my reading that it was the largest city on the Oregon coast. It still was nothing like Seattle. Not even close.

We came up over a hill and I saw the ocean. My heart sang at the expanse of slate blue water to the horizon. I cracked the window down to let in the sea air.

"Brrr — can you roll that back up?" Keena said. "It's February still!"

I laughed as I obliged. "I needed to smell the ocean. I hadn't realized how much I missed it."

"We'll be there soon." Keena smiled.

We pulled into a small parking lot behind grass covered sand dunes, the ocean just on the other side of them. Since it was a weekday, there were only a few other cars scattered about. I pulled on a windbreaker and a wool hat and got out of the car. Keena was still putting on more layers. I turned my head upward to the cloudy sky. Gray clouds hung low, looking like rain. I smiled.

She got out of the car and after making sure it was all locked up, turned to me.

"Ready?"

"Are you sure you can walk?" I gestured to her many layers and laughed.

"I'm from the South! This is beyond frigid to me," Keena laughed back.

"This was a really good idea," I said as we walked up the sandy path that led to the beach.

"You seem happier than I've seen you in a while. We need to remember to get you out more often," Keena said.

At the top of the little dune, I paused and looked out at the beach. The wind was stronger on this side, blowing like crazy. It energized me. I ran down the sand and toward the water like a golden retriever off leash.

Keena called my name, but I didn't stop until I was right at the edge of the water. The waves crashed and I watched the foam surge toward me, making little patterns in the sand. I wanted the wind to blow even harder. A big gust came driving across the sand at me. I looked up at the clouds and felt an urge to pull the rain out of them with my hands.

"Reva!" Keena tapped me on the shoulder, speaking loudly over the roar of the wind and the surf. "You took off like a bat out of hell. I can't run that fast. In fact, I prefer not to run."

"Oh, sorry. I'm just excited to be here," I yelled back, not remotely sorry.

"It's okay, I'm glad to see you excited. Come on, let's take a walk before it starts raining."

I pulled back on the storm wishes in my head. If it rained or was too windy, Keena wouldn't want to stay, and I wanted to be out longer. We walked down the beach in silence. The wind subsided.

We walked for an hour, looking out at the sky and the waves while picking up little rocks or flotsam that caught our eye. Keena said it was good to bring these to the altars, offerings to the goddess of our choosing. One rock in particular snagged my attention, dark gray with a series of holes through the middle that had worn through so they almost all connected. It reminded me of a cloud. As I bent down to pick it up, the ruby ring on my finger shifted in temperature suddenly, becoming cool and icy. I looked at the ring, curious, but the sensation was gone. My hands were cold, that must be all. I put them in my pockets with the cloud rock.

As we walked back off the beach and the noise subsided, Keena asked me, "What happened back at the store with you and Lonnie? I got so angry at her I forgot to ask you."

"I saw something when I shook her hand. It was really weird." I hoped that'd be enough for her as I waited for her to unlock the car.

"Tell me more." Keena wasn't going to let me off the hook. She slid into the driver's seat and unlocked the passenger side.

I sighed and got in the car. "I saw what I think was her as a young woman after a car crash. Like I was seeing her worst memory or most painful."

"Like when you saw mine when we first met?" Keena asked.

I looked over at her.

"Yeah. But unlike with you, I don't think Lonnie knew what was happening."

"She may have wondered why she thought of it but yes, she didn't know like I do. But she's not a witch."

"Just a bitch."

"I'm sorry I lost it and called her that. She's not that bad. She just doesn't understand Darcy. I think she's fascinated by her, and it makes her uncomfortable."

"Hey, are you trying to change the subject?" I recognized the tactic. I used it a lot. Redirect.

"Perhaps." Keena smiled and started the car. We drove out of the parking lot in quiet before Keena spoke again. "I saw it, too, what you saw about Lonnie. It's a skill of mine, to read people's emotional experiences. I've never met anyone before who was able to do it as well."

"I'm not sure what it is but I hesitate to call it a skill I have yet. Two weird occurrences could be a coincidence."

"You really sell yourself short, don't you?" Keena glanced at me as we drove along, passing beach houses and little tourist-driven businesses. A bead store, a closed ice cream store.

I considered what she said. "I guess so. It's just so new, I'm not ready to latch onto anything yet."

Keena didn't respond. We drove to a grocery store and went in to get some of Sora's requested items. As we were walking the aisles, a thought occurred to me.

"If you can —" I stopped, not sure if talking about witchy skills in public was a good idea. I plunged on with carefully chosen words. "If that is your skill, what do you know about me?"

What unspoken secrets was Keena able to see?

Keena smiled. "I try not to use my skill on my housemates. Makes for a bad roommate situation."

We walked on but I knew she was evading the question. I worried about what she may have seen; if she knew what I was hiding. If she knew what had happened to Anthony. I decided to let it go for now. I was confident she wouldn't be talking to me if she had seen that.

We drove out of the grocery store parking lot and came to an abrupt stop on a one-way street when the car in front of us slammed on their brakes. Looking ahead a few cars, I could see a crowd of people walking in the street.

"What's all this?" Keena said, her brow furrowing.

I caught a glimpse of a familiar sign. "White Pride" in sloppy red letters on white cardboard. Others came into view. "White is Right." "Go Home!" "Pride Power." The angry faces of men came into view as the march surged our way.

"This bullshit was going on when I came in a few weeks ago." I looked over at Keena. Her face was distorted in horror.

"I've never seen it like this before. It's not the friendliest town to what they think of as outsiders, like a lot of rural Oregon, but it's never been like this." Her voice came out strained.

Cars honked in front of us, but I couldn't tell if it was in solidarity or frustration. I hoped it was frustration. There was no visible police presence as the crowd surged ahead through all the stopped cars.

I looked out at the crowd of awfulness pushing forward. A man at the front caught my eye. He looked familiar — the same man who had shouted "witch" that first night. His eyes shifted, even from so far away, and locked on our car.

Keena looked around frantically as the white supremacists came closer. "We're stuck. I was hoping we could reverse and go another route but there's no room."

I looked over at Keena with her brown skin, felt her anger and fear. I heard the echo of the witch chant from them the first night I saw them. Fear clutched at my stomach. And so did a boiling anger. Anger at their presumption, their disregard, their hate.

My rage built. The air inside the car grew stagnant and humid. A gust of wind blew off the ocean, up over the cars and tearing at the hateful signs. I watched them whip and smiled. Another gust of wind came, even stronger. The steady march that was headed toward us slowed as the wind pushed them back. The man kept coming, struggling less than the others.

"Why is it a million degrees in here?" Keena said, her voice worried and far off. She rolled down her window a crack and the heat and stagnant air rushed out. The clouds above us darkened to a deep angry purple. The ring on my finger heated up until my whole body felt like it was burning with a fever. I opened the car door. Keena screamed my name, for me to get back in the car.

As soon as I was outside, the fever broke. A huge streak of lightening flashed across the sky. Thunder rolled deep and loud. I looked at the paused march, the men and women staring up in confusion. The ring on my finger suddenly felt cold and wet. I clenched my fist, my palm damp with sweat.. Another loud thunderclap and the sky opened up. Rain drops the size of pennies began falling, and then it was pouring. I stood there in the pouring rain and saw the same man watching me as the crowd around him ran in different directions. We stood eyes locked for a few seconds before he turned and walked away calmly.

I got back in the car, my jeans darkened and soaked from the rain, my wet hair plastered to my head. Keena was looking at me like I was a crazy person. In front of us, the marchers had disappeared as fast as the rain had started. The cars in front of us started to move. Keena put the car in gear and slowly drove forward. We passed a fallen sign with "White Pride" in red bleeding into a puddle of soggy pink.

Finally, I turned to Keena and broke the silence.

"Looks like someone rained on their parade."

Chapter 8

The storm seemed to follow us home, the windshield wipers frantically working as the rain poured down. Keena and I drove in silence; neither of us wanted to talk. I felt drained, like that little bit of an outing had been more than I could handle. I was still recovering, and I had overdone it.

As we passed through Silverdale, I looked at the tavern and felt an urge to stop. To have a beer at a sticky bar surrounded by glowing neon beer signs and the sound of conversations all around me. It wasn't a bar I was missing, but a city. Seattle.

"Reva." Keena broke the silence as we turned onto the farm's road. "What the hell happened back there?"

"What, the march of nastiness?" I replied.

"No. The storm. You."

"I don't know what you mean." The exhaustion was coming on stronger now.

"Don't give me that. You felt it. The whole car changed. You changed. I felt a strange energy coming off you, pulling at me."

"I was angry." All I wanted to do was close my eyes and sleep.

"Reva," Keena said softly. "I think you started that storm. I'm not sure how, I've never seen magic like that. But I really think you did that."

"That's not possible," I scoffed out loud but a sense of dismay curled around me. It couldn't be possible. "No one controls the weather."

"I'm not sure control is the right word," Keena said as she pulled up to the house. I glanced over at her. She looked worried and maybe a little scared. "Has anything like that ever happened to you before?"

"No," I said. Yes, I thought. Just once.

I hated even thinking about that storm and who it took.

"Reva, I think you're lying to me," Keena said, the disappointment thick in her voice. "I'm going to let the others know. Even if you don't think it was real, I felt it."

She got out of the car and walked to the house without waiting for me. I pulled myself out of the car slowly. I felt like I had hiked for hours, all uphill with no water. But without the sense of accomplishment that comes with such a hike. Just the bone-weary exhaustion.

I walked into the house, the warmth hitting me. I could hear Keena in the kitchen, her low voice mingling with others. Sora's bright and airy, Darcy's low and melodious. And another one, gravelly and slightly fierce. Alex. I couldn't face all of them. I definitely couldn't face Alex, the roommate I knew the least. And trusted the least.

I trudged up the stairs. I heard the kitchen door open below me as I reached the top landing. Sora called out my name, but I ignored her. I walked into the bathroom and proceeded to gulp water from the tap like a person dying of thirst. After a moment of resting against the clawfoot tub, I managed to get to my room.

The cats swirled at my feet as I came in, almost tripping me as I headed to my bed. I sat on it and pulled my shoes off, letting them land with a clunk in a sandy mess. I took off my wet clothes and curled up in the covers. I lay there, waiting for sleep that didn't come. The cats hovered around me, purring and kneading. And finally, I let the thoughts I had been pushing away come back.

The day of the first storm was placid and gray. And I was so heartbroken.

I hadn't wanted to feel that way. I hadn't wanted to find out the truth. If I could have, I would have rewound back to the night before and not snooped. Not found that text on Anthony's phone.

We had been living together for a few months. He had insisted we move in together, had won over my reluctance but not the cats, they had never warmed to him. Everything had been moving so fast, but I couldn't lie when he asked if I was falling in love with him.

"We're everything together, baby. Why wait?" He called me "baby" a lot and I loved and hated it in the same breath. He was nothing like past boyfriends. I had favored boys who were distant and self-absorbed; if I could win them over, I was worth being loved. It was a game I would never win. Anthony changed all that.

We met at a bar, standard cliché meeting. I was there with work colleagues, single and enjoying myself. When I saw him watching me across the bar, there was a spark. Also a cliché but best way I can describe. I felt a magnetic attraction to him, more so when he came over and our hands touched in a greeting shake. Almost like he knew the touch was part of it, the deal sealer.

We moved fast, professing love within weeks. I was under a spell. Little did I know, I wasn't the only woman under his spell. I ignored the signs, the late nights with thin excuses, the lack of information about himself while he asked all about me. What can I say, it was nice to be the center of attention in a relationship for once. I told him about my difficult childhood, my shitty relationship with my mother, my mental health issues, and my strained relationship with my aunt. I never told him about the magic, about witchcraft. I had buried that all deep away.

One night after he came in later than he had promised again, I looked at his phone while he was in the shower. He was a big believer in no secrets. He had shared the pass code to his phone early on and I had felt the need to share mine, to show we were equal in our trust. I had never needed to use that trust before. I had thought he had nothing to hide until that night.

I had reasons beyond his late arrival, dodged kiss, and going straight to the shower. A credit card statement for a card in my name had been forwarded to our address from a PO Box. A credit card I had never signed up for and certainly not with his name as joint as the statement showed. The charges were for places we had never been and items I had never seen: fancy restaurants, hotels, jewelry, clothing, a dock fee for a marina. It all felt fraudulent, but I was hoping the fraud wasn't my own boyfriend.

There weren't many texts on his phone, which was more suspicious to me; there was only a history of texts from me. Nothing from friends or work. I dug deeper, glad he was prone to long showers. I was beginning to think I was imagining it all when a text message popped up. I clicked on it without pause.

Miss you already. Can't wait to have you again.

I stared down at it, willing it to be something other than what it was. And then I tapped back a message.

Miss you too baby.

I watched the little dots of someone typing and waited. I hoped for a friend to scoff back at being called "baby". Something other than what I knew was coming.

Didn't think I'd hear from you, lover. You said you were going back to the bitch.

I didn't even pause, immediately responding and hoping I sounded like Anthony.

Had to, didn't want to. Bitch is in the shower, got a few minutes.

The response back was fast.

I know, lover. Hurry up and get the money. I'm tired of you being away with that ugly witch.

The last word made me drop the phone like it was burning. It landed beside me on the couch. How did they know, I thought. How did they know? A panic rose in my chest before calm washed over me. Witch was just a variation on bitch for a lot of people. The tramp in Anthony's phone didn't know. He didn't know.

The calm faded quickly as I heard the shower go off. My boyfriend was not who I thought he was. My throat ached with confusion.

Anthony came out of the bathroom whistling some bad '90s tune, a song I couldn't place but was familiar. A song written by men and played by men all about the evils of a woman. Those were his favorites, something I had thought was cute, an ironic love of throwback music.

He strolled out into the living room in a t-shirt and jeans, his black hair wet and clinging to his neck. He came and sat on the couch next to me, throwing his arm around my shoulder to pull me into a hug. I was rigid like a cardboard cut-out before I pulled away and got off the couch, walking to the window to look down at the street below. I didn't know what to do.

"What's wrong, baby?"

I was silent, not knowing what to say.

"Look, baby, I'm sorry I was late. Work was a crush and then Joannie made me stay late." His boss was often the source of his excuses but now I wondered, was she even real?

I stayed quiet, let him rattle on until he petered out when I didn't respond. Usually, I responded by now.

"If you're gonna be such a bitch, maybe I shouldn't have rushed home." His tone immediately became sulky and accusatory. I doubted for a few seconds. Was I being too much of a jerk, expecting too much? Maybe the woman in the phone was a wrong number.

Soft fur touched my leg, making me jump. Tuna was rubbing herself around my ankles. She meowed loudly, bringing me back to my senses. I turned to Anthony.

He had found the phone sitting next to him and was looking at it, his face contorted into anger.

"You looked at my phone." Accusatory but not a question.

"I did." I tried to keep my voice cold but it wavered. Kiz joined Tuna in the ankle chorus. Had I fed them? Fine time for them to suddenly need food.

"Don't you trust me, baby?" He looked at me with a pleading look. If I hadn't been watching carefully, I would have missed the split second between the indignant anger and the hurt look, the split second of condescension.

"No. I don't." My voice went up an octave. I wished for more control. "Not anymore."

His eyes returned to the phone.

"Why did you respond to this crazy person? You pretended to be me, that's pretty shitty." He looked at me, mixing indignant and hurt.

I nodded, fighting back tears. "It was pretty enlightening to be you for a few seconds."

"You don't know this woman. She used to bartend at this club I went to, we hooked up once, well before you, but she turned out to be crazy. Real piece of work. I had hoped she would have forgotten me, but you seem to have woke the monster by responding to her." He was watching me carefully as he explained the tale.

I wanted to believe him. If it was my fault, everything could go back to normal. But the credit card statement said otherwise. Too much was adding up to be a series of weird coincidences. The cats meowed even louder, yowling. Tuna got on her back legs and reached her claws up to land on my thigh.

"Ow!" I batted her paws off my leg to which she responded by batting back, claws out and drawing blood. I looked down in surprise at the scratch. Tuna could be grumpy and lash out but never over second dinner. A wave of anger, strong and clear, tore through me. I looked down into her blue eyes. She looked right back at me and yowled like a Siamese with a megaphone.

"GOD DAMN IT! Shut those fucking monsters up!" Anthony grabbed a book lying on the coffee table and threw it toward the cats. They scattered, diving under furniture, and the book hit my ankles.

The pain shocked me, not because I was that hurt but because the force clearly would have hurt the cats. Hot rage filled my head, and a guttural scream tore through my mouth.

Anthony froze, confused. I picked up the book and threw it back at him with all the force I had. He ducked and leapt off the couch.

"You're a fucking crazy bitch!" he yelled as he backed away from me.

"I know about the credit card, Anthony!" I screamed. A flow of words tore out of me, most of which I couldn't remember seconds after they left. He looked at me with fear at first and then something changed on his face. And he started to laugh.

"You always were a bit of a wild card, the only thing I liked about you. Too bad you didn't let this side out more, you would have been a better lay." He had retreated to the hallway, hastily sliding on his boots and grabbing his jacket.

"GET OUT!" I screamed, picking up his abandoned cell phone and throwing it at him. He caught it, laughing. The scorn on his face as he closed the door broke me. Cheating on me, that was bad enough. But to be with someone who pretended to love me, who actually thought I was all the things I feared, that cut deep.

I didn't fall apart right away after he left. My anger was a hot burst of energy, driving me to pull all his clothes off hangers and out of drawers and into garbage sacks where I poured ketchup, soy sauce, all the condiments from the fridge into each. I found his laptop next, hitting it against the laminate countertop in the kitchen, watching in satisfaction while the laptop smashed to pieces and the countertop cracked.

I burnt out as fast as a birthday candle, turning into a puddle of wax on melting frosting. The cats came out to comfort me as I cried for hours. The next-door neighbor banged on the wall at some point, which I ignored. Finally I collapsed into a shallow sleep.

A knock on my door brought me out of my memories of Anthony. I waited under the covers of my little twin bed, hoping they would go away. I felt utterly spent. The knocking came again.

"Go away," I croaked. I doubted they heard me.

"Reva?" Sandra called through the door.

"It's us, we want to talk to you." Sora's voice came next.

"Go away." I raised my voice, though it came out faint and scratchy. What was wrong with me? I hadn't locked the door. I thought about getting up and doing that to make my point but the idea of moving even my arm didn't seem feasible, let alone getting out of bed.

"Reva, we need to come in," Sandra continued.

"No."

"Let's just open the fucking door." A gravelly voice came loud through the door. Alex. Followed by the door banging open, the hall light cutting through the dusk shadows in my room. I was surprised the light was all gone; it must have been almost 5 p.m. now. I had crawled into bed about two hours ago.

I watched the darkened figures in the doorway as they came into the room. Sora was softly scolding Alex for barging in. Sandra held a tray in her hands which she set on the side table I had set up as a desk. She walked over and sat on my bed.

"Reva, we have to talk. Keena told us what happened."

"The news told us what happened," Alex broke in. "Freak lightning storm with torrential rain in a localized area of Coos Bay."

"Alex, stand down." Sandra pointed to a chair. Alex backed up slightly but didn't sit. She did stop talking.

Bright light flooded my face. Sandra had turned on the bedside lamp.

"Oh no. Oh, Reva, this is bad. You're in much worse shape than I thought." Her face furrowed. Sora's appeared next to hers with the same concern.

"Get the elixir. I'm so glad you thought to make it up earlier. It needed a good half hour to set up properly." Sandra waved her hand and Alex handed her a small green bottle. Sandra pulled the top off, taking a dropper out. "I didn't know it would be this bad. Get the cats off. Alex, get ready."

I should have felt more alarm than I did. I opened my mouth to try to tell them all to leave me alone, but nothing came out.

"Don't try to talk, Reva," Sandra said as she fiddled with the dropper, prepping it.

"You used the last of your energy to tell us to fuck off." Alex loomed over me. I caught a note of amusement in Alex's voice. I felt Sora pulling the cats off me, their meows almost like whimpering. The whimpering kept going as their warmth left me. The sound was coming from me.

"Shhh, it's gonna be okay. They did as much as they could. We have to bring in the big stuff now," Sandra said, petting my head. I wanted to brush her hand away, but I couldn't move. Someone pulled the covers off me, leaving me exposed in just underwear and a t-shirt to the cold air.

I felt a new, heavier weight on top of me. Alex had crawled on the bed and was sitting on top of me. She grabbed my wrists and pinned them to the bed, holding me down. I was limp, unable to fight back at all even though my healing wrist twinged in pain at the pressure. I turned my head away from Sandra to look at Alex. Her face was unsmiling, set in hard concentration.

"This is going to be rough. But we'll get through it," Alex said in her brusque manner. I felt strangely reassured. She turned and called out. "Keena, Darcy, get in here. Hold her legs."

I heard movement next to the bed, felt warm hands on my ankles. Heard snippets of an argument.

"This is a bad idea."

"Keena, just ride through it."

"I don't want to see what I'll see though. Not without permission."

"It can't be helped, Keena."

"We'll lose her, we have no choice."

"Sandra, do it now!"

My vision blurred, the world going soft and gray. I felt a touch on my cheek and a whispered apology. A drop of liquid hit my right eye. My body relaxed into a puddle. Then pain exploded in my eye, like a piercing needle straight into my brain. My muscles tensed, more pain spreading through my body as I bucked. The warm weight of the other witches pressed down. The pain tore through me, and I found my voice to scream.

The pain receded as quickly as it had come. I blinked a few times, tears rolling down my cheeks. Alex still held me down, her face covered in beads of sweat. She met my eyes and held my gaze for a few intense seconds before nodding.

"Time for the second drop."

"No!" I choked out the word and struggled against her. "No, no, no."

"This one doesn't hurt," Sandra said. I continued to struggle before realizing I was no match for Alex and the other two holding my legs down. I squeezed my eyes shut.

"Come on, Reva. I promise it won't hurt," Sandra implored. "I know you don't trust me right now but please."

I kept my eyes shut.

"Look, the other way we do this is up your left nostril and it will hurt worse than the first eye," Alex said.

I tentatively opened my right eye and looked at her. She was smiling.

"Alex, you have the worst bedside manner," Sora chided.

"I'm specialized in hard magic. Bedside manners don't matter." Alex shrugged, still smiling.

"Not true. Don't lie to her, Alex," Sandra said. "Reva, we won't put it in your nostril. It doesn't work that way. But if we don't finish, you won't regain your strength for weeks. It will be like having a really bad flu for a month. Trust me, it won't hurt like the first eye."

I let my muscles relax and felt a body-tired ache flowing through, exactly like the muscle aches of a flu, the worst flu. The idea of being sick for a month sunk in. I weighed out the option of the pain I'd felt and a month of exhaustion and flu-like symptoms. I opened my left eye.

"Good girl. Thank you." Sandra breathed out and I watched the dropper move over my face. A drop of liquid dropped in my eye quicker than I could blink. I braced myself for the pain but instead a warm tingling sensation flowed through and down the rest of my body. It wasn't painful per se, but it also wasn't comfortable. It passed within seconds. I sank fully into the bed.

"Excellent. Good work," Alex said as she squeezed my wrists before letting go. Keena and Darcy had already released my legs. Alex climbed off the bed and stood next to me. "Try to sit up."

I wanted to stay where I was and close my eyes, drift off to sleep, but knew that would be impossible with everyone in the house watching me. I sighed and pulled myself up to seated position. It was remarkably harder than I wanted to admit. My core muscles were sore, my arms were stiff, and I felt cold all over.

"Here, drink this." Sora held out a mug with steam coming off it. I eyed it suspiciously.

"Just herbs and honey. It'll be sweet and a little grassy in taste but that's it. It'll help with the chills." Sora smiled. I took the mug and sniffed it tentatively.

"It's only Alex's potions you have to watch," Darcy said to me with a small smile as she laid a robe next to me.

"Hey, I'm working on hard magic," Sora said a tad sulkily.

I took a sip. The liquid was warm but not too hot and sweet with an herbal flavor.

"You're learning it well, too," Alex said to Sora.

"I meant it as a compliment, Sora," Darcy said, her smile fading.

I took a bigger sip. It seemed to help.

"You'll no doubt surpass me on the potions," Alex said to Sora. "You have a more adept touch, and you know the follow ups like this. Which is what Darcy was referring to. I'm all punch, nothing else."

"I'm not all soft, you know," Sora mumbled but with pleasure in her voice at the compliment. I could imagine a compliment from Alex was rare.

I came back to life as I drank the liquid. The chills disappeared and the aches faded to a dull reminder. Sandra was sitting next to me. I turned to look at her and saw lines of worry etched deep in her features.

"What's hard magic?" I asked. It still felt hard to talk, my voice a little rusty. "Difficult?"

"It is difficult but that's not why it's called hard. It is often confused with black magic because of the potency and the —" Darcy cut off, searching for the right word.

"For the physical intensity and tax it takes. It is the magic that most often has pain as part of the threshold," Alex finished.

"For who?" I asked, turning toward Alex.

"For everyone involved in the spell," she responded. She was drinking a mug of the tea as well. She was the only one, though. Everyone else stood awkwardly around the bed, besides Sandra who had begun petting my hair again. Darcy looked at me with curiosity and Sora with an almost awe. Alex looked tired. And Keena. She wouldn't even look at me, her eyes cast down.

"What is going on?" I asked. "What just happened?"

"There's a lot we need to talk about, Reva," Sandra said. "We have questions for you, too."

"A lot of questions." Alex looked at me. All around me, the other witches nodded. Questions, but would there be any answers that any of us liked?

Chapter 9

The questions waited while we made our way downstairs for dinner. It was around 8 p.m., a late dinner but not midnight like I felt inside. Walking down the stairs was hard, my leg muscles threatening to quit each step. Alex, below me on the stairs, was going slow, too. I thought back to what she said, the tax required for hard magic.

She looked back at me. "It'll get easier. Stairs help bring the blood back in but walking down them is a real bitch after a spell like that. Better than going up, though."

I nodded and focused on getting down, hoping it would get easier in time for when I had to walk back up them later.

As soon as I walked through the kitchen, the hunger hit like a storm. I collapsed at the table and looked around for a piece of bread. With butter, big slabs of butter.

Darcy put a big plate of spaghetti in front of me with crusty garlic bread tucked into it. The smell of tomato, garlic, and parmesan cheese hit my nostrils. I wanted to put my hand into the steaming pasta and shovel it into my mouth. Darcy took my hand and put a fork in it.

"I know that look. Try to use utensils." She laughed, a lovely sound which didn't happen enough.

I disregarded all table manners and ate with ferociousness. As the carbs hit my bloodstream, I slowed in my eating and became more aware of the table. Alex's plate was empty, and she was getting up for seconds, waving away Sora's insistence on helping.

"Thank you for making spaghetti, Keena," Alex said as she heaped more onto her plate from the counter. She came back to the table with four pieces of garlic bread, two of which she threw on my plate before sitting down. I picked one up and began to munch on it.

"Thanks," I mumbled.

"I know it's your go-to meal after spells like that," Keena said. She still seemed distant, and her own plate of food was mostly untouched.

"Keena, eat. Swallow some spaghetti with that guilt," Darcy said to her.

Keena smiled wanly and picked up her fork.

"Guilt?" I asked between mouthfuls.

"Keena thinks she's to blame for what happened today in town," Sora said. "Which isn't possible."

"It's not just that." Keena looked away uncomfortably.

"Right, your big mouth," Darcy teased even as Keena blanched.

"No. As bad as she feels about outing you, Darcy, Keena is not looking forward to the next step in this process," Alex interjected.

"I already said it wasn't a big deal. We all thought Sandra had told Reva." Darcy quickly tried to soothe Keena. "I'm not ashamed of who I am."

"I completely forgot to mention it," Sandra sheepishly said as she picked at her spaghetti. "It's my fault, Keena. And Darcy, I'm so sorry. I should know better."

"Hold it!" I shouted. The conversation was getting away and confusing me. "What do you mean by the next step?"

Uncomfortable silence descended around the table. Everyone was looking away from me suddenly, even Sandra. Everyone except Alex who had just taken a big bite. She looked at me and after swallowing, answered.

"You know Keena's skill in reading past traumas living inside us." She waited for me to nod. "She does a remarkable job blocking that skill without prior consent. But that blocking is harder with touch and impossible with certain spells. Spells like the one you just went through."

The hairs on my neck stood up. Keena knew. She had seen the worst of me.

"No." I whispered it, a wish for it to be a lie.

"I'm sorry, Reva." Keena looked at me for the first time. "I think it was particularly impossible with you sharing a piece of the same skill."

"So you saw it all," I said. I pushed my plate away, the meal sitting in my stomach like concrete.

"I don't just see, Reva. I feel what the other person felt." She looked at me, my own misery and guilt reflected in her face. She knew what I had done. I couldn't hide anymore.

"The next step is for you to tell us or for Keena to tell us," Alex said.

"This isn't how we do things." Sandra stood and scooted Darcy out of her seat to sit next to me. She tried to take my hand, but I pulled it away. "We don't usually go this fast or require a witch to spill her secrets, relive pasts she wants to forget."

"So what's different?" I asked but I knew. I was different. My secret wasn't a bad accident or something done to me. It was something done to another. By my hand.

"The difference is you and your power," Sora said softly. I looked up at her. I felt closest to her. I was going to hate losing her friendship.

"Come on, just get it all out. You'd be surprised what we've heard," Sandra said, reaching out for my hand again before pulling back. I had my fists clenched on my lap.

"And you'd be surprised at what we've done ourselves." Alex looked at me, the hardness in her eyes shifting to a kind of understanding. For a moment I felt better, but I shook that off. Her secrets, whatever they were, didn't entail murder. I took a big breath and told them all about Anthony.

It was a relief at first, to tell about meeting him, falling for him, and his betrayal. My audience was receptive, adding in commentary I had needed, the words of girlfriends who help you get over heartbreak.

"What an asshole." From Darcy.

"Your cats knew he was trouble." From Sora.

"You deserved so much better." From Keena.

Choice words about the size and qualities of various body parts from Alex.

Tongue clucking and squeezing of arms from Sandra.

But then I came to the end of the story, to my crime.

I woke up the next morning after he had left to a gray overcast day, a broken heart, and simmering anger. I didn't know what to do next. I lay in bed for an hour, wishing to be unconscious again. Finally I pushed the cats off me where they had been curled up, surprisingly quiet, and stumbled out into the living room. The wreckage of the night before lay everywhere: the smashed-up laptop, the bags of clothes with unpleasant sweet and vinegary smells of condiments wafted around. I felt frozen again. Not a dream. I had fallen in love with a lie.

I took a shower and fed the cats, trying to right myself. I made coffee but wasn't hungry. Hungry was for the happy, I thought, watching the cats hoover up their kibble. I checked my phone, hoping there would be something from Anthony. An apology, an explanation, even another lie. Instead, I had an email from my bank. For an overdraft.

Jittery and the coffee burning in my gut, I turned on my laptop and logged into my bank account. Everything was gone. My savings, my checking. Nothing was left.

A frantic phone call revealed I had transferred everything but five hundred dollars the day before to an account in another bank. One that had my name on it allegedly. Of course, I hadn't. Anthony or maybe the woman from the text had completed it. The five hundred had been withdrawn last night by ATM.

The people at the bank heard my story, my pleas, and sent me to the fraud department. I spent hours on the phone, explaining and being transferred to the wrong places. I put in a police report over the phone, the Seattle police not interested in coming out in person for a non-emergency crime. I was scolded for busting up the laptop, but I was confident nothing would be on there. Anthony was a petty criminal but he had been thorough. I was baffled at why me and my meager savings. Was I that easy of a mark?

I sat looking out at the gray sky and the Sound out in the distance. One my favorite things about Seattle was how it was impossible to escape the water. I remembered the credit card statement and the mysterious marina charge. A quick internet search and I had the phone number of the marina. One call later, I had the dock address and which slip Anthony had registered his boat. He hadn't been clever enough to change the name.

And here's where I made my first mistake of that day. I didn't call the police and give them the information. I knew he'd be there, a firm knowing I couldn't ignore. I wanted to confront him myself. I left the apartment and headed to the marina.

The sky remained the pale gray when I pulled up to the dock and parked. The late afternoon light filtered through and hit the placid water. A typical October day in Seattle. I got out and walked onto the docks, not knowing where exactly I was headed but sure I'd know.

A boat was idling down one side dock. I turned and headed for it. A figure untied the last of the ropes, setting out to sail. As

I approached, the figure turned into Anthony. He turned and saw me. I watched his features twist in surprise.

He quickly freed the last rope and jumped onto the boat. I ran down the dock as fast as I could. He was at the wheel, maneuvering the boat out of the space, lightly scraping the boat on the right in his haste. Running, I hit the end of the dock by the slip and for a split second, thought about jumping the gap and onto the boat. I paused, panting at the sudden burst of exertion. The boat was too far, and I would only make more of a fool of myself, sure to fall into the calm deep water.

Anthony paused the boat in the water with the motor running to come out on the deck to watch me. He was laughing.

"You always had more spunk than most of them!" he yelled across the water.

"You asshole!" I screamed, immediately wishing I had come up with something more clever and cutting. "You fucking asshole!"

He laughed again.

"I'll be waiting for you with the police," I yelled.

"I won't be back here." He shook his head at me as if I was exceptionally stupid. "Take care, babe."

A woman came up from below deck of the boat and curled herself around his arm, glaring at me. She was short with close cropped hair. He turned away and walked back into the boat. She stood there, watching me. As the boat pulled away, she flipped me her middle finger.

I should have called the police. I should have walked away. There were so many things I should have done. Instead a deep scream of rage came out of my throat and my vision darkened around the edges. A gust of wind whipped through the harbor. I could taste it suddenly, the wind heavy with salt and sea and something else. Something dark that wrapped around the back of my throat.

The gray ceiling of clouds above pulled together and darkened, moving closer to the sea. The gusts of wind grew stronger and closer together, blowing fiercely at me. I stood unmoving on the edge of the dock. The dark clouds opened up and rain began to pour down. All I wanted was for the wind to blow Anthony back. I screamed into the wind until the dark taste in my throat became raw pain.

Time passed but I was unaware of it as the storm raged around me. At some point, someone from the marina found me and steered me back off the floating dock as it rocked violently from the waves. A warning had gone out about a freak unpredicted storm. Boats had hastily returned and moored. There was a frantic energy of people scrambling to cover.

Deep exhaustion hit me as I walked slowly toward my car, ignoring the rain. I managed to drive home and slide into the elevator, soaked to the core.

Inside my apartment, I collapsed and stayed in bed for days with what I assumed was a flu. The storm passed quickly as the night came on. A storm in October wasn't unusual for Seattle but it hadn't been predicted for that Tuesday afternoon. I had a deep sense of responsibility for the storm, though that seemed crazy. I slept and had nightmares of capsized boats and drowned bodies. The news didn't report on any deaths from the storm or any missing boats, but I was racked with guilt. I felt deep down he was dead. That the woman on the boat with him was dead. And I was responsible.

Eventually I called the police and reported the marina information I had on Anthony. I gave a description of the short-haired woman on the boat with him. The cop assigned my case scolded me for not reaching out sooner, took down the information and hung up.

During that time, the flu turned into a depression and anxiety. I was broke, using my dwindling paycheck for rent and buying groceries or take-out with credit cards. Not that I was eating much. I stopped going to the two classes I was taking, unable to imagine writing history papers. I was still making it in to work some of the time, but my performance was sub-par. I expected any day to be called into the boss's office to be put on a performance plan. If I was lucky.

A few weeks after the storm, plainclothes police came to my door. The two men identified themselves as detectives, though even without uniforms they had that cop look to them. I invited them in, watching their noses wrinkle in disgust at the state of the apartment. I had managed to drag the garbage bags of Anthony's condiment-covered clothes down to the dumpster but that was it. His broken laptop was still on the kitchen counter. Take-out containers and dirty laundry were strewn about. The detectives decided to stand when I offered them a seat. I couldn't blame them. The only clean places to sit were covered in either cat hair or an actual cat. Tuna and Kiz had glared at the strangers from their sleeping perches but stayed in the room as if they too didn't have the energy to react to anything.

That changed when the shorter detective handed me a photo. A teenage girl smirked back at me, her eyes rimmed dark like a racoon and her hair bright red, flipping off the person holding the camera. But I recognized her instantly. The woman from the boat, younger by maybe five years.

"Do you recognize her?" the taller detective asked.

I nodded. They told me the briefest of information. Her name was Kelly Strickland. That her parents hadn't seen or heard from her in weeks. She had reconnected with an old boyfriend months before. A man her parents had disapproved of, had encouraged her to leave. A man named Tony.

"Anthony." It wasn't even a question. I knew it was the same.

Anthony Michael Ricci. Not Anthony Mitchell Russo as he had told me. He was also missing. Along with five other women's money.

"It took us a while to connect the different cases since he used different names, but it looks like the two of them had a couple of scams going," the shorter detective explained. It sounded as close to an apology as I was going to get that it took them weeks to connect reports of theft by several Anthony-Tony-Michael-Mikes.

It appeared I was the last person to see Anthony and Kelly. The police were convinced they had sailed through the storm and landed in another port close by, escaping. The boat hadn't turned up at any marinas within reasonable sailing distance yet, but the detectives seemed sure it would as they walked out the door.

Two weeks later, Kelly's body was found on a rocky beach of Bainbridge Island. I felt nothing when I found out. I was numb. Any feeling was gone, which I took as a sign to take it the rest of the way. I tried my first suicide attempt.

Chapter 10

The witches had gotten quiet as the tale progressed. I didn't want to see their faces, so I kept my eyes down on my empty dinner plate.

"You pulled a storm from the sky." Sandra spoke first. I looked over at her. Her face was twisted in concern and surprise, the lines on her face deeper than usual. I had aged her a few years with my confession.

"Sandra, maybe that's not the right thing to focus on right now," Darcy said quietly. "Reva, did they ever find Anthony?"

I shook my head, looking back down at my plate.

"And the boat? Any sign of the boat?" Sora asked.

I shook my head again.

"And you think you're responsible for the young woman's death?" Alex asked. I looked at her. Her face was calm and open.

I opened my mouth to speak but closed it. I couldn't say the words out loud. I nodded.

"Did it occur to you perhaps that toad who lied and stole from you pushed her overboard in the storm? That he's the one who took her life?" Alex pressed on.

The idea sunk into me. It had drifted around my head before but had never stuck. And it didn't matter. "I still started the storm. If he did, I gave him the cover to get away with it."

Alex drew in a sharp breath. "You're taking on more than you're responsible for."

"You don't know what happened on that boat, storm or not," Sora broke in.

"Reva." Keena spoke for the first time since my story. She would have already seen it, felt it. I couldn't look at her. "I know the guilt you feel and the anger that burns over the guilt which compounds it back. Feeling guilty doesn't necessarily make you guilty nor does it atone for what you are responsible for. You might never know what happened on that boat. But you do know how the storm started. You have to stop neglecting your power and learn to control it."

I started to cry. I hadn't wanted to break down, but it was too much. Sandra pulled me into her arms. I held myself rigid for the first few seconds before I melted against her. It felt good to have someone who loved me holding me.

"Let's get you to bed. I think that's enough for tonight," Sandra said as she pulled me up with her from the table. She steered me and we moved together slowly across the kitchen to the door.

"Bit harsh, Keena," Sora whispered behind me.

"You weren't there today, Sora. The power she has can't keep being ignored, or something worse could happen," Keena responded. Alex said something, but it was lost as Sandra and I went into the hallway, the door swinging closed.

Climbing the stairs was worse than going down had been. My body was exhausted but Sandra patiently stayed by my side and gave me small words of encouragement. We got to my bed where I collapsed into it.

"Where are Tuna and Kiz?" I mumbled as Sandra tucked me in.

"You pulled a lot of energy from them earlier today. They'll come back when they have recharged," Sandra said nonchalantly. I imagined their tails as little electric cords, plugged in somewhere to recharge them.

"How?" I murmured.

"How did you pull energy?"

"How do cats recharge? Little batteries?" I was fading, sleep pulling at me.

"Mostly through sleep, heat, and food, like a lot of us." Sandra laughed. "I saw them down in front of the fire. They'll be okay."

"Sandra." My eyes were shutting, I wasn't going to be awake much longer.

"Go to sleep, Reva."

"I'm sorry." I don't know how coherent I was or if she heard me, but I felt it. The last thought I had before I fell asleep was how much I had missed her and how much I regretted pushing her away.

"Rise and shine." A gravelly voice and a sudden burst of light pulled me out of a deep sleep the next morning. I squinted against the sunlight coming in through my windows, courtesy of the curtains being flung open by a redhead. Alex.

I turned over and pulled the covers over my head. "Why are you here?"

"I'm here because it is almost eleven in the morning, and you need to move your body." She came over and pulled the blankets out of the end of the bed, exposing my feet to the air.

"Hey!" I sat up to throw the covers back on my feet.

"Get up." Alex marched over to my dresser and started opening drawers, rifling throw them.

"What the fuck ..." I swung my feet over the side of the bed, cringing at the soreness of my muscles. I gritted my teeth and pulled myself out of bed. I moved as fast as I could and slammed the drawer Alex was in, narrowly missing her fingers as she pulled back abruptly.

"Good, you're out of bed." Alex turned to me nonchalantly and threw a pair of workout pants in my face.

"Get out." I threw the pants on the floor and started back to the bed.

"No such luck, buttercup," Alex said. "You'll feel worse if you don't do a little exercise. Trust me."

"Trust me, says the woman who held me down and inflicted the worst pain on me last night," I said as I sat on the bed. I desperately wanted to curl back up into it, but my muscles were warning me I would regret more sleep.

Alex laughed. "Fine, don't trust me. Trust your body."

I sighed and crossed my arms.

"Get dressed in something you can sweat in and meet me downstairs." She turned and left, slamming the door behind her.

I debated whether to follow her instructions. I felt like a child who knows the adult trying to persuade them to join an activity is right but who keeps saying no despite it all. After a few minutes of internal debate, of lying back down and then pulling myself up, I found workout clothes and made my way out of my room.

The house felt lively though I couldn't hear anyone. I walked down the hall and jumped in surprise when Darcy's door opened. She strode out, not at all surprised to see me.

"Good morning. How are you feeling?" she asked as I waited at the stairwell for her.

We started down the stairs, my thigh muscles resistant the whole way.

"I'm —" I paused. I was going to say fine, but social niceties were neither required nor a worthwhile lie. "Sore. I'm really sore. It's like a hangover times ten."

"Mmm, not surprising. Alex loves spells that require a hard workout after. It's her thing. Don't let her fool you with 'hard magic' requires jumping jacks and burpees, though. She just loves cross-fit." Darcy shot a wry smile my way. I grinned back before grimacing as my shins joined in the pain party in my legs.

"I heard that." Alex was waiting at the bottom of the stairs, holding two glasses of brown liquid. "Hard magic does take a physical toll. You can do yoga instead, but it'll take you twice as long to recover."

"Not true. Not if you actually do the breathing and have the patience for it," Darcy said, still smiling.

"Pfft — yoga is for suckers," Alex said dismissively. Darcy laughed and I realized this was a well-worn banter between the two of them, one they both enjoyed.

We reached the bottom of the stairs. Darcy darting down the last few steps with graceful speed. I felt a small wave of gratitude that she had walked with me. She had disappeared into the kitchen before it hit me she was awake before noon, something I hadn't seen before.

"Drink this." Alex shoved one of the glasses of brown liquid in my face.

"What is it?" I said, not taking it.

"Protein drink. It'll hydrate you and give you something to get through our workout before breakfast." She took a big swig of hers.

"Ugh, no." I pushed the glass back. My mother had gone through a protein drink phase while dating an aggressive and attractive gym rat. She had made me drink them with her, her attitude being "why suffer alone when you have a child to join you?" Many of my childhood experiences involved some variation of that attitude.

"Don't worry. I didn't make it. While I can and will choke down that chalky stuff, this is magic." Alex took a big swig from the other glass and shoved the offered glass back at me.

"Actually magic?" I was both thirsty and hungry. Not quite as bad as the night before but more than usual. I had forgotten that the months of depression had robbed me of my appetite. It was almost novel to feel it so acutely.

"As much as anything Sora makes. She has a knack for making these taste like chocolate malts. She perfected it out of deep concern after tasting my original version."

If Sora had made it, that gave me hope. I took the glass and sniffed it. Chocolate and malt. I took a tiny sip. It tasted exactly like it had been made of chocolate ice cream with a healthy scoop of malt. I took another sip and then a big chug.

Alex raised her eyebrows at me in a "see-told-you" way and drank the rest of hers. I savored mine but it went down easy. She took the glass from me when I was done and placed it on a side table in the hall.

"Okay, let's get outside and get a little exercising in." Alex gestured to the front door.

"Shouldn't we take those back to the kitchen?" While I was more at home here, I wasn't okay with leaving dirty dishes for others to come across.

"No, if we go into the kitchen, we'll get pulled into the Imbolc preparations. We'll take care of them on our way back in." Alex moved toward the door, me still in her path. She was like a herding dog. I let her guide us out. I didn't want to find out her version of nipping at my heels.

The cold air felt clean on my lungs as I walked onto the porch. Alex was already in the driveway, jogging in place. Clouds hung low and gray overhead but it wasn't raining.

"Come on. Let's start with a slow jog." Alex motioned at me. I walked down the steps and fell into place beside her. I could do a slow jog.

Alex quickly moved ahead of me as we trotted toward the fields.

"I said a slow jog not a glacier plod. You walk faster than this!" she heckled as she turned around and jogged in place waiting for me to catch up.

"Running isn't my favorite thing," I said but picked up the pace.

"Better." She gave a nod of approval.

We continued in a slow loop around the fields, dodging piles of manure and Alex still outpacing me. Finally I had to stop, bending over to put my hands on my thighs. I wished I had water as I tried to catch my breathe.

"Nice work. How are you feeling?" Alex said as she ran back up to me.

"Done."

She laughed.

"Fair enough. Let's walk back. This is as good a start as any."

We walked side by side through the field in silence. I was surprised at how far away the house looked. We had traveled farther than I expected. I had forgotten exercise could do that, could turn off my mind so I lost track of some measurements: time, distance.

As we got closer to the house, Alex headed toward her trailer. I paused, unsure, until she waved me over.

"You need water. This is closer."

She unlatched the gate on the fence around her trailer and walked in. I started to follow but a low growl from inside stopped me in my tracks. Alex's dog stood in front of me on the other side of the fence.

"Friend, Flame. Friend," Alex called out in a low firm voice. Flame stopped growling but looked at me suspiciously. "Come in, Reva. Flame will behave."

I cautiously walked inside the fence. The dog trotted over to the door where Alex had disappeared inside and sat in front of it.

"Flame, move." Alex came out of her trailer carrying two glasses of water. Flame moved aside so Alex could get by but didn't stop watching me. "She's too good of a guard dog."

I took the glass from her outstretched hand and gulped it down, choking as I took too much in. The glass was empty in seconds.

"Easy there." Alex chuckled and handed me the second glass. I didn't even hesitate, chugging that one too.

"Thanks," I croaked out when I could talk.

"We'll do this again tomorrow. Earlier this time." Stated like a fact not an offer.

"I don't —" I started to protest.

"No getting out of this. You need to be active, to train your body so you can better control your magic."

"What does being in shape have to do with magic?" I headed back toward the house. Alex fell in step with me, and Flame followed, ending up striding along silently next to me. I felt uneasy.

"She won't hurt you. She's trained to know who to protect," Alex said.

"How?"

"Magic."

I turned to see Alex grinning.

"But back to your question. Everyone has their own idea of magic before they actually try it. Some believe it is all in the head, the spirit. Others in the heart, the emotions. All trying to distill magic into one place, one thought, one way. Never works. Magic is as complex as we are. Each part of who you are has to be tended to. And the physical body is included. Strong of mind, strong of body, strong of magic."

"That's a good tag line. You should start your own gym," I said.

"If I liked people more, I'd consider it," Alex said wryly.

"Does it have to be running?" I asked as we walked up the back steps of the house.

"No, but I think you liked it. Despite yourself."

Walking into the bustle of the kitchen fortunately robbed me of having to respond. I would have hated to admit out loud that she was right.

Clouds of white powder hung in the air of the kitchen. Every surface was covered with dishes and food in various stages of prep. And in the center of it was Sora moving at inhuman speed whisking something in a huge bowl she carried while shouting instructions to Keena, who looked wilted while she pummeled a ball of dough. I half expected broomsticks to come waltzing in with buckets of water like the famous Disney wizard scene.

"Good morning." Keena smiled at Alex and me. I smiled back, uneasy. I wasn't sure how I would be greeted after the previous night's confession. Her words to me still stung but I also recognized I owed her an apology for the various ways I had put her in difficult situations the previous day.

"Is there breakfast somewhere in this mess?" Alex lifted a dishcloth covering a pan.

"Don't touch that!" Sora swooped over and managed to swat Alex's hand away while still holding the huge bowl and whisk. "That's rising and cannot be disturbed."

"There's pastry and coffee in the green room," Keena said, an amused note in her voice as she watched Sora tend to a bubbling pot on the stove while placing the huge bowl down and continuing to whisk.

"Pastry? That's breakfast?" Alex made a face of disdain. I silently thought it sounded good.

"I put a few rashers of bacon on the sideboard." Sora pointed to the door exiting the kitchen, the underlying message of "get out" abundantly clear.

"Rashers? Are we British again?" Alex strolled through the kitchen and grabbed a blue dish with a hen-shaped lid on it.

Sora paused in her whisking to lift a solitary middle finger at Alex.

Alex caught sight of the gesture as she pushed the door open with her back and laughed.

"Thank you, Sora!" she called out and motioned for me. "Come on, Reva. Let's get out of here before we're put to work."

Keena nodded a warning my way. I walked as fast as I could out of the kitchen and followed Alex across the hallway and into the green room.

I had been avoiding the green room since the vision. The space was lovely, and without the lingering memories of bone-chilling evil, it would have been my second favorite space behind the library. I trailed behind Alex pushing plants out of my face as she carried her bacon to the table. She was already munching on a piece when I sat across from her. The table in front of us was laden with a plate of pastries covered by a domed net, a full coffee service in antique silver dishes, and a pitcher of orange juice. Fresh-squeezed, I discovered after I poured a glass and took a big sip.

"Sora loves holidays. Always does it up," Alex mumbled through a second piece of bacon. "Here, you need some protein to go with all that sugar you're about to consume."

I took a piece from the dish she offered across the table.

"I've never been big on holidays. You?" Alex asked.

I shook my head. "No, I only got to celebrate when I was with Sandra. Ginny — my mother — wasn't very —" I stopped, searching for the right word that wouldn't expose too much of me.

"Stable?"

I nodded. That was putting it mildly, but it worked.

Alex looked at me with understanding. "I don't talk to my birth family anymore. They were a fucking mess. It does a number on you."

"Birth family?" Was Alex adopted?

"Family of origin. Whatever you call it. Family can also be who you choose. I've chosen, created, and been found by all sorts of families."

"Oh." I had so many questions, but I sensed Alex shared what she wanted when she wanted, and any pressure shut her down. "I still talk to Ginny. Sometimes. I only have her and Sandra."

"That's not true." Alex grabbed the last piece of bacon and stood. "I'm going to go change and give Flame a treat."

"What do you mean that's not true?" I asked, standing as well. I didn't want to be alone in the green room. Just in case. And I could use a shower.

"Grab yourself a pastry. Sora has an amazing feast planned but it won't start for hours." Alex gestured at the plate.

I grabbed a cherry cheese Danish and then a croissant as well. Better to be armed with too much pastry instead of hungry.

Alex walked past me, on her way out. I stood and followed her. As we left the green room and she headed for the front door, a clear way to avoid the frenzy in the kitchen, she called over her shoulder without turning.

"And to answer your question. You have us."

Chapter 11

I spent the rest of the day in my room, eating pastries and thinking. Tuna and Kiz had reappeared from their recovery sleep and curled up on my lap and next to me, mostly to beg with intense cat stares for pastry. I thought about Alex and her parting words. I had expected a different reception to my confession. What I had expected would shove the others away had brought them closer. Well, some of them. I didn't know where I stood with Keena or Sora. The new friendly Alex would take some getting used to; I was only now realizing how much of an enemy I had made her in my head without even realizing it.

Mostly I thought about the thing I had been avoiding for so many years. Magic. My own magic. I sat in the sun trying to imagine having enough control to pull a storm out of the sky intentionally. It felt surreal, like something that happened to someone else despite the recent events in town, the vivid memory of heat building in me before the storm broke.

After a while wallowing in my thoughts, I pulled out the Quinn book of shadows. Sandra had encouraged me to keep it with me.

"It belongs to you now," she had said when she had found me carefully putting it on a shelf in the library wrapped in a clean white tea towel.

"It's old enough to be in a museum," I balked.

"Not everything is meant to be kept in a glass box. Take it to your room."

I pulled it from my own personal bookshelf and unwrapped it. It needed its own special bag but when I had asked Sora to make me one, she had shaken her head and said I needed to do it. I had exactly one Home Economics class with sewing in my past and had gotten a C only for effort; none of the skills had stuck. I ran my fingers over the magical stitching on the book, marveling at the skill and care put into it. A light pulse thrummed on my fingers under the stitches. I had noticed it before, but it seemed stronger today. Was the book waking up, or was I waking up to the magic?

I opened the pages, flipping delicately through it. After I had found the book, I had spent a few days making notes with the intention of a whole research project: genealogy searches, family trees, historical events. That petered out after a day or two. Despite being in a better place, I was still struggling with the inertia of depression that tears down grand plans into little bits of confetti impossible to piece together.

I opened to Oona's page. The text remained the same, the short paragraph introducing her book of shadows. Oona was an intriguing and hidden presence that routinely frustrated me. There was so little known about her.

Sandra remembered a few rumors passed down in the family: that Oona had been unusually independent for a woman of her time, and that she had killed herself shortly after her second daughter was born.

I turned to the next page, the first of the blank pages, hoping maybe something would appear. Nothing. The yellowing paper was empty as always. I sighed and touched my hand to the middle of the page, breaking my historian rule of not touching the fragile pages.

There beneath my fingers, marks appeared. Faded gray ink, fragments of letters. I pulled my hand back in surprise. The ink started to fade. Shoving down all my preservation knowledge about protecting old artifacts from the oils on my skin, I put my whole hand on the page.

And waited. Nothing happened. I pulled my hand back in frustration. Breathing out a big sigh, I recalled the magic lessons I'd had with Keena. Intention of thoughts was a big part of magic, she had said.

"You can't just wave a wand and 'poof'! Magic comes from deep within us and requires us to focus to pull it out."

I took a few deep breaths and let them out as slowly as possible, a technique Keena had showed me after I had said meditating made me squirmy. I put my hand back on the page and closed my eyes, continuing the breathing. Every time I was tempted to peek open an eye and see if it was working, I focused back on counting breaths.

Finally I opened my eyes and looked down. The page remained blank. I pulled my hand off despondently and there underneath in the same faint gray ink were the words:

Welcome, Stormweaver.

I held my breath and waited. The words stayed but nothing else appeared. Stormweaver. Was that Oona? Was that me? I stared at the words wishing for more.

A knock on my door startled me out of my head. I jumped, disrupting Kiz who had been fast asleep on my lap. He meowed grumpily as I shooed him off and went to the door holding the book.

Sandra was on the other side, smiling and dressed in all-white flowing clothes.

"Happy Imbolc. It's time to honor the Goddess."

"Oh. Right. Yeah. Look at this!" I held up the page of the book to her.

Sandra leaned over and her eyes got wide.

"When did this happen?"

"Just now," I said excitedly.

"Just like that?" She reached out to touch the page. I instinctively pulled it away from her. Sandra looked momentarily hurt before pulling back her fingers.

"Sorry. I don't know why I did that."

"It's okay. I think you're listening to the book. I just wish it liked me, too." She looked at it wistfully.

"It didn't just happen. I mean, it did just happen but not without me touching it. And concentrating," I said.

"Stormweaver. I haven't heard that phrase in a very long time. Hadn't thought about it until yesterday," she mused.

"You've heard it before?" I asked eagerly.

"I have. Come on, I'll tell you about it later. We can't keep the others waiting." She motioned for me to follow. "Leave the book here."

I reluctantly rewrapped it in the white towel and set it on my bed. I would try again later to unlock more words. The delight in a book full of hidden secrets was like catnip to a history buff like me. It was better than finding a letter written in disappearing ink.

"Will the others be joining us?" I asked Sandra, thinking about the other commune women who I never saw at the house despite being told they used the library.

"Yes, everyone will be there." Sandra smiled.

"I haven't seen Sunray and Lily since I first got here. It will be nice to catch up." I thought about my awkward departure from their house last time, running from Lily's intrusive but well-meaning questions about my health.

"Oh, no. None of the sisters will be there. Just the six of us." Sandra's smile faltered for a second before she turned to leave. "The others do their own thing on the smaller holidays now."

I followed Sandra downstairs, wondering if I was underdressed in my jeans and long sleeve t-shirt as I watched her skirts flow like she was channeling Stevie Nicks. My fears were confirmed as I entered the kitchen and saw Sora in a simple white dress and Darcy looking like a ghost in a stunning white sheath with white feather trim around the neck and hem.

"Should I go change?" I asked hesitantly.

"No, you're fine." Keena's voice came from behind us as she entered the kitchen. She was wearing loose flowing pants printed with vibrant green and yellow tropical leaves and a simple white shirt.

"Every witch dresses to her comfort for our holidays. Some of us like the opportunity to dress up more." Darcy smiled at me. Given how impeccably stylish she looked every day, I could understand it was important to her. And then I remembered Keena telling me how unsafe Darcy felt off the farm and realized it had even more meaning to her. That made me feel worse, like for her I should try harder even as she gave me a pass.

The back door opened, and Alex strode in with the dogs, wearing her usual black cargo pants and a sleek pullover in green. She looked like she did every day. I relaxed a little. Both dogs ran over to the hearth and sat in front of the fire. I could see Bear was trying hard to be a good dog, second guessing himself as he sat up and looked at Keena.

"Bear, sit," Alex commanded before turning to the rest of us. "What's going on in here?"

"Reva was feeling under dressed," Darcy replied as she pulled the last bowl off the counter and placed it on the table. "Everyone sit."

We took our usual seats.

"Pff, don't worry about it," Alex said to me. "Imbolc is not my favorite holiday and not everyone looks good in white. It turns some of us downright ghoulish."

"I hope that wasn't directed to me," Darcy responded.

Keena laughed. "Darcy, my love, if anything ever makes you look like a ghoul, you will still be a stunningly stylish one."

"Not directed at you," Alex clarified. "You would make a paper bag glamorous. I, on the other hand, do look terrible in white."

Sora joined in the banter. "I don't think you give yourself enough credit, Alex. With the right shade, it could work. And it'd make your hair really pop!"

Alex snorted. "Optimism won't save everything, including my pale-ass skin in white. The red hair doesn't save it. I just look like a dead redhead."

I felt more at ease listening to them and appreciative of Alex yet again in one day. The table was set with a stunning feast: buttery mashed potatoes, braided loaves of brioche bread with fresh whipped butter, roasted carrots and turnips, a white shredded salad which I learned was celery root, creamed kale, and onion cheese tarts. I waited, expecting some sort of prayer or thanks but everyone started passing dishes to each other. We ate with relish and talked in between bites.

As the last forkfuls were consumed and chairs pushed back, the conversation died down. I felt comfortable sitting in silence with these women, something that surprised me. I had always considered myself a loner at heart but perhaps that wasn't the sum of who I was at all.

"Thank you for all the hard work on the meal." Sandra broke the silence. "Shall we get the ritual started?"

Everyone nodded and stood, moving out of the kitchen into the hallway. I followed behind Darcy as we all trooped into the altar room. The room was draped in white cloths everywhere and all the candles were lit. The middle of the room was cleared of the usual cushions and the rug had been rolled up and pushed to the end of the long rectangular room. The floor underneath was the old wood of the farmhouse but stained a glossy black with a painted circle with a pentacle inside in white. The witches gathered around the outside of the circle. I hesitated, not knowing where to go.

Sandra grabbed my hand and pulled me over next to her. To my left was Alex. I expected her to look out of place with all the white clothes on the other witches and the white décor all around, but she didn't. I hoped I didn't either, though I felt like I didn't belong. At the next holiday or ritual, I promised myself to ask Darcy what would be best to wear. She looked right at home in her white gown.

Sora passed out unlit white column candles for each of us. I took mine and held it awkwardly until Sandra gently showed me how to cradle it in my left while holding it upright with my right. No one spoke but the silence was comfortable.

Keena began to hum in a low beautiful tone. Sora joined in at a higher pitch followed by Darcy, Sandra, and to my surprise, Alex. She winked at me as she started to hum low but on pitch. I swallowed and hummed quietly with them.

The humming vibrated in the air around us, and the air shifted. It felt like that swelling sensation at a classical music concert right before the opening notes start. Sandra touched the wick of her candle, and a flame sprang to life. I watched Alex do the same thing though the flame shot up higher for a second. I worried that all of the witches were able to light the candles with their fingers, but then Sandra and Alex lit the candles of the others. Sandra turned with a smile and lit mine last. Darcy stood across from me. The shadows behind her flickered in the candlelight as if they were alive.

We stood humming with our lit candles and then all the witches bent down to place the candles inside the circle in front of us. I was a half a beat behind everyone else's movements. Then everyone stopped humming.

Sandra's voice filled the room. "Welcome the return of the light. We honor Brigid, keeper of the eternal flame. We ask for her strength in —"

My vision went black, and Sandra's voice cut out. I stumbled as I tried to recenter myself, letting go of everyone's hands. My vision came back for a second and I saw Darcy across from me pointing. Her mouth was moving, but I couldn't hear anything.

As my vision went black again, someone slipped their hand into mine and grasped tight.

I felt the cold before the fog poured in around me and I was back in the forest. The cold was chilling as the first time I was here, creeping deep into me. Except for my hand, which felt warm like it was still being held. When I looked around, there was no one with me. I squeezed my hand. The phantom hand squeezed back. I took a deep breath and tried to relax. I wasn't here. I wasn't all alone.

The wailing started around me, same as last time. Banshees. I shivered, the cold seeping deep into the soles of my feet and running up my legs. All I wanted suddenly was to curl up on the ground and give up. The warmth of the one hand clasping back into reality was the only thing that stopped me.

The banshees' wails increased in pitch and volume, whipping up from the sound of grief to hysteria. My body responded immediately to their frantic screams. My breathing became shallow and fast, my pulse raced, and my muscles tightened. Panic was overtaking me. I turned my head in all directions, looking for them but seeing nothing in the fog and the dark.

The warmth on my one hand intensified, not uncomfortably. It grounded me, my breathing slowed though my body stayed tense. The wails receded as a new sound came through. Humming.

The witches were reaching me in my vision. I squeezed my hand in hopes the other side felt it. In response, the humming increased in volume and the wails disappeared. I closed my eyes and waited. Surely this would pull me out. I trained my focus on the humming, imagining the room. I would be back there.

I opened my eyes to fog and the dark trees. The panic welled up in me again. I whirled toward movement to my right.

A shadow stood in the dark. I took a step backwards. It moved forward, a creature with horns coming into view. My limbs grew cold. I wanted to run but I was frozen with fear. The creature moved toward me and as it stepped out of the fog, I recognized the Evernia stag with the lichen covered horns and the ghost eyes. He stopped a few feet in front of me. I took a tentative step forward. He stayed still. I took another until we were no more than one foot away from each other.

We stared at each other for a few seconds before he shook his head slightly. My eyes caught on something hanging off his antlers. A small metal ring with a key. I reached out my hand and the deer shied his head back slightly. I paused. I had moved too fast. I reached out again, slower this time. The Evernia waited while I slipped my fingers through the ring and delicately pulled the key off his antler.

It looked like an ordinary house key on a standard metal ring. I felt what might be letters or numbers raised on the surface of the key but couldn't see clearly in the dark. I looked up and the Evernia had vanished. I clutched the key in my right hand tightly. Now maybe I could go home.

The humming had faded but the banshees hadn't started up. I turned around in a circle. Nothing but trees and fog. I closed my eyes again, concentrating on imagining the witch house. If I had been wearing ruby slippers, I would have clicked my heels together.

Rustling came from behind me. I turned around, hoping the deer had returned and dreading what else could be there. A figure stood in the distance. I breathed in sharp and short. The figure stepped closer.

The figure was a man, ordinary looking with dark hair and a full beard. He seemed familiar and surprised to see me. We looked at each other for a moment before recognition dawned on his face. And I recognized him as well. He was the leader of the hate parade, the one who had watched me before walking off.

A smirk crept onto his face, and he took a step forward. I took two steps back.

"I didn't think it'd be so easy to find you." His voice rang out, low pitched but strong.

"I didn't know you were looking for me," I replied. Who was this asshole?

"Oh, I'm not the one looking for you. *It* is looking for you." His smile widened, showing a mouth of teeth filed into points. His smile stretched across his cheeks unnaturally until the ends of his mouth were at his ears. *Who* was no longer the question. *What* was this asshole?

I was about to ask what was looking for me but then I felt it, the icy cold creeping up my spine. It was back. The evil had returned. I panicked and took off running, veering to my right. I heard footsteps behind me and the snap of twigs underfoot. I kept running, hoping against hope to outrun it all. I had to get out, but all around me were trees and fog and behind me I felt the evil creatures. My mind raced with panic. All rational thought fled as flight took over.

The fog collected around me until I couldn't see. I slowed to a halt. Laughter sounded to my left. I spun that direction but couldn't see. The fog had closed in. Then the wailing started up again, all around and mixing with the laughter.

I closed my eyes and tried to slow my panicked breathing, but it only came faster. I was hyperventilating and a different darkness was closing in on me as my vision started to blur and narrow.

Stormweaver.

The word was faint and distant, but I heard it. I thought back to the day of the parade and the storm, the feeling of water on my palms when I picked up the rock on the beach, the electric energy building inside the car. And as the darkness took over, I felt the spark deep inside. I pulled all my energy to it as it shot out blue and violent into the black.

Chapter 12

I opened my eyes to whispering voices and dim shadowy shapes dancing above me. As everything came into focus, I recognized the voices of my fellow witches. I was on the floor looking up at shadows from the candlelight. Someone was holding my hand. I breathed out a huge sigh of relief.

"She's back!" Sora exclaimed from somewhere off my left shoulder.

"Thank fucking Christ," Alex muttered. I looked over to see her holding my hand. She gave it a squeeze when she saw me looking.

I tried to sit up but immediately felt nauseated. I plopped my head down onto the wood floor.

"Don't get up yet. It's too soon. But lift your head a little." Keena's soothing voice came over my right shoulder. I picked up my head and she slid a thin pillow under it.

Sandra sat on my right side, her brow worried into a series of knots. She gave me a weak smile and patted my right arm. Her mouth opened as if she was going to say something and then closed again.

"What happened?" Alex asked.

"It seems a bit soon to be asking that," Keena interjected. "Let her recover."

"We need to know if we're safe. Something could have followed," Alex replied and squeezed my hand.

"Followed?" I croaked out. My voice was hoarse, and my throat ached. I felt like I had the beginnings of a flu. I kept talking when Alex didn't answer me. "I was back in the dark forest. With the banshees."

"We heard them," Sora replied softly.

"That's why you started humming," I said.

Alex and Sandra nodded in unison.

"I'm so glad you could hear us." Sandra's voice cracked with emotion as she spoke. "Thank goddess you could hear us."

"I felt Alex's hand, too," I replied.

"What did you see?" Darcy asked, concern coating her words. "Did the evil return?"

I shook my head. "Not at first. I saw a guy I recognized from the hate parade in town. But he wasn't a man. He had a mouth full of pointy teeth that went ear to ear."

"Demon seeker!" Alex drew her breath in sharply.

"What's a demon seeker?" I asked.

"It's a type of demon possession. Demon energy gets absorbed by a human who then turns partial demon, at least in the Other Realm," Alex said. "Which you seem to be visiting too frequently. That so-called vision in the green room was the Other pulling you in."

"Enough. We're all worried but I think Reva needs to rest." Sandra reached out and grabbed my other hand. Her worried look turned into a confused frown. I had forgotten I was clutching the key from the Evernia.

"What's this?" She withdrew her hand quickly, leaving the key in mine.

I held it out on my palm. "It came with me from the Other, I guess."

"DROP IT!" Alex screamed. The others scurried away from my side.

"But —"

"Put it down now!" Sandra commanded.

I put the key down. I couldn't see their faces, but I felt their panicked energy.

"The Evernia stag gave it to me," I said quickly.

"The Evernia was there?" Sora asked. Alex snorted in disbelief.

I pushed myself up onto my elbows, pausing to let the nausea pass before sitting up. The other witches were about six feet from me so they couldn't stop me from getting up.

"Yes, the same stag with the ghost eyes came out of the forest and the key was on its horns."

"No, that's not possible. Sounds like a demon. We need to destroy the key," Alex said.

"It is possible," Darcy interjected. "It's infrequent but in urgent circumstances, some cryptids will enter into a demon-possessed space in the Other."

"And give an object to take back? That sounds like demons," Alex argued.

"I've experienced it once before and it wasn't a demon. It can happen," Darcy said firmly before turning to me. "Did you feel the same energy from the Evernia as the last time?"

I nodded slowly. "Sort of. Not as calming but it did feel like the same stag. He seemed nervous to be there."

"Sounds right," Darcy said.

"I don't trust it," Alex said.

"Darcy is our resident expert in the Other Realm," Sora said. I hadn't heard that before, but I hadn't spent much time with Darcy. Yet. I suspected I was about to be getting more lessons from her.

"Darcy may have a gift in visiting the Other but she's still young. She hasn't been around demons as much." Alex crossed her arms, staring at the key on the floor next to me like it was going to change into an evil creature at any second.

"I may be young, but I have visited the Other a lot more than you, Alex." A hard note crept into Darcy's voice. I wondered if this was an ongoing fight between the two of them.

"Not the demon realm," Alex retorted.

"Just because I don't take stupid risks like baiting demons doesn't mean I don't know about them." Darcy's voice got louder. I hadn't heard her angry before.

"I don't bait demons —" Alex started in.

"Stop. Both of you, just stop," Sandra said, cutting off the fight. "We don't have the energy or time for you two to argue. If Reva trusts the key, we'll have to for now until we get an outside opinion."

"Outside?" I asked. I didn't like the sound of that.

"The tribe? They won't help us," Alex said dismissively.

"They have little reason to." Keena spoke up softly for the first time.

"Yes, the tribe. I'll contact Wynona. We are still friends, you know," Sandra said. "In the meantime, we'll put the key in something to contain the energy just in case. Darcy, do you still have that obsidian box?"

Darcy nodded and left the room to get it. I watched her glare at Alex on the way out. Alex didn't notice, all her energy focused on the key sitting beside me.

"Reva, I think you need a cup of tea." Sora walked over to me and held out her hands to help me up.

"Will it taste bad?" I asked.

She laughed and shook her head. "How about chamomile and lavender?"

"Sounds good." I stood, shaky at first, but followed her into the kitchen.

I sat at the table while Sora buzzed about, putting a kettle on. Keena had come with us and was sitting across from me, a worried furrow in her brow.

"Do you need help, Sora?" she asked.

"No, you'll just get in the way. I need to burn off some energy after that," Sora said from behind me. I heard her getting out cups. "We've never had something like that happen at a circle."

"Well, you've never had me here to ruin it," I said, shame creeping in.

"Don't say that. You didn't ruin it. Something else did." Keena reached across and grabbed my hand.

"If it's never happened before, and now I'm here …" I trailed off.

Keena shook her head. "You're not the cause of it but you're a draw. Evil like that has always been around and it didn't pop up overnight because of one witch. I think you're special but come on." She smiled at me.

I returned the smile. "I'm special?"

"Don't let it go to your head," Sora said with an amused note, putting down a pot of tea and a few mugs in front of us. Keena winked at me and poured a big mug of tea for each of us. Relieved, I let some of the worry that she hated me slide away.

Sandra, Alex, and Darcy walked into the kitchen, whispering fiercely with each other. They plopped into seats around the table. Darcy carefully placed a black glass box on the table. The edges of it were irregular. The obsidian box.

"Is that actually obsidian?" I asked as I took a sip of my tea. It was calming me down.

Darcy nodded. "Obsidian is highly protective against negative magic. It will keep it contained until we know more."

Sora plunked a bottle filled with amber liquid on the table next to the tea pot, followed by a large white coconut-covered cake.

"Let's not skip the cakes and ale end of the ritual just because it went sideways. Can't let the demons stop all the fun." She put out a stack of plates. "Though I decided we needed a stronger spirit than ale so got the whiskey out instead."

I had forgotten about the cakes and ale tradition of ending a ritual. Normally it was done in the circle with a blessing to close out the energy. I had loved it when I visited Sandra as a kid and there was a cakes and ale time. Usually for me it meant apple juice and oatmeal raisin cookies, but it had made me feel special and included. It warmed me to see the tradition again in a different form.

"I'll skip the cake but definitely take the spirits." Alex pulled the bottle towards her and poured a healthy glug of it into a mug set out for the tea. "Thank you, Sora. You always know what we need."

Everyone agreed with a chorus of thank yous. Sandra pulled the cake over and started slicing after gesturing for Sora to sit.

"You do so much, Sora. Let me cut you a slice." Sandra cut a big chunk of the cake, all white and filled with what looked like custard. She put it in front of Sora who happily sank her fork into it.

Soon we were all eating cake and sipping on tea or whiskey. Or tea spiked with whiskey for Sandra and Keena. I stuck with the tea but couldn't resist the cake, which was like eating a coconut covered vanilla cloud. I wasn't even that fond of coconut, but Sora was magic with food. Maybe literally. I smiled as I lifted another forkful to my mouth.

The silence at the table eventually gave way to speculation and then planning on what to do, based on what I had told them about my unplanned trip to the Other. The tribe that Sandra had mentioned earlier came up again, a reference to one of the local Native American tribes in the area.

"They keep to themselves, understandably," Keena said. "We respect that, particularly since a lot of witchcraft practitioners steal from their traditions far too liberally."

"It wasn't always like that," Sandra said. I detected a hint of defensiveness in her voice.

"You're right, it was worse," Keena said, a hard tone behind her words.

"Look, I had a good relationship with the elders for years. We learned a lot from each other, and we were friends," Sandra responded.

"Not all of the tribe agrees," Keena said.

"I'm aware of that." Sandra looked away. "I'm not welcome by the younger generation. I know my place now and I acknowledged the wrongs."

"Not fully to their satisfaction though," Darcy said. "Is it a good idea to call on them?"

"I'm not sure what else to do." Sandra sighed in exasperation. "In the hubbub of dinner, the ritual, and then this whole mess, Reva and I forget to tell you something."

"We did?" I looked up in confusion from my cake. I had been listening, not wanting to intrude with questions in what seemed like a delicate topic.

Sandra nodded. "You told me right before dinner the ancestor diary had opened up again with new words."

"Right." I hadn't forgotten exactly but it certainly paled in comparison to the rest of the evening.

"What word?" Alex said forcefully as Darcy chimed in at the same time excitedly.

"The diary has new pages?"

"Stormweaver." Sandra and I said it at the same time.

Silence descended around the table for a brief second before everyone started talking at once. Sandra yelled out for everyone to stop.

"Stormweaver?" Sora said after a pause.

"It said 'Welcome, Stormweaver' in the pages." I looked up at their confused faces.

"I've never heard that word before," Alex said, sounding angry she hadn't.

"Me either." Darcy spoke up and Keena nodded her head.

"I have," Sandra said. "It is a rare power. Very rare. There were rumors our ancestor Oona possessed the power, but there are a lot of rumors about her I suspect were exaggerated."

"Might want to rethink that," Alex quipped.

"Is it a bloodline power?" Darcy asked. It was during conversations like these I wished I had more training in witchcraft. I didn't know there were bloodline powers. I made a note to ask Darcy more about it.

"I don't know," Sandra admitted. "I've heard of storm witchcraft in Norway during witchcraft trials in the 1600s after a sudden December storm sank village boats. But we also know most of the women killed weren't witches. The only other time I heard of it was with tribal lore."

"What's the tribal lore?" Keena questioned Sandra. I felt tension between the two of them again. Keena clearly had a different view on the issues surrounding the tribe.

"They didn't tell me much. It was just a word used, stormweaver. It sounded rare for them, too. I had asked Wynona about it as I heard rumors about Oona. But that was the time of my falling out with them so ..." Sandra's words drifted away. She looked pained at the memory.

"Well normally I'd say respect the tribe's wishes and stay away, but we do have a lot going on they should know about. The demon seeker alone should be reason to give them a heads up," Darcy said softly.

"Well, that's settled then," Alex said, taking charge. "Sandra will reach out to get a meeting. Meanwhile, you, Reva, have a lot of work to do to stay safe. A lot."

I looked Alex in the eyes and nodded. The reality of what was happening felt so far away and so immediate all at the same time. I realized I was in a state of shock with how distant I was in all the conversation, eating cake and drinking tea while everyone swirled around me, but I was going to have to face it all: I was a stormweaver, whatever that meant. I had a rare and terrifying power I couldn't control yet, and a terrible evil was lurking, actively hunting me.

Chapter 13

The next few days I began what could only be described as Witch Bootcamp. Alex woke me up before it was light out and had me running with the sunrise, followed by a series of torturous exercises including something called burpees that I hated deeply.

"It's one of the best exercises, it uses your whole body!" she would yell next to me. To her credit, she always did every exercise with me.

After the third day, my body was waking up even before I heard her stomping down the hallway. And I felt good after the exercise, having more energy throughout the day.

Keena and Sora worked together with me in the late mornings and afternoons, going through magical theories in various areas. They both claimed they were learning with me, which mostly seemed like bullshit, but it was surprisingly fun. It was like being back in college, arguing and discussing magical theory as intensely as any group of history or philosophy majors. My perception of magic shifted as I began to understand it was both knowable and unknowable all at the same time.

One evening a few days into Witch Bootcamp, I was in my room after dinner, settling in to read a history on elemental magic, the magical area that seemed most apt to my storm skills since it was about controlling the elements like air or fire. Or would be once I figured out the control part.

Someone knocked at my door. When I opened it, I was surprised to see Darcy. Since the Imbolc ritual, I had only seen her at dinner. Her day-to-day schedule was more of a night-to-night schedule that I didn't understand.

"Good evening, Reva. Are you ready to start your night lessons?" She smiled at me, clearly enjoying being a little cryptic.

"I — uh. I wasn't expecting night lessons. I was just settling in to read before going to bed."

"Well, all of that will have to wait. These are critical lessons for you. On the Other."

That certainly paused the excuse I had ready on the tip of my tongue to bow out of these lessons. I had thought on and off about both the visions I'd had, trying to understand them with the Other. The obsidian box with the key sat on a shelf in my room taunting me. When I had asked Sandra about anything related to that, she waved me off. So did everyone else, except Alex who told me point blank she wouldn't discuss the Other with me and made me do an extra burpee for asking. I had tried to find books on it, my usual go-to for research, but nothing had come up.

"I know you've been wanting to learn more. Both Keena and Sora told me you've asked a lot of questions. I'm our resident expert on it." Darcy smiled. "Come on, let's get started."

She walked down the hall with confidence I'd be right behind her. And she was right. I put on a robe and a pair of slippers over my t-shirt and pajama bottoms and followed.

Down the hall, Darcy waited at her black door, which she opened with a flourish and motioned me into the only room in the house I hadn't been inside yet.

Her room was as dark, gothic, and glamorous as her wardrobe. It was larger than any of the other bedrooms as well. Black velvet hung in swags over the windows and puddled down to the floor which was covered in a large floral Persian carpet. A room divider covered in golden skulls lay across one third of the room to the left. In front of it was a huge desk covered in a colorful chaos of tools, feathers, and beads, with a card catalog cabinet next to it, the drawers cracked open with ribbon and other flotsam peeking out. To the right was a lovely sitting area with worn Victorian velvet chairs and a settee. Nevermore was perched on a metal coat rack shaped like a leafless tree. He looked at me suspiciously with his beady eyes as I walked in.

"Take a seat," Darcy said as she closed the door and glided to a green chair. I felt ridiculously underdressed in my tattered robe and shabby slippers but sat tentatively on the edge of the red settee, running my fingers over the threadbare velvet.

Darcy laughed. "Reva, relax. I don't bite."

"I'm not worried about you biting," I said as I realized the carpet's floral patterns formed skeletons.

"Nevermore only bites me," she said. "I promise."

"What about that?" I asked, pointing to a taxidermy badger poised viciously on a table next to my right elbow.

"The dead don't bite," Darcy said with a grin.

"What about zombies?"

"They are technically undead." Her face went serious.

"Fair point." I hoped zombies were just folklore, but asking would likely lead to an answer I wasn't ready for. "I've never been in your room. It's lovely. Must have taken a while to find all of this stuff."

Darcy smiled shyly at the compliment. "It did, but it was worth it to bring my vision into reality. Sandra helped with sourcing the larger items and helped me modify some of it, like the room divider."

"What do you make there?" I gestured toward the desk.

"My jewelry. I have an online shop that does pretty well. Magical jewelry is in high demand out there. The internet really opened up the market."

"Magical jewelry?" Of course, I thought as the question came out of my month.

Darcy got up and rummaged around on her desk. She returned holding a few small boxes, opening the first one and handing it to me.

"Don't touch it but you can look. I've been commissioned to make this piece for a love witch."

Nestled in the box was an elaborate silver filigree necklace dripping with pink and iridescent stone tear drops. I immediately reached out for it before remembering her warning and pulling back.

"That's stunning!" I exclaimed.

"Rose quartz and moonstone. Not the most unusual stones but very effective," Darcy said modestly.

The next box had a bat-shaped choker studded with shiny black stones — a happiness necklace with black tourmaline; and the one after that, a bracelet shaped as an ouroboros in gold with green emerald eyes. I was gobsmacked at their beauty and Darcy's talent, telling her so over and over as I sat on my hands.

"Sorry you can't touch them. After a certain point in the making, energy from others can muddy the pieces. I cleanse and recharge each piece before sending them off and always wear gloves during that process."

"Cleanse and recharge?" I knew she wasn't talking about physical cleaning. I had picked up enough knowledge in the past few days.

"Depends on the piece. Could be sage smoke and moonlight. That's the most common ritual I use but there are others."

I could have looked at her work all night, but Darcy snapped the last box shut and put them away before returning to sit in front of me.

"Shall we get started? Ready to go into the Other?"

"What?" I stared at her. She said it as casually as one would suggest going to a corner store. "I can't just go into the Other. And if I could, why would I want to?"

"There are a lot of parts of the Other, just like in this realm."

"Oh." I contemplated that. "Nice places?"

"They're like any place. Some are better suited for us than others, but all have their beautiful and their dangerous aspects. Like a desert or a jungle."

"But how do you go?"

Darcy smiled and leaned back. "It's my talent, my main magic. You are a stormweaver. I'm a realmwalker."

"Realmwalker." I parroted back as she nodded. "So you can visit the Other whenever you want?"

"Like your magic, it takes a while to learn and command. But generally, yes. The Other and hypothetically realms beyond."

"There are other realms other than the Other?" I winced at how many times I used the word "other" in one sentence.

Darcy laughed, understanding the reason for the wince. "Other realms other than the Other. Yes, but not that have been recorded consistently. No one knows for sure if there's anything past that. We describe it as layers or rings but that's probably just how we're able to categorize something so incomprehensible."

"How often do you go?" I was stalling. All I saw in my mind was the darkness of the forest and the obscuring fog.

"Often. Come on, let's go in. I promise I'll take you to a nice part of the Other." Darcy reached both hands towards me, offering me to take them. Her nails were painted a deep black that shifted to red as the light caught them. After a pause, I reached out and took her hands.

"First step, close your eyes and empty your mind." Darcy closed her eyes.

I sighed and followed suit. My mind, however, was far from empty.

"Reva," Darcy said. "I want you to count your breaths. It will help. I can't pull us in together if your mind is cluttered."

"My mind is always cluttered." I started counting, one on the in breath and two on the out breath. This went on for what felt like forever with gentle reminders from Darcy to stay focused.

Eventually the black of my closed eyes faded to a gray blue and I felt a shift in the air, like moving through a curtain made of static.

"Open your eyes, Reva," Darcy's voice cut in.

I opened my eyes, bracing myself for the dark. Instead, I was standing on the edge of a small meadow surrounded by towering pine trees. There was a warm orange glow all around like a sunset, but no one direction seemed the source of the light. The air felt heavy and still but warm.

I sighed audibly in relief. Darcy walked forward into the meadow, moving through the knee-high grass. It shifted around her in an odd way, parting like water rather than grass. I took a tentative step forward and watched the grass move out of my way before I touched it. Fascinated, I bent down and reached my hand out.

"Don't touch the grass, Reva." Darcy's voice was firm. I pulled my hand back and looked up at her. "When something here doesn't want to be touched, respect that."

"What would happen if I touched it?" I asked.

"It will feel like stinging nettle here and give you a mild case of pinkeye back in our world," Darcy said.

"Pinkeye? How the hell does that work?" I pulled my hand back fast.

"I'm not sure. What happens to you here in the Other physically won't happen directly to you back in our world." Darcy paused. "But you will be affected somehow when you get back. Stinging grass on your hand here means an eye infection there."

"Is it always a bacterial infection of some kind?" I wondered what else could hurt me here in a weird way.

Darcy shook her head. "No, it's not that straightforward. Sometimes it's the same, like with the sting grass. Sometimes it changes around depending on the nature of the injury here. A cut on your finger for example could mean a mild case of depression when you get back. Sora's been cataloging all the reactions to try to pinpoint remedies and reasons."

"A mild case of depression?" I tried to sound nonchalant but could hear the anxiety in my voice. If I was clumsy here, would I sink back into the depths of depression when I returned?

Darcy saw my face and frowned. "Sorry. That was a bad example."

"No. It isn't a bad example. It just hits home a little hard for me. But it's good for me to know." I paused, trying to figure out how to ask my next question. "If the cut on the finger is mild depression for some, could it be worse for others? Regardless of the cut here?"

"No, it's usually a similar energy exchange. Sora knows more." Darcy turned away suddenly and waved me forward without answering me further. "Let's get out of the grass."

I reluctantly followed her to the other side of the meadow. I had been expecting something more from the meadow — magic butterflies, startling flowers, but it seemed to just be the no-touch grass. As we approached the trees, I hesitated. The forest looked dark and foreboding as we got closer. A path waited for us on the edge, weaving around the trees until it disappeared from view.

"Are we going in there? I'd rather not," I said when I caught up to where Darcy was waiting for me.

"Looks are deceiving. I think you'll be okay." She smiled encouragingly and walked out of the meadow into the woods.

"What if it's the same forest from my visions?" I stayed where I was.

"We can stop calling them visions now. And this forest isn't the same as the one you went to. I come here a lot. I know it well." Darcy took a few steps into the woods and looked back at me.

I mumbled a few curse words under my breath and stepped into the forest. The air shifted as I left the meadow. A light breeze that smelled like wet earth and salt hit my face and the light turned a golden green, more a late afternoon in a forest than the sunset of the meadow. I relaxed. This place felt more like the forest behind our house.

All around us was a low carpet of what looked like clover, dense emerald green. When I paused and looked closer, I could see it rippling at random intervals that didn't align with the breeze, like water after a skipping stone went across it.

"What are these plants? Why do they move like that?" I asked Darcy.

She shrugged. "I don't know. Nothing here is in a taxonomy we understand."

"Has anyone tried to? Like write a book or map it out?"

Darcy shook her head. "The Other is meant to be experienced, not categorized. Unless you're Sora."

We passed through the trees onto the shores of a large lake. I followed Darcy out onto a black pebble-covered shore. She stopped about a foot from the water. Above the trees, the sky had turned a deep stormy purple. The water of the lake mirrored the storms clouds.

"I call this Storm Lake." She sounded sheepish. "I don't know its real name. Forgive the simplicity. I was pretty young when I found it."

"Simple works." I looked out over the water, waiting for something to happen. A light breeze rippled the water for a few seconds but then everything went still again. "You've been coming here since you were how old?"

Darcy shrugged. "Six maybe? Five? A long time."

"How did you stay safe?" I asked, looking over at her. Between the terror of my unplanned visions to the night forest and the sting grass, I couldn't imagine a small child being here.

"I didn't." Darcy walked away. I thought I had offended but she stopped at a large boulder and motioned me to follow her. A similar size rock to hers sat on the other side of her. I sat on it, expecting hard rock under my ass but finding it surprisingly yielding. We sat in silence looking out over the lake.

"I survived but I wouldn't say I was safe. Remember what I told you about how what happens to you here shows up in some way back in the other world?" Her voice was quiet and steady, but I could hear the emotions trying to edge out behind the words.

"Yes. Sting grass equals pink eye," I responded.

"I —" She stopped again. "I almost died here. I don't know what would have happened if I wasn't a realmwalker, able to pull myself out. Back in our world, I came back very ill. I was a traveler there, too. Hopping trains, never stopping. My friends ..." The word "friends" caught at her throat like she had trouble saying it. "... they left me. On the side of a road. I was eventually brought to a hospital by people who found me there. I would have died there too but for Sandra."

I let her story fill in the quiet between us. I tentatively reached out my hand and put it on her forearm. She jumped slightly before giving me a sad smile and placing her long fingers on top of mine.

"Sandra figured it was a magic illness and started giving me secret treatments. Herbs. Eventually I was brought back from the brink, and she somehow convinced the hospital and the police to release me to her care. I guess it helped that I said yes and wasn't a minor." A small victorious smirk turned up the edges of her mouth. "That they knew of. I fortunately had an ID with a fake birth date."

"And Sandra nursed you back to health on the farm." I filled in the ending.

"All of them did." She paused again. "Until they found out the real me. Only Sandra and Alex were supportive. It caused a big rift."

I nodded. "Keena mentioned that."

"Keena wasn't here yet. She only knows the story Sandra told her. And Sandra being the peacekeeper that she is has tried to protect both sides."

"That sounds like Sandra," I said. Sandra would have been so upset to have to choose. In her ideal world, everyone would get along or every problem was fixable while staying together, staying friends. I knew that was one of the reasons my decision to leave hurt her so much. She had expected to work through it together.

The sky above us had been darkening to almost black but then turned a strange orange-tinged purple. An electric current pulsed through the air. I felt a cool pulse in my palms, and I flexed my fingers like one of my cats after a nap.

"This is why I brought you here. To see if the sprite shadows would appear." Darcy smiled, looking down at my hands like she could tell what I was feeling.

"Sprite shadows?" I asked. Smaller cryptids, I knew, would just be weird little animals. Maybe even insects. I had been studying them with Sora.

"Sprite shadows are ..." Darcy paused and looked thoughtful. "Hard to describe. Do you know about sprites in our world?"

"Fairies?" Sprites was a word I had heard used interchangeably with fairies.

"No. The scientific term. It's a type of lightning, large scale electrical discharges. They are beautiful red flashes that are hard to catch. Here in the Other, I think of sprite shadows as a combination of that lightning and the memory of the other sprites, the fairies you mentioned. Though not really like fairies."

"Oh." I didn't fully understand but gathered enough that they sounded like something I very much wanted to see.

"Just watch the lake."

"Not the sky?"

Right as I asked, I saw a vivid purple light from the corner of my eye. I spun towards it, but it was gone. Darcy laughed. I looked out over the lake, energy buzzing through me like caffeine.

Minutes ticked past and nothing happened. I still felt the hum around me, though. I took a deep breath to try to pull some calm into my increasingly jangling nerves.

Brilliant red light suddenly danced across the lake in front of us. In the split second it was there, I saw what looked like an elfin figure running. A rumbling noise that almost sounded like words echoed around us.

"Oh!" I exclaimed and turned to Darcy. She was beaming.

"Told you. Hard to describe, right?"

"Yes," I said distractedly while turning back to the lake. I wanted to see more.

Three distinct flashes in a white blue like lightning appeared in front of us. These three seemed clearer — three nude women with long hair dancing. They spun toward each other and grabbed hands before dissipating.

"Wow! I've never seen three at a time before." Darcy looked at me. We were both grinning like fools. "They must like you!"

I suddenly felt shy at the thought of these lightning beings liking me, at them putting on a show for me. My old feelings of doubt and self-loathing the depression had magnified reared up. I tried to shrug it off.

The sky shifted above us again, this time the clouds churning and the orange color deepening. The sprite shadows all briefly lit up in small flares of purple, red, and white before vanishing. Their electric pull left, and my elation with it. I felt tired and small. Worthless. I frowned at the word. I wasn't worthless. Where had that come from?

Darcy stood in alarm. The sky turned from orange to red, like the sky from a forest fire. The light faded, and a deep fog formed from the middle of the lake. A bitter cold blew towards us. Not like a wind. Like the breath of a monster.

Darcy gripped my arm so hard I would have cried out but for the lack of feeling in my mind. Physical pain didn't matter. The fog rolled towards us at an oddly fast pace. Darcy screamed my name and then everything went black.

We were sitting in Darcy's room back on the farm. I had slumped to the floor from the couch and Darcy was flung back in her seat. Both of us were breathing heavily.

Darcy moved first, groaning as she sat up. She got up, steadying herself against the chair arm as if she was dizzy. She gestured for me to stay put, a single pointed finger I understood immediately. She stumbled to a mini fridge I hadn't noticed before, hiding under the worktable. It was black but seemed out of place in the space Darcy had crafted.

She pulled a small can of something out, opened it, and tossed it back, gulping loudly. I watched her, feeling distant from everything. It was as if everything here was on a small television across a dingy motel room.

After finishing the can, Darcy brought one to me. She got down on the floor next to me and held the can out.

"Drink this." She looked me in the eyes, and I saw the concern etched on her face.

I tried to lift my arm. It flopped next to me. Did it matter? Did I really have to do anything?

"Reva." My name had a sharp edge to it, the "v" cleaving through the fog.

I lifted my arm this time and managed to grasp the can in my hand. I hesitated, unsteady though I was still sitting. I managed to lift the can up to my lips and drink.

The taste of coffee, sugar and milk filled my mouth. I choked in surprise but kept drinking. I finished the whole can with barely a breath between chugging.

"It'll hit soon." Darcy stayed next to me, watching me.

The caffeine and sugar hit my bloodstream and I started to focus again. The world around me stopped feeling like a distant show. I could move my body. I sat up a little, expecting Darcy to scold me but she moved out of my way and looked at me with encouragement.

After a few seconds, I could think and speak again. I hadn't missed the ability until it returned.

"What ... what happened?" I asked, surprised my voice wasn't shaky. I pulled myself back onto the couch.

"Where to start?" Darcy said as she moved to sit in her chair. "I guess your demon felt you and came to find you in the Other."

"Why didn't it feel me when I first got there? Is the Other where demons are from? Why did that taste like coffee?" The questions spilled out from me like my mouth was a stuck faucet wrenched open again.

Darcy watched me with amusement on her face. I was struck by how calm she was. The last two times I had been in the Other with the demon, I'd been surrounded by the whole house.

"I'll start with the easy answer. It tasted like coffee because it was. When I have a run-in like that in the Other, I have found having something caffeinated with a lot of fat and sugar works better than any magic potion could. If it's not urgent, I usually make a Vietnamese coffee or a Thai iced tea. But I keep canned iced coffee drinks for emergencies."

"Huh." All the burning questions I had suddenly evaporated. Caffeine, fat, and sugar seemed like a prosaic magic potion for recovering from demons.

"As to why the demon didn't find you when you got there, I'm not sure." Darcy watched me, clocking my reactions like a nurse watching a patient coming off a sedative. "If I had to guess, I would say something you did called it. Were you feeling any of your magic?"

I nodded. "When the sprite shadows showed up, I felt it. Is that what calls the demon?"

"I don't know. Something spoke to it. I think it's good news, though, that it doesn't detect you immediately when you arrive in the Other."

"Is that what you expected?" I looked at Darcy, absorbing the knowledge she must have. I didn't need the nod she gave me. She had brought me into the Other with that possibility known. "What would you have done?"

"We would have left immediately."

"And you would have been able to do that? What if it had been waiting and attacked?"

"It didn't any of the times you were there by yourself. Demons don't really work like that. They don't attack like a predator on the hunt." She paused. "They're more like star fish. They want you close enough to envelope you in their stomachs and then digest you."

I shuddered though a slow lumbering star fish should have been more reassuring than a lion comparison.

"The Other also isn't the demon realm, so they're visitors there, too. They can't have dominion over more than a small part of the Other. Our world is actually much more fertile of a place for them to infect."

That wasn't reassuring either. I perked up despite the news. The caffeine was hitting my bloodstream, strangely calming and enlivening at once.

"I see the caffeine is doing its job. You should probably head off to bed."

"I can't imagine sleeping right now. I feel like I could read a thousand books." I stood.

"You have about ten minutes before it wears off and leaves you exhausted. Trust me and go get some sleep. You're going to need to get as much as possible so we can go back to the Other."

"Back?" My voice went an octave higher than I meant. I had no intention of ever going back to the Other.

"Yes. This demon can pull you into the Other somehow without your permission. It must take a lot of energy for it to do that but once it gathers enough, it will do it again. So before that happens, I want you to become familiar with the Other and try to protect yourself there."

"Can't you just go in and pull me out if that happens?" As soon as I said it, I realized it must not be possible. Or surely she would have helped me before. I hoped she would have.

Darcy shook her head sadly. "I wish I could but if I went to the Other, I'd have to know where to find you in it. It would be like knowing you're on the continent of South America but not even which country."

"But you could go to Storm Lake. And the demon went there." I felt the beginning of exhaustion at the back of my eyes. Darcy was right. I was going to crash soon.

"The demon likely would have pulled you through the lake to another part of the Other. I'm still learning realmwalking. Most realmwalkers learn from family members. If you don't, you have to find an apprenticeship, which is very hard even if you aren't like me. I don't have the chops to chase a demon in the Other. Not alone." Darcy's face dipped down into a muddle of sadness and anger. She knew her limits and hated their existence. I felt a stab of shame at having pushed at her.

"Sorry. I didn't mean to be a jerk," I said as a wave of exhaustion hit so hard, I was surprised I wasn't swaying on my feet.

"You weren't a jerk. You're scared and want answers. It's understandable with what stalks you. I can't help the way I want to." I heard her unspoken sentences after she stopped speaking. Not just the way she *wanted* to. The way she was *supposed* to. If she had the support she needed from other realmwalkers. That the body politics of this world impacted another realm. I felt anger on her behalf and shared her frustration at the impotence of the situation.

"You should go to bed. If you don't hurry you may not make it down the hall." She gave me a half smile. Apology accepted and understanding half smile.

I nodded and walked toward the door, the tiredness at my heels. I needed to hurry. I stopped at her door and turned.

"Thank you for taking me to the Other," I said before walking out and down the hall to bed.

Chapter 14

My head was pounding, and I felt vaguely nauseated as I came to in my bed. As I lay there trying not to move, the pounding in my skull got louder.

"Reva?" A faint call through my door followed by knocking. I guess my head wasn't literally pounding.

"Come in," I tried to say. My mouth felt like it was covered in a carpet. A carpet coated with fur. This was becoming a trend I didn't like, waking up feeling like crap.

I turned my head as the door opened and Sora came in carrying a tray. Cinnamon scent filled the room and strangely held the nausea at bay.

"Good morning," Sora said in a chipper but soft voice. "Darcy let us know you had a run-in last night in the Other. I have something to perk you up."

"Is that why I feel like this?" I tried to sit up before flopping back down and immediately wishing I hadn't.

"Yep. Here, let me help you." She set the tray down and helped me into a sitting position leaning against the headboard.

"Thanks," I mumbled. Sora held out a big warm mug of something. I took it and drank without much thought. Sweet cinnamon and lemon flavors filled my mouth. I took a few more sips. The pounding in my head receded.

"I was expecting coffee, but this is nice, too. What is it?"

"Secret family recipe for magical hangovers. It's mostly an herbal tea." Sora shrugged and smiled.

"Is that code for 'you wouldn't drink it if you knew what was actually in it'?" I hadn't heard Sora be secretive about a recipe before. She laughed.

"Maybe. You want to know what awful thing is hiding in it?"

I shook my head. "No, when something is working as well as this is, I'm okay with not knowing."

"You're different than Alex in that way, then. For someone who gets into as many magical fights as she does, you'd think she wouldn't be so picky."

"Alex gets into magical fights?" As I said it out loud, I realized it wasn't that odd of a thought. Well, not the fight part. I still didn't have a good feel for what magic Alex possessed.

"Alex is our bruiser. She's out mixing it up all the time."

"What about Darcy? She goes into the Other a lot." I suddenly felt famished. "I feel like I could eat four breakfasts."

"Darcy isn't weird about ingredients like Alex. She also learned a lot of her own tricks on healing that she shares. We collaborate often." Sora handed me a giant cookie studded with chocolate and oats. I eagerly took a huge bite only to be confronted with the flavor of banana.

"Banana?" I said through my mouthful. I chewed and swallowed. "I don't love banana."

Sora rolled her eyes. "Now you sound like Alex. The potassium in them is really helpful in circumstances like this. Finish it and the tea, then you can come down for a full breakfast."

I ate the rest of the cookie with no enthusiasm but gulped the tea like it was going out of style. Sora took the tray from me and told me to come downstairs.

"I should go work out first. Before breakfast. I don't want whatever punishment Alex cooks up for me because I missed today." I had tried to miss exactly one morning workout session when I wanted to sleep in one morning. Alex had upped the burpee and squat sets in punishment after she had dragged me out of my reluctant bed. I hadn't been able to walk down the stairs without grimacing for days after.

"You're skipping today. Alex confirmed, I promise," Sora added after seeing my face. "Sandra is taking you to see Wynona today.."

It took me a minute to remember who Sora was talking about. "The Native American tribe? I'm going to see them today?"

"Not the whole tribe. Just Wynona. Come downstairs when you're ready."

After lingering in a hot shower for longer than I meant to, I went downstairs to the kitchen. Sora, covered in a light dusting of flour, was kneading a ball of dough . She was so engrossed, it was like she'd never been in my room less than an hour earlier.

"Your breakfast is under that bowl on the side counter," Sora said without looking up from her work. Sure enough, under an upturned big metal mixing bowl was a large plate with a huge slice of quiche, sausages, and toast.

I grabbed homemade jam from the fridge and sat down to my breakfast. Much to my surprise, everything was still hot.

"Did you just finish it as I walked in? How is it still warm?" I asked through a mouthful of toast and the newest jam flavor, Oregon grape from berries harvested in the woods. It did taste like grape but with a wild floral edge.

"Magic," Sora said without a hint of humor or teasing.

Sandra waltzed in as I was finishing the last sausage, Kiz and Tuna swirling around her as the door opened and almost tripping her as they crossed in front of her feet.

"Cats! I swear," she said as the two of them rushed toward me like they had sausage radars. I guess they did, as they started purring and rubbing against my ankles. I sighed and dropped two pieces in opposite directions. Fortunately, they both went after different pieces and were satisfied without having to fight each other.

"You ready, Reva? We have a bit of a drive. Wynona lives out in the direction of Coquille."

I finished my last bite of quiche and nodded.

We headed out of the house and got into the purple van. I hadn't driven in it since Sandra had picked me up all those weeks ago in Seattle. It was hard to believe it was the end of February. Only and already — time had bent in strange ways with all I had experienced.

"It's weird being back in this seat," I said as we pulled away.

Sandra looked over at me and patted my hand. "I'm so glad to have you back."

We rode the rest of the way to Silverdale in silence. As we entered the town, a strange sensation ran over my skin, giving me goose bumps. I looked out the window as we drove by the market. A man sat on one of the chairs on the porch, his face obscured by shadows, yet I felt his eyes follow me as we rolled past. I shivered.

"You cold?" Sandra asked. "I can turn up the heat."

I shook my head. "No. I'm okay." I started to say more but the sensation and the town were behind us. Surely just my imagination, my paranoia.

We drove the next forty minutes in a silence that was awkward yet comfortable. We both knew there were more layers of conversation to have with each other but there was no rush. Seven years of catching up would take more than an hour's drive but there was a confidence in the air between us that we wouldn't lose time again with each other.

Sandra turned off the highway onto an unremarkable road that meandered through newly planted forests and pastures for a while before turning again onto a small dirt road. Big ruts and mud puddles slowed the van to a crawl.

"I know Wynona likes to keep folks out, but she really needs to get work done on this road," Sandra said as she gripped the steering wheel and ran the van over a fern to avoid what seemed like a small lake in the middle of the road. "She's going to be pissed about that fern."

I looked back but as unable to tell which fern amidst all the others. We continued deeper into forest, the trees changing into old growth dripping with moss. Eventually we stopped at a small gate made of barbed wire and wood. Sandra took off her seat belt and opened her door.

"I can get the gate," I said, taking off my own seat belt. "You're the driver, you shouldn't get out."

Sandra shook her head. "Only known invited guests can open the gate. I'm not even sure if I'll be able to do it. She knows I'm coming but ..."

She trailed off as she left the car and went to the gate. I was puzzled for a few seconds before remembering Wynona was more than just one of Sandra's old hippie friends. Of course the gate was enchanted, even one made of rusted barbed wire.

The gate allowed Sandra to drag it open and drive the van through. After closing it, we continued. The dense forest loomed over us, blocking out the overcast sky so it appeared to be on the verge of dusk. We turned a bend in the road and the forest lightened up, trees sparser above a sea of blackberry vines that scraped the car.

"She could be a little more welcoming," Sandra said with gritted teeth. "We just had the moons repainted on the van last summer. I'll have to touch them up after this."

We drove around another turn and started down a small hill. I could see where we must be headed at the bottom. A small white house was there, tilting off its foundation as half its roof was consumed by blackberries. A few cars in varying states of disrepair dotted the area, all succumbing to the march of the blackberries.

"She lives there?" I asked, pointing to the white house. It looked like a light cough would blow it over.

"What? No, she lives there." Sandra pointed the opposite direction of the dilapidated house to a large mound of blackberries. Underneath the mound was a double wide trailer with a small porch. As the van rolled closer, a shadow moved on the porch and a man came out onto the steps.

"Fu- ... fudge. Mikhael." She breathed out as the car came to a stop. For Sandra to almost curse meant she was pretty upset.

"Who's Mikhael?" I said as I looked at the man. He had a presence that made him appear taller than he actually was, and his face was burned into a scowl. His brown hair was pulled back in a ponytail. "He seems friendly."

"He's not," Sandra said, ignoring my sarcasm. "He's Wynona's nephew. Quite protective of her. Bit of a jerk."

She got out of the car and three white and gray dogs came rushing off the porch barking like mad. Sandra backed up to the car door but didn't get back in. I, on the other hand, stayed firmly inside, watching in horror as the dogs rushed at her.

"Alto, Strato, Nimbus!" the man on the porch called out, and the dogs immediately turned, running to line up at his side.

"Nice way to greet a guest, Mik," Sandra said. She motioned for me to get out of the car. I slowly opened the door but waited to see if the dogs would run out again. They tensed with perked up ears on their fluffy heads but didn't move.

"You're not my guest. And my name is Mikhael to you." Mikhael crossed his arms and glared at Sandra, which was impressive given his already scowling face.

"I'm your aunt's guest, so that makes me your guest, too. And you scared my niece!" Sandra waved over the hood at where I was slowly getting out.

"No, I'm fine. It's fine," I called out, worried there'd be a tremor in my voice. I didn't dislike dogs, but strange dogs always made me nervous. Those that ran barking at people even more so. But hell if I'd let Mikhael know that.

"The stormweaver?" he said with a tinge of dismissiveness.

Mikhael shifted his gaze over to me and his features changed. His face opened up a bit and the hostility receded to wariness. He was almost handsome when he dropped the tough guy look. Our eyes met and a strange electrical current zinged through the air between us. We both flinched back in surprise and dropped our eyes.

"Yes, this is our stormweaver," Sandra said with a touch of smugness.

"I didn't realize you were bringing her on this visit." Mikhael directed the dogs behind him and gestured us to come up on the porch.

I followed Sandra up, glancing nervously at the dogs.

"Lot of blackberries out here," I said stupidly before thrusting my hand out to him. "I'm Reva."

Mikhael looked at my outstretched hand but didn't make a move to take it. I dropped it by my side, feeling even more awkward.

"Sorry," I mumbled at the same time he muttered something.

"No. My apologies. I don't shake hands," he said, looking at the ground. The dogs behind him all cocked their heads in different directions.

"Oh, sorry. Is that a — Native tradition?" I asked with immediate regret. His head snapped up and a look of irritation was back on his face.

"No. It's a personal tradition." He looked at me with a frown and our eyes locked again. The same electric feeling filled the air between us before we both looked away again. Behind him, the dogs began to whine.

"Okay, enough you two." Sandra's voice was filled with amusement. "Good thing you didn't shake, or sparks would fly!"

She laughed and led me inside, not waiting for permission. I turned to ask Sandra what the hell was going on, but the inside of the trailer distracted me.

We stepped into a small dimly lit entryway that looked like it was made from blackberry canes growing from, surprisingly, a stone floor up into an arch. I reached out to see if they were real when Sandra tugged me forward.

I followed her through the archway into a large room with sunlight flowing in through big stained-glass windows in abstract yellows and oranges on either side. A big live-edge wooden slab table graced the middle of the room with drying herbs hanging above it in rows. At the end sat a petite woman with long gray hair, dressed like Stevie Nicks.

"Sandra!" The woman's voice rang out in the space, light and airy like a songbird.

"Wynona!" Sandra rushed forward and they hugged, bracelets clinking.

I heard Mikhael step up behind me. I looked over my shoulder at him and caught him staring at me with an odd look on his face. He quickly turned his head away.

"Reva, come meet my dear friend," Sandra called me over. "Wynona, this is Reva. My niece."

I stood in front of Wynona, marveling at how tiny she was. Five foot at the most. Up close she looked younger than Sandra by a few years and was sporting purple lipstick that suited her brown skin perfectly.

"So this is your niece! Reva, I've heard so much about you. Glad to meet you in person." Wynona took my hands in hers. Gemstone rings covered her fingers. "Let's sit and get to know each other."

I took the seat next to her and Sandra next to me. Wynona stayed standing as she poured us each a cup of dark tea from a funky clay pot shaped like a rose.

"Mik, get over here! What are you doing sulking at the end of the table?" Wynona's voice went straight into Auntie-tone, firm and as if he was a misbehaving eight-year-old. Mikhael's face darkened in embarrassment, and he walked over, taking a seat across from Sandra.

"Why are you sitting so far away from me? And this pretty young stormweaver! Come, sit next to Auntie." Wynona firmly patted the table across from me, the sound of her rings hitting the wood echoing through the space.

Mikhael defeatedly moved seats with a sigh. I turned to Wynona. "This space is stunning! I love the windows."

"Wynona is a very gifted space-shifter. The best, really," Sandra piped up.

"No, I'm adequate." Wynona preened.

"Nonsense! You're the best and you know it. I have never seen such talent. And then to pair it with your decorating skills!" Sandra exclaimed. "You decorated famous musicians' houses!"

"Pssh, in the '70s. Not anytime recently." Wynona batted the compliments away with wave of her hand and a delighted smile.

"You are world class, Auntie," Mikhael chimed in, grinning at his aunt. He looked over at me briefly and gave me a smile before looking back at his aunt. The game of flattery went on a few more rounds where I learned of at least two famous people who Wynona had dated, one of whom I had never heard of but feigned being impressed with. Eventually it turned, though.

"Too bad all your spell work and money were stolen by that criminal," Mikhael said, a sudden bitterness injected in the conversation. "Thanks to you, Sandra."

"I didn't know he was going to do that!" Sandra responded. Mikhael started to say something, heat in his voice as Sandra opened her mouth to talk over him.

Wynona slammed her hand on the table, startling us all with the power in her small frame.

"That was unfortunate but it's water under the bridge. Sometimes we trust the wrong people." Her voice was hard and final. Both Sandra and Mikhael glowered at each other from across the table. Wynona turned to me.

"Reva, your aunt says you're a stormweaver. We haven't seen a full stormweaver in many generations in our tribe. Tell me about your magic experience."

The heat in the room seemed to creep up. It was like being at a job interview, with sweaty pits and suddenly tongue-tied.

"She's really just getting started. See, she came back in January —" Sandra filled in for me, sensing my distress.

"Her words. Not yours, Sandra," Wynona cut her off, her voice still hard. I wondered what exactly had transpired between them so many years ago.

"I —" I took in a deep breath and started again. I told Wynona of the most recent storm I had pulled from the sky at the hate parade in Coos Bay.

She nodded. "We've been hearing of the white power group forming there in recent months."

Mikhael scoffed. "That shit isn't new. Their boldness is new."

Wynona agreed before turning back to me. "Any other times?"

I hesitated again before telling a truncated version of the storm in Seattle. Wynona watched me carefully as I spoke.

"You're leaving a lot out." Her eyes narrowed at me. "But you have your reasons so I can accept that. For now."

I nodded, relieved. I wasn't ready to tell these strangers my worst secret. I never would be.

"We should tell you about the demon." Sandra spoke up softly. Wynona raised an eyebrow and after a nod from me, Sandra filled them in about the demon.

Both Wynona and Mikhael's faces were somber, and a few seconds of silence passed as Sandra wrapped up by ending with my trip to the Other the prior night. We all sipped at tea that tasted of blackberry and a soft vegetal flavor.

"You're a realmwalker as well?" Mikhael broke the silence, envy behind his words.

"No, I don't think so," I said. "It pulls me in."

Wynona looked at me thoughtfully. "Tell me about any other odd interactions you've had recently."

"Magical interactions?" I asked.

She shrugged. "Any. Sometimes magic is involved in the most ordinary of interactions."

"How about your interactions with the Evernia?" Sandra interrupted. "I brought the key."

"You brought the key?" I parroted in confusion as she pulled the obsidian box from her purse. "You went in my room and just took it?"

Sandra turned red. "You'd had a rough night in the Other. I figured you wouldn't want to run back upstairs to fetch it and I was already up there."

"You two can bicker later. Tell us about the Evernia. Did you really see one?" Mikhael interrupted this time. He sounded eager and skeptical at the same time.

I described all my encounters with the deer, watching Wynona's face and catching glimpses of Mikhael's. The electrical current between us could spark up if our eyes met. It was a strange feeling, confusing. Was I attracted to him?

"The Evernia gave you a key in the Other that carried over?" Wynona sat up taller at this information. "That's highly unusual. Let me see it."

"Do you think that's a good idea?" Mikhael said, eyeing the obsidian box with suspicion.

Sandra ignored him and slid the box over to Wynona, who studied it before resting her hands on top with closed eyes. She opened the box carefully and looked at the key before shutting her eyes again. Her fingers lightly grazed over the key.

"Wynona is very adept at reading magic currents in objects. Comes with the space-shifter gift." Sandra whispered loudly to me.

"Not just objects," Mikhael said. "People, too. That is why you brought your stormweaver."

"Hey, I have a name," I chimed in, ready to glare but quickly looking away.

"Indeed you do, Reva. It's time for you and me to chat. Alone." Wynona opened her eyes and closed the box. She slid it over the table to me before standing up. "Follow me."

I put the box in my bag, leaving it on my seat as I got up. I looked at Sandra who shrugged and Mikhael who was purposely looking away. I turned and followed Wynona through a beaded doorway at the back of the room.

Wynona led me through a warren of hallways, all with the same blackberry cane walls, until we came to a blue door. She took an old-fashioned skeleton key out of her pocket and slid it into a lock. It made a satisfying metal click and then she opened the door.

I looked through the doorway and my mouth dropped open in awe at what appeared to be the inside of a cave. Wynona stepped through and motioned me to follow. I closed my mouth and went through the door. My feet hit sand. Daylight shone in from my right where the cave opened up. The air, filled with the sound of waves and seagulls, smelled like salt and seaweed.

"Let's take a walk on the beach," Wynona said casually as if we hadn't walked through to the ocean from a landlocked trailer amid blackberry fields and forest.

"How —" I gaped around at the cave. Wynona had already started walking off. I ran to catch up.

"Space-shifting is a lot more than decorating for the rich and making grand homes out of blackberries and double-wides. If you're good, that is." A smug smile crossed her lips. She was that good. I could tell even from this limited interaction.

"How far can you shift? Geographically?" I asked.

"Everywhere within the continent. Crossing oceans is —" She paused thoughtfully. "Dangerous is the best way to put it. Possible, but with plane travel, not worth the risk."

I nodded as we walked out of the mouth of the cave and onto a deserted beach. Fog obscured cliffs and pine trees behind us.

The ocean and the sky were both slate gray. I felt a buoyancy in being there, like when I had gone to the beach with Keena.

"I like being at the edge of the ocean. Is this ... Oregon?" I asked. It didn't feel like it was only a few miles away. Maybe it was my assumption that Wynona would take an opportunity to show off her skills.

"It makes sense that you'd be drawn to large bodies of water. You can draw a lot of energy from them for storm magic." We were walking toward the ocean, across the dry sand. Tide must be out, I thought. "Today, we're at a beach I love in Washington state. Tomorrow when I take my ocean walk, it may be closer or further. I decide when I turn the key."

I nodded and we walked on in silence until Wynona stopped where the dried sea foam and kelp lay from the last wave. She turned to me and held out her hands. I placed my hands in hers and waited, looking down at her face. She was looking at me but also through me in an intense stare. We stayed like that as seconds passed. Minutes.

Finally she refocused and looked right into my eyes. The world shifted, like being in a video game with a short, sudden glitch. I had an urge to rearrange the sky. I flinched in surprise at the sensation. It felt dangerous. Wynona raised her eyebrows.

"You have another gift beyond the stormweaving, which is plenty as it is. You can feel and even take on another witch's magical trait, though it looks like only for a short time. And likely only with those that align with your own magic."

"Is that — did I just feel your magic?" I looked around. The glitch had disappeared.

"In a way, yes. Have you felt this with others?" Wynona dropped my hands and started walking along the waterline on the wet sand. I fell in line next to her and thought for a while.

"Maybe. I'm not sure." I was puzzled. "What sorts of magics align with mine?"

"Elemental, of course. So likely you'd be able to borrow fire from one of your fire witches." She must have been referring to

Sandra and Alex. "Empathetic magics, naturally, since this trait is categorized with them."

"What are other empathetic magics?" I asked.

"You're really quite unlearned on this. Sandra did describe the situation accurately." Wynona sighed. A ripple of irritation ran through me at the condescension, particularly as I couldn't argue. "A lot of healing magic, though not all. Emotional divining, some of the body arts —"

"What's emotional divining?" I interrupted. It sounded familiar.

"That's the ability to tell the future through someone's emotions. And read their past."

"I think Keena does that."

Wynona kept walking.

"What about realmwalking?" I asked, thinking of Darcy, of being pulled into the Other. Maybe I had been borrowing her magic.

"That's different magic and very rare. It has more in common with space-shifting."

"Oh." I felt a little disappointed with that news. That meant it was the demon pulling me in except for when Darcy had led me. "I had hoped I was borrowing rather than getting pulled in against my will."

"How would you borrow that magic? There are no realmwalkers here that I know of. Closest one is in Portland. And a bit of a prick," Wynona said with a small laugh.

"Darcy is a realmwalker," I said in surprise.

"Darcy? The runaway witch?" Wynona mirrored back my surprise.

"Yes?" I had heard of how Darcy showed up at the farm in bits and pieces but not all the details. That Darcy was a runaway did seem to be a puzzle piece to the incomplete picture of her. A frown crept over Wynona's face.

"Sandra sometimes gets so overprotective, she fails to see how she's holding back the very person she's protecting." There was a deep bitterness in her words that spoke to past hurts. She stopped and turned abruptly. "Time to get back. We should rescue Mikhael and Sandra from glaring at each other."

We walked back in quiet, each with our own thoughts until Wynona spoke.

"What do you think of Mikhael?"

I paused, not sure exactly what to say before going with blunt. "Are you trying to set us up?"

She laughed, one of those laughs that sounds like notes in a song. "I'm his Auntie. I'm always trying to set him up. He is terrible at first impressions with a sweet center under all his bluffing. But no. I'm not asking for that reason. Did you notice anything —" She paused, searching for the right word. "Odd. Anything odd when you met him."

Heat rushed to my cheeks. I didn't want to tell her about the weird electric feeling as she'd just admitted to always trying to set him up. "He sicced his dogs on us when we showed up."

"That's not odd. The Cloud Pack is very protective of him. And he's not fond of Sandra, as you gathered. It was only for show. What else?" Wynona waved me on. I got caught on the Cloud Pack but remembered the dogs' names were cloud-based. It made me smile before I continued.

"He didn't shake my hand upon meeting me."

"Ah, that's normal for him. He has to be careful with touch due to his magic. He's a lightning witch. Sometimes known as an electric witch. Rare in the elemental magics but not as a rare as you."

"Lightning witch?" I had so many questions swarming through my mind, including whether men could be witches. I guess they could, who was I to question a more powerful elder witch. And I felt relief at the confusion I'd been feeling. Mikhael and I had a literal electric current between us because of magic. At least, I thought it was relief. Not disappointment. Nope.

"There is a weird electrical charge between us," I said, hoping Wynona wouldn't go into Auntie Matchmaker mode.

She smiled widely. "I knew it! I was hoping that would happen. It's why I invited him. He thinks it was to protect me.

But I knew if you were a stormweaver like Sandra claimed, there'd be simpatico magic."

We walked back up the beach to the cave and the house beyond, each of us lost in our own thoughts.

Chapter 15

The visit wrapped up quickly after Wynona and I returned. Sandra and Wynona hugged and made noises about seeing each other soon. Mikhael avoided my eyes while I tried to catch them to recreate the electric sensation.

They both walked us out onto the porch where the Cloud Pack rose to greet everyone with wagging tails and a few short, excited yips. I patted a light gray fluffy one on the head as we walked out.

"That's Strato," Mikhael said coming up next to me and squatting down to let Strato lick his face. He wasn't even facing me but being close by a few inches, I could feel the electrical pull and a crackle between us like warm water on the back of my hand. Close like this, I could feel it as magic. He jumped up suddenly and took a few steps back.

"Sorry. I didn't mean to get so close," he mumbled. "I hope that didn't hurt."

"No. It's fine. That didn't *hurt*?" The last word came out of my mouth with a question mark not because I wasn't certain, but I was baffled at the idea that it could hurt. It had felt right.

Mikhael gave me a questioning and skeptical look of his own. He opened his mouth to speak.

"Okay, time to go!" Sandra interjected, cutting the moment short. Mikhael turned away to his dogs, corralling them to stay on the porch. I followed Sandra reluctantly down the steps, looking back on Mikhael.

As we reached the car doors, Wynona called out.

"Nice to meet you, Reva! Hope to see you again very soon. By the way, that key from the Evernia is a post office box key. No magical threat on it."

I thanked her and started to get into the car when she called out again.

"And Sandra?" Wynona chirped from the porch. "Next time, bring your realmwalker. I very much want to meet her."

Sandra paused from getting in the car to look at Wynona and then over at me as I slipped into the passenger side. She waved but said nothing and got in. Chilliness came off her but we both stayed quiet.

As we approached the stop sign at the main road, Sandra rolled the car to a stop and turned to me.

"Why did you tell her about Darcy? Did you tell all of her secrets?" Anger and coldness dripped off her words.

"Why is Darcy being a realmwalker a secret?" I snapped back. Her anger didn't seem fair. "I don't understand. You told her I was a stormweaver."

"It's different. Wynona is a space-shifter, one with a big ego. Realmwalking and space-shifting together are a dangerous mix."

"How was I supposed to have known that?" A huge ball of frustration filled my chest. "Wouldn't that be Darcy's decision anyway? She's an adult. Maybe having someone with similar magic could help her."

Sandra's face was squinched in fury, her mouth a hard line. "Darcy needs our protection. She's very vulnerable to hate, judgment, being taken advantage of —"

"Wynona doesn't seem like a bad person. You two are friends," I pointed out. The conversation was getting confusing.

"Wynona and I have a complicated friendship. Always have. We're like sisters. She's actually a lot like your mom." Sandra pulled the car out onto the highway, a decisive move to end the conversation. I felt stung that Sandra would compare Ginny to Wynona. Wynona had made me feel welcome, given me support and, though it made me uncomfortable, was trying to set me up in some magical way with her nephew. None of those were things my own mother would do. And I couldn't forget Sandra had clearly brought someone into Wynona's life who had hurt her. I might not know the details, but I knew enough that Sandra didn't get to play innocent.

"Maybe you're the one in that friendship who is like Ginny," I said quietly after a few moments of silence. "You're punishing me for your own mistakes and decisions. Just like she does."

Sandra didn't respond. The iciness coming from her shifted to include a fiery heat. It was like being rubbed all over with triple strength Bengay cream. She was using her fire magic in anger, which pissed me off. I had felt it before as a kid but never realized what she had been doing, since it hadn't been directed at me.

The clouds above us had been darkening and finally opened up. Rain splattered on the windshield as Sandra turned on the wipers. I felt heartened at the rain. The cool damp feeling in my palms returned and this time I concentrated on that feeling and my intentions. The rain fell harder. A small smile crept onto my face.

Sandra turned the wipers up a level. "Don't be a child, Reva. I'm driving."

"I don't know what you're talking about," I said. "Didn't the forecast call for rain?"

The heavier rain made the sky dark in the fading afternoon light. We had been at Wynona's longer than I had realized. Sandra turned on the headlights but didn't say anything else.

A pair of headlights came on behind us suddenly. Sandra jumped. A car, likely a truck from how high the lights were, had come up fast behind us without either of us noticing. The truck was really riding our bumper.

"I didn't see them approach," Sandra remarked.

"You must have been too focused on your icy-hot game," I said, too pissed not to be petty.

"I don't know what you're talking about," Sandra retorted, mimicking my voice.

The truck accelerated and came even closer. The headlights reflected off the rear-view mirror, blinding as the sun.

"That asshole just turned his brights on!" Sandra exclaimed. The van slowed a little as she tried to adjust the mirror. Suddenly the van jolted forward violently.

"He rear-ended us!" I yelled and froze before fumbling in my purse for my cell phone.

"He's trying to run us off the road," Sandra said with a strange mix of fear and calmness in her voice. "Is your seat belt on?"

"I'm calling the police!" My hands trembled and little electrical pulses came from my fingers. My phone slipped through my fingers and onto the floor, sliding under the seat.

"SEAT BELT?!" Sandra yelled.

The truck hit us again. We weaved into the other lane and back, the tires skidding in the gravel shoulder. Sandra pressed on the gas, and we shot forward as she wrestled with the steering wheel. We got back on the road, but the truck had sped up and was now next to us in the other lane. Everything was happening so fast. We were going so fast. The truck slammed into us from the side and the world turned upside down.

Sickening loud crunch. Glass diamonds in my hair. A burnt powder smell. Metallic wet taste in my mouth. My breathing stopped and sped up at the same time. Fragments, everything was in fragments. Sandra. Where was Sandra?

I was sitting in wet grass and wet mud. Rain poured down from the darkening sky. My name was being called in the distance. Sandra. I needed to find Sandra, but I couldn't move. I wasn't sure where I was.

"Reva! Sandra!" a voice called out. I couldn't see anything in the gloom. A dark shape obscured my vision. I put my hand out and felt the shape. Cold wet metal. My mind connected the dots. I was next to the van. The van was upside down.

I tried to call out but felt choked. I coughed, wet and hoarse, before calling back.

"Here! I'm here."

The sound of a man's voice calling my name. I remembered the truck and stopped trying to respond. Had the person returned to finish the job? I tried to stand, slipped in the grass and the mud before shakily getting to my feet. I wouldn't go down without a fight.

"Reva!" The voice was closer. A blinding light swung around the van and into my eyes. "Are you okay? Where's Sandra?"

I didn't respond. The flashlight lowered and I saw the dark outline of the man, the steady rain obscuring him. Dogs barked in the distance. I backed up, slipping a little, and held my hands out in front of me. The fight I was so sure I had in me vanished and I sagged against the van. The man rushed forward and caught me. A warm sensation flooded through me.

"Shit," he mumbled. "Are you okay?"

I recognized his magic before his voice. Mikhael. I tried to say his name and it came out as a mangled sob.

"It's okay. Help is on the way." He started to pull away and I grabbed onto him. He came around to my side and wrapped one arm around me in support. Together we limped through tall dead grass toward a pickup truck with three barking dogs. When we reached it, he pulled open the passenger side and helped me clumsily climb up. I sat facing out, my legs dangling. I tilted my head to the right and laid it on the back of the seat.

"Stay here." He instructed and whistled three times. One of the dogs in the back jumped out and headed out into the grass. Mikhael followed.

I closed my eyes and time passed. Rain beat a song on the roof of the truck. Red and blue flashing lights probed through my eyelids. A flashlight made them pop open. A man in uniform stood by the open truck door, asking me questions. I mumbled answers I couldn't remember. I asked my only question, but he didn't answer. Shouts in the distance and he was gone. The man in the uniform was replaced by a young woman with a short haircut in a rain covered fleece jacket. She asked me questions about my body, about pain. I answered and asked my question again. She ignored it so I closed my eyes to her and the lights.

"Reva." A gentle familiar voice. I opened my eyes and Wynona was standing in front of me. "Make the rain stop."

I looked at her in confusion. I didn't control the rain. My voice was a whisper after all the questions but finally I asked mine. "Sandra?"

"Sweetheart, we need the rain to let up. It'll make pulling her out of the van easier." Wynona grabbed my hands and looked at me hard.

"Is she dead?" My voice was hoarse.

Wynona shook her head. "No. But it's bad."

I closed my eyes. "I can't."

"You can. Let's start with the rain. Concentrate and pull it back up into the sky." Wynona responded to everything contained in my two words. "Think of the clouds parting."

"I can't." I wanted to say I only knew how to start the storms. How to bring the rain and the wind. I couldn't control it. All I could do was cause chaos.

"You can, Reva. Close your eyes and concentrate." Her voice continued to guide me. "Imagine the clouds and the water in them. Now pull them apart slowly."

I concentrated and felt the coolness on my palms but without the damp sensation. I imagined the clouds as she said and tried to will the rain to stop.

"Good girl." Wynona patted my hand. "You can stop now."

The rain had softened. The staccato beat on the roof slowed to a light patter. I breathed out.

"Okay, pull your legs up into the truck," Wynona instructed. I turned and pulled myself the rest of the way into the truck, sitting the correct way. "Mikhael is going to take you to the hospital."

"What about Sandra?" I couldn't leave her. Not out in the van by herself.

"I'm here. I'll ride with her when they get her out."

I wanted to resist, to stay but instead I nodded, and she shut the truck door. My eyes closed. I heard the dogs jump up into the back of the truck, panting and the click of their toenails on the metal of the truck bed. Mikhael slid into the driver's seat next to me, setting my purse next to me. I felt him look at me before starting the truck and driving us to the hospital.

Chapter 16

My time at the hospital was brief but felt like eternity. Mikhael had helped me inside and left as soon as "my coven" as he called them arrived. I didn't have a chance to thank him as Sora, Keena, Darcy, and Alex surrounded me in the tiny hospital room made of glass. An ER nurse eventually showed up to insist that only two of them could be back there. Sora and Keena stayed as a series of tests were run, holding my hand and a silently agreed-upon quiet, only a few words murmured here and there.

I had several cuts, whiplash, and bruises but no internal bleeding and shockingly no broken bones. My head and neck hurt the most from the impact but the ER doctors rotating through had remarked on my amazing luck. When I asked about Sandra, I'd get a concerned smile and a pat on the hand with little information other than she was in good hands.

Darcy traded off with Sora at one point and had more of an update.

"She's in surgery. Head trauma is all they said. We have no idea on how critical, but Alex was able to pry a little bit more out of Sandra's coworkers here. If she pulls through the surgery, she'll be in intensive care." Darcy had streaks of black down her cheeks as she spoke. All I could think of were the words "if she pulls through" but felt frozen inside. No tears rolled down my cheeks and I felt all the worse for the lack of them.

At some point among the beeping, the tests, and the changing of bedside witches, a police officer showed up to talk with me. He was the kind of guy who should be tall and thin, but he had a large gut that hung over his pants, pulling his whole center down like the permanent frown on his face. He sent Keena and Darcy out of the room with an obvious sneer. I disliked him immensely.

"I'm Officer Dawson," he said, standing over me, closer than I would have liked. "I have a few questions about the accident."

"It wasn't an accident," I said.

"Your aunt purposely drove off the road then?" He raised his eyebrows.

"A truck ran us off the road." A tired feeling spread through my body at the memory.

"I see. Were either of you drinking?"

"What?" I looked at him with a frown. "No."

"No whiskey in your teacups? A flask you were handing back and forth?" He winked at me.

"No!" Anger pressed at my throat.

"Okay, calm down little lady. You weren't drinking. What about your aunt?" He put his hands up in front of him, the classic "just doing my job" pose.

"She wasn't drinking. Why are you asking me these questions?" My voice rose in volume. I suddenly felt alone and trapped with him. He smirked at me.

"Just trying to understand what happened. Tell me about this 'truck that tried to run you off the road'." He did air quotes when he spoke.

"It was white or light colored, tall as if it had those jack-ass tires on it that men with big egos have when they're trying to compensate for something." I spat the words out and watched his smirk turn to a frown.

"No need to get fresh. Be respectful when speaking to me." His voice hardened.

"I'm just describing what I saw," I sneered back at him.

"Now look here —" He leaned in so close I could smell his breath, sulfur and onions.

"Dawson!" A stern shout came from behind him. He spun around and I looked past to see a short, round, gray-haired woman in purple scrubs holding a clipboard. "What the fuck are you doing back here?"

"I had to get this young woman's statement from the accident," Dawson stammered as the woman put her hands on her hips.

"Don't give me that shit. Her statement was taken at the scene. By Hal." She emphasized the name Hal, implying Hal was higher up than Dawson. And wouldn't take too kindly to Dawson's actions.

"He sent me to follow up," Dawson said meekly. Even as he spoke, he walked out like he knew it didn't matter.

"Like hell he did. You're just up to your usual bullshit. Get out of my hospital." She pointed down the hallway where the exit was.

Dawson hurried out as she watched him. He kept his head down as he passed her, trying to make a wide berth around her in the tiny space. She looked ready to reach out and slap him. I hoped she would, but she just glared at him, watching until he was out of sight.

"I'm Linda," she said turning back to me. "Sorry about Officer Dickface."

I laughed for the first time in hours which suddenly turned into tears. Sobs escaped me as I desperately tried to shove them back down.

"Oh shit," Linda said softly as she rushed up to me and put her arm around me. She rocked me gently as I cried. I wanted to stop, didn't want to be crying with this stranger however much I appreciated her, but I couldn't stop.

"Reva. It's okay." I heard Sora's voice next to me and felt another arm around me. After a time, I calmed down. The sobbing slowed, then stopped.

"Damn, honey. You've been through a lot," Linda said as I quieted down. "Sorry about that. An ill-timed joke on my part."

"No." My voice was hoarse and trembled, but I kept going. "Thanks for running Officer Dickface out."

"Oh, my pleasure. He knows better than to come in here after the front desk tells him no."

"Who's Officer Dickface?" Sora questioned, her head tilting to the side.

"Just this officer who came in and made Keena and Darcy get out so he could ask if Sandra and I had been drinking," I told her.

"What?!" Linda's outrage echoed through the hospital. "His supervisor will be getting a call in the morning."

"That's awful!" Sora said. "Why would he ask that?"

"He didn't seem to believe we were run off the road by a big truck. On purpose."

"You were run off the road?" both Sora and Linda exclaimed at the same time. I hadn't told the witches what had happened, not that part. There was so much I needed to tell them.

"Well. I was about ready to discharge you but let me make a quick call. I think someone should follow you all home just in case." Linda looked ready to spit bullets at anyone who defied her. She turned to Sora. "Help her get ready to go. I'll be right back."

"Wait. How is Sandra?" I asked. "We're not getting very much information."

"Oh, honey. We're not supposed to tell you much — HIPAA and the like — until we get doctor approval. She's well-loved here, one of the best nursing aides we have. We're going to do everything we can for her." Linda patted my hand, somehow making the gesture meaningful and warm rather than cliché and perfunctory.

The check-out process took another hour during which time all the witches trooped back in sets of two to ask questions about the truck that ran us off the road. Alex was the most intense until Darcy literally pulled her back from my hospital bed. Alex had already heard about Dawson, who she said she'd had run-ins with before.

"He's a real pig, the sort of good ol' boy protege who never should have been made a cop but who's daddy or uncle or related fuckwad got him in and keeps protecting him," Alex relayed as she helped me up from the hospital bed. I was relieved to be leaving but I was incredibly tired. Everything ached as I walked, and I felt the stitches in the cut on my arm and ankle. More stitches. I ran my hand over the healed scars on my wrist. A heavy feeling settled on me as we walked out into the rain.

We piled into the two cars, Alex driving one and Keena driving the other. I rode with Keena, Darcy in the front passenger, me settling into the back seat   clutching my purse. I was relieved to see my cell was usable with just a cracked screen but dismayed that the obsidian box was shattered, shards of black glass and the key rolling loose at the bottom. I would have to deal with that later.

A cheerful man with a full white beard like Santa Claus and a young man who looked like his son drove behind us in a big SUV as escort. I didn't catch their names but was grateful for the consideration and care.

I was worried I wouldn't be able to tolerate riding in the car after what had happened, but I fell asleep. I woke up at the house, shaken gently by Keena. Our escort had apparently turned back at the main drive. It's good to be home, I thought as I climbed up the steps.

I slept most of the next day, waking up in the late afternoon. Sora updated me on Sandra as I came downstairs with an incredible hunger from so many skipped meals the day before.

"She's in intensive care but the surgery went well. Alex is there now."

I felt relief and guilt as I ate the grilled cheese sandwich and tomato soup Sora put in front of me. She seemed to know exactly what comfort food I needed.

For the next few days, everything was a blur of off schedules. I slept a lot, a nagging worry about whether my depression was returning following me like a puppy. Sora baked copious amounts of cookies and muffins for the hospital staff, which either Keena or Alex delivered. According to Alex, some of the commune sisters were all taking turns sitting by Sandra's bedside as well. Darcy disappeared into her room, only coming out for dinner and updates on Sandra's condition.

"Why don't you or Darcy take on shifts at the hospital?" I asked while sitting at the table with Sora, immediately regretting the words as they left my mouth. I hadn't taken on any of the shifts either and had no excuse. Her face tensed but she went on kneading the dough for cinnamon rolls she was working on.

"Both of us have recent bad memories of hospitals. I with my parents' car wreck and Darcy from her illness." Sora didn't look at me and bashed the ball of dough under her hands with extra force.

"I'm sorry. I didn't think. That was clumsy of me," I said after an awkward silence.

"I like you, Reva," Sora said sharply. "But sometimes you're a bit selfish."

I left the kitchen and spent the day in the library, feeling like crap on someone's shoe. On Sora's shoe specifically. And Darcy's. Eventually I went back to the kitchen and apologized.

"I'm sorry, Sora. That must have been hard for both of you to be there. Particularly hard for you."

"I'm sorry, too. I didn't mean to unload on you like that," Sora replied.

"You don't owe me an apology. How are you doing?"

"I'm okay. Worried sick, of course." Sora was making cream cheese frosting for the now baking cinnamon rolls. The whole house smelled sweet and warm. "It's funny. It was both harder and easier than I thought. Hard to walk in there, not knowing whether you two were going to be okay or not. But once I was there, I went into a different mode. My healing magic kicked in and I was ready."

We talked for longer, me mostly listening as Sora told me about her parents and what she might want to do with her magic. It was nice to get break from my own thoughts. We laughed and tore apart fresh cinnamon rolls with sticky fingers, getting to know each other better.

Later I knocked on Darcy's door. She opened it, her face long and paler than usual. There were dark shadows under her eyes. She had no makeup on, which made her look young and vulnerable.

"I wanted to thank you for coming to the hospital. That can't have been easy," I said, jumping straight into it.

"Thank you." She held the door wide and invited me in.

We took the same seats as when I had been here a few nights before when she took me into the Other. It was hard to believe it was so recently. We sat in silence for a while. Darcy wasn't going to be as easy as Sora to apologize to.

"How's Sandra?" She broke the silence.

"Better. I hear. I haven't been to see her. Alex said she's awake now sometimes. The surgery went well but they don't know how she'll recover. Her pelvis is fractured as well. She's in a lot of pain but they're keeping her comfortable."

Darcy nodded but didn't say anything for a bit. "I bet she hates that. She always takes care of others. She hates being the one needing care."

"That sounds like Sandra." I smiled.

"She's so protective of us all she forgets to take care of herself sometimes," Darcy said. A thought pushed into my head that I didn't want. The argument we'd had before the wreck. I felt a frustrating mix of guilt and confusion about it. I grappled with what to tell Darcy, since Sandra hadn't wanted her to be introduced to Wynona.

"I don't want to lose her. She's the first person who felt like real family." Darcy broke down into tears. I quickly rushed to her side and hugged her. She quickly wiped away the tears after a few moments. I sat back down across from her.

"Sorry. Sandra was the first person who gave a crap about me. And it kills me I can't go to the hospital to see her," Darcy said, fishing out a black handkerchief from a side table drawer. "I managed to get through that night when you were both there, but it definitely wasn't easy."

I felt bad I hadn't noticed her struggle that night, though I had been in shock. I was also avoiding going to see Sandra. None of the witches had pushed me, but I didn't feel like I had as much of an excuse. No one I loved had died in a hospital like Sora had experienced. And I hadn't almost died in the hospital like Darcy had. I made a silent vow to go see Sandra the next day.

The next day passed, and I put off my promise. And the next day. Still no one pressured me to go but I felt self-conscious like they were watching me, talking behind my back. Finally I got up my nerve and approached Keena.

"I'd like to go visit Sandra with you tomorrow," I said over dinner. We were missing Darcy, who was in her room again, and Alex, who was at the hospital. And Sandra of course. Keena had cooked to give Sora a break from her frenzied kitchen activity. Both of them looked fatigued, Sora with puffy eyes and Keena with the corners of her mouth turned down. I had seen dark circles under my own eyes in the mirror that morning.

"Sure. If you feel up to it." Keena gave me a wan smile before going back to eating her potato cabbage soup. It was hearty and simple, nothing I would have chosen to eat, but Sora had drizzled balsamic vinegar and dusted it with parmesan cheese, and I couldn't complain.

"I need to go."

"It's okay to take it easy, Reva. You were run off the road by some pyscho. You are still recovering in a lot of ways," Sora said as she shredded a garlic miso roll on a plate in front of her.

She didn't seem to be eating much, though I hadn't been paying as much attention as I should have been. Despite my apologies to Darcy and Sora, I had gone back to my own self-absorbed state. I had spent the last few days replaying the moments leading up to the wreck in my mind, both trying to remember something about the truck that hit us and going over the argument between Sandra and me. In the better moments, I mused on the conversation with Wynona. I had learned a lot about my magic in that short span of time, but it seemed inaccessible and unimportant now. And sometimes I had thought of Mikhael.

The day after the wreck, Alex had slipped a business card to me.

"You get in a car wreck and still get some dude's number. He's a good guy." She had winked at me half-heartedly and the teasing felt forced, but I had smiled. We were all trying to maintain normalcy in the small ways even as we failed at it.

The card was for Mikhael Gray, Electrician. That made sense. A phone number and an email address were listed but nothing else. No scrawled note on the back. Just the bare facts. I had held onto it but didn't even attempt to call or email. I had no idea what to say. I could start with thanks, but even that seemed hard.

I was shaken out of my thoughts at the dinner table by Alex coming in the backdoor looking as pale and tired as the rest of us. She took a look at our faces as Flame trotted over to sleep in front of the fire.

"Soup?" Sora asked without her usual pep.

"No. I can't stand cabbage. Grew up with too much of it," Alex replied while flopping onto the bench across from me. "What I could use is a stiff drink."

"I have pear brandy," Sora said without enthusiasm.

Alex shook her head. "I need to get out. Get a cheeseburger and fries. A few whiskeys. No offense to your cooking, Keena."

Keena shook her head. "None taken. We're all on autopilot these days. Fries sound good."

"A drink in a bar sounds nice," I said. I hadn't been in a bar in forever. Not since before. With Anthony. I missed the feeling of being surrounded by noise and strangers, the short-lived comradery built like fragile toothpick structures, held together with alcohol and revelry.

"Let's go to the Rubber Bucket then." Alex popped her hand on the table, startling us all.

"The what?" I asked.

Keena rolled her eyes. "The Rubber Bucket is Alex's nickname for the tavern in Silverdale. Officially it's the Rusty Bucket."

"Oh." I waited for an explanation from Alex, but none came forth.

"I'll pass," Sora said. "I want to get up early and bake donut muffins."

"Me, too," Keena said. "Not my scene."

"Ah, come on! You all deserve some lukewarm fries and watered-down whiskey," Alex cajoled. She had a strange energy about her that I hadn't seen before.

"Nope. Once was enough for me. I don't feel welcome there," Keena said firmly.

"I hate bars," Sora said.

"You two are party poopers. Come on, Reva. Let's go."

I looked down at the old University of Washington sweatshirt I was wearing and my faded, most comfortable jeans. "I should change first."

Alex laughed a little too loudly. "If you change into something else, you won't fit in there. This outfit is perfect. It's a redneck bar in a tiny town. On a Thursday no less."

She got up and walked to the backdoor to put her raincoat back on. Keena turned to me and said quietly, "You don't have to go. She gets like this when stressed."

"I heard that, Keena. Stop trying to talk my companion into not going."

"Go. One of you should be a designated driver," Sora said with concern in her voice. I was picking up that the shift in Alex's behavior wasn't new to them, but it was worrying.

"It's just down the road. We don't need to worry about that. We're not going to drink ourselves into a stupor," Alex said firmly in a voice that suggested she expected to do exactly that.

I shrugged at Keena and Sora before getting up and finding my coat, changing out of my old comfort sneakers into boots and following Alex out into the dark night.

Outside the air was damp and cold but a low cloud layer kept it from being too cold. It was the kind of night I loved in Seattle, everything wet from the rain so the city lights reflected off the streets. Here in the country, it was dark, but the clouds had a surprising luminous quality. I had thought that only happened with the reflecting of so many lights. They weren't the odd orange color clouds over cities take on, but they had a warmth to them.

Alex drove us in her beat-up old pickup, one of those that looks like a toy. We pulled into the gravel parking lot of the tavern, and I felt a sense of foreboding.

"Maybe this isn't such a good idea. We could be drinking a nice glass of something back in front of the fire in the library."

"Oof, Reva. Listen to yourself. That sounds boring. Come on. I know Carl, the bartender. He's usually working on Thursdays. He'll treat us right." Alex got out and slammed the car door before walking purposefully toward the glowing beer signs at the entrance. I sighed and followed her.

The tavern was a small narrow room with a bar running down one side and booths down the other and the back in a "L" shape. A scarred pool table was scrunched off to my right by the door. The place was lit with various old beer signs, from neon to the glowing plastic depicting landscapes behind the brand. A few men sat on bar stools that had seen better days. Frankly so had the men.

"Alex! How are you, sweetheart?" A burly man in his fifties stood behind the bar wearing a trucker's hat over a long brown ponytail and sporting a red and black checked shirt. He looked like he'd stepped out of a beer advertisement, complete with full beard and grin. "Who's your pretty friend here?"

"Carl, if you ever call me sweetheart again, I will rip your balls off," Alex said cheerfully. "This is Reva. Sandra's niece."

"Oh." Carl's demeanor went serious as he turned to me. "I'm sure sorry to hear about your aunt. She's a swell lady. Can't believe some asshole would run you gals off the road."

"No one wants to talk about it, Carl. Two whiskeys." Alex held up two fingers before turning to me. "What do you want?"

"You don't get two drinks," Carl scoffed as Alex laughed. "Not after last time."

"Whiskey sounds fine," I lied. I hated whiskey, most hard liquor, actually, but didn't want to order a glass of wine in a bar like the Rubber Bucket. Rusty Bucket, I corrected in my head.

"I'll wait for Slow Hand Luke here to pour us our drinks. Grab a booth, why don't you?" Alex settled onto a bar stool. I sighed again and walked past her to the furthest booth in the back across from the bar. I slid in, catching my jeans on taped vinyl. The table at least looked wiped down. I tentatively touched it and was relieved it wasn't sticky. Then felt guilty. Carl seemed nice. I was judging a book by its cover.

Alex plunked a glass of beer down in front of me and two glasses of whiskey opposite before sliding into the booth.

"I'm not sharing my two whiskeys so this is for you." Alex gestured to the beer. "I got us a basket of fries. I know you've eaten cabbage soup already, but I am willing to share a few to erase the taste."

"It was pretty good. Sora added a few touches," I defended the soup and Keena in turn.

Alex sighed and downed a gulp of whiskey, her face screwing up as it went down.

"Relax, Reva. I'm just decompressing."

"I see." I took a sip of the beer and was surprised at the light citrus flavor. I took a bigger sip.

"Good, right? Local brewery in Coos Bay does a nice job. And you probably thought you could only get a glass of piss here."

"I'm surprised," I admitted. We sat in quiet until Carl strode up with a large plastic basket of fries and a red plastic bottle of ketchup.

"For you, my Queen," he said as he delicately set them both in front of Alex.

"Queen. I'm tepid about that nickname but it will do for now." Alex grabbed up the ketchup and squirted it all over the fries before grabbing a saltshaker to top it off with a good shake. Carl watched in horror and amusement before shaking his head and marching off.

"Dig in." Alex began putting fistfuls of ketchup-soaked fries in her mouth. I grabbed one or two to keep her from pestering me. They were average bar fries, salty and sweet with ketchup.

"How are you doing, Alex?" I asked. I hadn't seen much of her over the past few days, just in passing with an update on Sandra. It had been almost a week since the wreck.

"I'm drinking my feelings, Reva. That's how I'm doing." She had finished off one of the glasses of whiskey and half the fries before slowing down to a normal pace of consumption.

"I haven't just been at the hospital," she said, staring out the window into the darkness beyond the reflections of us. "I've been trying to figure out who was behind it all. What son of a dickwad ran you off the road."

"Oh." I hadn't thought anyone but the police were looking into it. And while I hadn't talked to Officer Dawson again, the other officers when they had called me had been halfhearted in their questions.

"Yeah, it's a cluster. There's some bad shit going on in town. Hate parades like the one you and Keena ran into. Protests, the fuckers call it. It sounds like it's even in the churches." Alex frowned, the lines on the bridge of her nose crinkling. "And I'm not a church lover by any stretch but that seems sick. To be spewing hate from the pulpit. Not exactly what the big man Jesus had in mind."

"Is there a ringleader?" I asked, thinking about the man in the Other. The one with the pointed teeth and too wide smile. I shuddered.

"The demon seeker?" Alex shook her head. "There isn't a clear identified leader, which worries me. That means whoever is in charge is smarter than usual. And that does sound like the workings of a demon."

We sat in silence a minute before Alex shifted gears. "Enough about that depressing shit. You never told us how meeting Wynona went. She's intense but good people."

"You've met her?" I hadn't thought any of the witches had met Wynona. I realized sheepishly I had hoped I was the only one, like I was special.

"It's a small town, Reva. I know Mikhael, too." She grinned at me over the basket of fries which was now empty save for smears of ketchup and mangled rejected bits of potato.

I ignored her teasing over Mikhael. "It was interesting meeting Wynona. I hadn't heard of space-shifting before. Certainly never experienced it."

Alex looked at me in surprise. "Wynona is a space-shifter?"

I nodded slowly. "Yes. If you've met her, how did you not know that?"

"I met her under non-magic pretenses in the community. The Coos tribe is pretty secretive about their powers. Too many white folks stealing their spells and knowledge to use against them. Takes a lot to trust one of us usually. But I guess since you went with Sandra that makes sense."

"They have an odd relationship," I said, musing on the easy closeness between Wynona and Sandra but also the tension.

"Yep. They had a big falling out in the '80s. Sandra introduced some magic lawyer who completely ripped Wynona off. She was a big shot, had a well-known design business with famous customers. He took everything she built. The asshole stole from Sandra, too, but she bounced back easier. Wynona never forgave Sandra for it. The tribe certainly didn't. Sandra has been banned from tribal involvement since."

"Magic lawyer? Those two words don't seem to go together." I mused on the story Alex was unfolding. I could understand Mikhael's dislike of Sandra more. If someone had introduced me to Anthony, would I feel the same way toward them? No one had, though, so I had only myself to blame. And I had taken great lengths to punish myself.

"That's shorthand, not exactly correct. There are people in the magic community who allegedly can help you essentially copyright your spellwork. It is well established in potion work since that has a process and ingredients, but in other magics, the copyright idea doesn't really work. Mostly it's a way to steal from other witches. That didn't come to light until the '90s though."

I nodded through her explanation and sipped my beer slowly. Exploitation happened everywhere, even in magic.

"Sandra got a settlement out of the whole thing, but Wynona didn't. The groups who were policing all of that in the '90s for the witch community claimed they couldn't help Wynona due to tribal law. Which is racist bullshit, of course. An excuse not to right a much bigger wrong."

"Why didn't Sandra share?" It seemed unlike my aunt to not give back some of what Wynona had lost. Sandra was the sort to give you her sweater if you were cold, never minding if she was also cold. Or at least that was the Sandra I knew.

Alex shrugged. "Don't know. Maybe she tried. Maybe she didn't. She doesn't talk about it much. She invested the settlement and used it for a down payment for the farm."

"How is she really doing?" I changed the subject. I wanted to think the best of my aunt. This line of conversation was convincing me she shared more traits with my mother than I wanted to believe. Which made me wonder about myself.

Lines creased Alex' forehead as she took a drink of whiskey. "Not good. Better than she was, of course. But it's going to be a slow recovery. Not sure she will fully. The old biddies are slipping in herbs and spells when they visit, but witchcraft can only do so much."

"Will she walk again?" I asked, looking down at my beer.

"Doctors think so, but she might need a cane. It's going take a lot of physical therapy. It's the head injury I'm worried about. We don't know how much damage was done and the long-term effects." We sat in silence until Alex drained the last of her whiskey.

"I'm going to take a piss and get another. You want anything?" She got up and made a show of stretching. I caught Carl looking at her from across the bar. Someone had a crush.

"No, I'm good."

"You sure? You've been sipping on that beer so long you should buy it a drink." Alex laughed at her own joke and headed to the restrooms on the other side of the bar.

I took another sip of my beer while looking at my reflection in the window, thinking about Sandra and what future lay ahead for her. And whether we'd ever figure out who had run us off the road. I knew there was a person or people behind the wheel, but I felt sure the demon was there with them.

The door to the tavern opened and a cold blast of air came in, reaching me all the way in our booth. I shivered. The foreboding feeling crawled up the back of my neck. I turned and saw three men standing in the doorway. The first man was familiar but took me a second a place as Officer Dickface né Dawson. The second guy was no one I had seen before, and the third guy stood in the shadows behind the two. Dawson was scanning the room until his eyes fell on me and an awful grin filled his face. He turned and said something to the man in the shadows.

The man stepped forward in front of Dawson and I recognized him immediately. The demon seeker.

Chapter 17

He looked like an ordinary man, medium height with brown hair tucked under a baseball cap. His face was generic, neither handsome nor unusual, just average with five o'clock shadow. Something beneath all that normal was disconcerting. He looked at me and smiled wide. I recoiled as I saw for a split second the pointed teeth but then they turned back to ordinary human teeth.

"Dawson. What the hell are you doing in here?" Carl said sternly, walking to the end of the bar by the door. "I told you no coming in and harassing the customers with your cop bullshit."

"Relax, Carl. I'm just here as a regular citizen tonight." Dawson bucked his chin up as he threw his hands out in innocence.

"Man came here to drink. Is that a problem?" The demon seeker turned his gaze from me and looked at Carl. I watched as Carl took a step back and deflated a little.

"No problem as long as Dawson keeps his hands to himself. I don't want a repeat of last time," Carl said before turning away quickly to dry some glasses.

"Excellent." The demon seeker turned and walked toward me, the other two men following. I felt frozen in the booth, but I wanted to run.

The group of men reached the booth and stopped. The demon seeker slid into the seat across from me where Alex had been. Where was Alex?

"Well, hello there." He smiled at me again, the skin stretching slightly too far for a split second before righting itself back into a human smile. "I've been waiting for a chance to see you face to face. Here in this realm."

I didn't say anything. Up close I could feel the cold power seeping out of him. To say it gave me chills would be an understatement. Shivers ran all over my body.

"How's your aunt? Damn shame about the wreck. Some in town are saying the wrong person ended up in the hospital." As he spoke, I knew it was him. That he was the one behind the wheel of the white truck. And I was the intended target.

"Who are you?" I asked, finally finding my voice and hoping it came out strong without the trembling I felt inside.

"Is that really what you want to ask? My name doesn't matter." He watched me, putting his hands on the table and slowly drumming his fingers.

"If your name doesn't matter, why won't you tell me?" I pressed myself against the back of the booth, wishing for an escape. Dawson and the other guy stood in front of the booth, blocking any exit.

"How about you call me Damien?" He laughed. "Do you know the roots of the name? It means 'to subdue'."

The cold swept over me again. I looked up and made the mistake of looking into his eyes. Ordinary brown eyes but with something lurking just out of sight, like movement in your peripheral vision. I couldn't look away, much as I wished I could.

"I know of another name you may prefer. Starts with an 'A'." He grinned and the pointed teeth showed this time. Dread filled me. I wanted to think of any coincidences that he chose the letter A, any other name than the one that popped into my head.

"HEY!" A yell from Alex came from behind the man wall. Dawson and the other fellow turned but stayed in formation blocking me in. "You fucking assholes — move!"

"No can do," Dawson said firmly in cop voice. "Police business."

"Police business my ass. Dawson, you piece of shit, move aside." Alex's voice was pure fury.

Dawson fell back against the table as if pushed. The ketchup container fell over, rolling on its side in front of me. Dawson launched himself off the table at Alex.

Irritation rippled over Damien's face, and he turned toward the fight breaking out. I immediately glanced down, anything to not be looking into his evil eyes.

I heard shouting and the sound of glass breaking. Someone yelled in pain.

"Fire! FIRE!"

"Fuck you! Don't ever touch me!"

"Dawson, you're 86ed!"

I grabbed the ketchup bottle in front of me and pointed it at Damien. He looked back at me as I squeezed with all my might and ketchup went squirting across the table. Red hit him in the face and he yelled in surprise.

I flung myself out of the booth, ducking the reach of the nameless third man and ran for the door. I heard Alex call my name and the sound of footsteps at my heels. I barreled through the tavern door and almost sent myself sprawling on the gravel lot.

"Reva!" Alex came running up from behind, almost ramming into me and sending us both to the ground. "Let's get the hell out of here."

We ran to the car, colliding again at the driver's door.

"You've been drinking!" I snapped, struggling to move her aside.

"Doesn't fucking matter right now — I have the keys, get in!" Alex wrenched the door open and flung herself into the seat. I debated arguing with her but started around the back of the car to get in the passenger side. The sight of a big jacked-up truck stopped me. That was the truck, I was sure of it. Even more sure I would see dents on one side of it where it had hit a van recently. I took a step toward it.

"REVA!" Alex screamed out the window and honked the car horn. I stopped. The door of the tavern opened, and Damien came walking out, the ketchup still on his face like a smear of blood. I turned and ran to the car. Alex had already started it, putting it into drive before I had even shut the door.

She drove the pedal to the floor so hard, we spun out on the gravel sending it flying onto other cars like hail. Alex drove us out of the parking lot without even looking for oncoming traffic. As soon as we were on the road, I looked back. Damien had walked out to the side of the tavern to watch us. He waved and grinned at me before the night swallowed him from view.

We drove back to the farm at a terrifying speed, checking the rear-view mirror for headlights behind us. Both Alex and I knew we were vulnerable to being run off the road by the big truck but we didn't say a word. The road stayed dark behind us.

Alex pulled the car up to the house and turned it off. Both of us sat there in the quiet, only the sound of the engine ticking as it cooled.

"You okay?" Alex asked finally.

I paused, not sure how to respond. I wasn't okay, not even a little bit.

"I'm okay physically. What did you do back there?" I thought of the commotion that had given me the opportunity to escape Damien. It had felt like his eyes were going to pull me into another world.

"I lit Dawson's sleeve on fire. Hopefully he thinks it was with a lighter. Though if he's hanging out with a demon seeker, that probably doesn't matter."

"What about the other guy?"

"I punched him before Carl and a few others got involved." Alex looked down at her left hand. "I need ice or better yet, some of Sora's balm. Hurts a little."

She opened the car door and walked into the house. I looked down the drive into the dark. No one had followed us, but I didn't feel safe. I got out and followed her in.

Sora was up baking in the kitchen when we walked in. She looked at us and without a word, put the cookie dough she had been rolling out aside and started gathering up jars from another cabinet.

"Reva, go get Keena and Darcy. We need a house meeting," Alex said as she sat in front of the fire. Flame immediately trotted to her side and licked her hand with a small whimper. I stared in surprise. I had never seen that dog display the slightest bit of affection ever.

"Reva. Go." Alex glanced up at me, urgency in her voice. I went upstairs and got the others.

We gathered around the kitchen table with a plateful of shortbread and hot chocolate that Sora whipped up after tending to Alex's knuckles. The beer I had earlier sat sour in my stomach, so I just watched everyone else enjoy the goodies. Except Alex who sat with a glass of water. Maybe she felt as bad as I did.

Alex waited while everyone settled in. "We're at war."

We took turns filling in the other witches on our night and what little we had learned. Everyone took in the information, and we sat in silence.

"Here I thought we were just getting a midnight treat," Darcy said sarcastically as she sipped her hot chocolate and delicately broke off a bit of cookie to go with it.

"Is war the right word?" Keena asked.

"What else would you call it?" Alex looked at her intently.

"Under attack?" Sora suggested.

"That's true." Alex leaned back and waited a second. "We need to fight back. That's what makes this a war. One of us is in the hospital and two of us were openly attacked in a public place. This is serious."

"Is attack the right word for what happened tonight?" As the words came out of my mouth, the question seemed silly. That had been a bold move on the demon seeker's part to approach me in a bar, and who knows what would have happened if I'd been alone.

Alex looked at me with open disgust on her face. "Dawson and that other creep were physically keeping you in that seat. I had to use fire magic, in public. You may have been talking but it wouldn't have ended that way, and you know it. Or you wouldn't have resorted to spraying his face with ketchup."

Sora giggled. "You did that?"

I nodded. "It was the first thing that came to my mind."

"We'll have to add ketchup magic to your skills," Keena said with a smile and we all started to laugh. A ball of tension in my chest uncoiled with it. Even Alex grinned and joined us.

"Pretty smart of you. I bet that demon seeker didn't expect to be foiled with a condiment."

"I'm sorry I questioned if it was an attack. I'm not sure why I did that," I said as the laughter subsided.

"Self-denial is a type of defense." Keena looked at me, her big brown eyes filled with warmth and understanding. "You've been attacked twice in less than a week. That's a lot for the mind to digest."

"Let's not forget you've been pulled into the Other twice with the actual demon. And it tried to get you a third time there," Darcy added.

The weight of it all suddenly hit me, and I sagged in surprise. I had thought about all that was going on, but I hadn't laid it out there. Although no one mentioned it, there was also my own struggle following the Anthony debacle. I frowned.

Damien knew about Anthony, or at least that was what he implied.

"The demon seeker called himself Damien," I said, deciding to ignore the concerned looks from the other witches after they had watched the reality of all the attacks sink in. "I don't think it's his real name —"

Alex snorted. I looked at her and continued. "But he said something else that was weird. He suggested he knew of Anthony."

I explained the conversation to them best I could remember.

"Well, that's creepy as fuck," Sora said vehemently. We all turned to stare at her in astonishment. It sounded more like something Alex would say. "What?"

"Nothing," Keena and Darcy said at the same time.

"It is creepy as fuck," Alex said with a smile I swear held a hint of pride.

"Are you sure he meant Anthony?" Darcy asked.

"He was cryptic, never said the name, just like he never said he drove Sandra and me off the road. But I was meant to pick all that up. It felt very intentional." I had second-guessed myself since the conversation but deep down nothing budged. I knew exactly what he had meant every step of the way.

"Stop questioning her intuition," Alex said forcefully. "We spend too much time being told not to trust our guts."

"Sorry," Darcy mumbled.

Alex sighed. "No, don't apologize. I get it. We have to look at all the angles here but who else would he mean? Me? Let's stay focused. We need a game plan because the attacks aren't going to stop."

"We need to fight back," Keena said with a fierceness I hadn't heard from her before.

Alex nodded. "Now you're getting the spirit."

We spent a few more rounds trying to talk about how to fight back but it quickly devolved into defense strategies.

"No going alone anywhere. We can't take the chance. I don't like to think what would have happened if there hadn't been both of us there tonight," Alex said.

"I don't know that anything would have happened without me there. None of you have had any trouble unless I'm present," I said with a sprinkle of guilt.

"I don't think you should go see Sandra, Reva." Darcy spoke softly without looking at me.

"What?" I didn't understand. Or maybe I didn't want to.

"Darcy has a good point. I don't think you should leave the farm for a while," Alex agreed.

"But ..." I struggled with what to say. Bitterness at the unfairness spread in my chest. I felt trapped. And I knew they were right.

"I want to see Sandra," I said, though there was a bit of a lie in my words. I dreaded seeing her and the awful guilt I would feel. If I wasn't here, Sandra would be walking and laughing, not lying in a hospital bed. But if I wasn't here on the farm, I didn't want to imagine where I would be. That was a dark place for my thoughts.

"I know you do. We all do." Keena reached over and grabbed my hand. I fought the urge to pull it away and let her hold it. Her hands were warm and dry. The touch pulled me back from the darkness in my mind. "Let us take this part. We have to keep you safe."

"You have to keep yourselves safe," I said, chastened.

"We will," Darcy said with conviction. "You're not the only one with monsters who have chased you."

I looked at her and wondered about her stories. There was a lot untold there.

"How will staying on the farm keep me safe? Won't they come here eventually?" I asked the question that nagged at me. The feeling I had looking down the drive earlier into the dark wondering if I'd ever feel safe again.

"There are wards on our land." Sora clarified when I looked confused. "Protections. Dawson and other humans could maybe come here but any attack would result in the land fighting back."

"What about Damien?" I asked. He was the one that worried me the most.

Alex shook her head. "A demon seeker would have to be invited. Dawson and crew in a sense as well, but they could come. Otherwise, we'd never be able to get packages delivered."

"We barely can as it is. That's why we get most of our stuff delivered to the store," Darcy explained.

"You're relatively safe here." Alex said firmly.

I loved being on the farm, but I also had relished the recent excursions off the grounds. Though when I looked at them, all had ended poorly. But I wasn't sure I wanted to give up that freedom — to go to the ocean and walk on the beach, to meet new people, to have a drink in a bar like a normal person. I scrambled in my mind for a reason to not be tied to the farm.

"Wait," I said. "I might need to leave for a good reason."

They all waited with skeptical faces.

"The key. I need to figure out the key." The words came out fast and unorganized. Alex raised her eyebrow. The others looked confused except for Darcy.

"The key the Evernia gave you?" she asked. The concern had not left her face. At least she remembered the key where the others had forgotten.

"Yes. Wynona looked at it. Said it's an ordinary post office box key."

Now they were all quiet for a different reason as they digested the information.

"Just a post office box? Not a safety deposit box? Nothing magical?" Alex asked finally.

"Yes, that's what Wynona said. It has no magical threat."

"Not on it," Darcy said with a frown.

"Why would the Evernia give you that?" Sora pondered thoughtfully.

"Sounds like the Evernia brought you useless trash." Alex didn't mince her words.

"Alex! It's from the Evernia. A stag. Who came into the middle of the Other where a demon resides," Sora scolded.

"Animals sometimes bring you things you don't need but they think you do. Like cats bringing you a dead mouse," Alex said.

Keena shook her head and spoke up. "No. The key has a purpose, but the Evernia are on a different timetable than us. That key may be helpful for you in two minutes or twenty years."

"And how are you going to track it down to a location? It could be any post office." Alex crossed her arms in front of her.

"Don't forget post office boxes in store fronts and such," Sora added.

"Were you going to go test every box, starting in town?" Alex asked.

"I — uh." I was going to do just that. I would start in Coos Bay and go from there. The plan had formed in my head in the last minute since bringing up the key, but I didn't say that out loud.

"You think the post office clerks will be okay with some strange woman testing every box with a key that doesn't belong to her?" Alex went for the jugular of my already pathetic argument. I hadn't even thought of that. The wind left my hopeful sails.

"The key does belong to her," Sora said. "But Reva, Alex is right. You can't chase it down. When the time is meant to be, the purpose of the key will become clear."

And with that, the conversation wrapped up. I would stay on the farm out of harm's way, and we would start planning on defense and attacks the next morning. I felt restless as I tried to fall asleep, hours after my usual bedtime. Part of it was the usual exhaustion from staying up too late combined with the surge of adrenaline and fear from the bar. But another part was a nagging feeling I had that staying on the farm was the wrong move. That I wasn't supposed to hide. But no one felt that way except for me. And I wasn't sure I could trust myself.

Chapter 18

The morning started with a big elaborate breakfast Sora somehow put together. I worried she wasn't getting enough sleep, channeling all her worry and concern into cookies and now a large breakfast slab pie filled with eggs and potatoes and leeks and cheese.

"It came together pretty fast — I had pie dough already made," she said, reading the worry for her on my mind. It still didn't answer how there was a full-service coffee tray and fresh-squeezed orange juice as well as bacon and sausage links.

"War room food — I like it," Alex had said enthusiastically when she came in, shining with sweat from her morning workout. I wondered how long I'd be able to get away with skipping the workouts. I even missed them a little. Or at least missed how they had made me feel after, more relaxed and energetic.

Keena came down dragging, but smiled at the spread. "You've outdone yourself, Sora. Let me make dinner. And let's call this brunch so no making anything for lunch either."

Darcy came down last, clearly unhappy to be awake at 10 a.m. The food perked her up, though she sat in silence with an almost glare on her face as the rest of us started talking. I recognized it was general not-a-morning-person-ness and nothing personal toward anyone.

Alex, on the other hand, was chipper and irritating. She was eating with gusto and even dropped a sausage down for Flame who obediently trotted over and ate it with as much enthusiasm as her owner. Keena's dog, Bear, immediately barreled over and started begging with no shame, even whining.

"Go lay down!" Alex commanded.

Bear slunk off from Alex and over to Keena who tried to slyly slip a piece of bacon to him. Alex looked over and shook her head.

"Never going to break the habit of begging if you reward him, Keena."

"Who could say no to this face? Look at this face!" Keena cooed and ruffled Bear's ears to his great delight. Bacon and head scratches — I wished I had that sort of enthusiasm for the little joys in life.

As if on cue, Tuna leapt up next to me on the bench and chirped for a piece of bacon, her paws reaching out for the piece in my hand. I gently batted her off the bench, but she jumped back up with eyes that proclaimed she had no fucks to give but I did have bacon to give so cough it up.

"Cats," Alex mumbled. "I fail to understand the appeal."

I tossed a small piece of bacon over my shoulder and kept eating as Tuna sped after it. Kiz immediately jumped up to take Tuna's place. I sighed and tossed another piece of bacon. There were certainly moments I agreed with Alex.

"How's Magpie?" I asked. I didn't know who was taking care of Sandra's cat.

"He's fine. Lonely but prefers his own space. I wanted to bring him in here but he's not okay with other cats," Sora said. Her own cat, much to my irritation, was snoozing in front of the fire rather than embarrassing her with begging antics like my own. "You should go visit him though. He'd love a lap to sit on for a few hours."

I nodded, not sure I could sit in Sandra's trailer, see and smell all the traces of her but knowing I couldn't see her for a while.

After breakfast, Alex herded us into the library for our war prep, as she referred to it. Darcy rolled her eyes as Alex pulled out an old white board.

"Don't roll your eyes, Darcy. We need a game plan," Alex said peevishly.

"Yes, coach." Darcy's response was a complete deadpan. Keena started giggling. Then Sora and then me.

"Fine. I don't have to do this. You all can let Reva die at the hands of the demon." Alex turned red in the face.

"Relax, Alex. We're just trying to lighten things up. We all know it's serious. That's exactly why we're reacting this way," Keena said calmly.

"I'm not!" Alex shot back.

"Right. You're just dragging Reva out for a night of drinking at the local tavern," Sora cut in angrily.

The air went out of the room for a second while we all waited for Alex to react. I expected her to blow up, scream, or storm off. Instead, she collapsed into a chair, crying.

We all watched in horror, feeling guilty we had caused our strongest witch to start bawling. We all spoke at the same time, apologies pouring forth.

"I'm sorry, Alex."

"I didn't mean to -"

"Alex?"

"It's all my fault."

The last one was me, but no one heard it as it came softly out of my mouth. Alex ignored us until the words petered off. Keena got up and squatted down by Alex, trying to pull her hands off her face. Alex fought her a little but collapsed in as Keena pulled her in for a hug.

Slowly the pressure and the emotion eased out of all of us. Alex sniffed and let go of Keena who knew instinctively to get up and pull a chair up next to her. We all sat in the awkward silence waiting.

"I'll go get us tea." Sora stood as if to go but Darcy pulled her back down in her chair.

"Sit, Sora. I'm not mad at you. I'm not mad at anyone." Alex's voice was hoarse and raw. "I'm sorry. I don't react well to these types of situations. I want to fix it all. I try to control everything."

Keena nodded and put her hand on Alex's arm. "Thank you for being there for us all."

Alex shook her head. "We have to figure this out together. No single leader. That's always the way things get fucked up. I'll stop trying to take charge."

"We were looking for someone else to take charge so we didn't have to think and face it all," Darcy said. "I'm sorry for hiding so much these past days."

"I'm sorry for baking so much and being unavailable," Sora said.

"You never have to apologize for your baking, Sora." Keena laughed gently before turning serious. "But you do need to take care of yourself. You're not getting enough sleep."

Sora nodded in agreement. The circles under her eyes were darker in the light of the library.

"Oh jeez. Are we really doing this?" Alex laughed wearily. "Who's next?"

"I'm sorry for checking out mentally on all of you. I haven't been available either," Keena said.

"This has been triggering for me, that something is hunting us."

"Just me. It's only hunting me, and all of this is my fault," I cut in, my voices ragged around the edges. "I should leave, take this thing with me so you all can go back to your normal lives."

They looked at me. Alex shook her head, but it was Darcy who spoke.

"We're witches, Reva. We don't have normal lives. And we don't abandon a sister."

"This is bigger than you, Reva," Alex said. "You leaving won't release the town from the demon. It just wins here while it continues to hunt you down wherever you go."

I quieted down as I digested the overwhelming thoughts that I had a group of people who cared enough about me to go to war with a demon, and that my running wouldn't fix anything. Grateful I had friends like these, I was also disappointed that running wasn't a viable option. It was like breaking up with a mediocre boyfriend; there was no reason to be sad over such a short-lived bad idea, but it had been something concrete and familiar that was gone now.

We dried our eyes and started to talk more about actions we could take to move forward. After we got through how to support each other to get enough sleep and heal, which took the better part of a half hour, we moved on to discuss tactical defense and fighting strategies.

"We need to lay all our magic out on the table and see what we have," Alex said. She had brightened up considerably and was in front of the whiteboard, ready to write it all down. "From there, we can formulate a plan on what we need to focus and work on."

Keena and Sora had various healing magic they were familiar with or working on, Sora being focused on physical remedies and Keena on energy healing. Alex also had the hard magic healing, though we all agreed that was last resort given the energy it took out of everyone involved.

"I'm also not sure if I'll be as good without Sandra. She reflects a lot of the fire magic back into me, which makes it work." Alex sighed as she made a column of healing magic with initials by it.

"Oh, maybe I could do that," I piped up. I watched them look at each other as if trying to figure out who would tell the newbie enthusiasm won't replace another fire witch. I had never told them about what Wynona had told me about my other magical gift. I had mostly forgotten it myself with everything that had happened.

"Wynona told me I have another magical skill. I can share another witch's magic for short durations."

Everyone was quiet until Keena spoke. "You're a para-empath then?"

"Is that what it's called?" Alex said looking at me with bemusement. "I've heard of it but there aren't many out there."

Keena nodded. "It is rare, so it's odd you'd end up with two rare magical gifts, but nothing is unheard of. Usually it pairs up only with certain types of magic that the witch has an affinity with."

"That's what Wynona said, that elemental magics and empathetic and sympathetic magics align. So I likely could take on the fire magic."

"What about the other types?" Darcy asked.

"She let me try her space-shifting magic, but it felt weird, like the world had a glitch," I said, watching as Darcy looked puzzled.

"Wynona is a space-shifter?" Keena asked. She looked as confused as Sora and Darcy.

"That's right, I forgot about that," Alex said.

"You knew?" Darcy's voice was quiet, but a lot of emotions lurked in her tone.

"Not until Reva told me last night. And then we got distracted."

Darcy looked at me. "How long did you know that?"

"I ..." I paused. "Only found out when I met her. And saw her house."

"But Sandra knew." Darcy waited for me to nod before abruptly standing and stalking out of the room, her anger trailing her like a boat's wake.

We sat in silence as Alex quickly jotted down the different magics she knew about us. No one knew what to say or whether to go after Darcy.

"We were fighting about it in the car. When the wreck happened," I finally said. "I told Wynona that Darcy was a realmwalker and she wanted to meet her. Sandra was mad at me."

"Talking about another witch's magic is tricky etiquette," Sora said. "Some cultures are very protective. I was always taught not to reveal my own or others' until there was established trust."

Keena shook her head. "Sandra and Wynona have known each other a long time, so the etiquette protocol isn't the issue."

"They don't trust each other, though," I said and added, "Not anymore."

"That's not a good excuse on Sandra's part, though. She brought you to Wynona. Why not Darcy? Darcy has been needing a mentor. None of us share the same affinity magic." Keena's voice held frustration. I didn't know how to respond as I had wondered the same thing. Why would Sandra take me and not Darcy? Was one of us a favorite and if so, which one?

"That's exactly why Sandra didn't." Alex sighed. "Wynona has a gift for reading magical skills. I knew that much from Sandra. A single meeting with Wynona for Reva to get insight in a skill Wynona doesn't have affinity for, no risk. Meeting another witch with the same magic affinity and a mentorship situation? Much more involved."

We went around musing on why that could be, with Alex telling the story of the falling out between Sandra and Wynona. Eventually the conversation trailed off as we finally accepted the only person with answers was Sandra. Those answers would have to wait.

"Should I go talk to Darcy?" I asked.

"No. I'll do it." Keena stood. "Are we good here?"

"Not even a little bit. We have no plan, no next steps," Alex said bitterly.

"Maybe it's time for a break either way," Sora said. "Let's talk after dinner."

Alex reluctantly agreed and everyone drifted out of the room on different agendas. I stayed in the library a while longer. Coming up with a plan to defend against the demon and its followers, let alone attack, was overwhelming. I wasn't sure we could do it at all, though I didn't see what choice we had.

The day passed and we didn't meet up after dinner because no one cooked dinner. Sora was still sleeping hours after what she claimed would be a short nap and we all agreed to not wake her up as we weren't sure how much sleep she'd gotten in the past days. Alex offered to make everyone sandwiches.

"Two pieces of bread, piece of meat and slap it together."

We declined and everyone ended up eating leftovers or a more elaborate sandwich of their own making. No one saw Darcy again that day, though Keena reported the two of them had talked. She claimed Darcy felt better about it all, but I was skeptical.

After a sandwich of cheese topped with an apple chutney Sora had made in fall, I grabbed the family diary to see if Oona had more to say and made my way out to Sandra's trailer to sit with Magpie. My own cats would have been supremely irritated I was letting another feline sleep on my lap, but they were passed out in an unbearably cute cuddle together on my favorite wool sweater. I debated saving it from the inevitable cat hair layer they were putting on it but decided to let them sleep. We all needed a break.

I walked outside, appreciative of the fresh air after I'd been cooped up in the house for days. I promised myself I'd get out more and started making plans to drive to the beach when I remembered I was sequestered to the property. Oh well, I thought. I could go for a walk in the forest. I could make the most of it, I told myself though I was having trouble swallowing my attempts at a self-pep talk.

The sky was the dark fading blue of dusk, enough light to navigate to Sandra's trailer without turning on the flashlight I had grabbed from the backdoor. I walked up to the trailer and heard meowing on the other side of the door. I opened it to see Magpie sitting on the threshold. He turned his black and white face up to me and meowed again. I stepped up into the trailer to feed him what I suspected was a second dinner but figured he could use some comfort food, too, with his mistress gone.

The trailer smelled like Sandra, sandalwood with a hint of dryer sheets. Immediately inside the door was a small kitchen she used only for tea and cat food, the rest of it for storage. Off to the right of the door was her bed, the once convertible dinette table permanently a bed with a real mattress and curtains from old saris hanging in front to cover it. I felt a tug to both pull back the curtains and curl up in it to wait for her return and another urge to turn away and leave her some privacy. The latter feeling won and I prepped food for Magpie, who was determinedly trying to trip me by rubbing up against my legs and meowing.

Across from the tiny stove and cupboards was a minuscule shower she had made into a closet and next to that a small functional toilet behind folded doors. The back of the trailer was a tiny sitting area with a small bench seat. It had a curtain of wooden beads in front of it. The seat overflowed with velvet cushions and a cozy throw blanket. I turned on the small reading lamp she had rigged in the space. I sat and after rearranging and discarding a few pillows to the floor, I felt cozy. And lonely. I knew Sandra would be happy I was there, keeping Magpie company, but it felt wrong as well.

Magpie jumped onto my lap as I questioned whether I belonged there and began kneading my stomach with his paws. I tried to redirect him to sit on my lap, but he was relentless, always coming right back to my stomach and staring me in the eyes intensely until I petted him into a purring frenzy. Cats. After what felt like forever but was only a few minutes, he curled up on my lap and began to drool.

I resigned myself to the damp saliva patch on my jeans and opened the journal. I had read and reread what was there. I hadn't tried to reactivate any new pages, but I hoped more would appear. I had done some stormweaving on the day of the wreck, including slowing the rain. Surely that would count for something in Oona's book.

I flipped to the page I had last activated, the one that had said "Welcome, Stormweaver." The page remained the same with just those two words. I had since tried to activate more of that page with the same deep breathing and concentration technique as the first time, but it hadn't worked. Oona wanted something more from me.

I put my hand on the page again and tried anyway. As expected, nothing happened. I snapped the book shut in frustration. I put my head back and closed my eyes. What was I doing wrong? Or failing to do altogether? I decided to do what I had done in my college classes when stuck on a paper — I would go back over everything I had learned, from the beginning. I started with my first day at the farm and the vision with the demon, even though my brain resisted going there. I walked through everything from there — the feeling at the ocean with Keena, the first storm, the second pull into the Other, the Evernia stag, the visit to Wynona, meeting Mikhael, the fight with Sandra where I pulled the rain down, the aftermath of the wreck when Wynona coached me to stop the rain. I forced myself to think about it all.

I felt a damp sensation under my hand where it rested on the cover of the book.

"Damn it, Magpie. That better not be you drooling," I mumbled and opened my eyes. Magpie was wheezing softly on my lap, unmoved by my inner turmoil. I pulled my hand off the book and opened it up to the page.

Welcome, Stormweaver.
Let us begin.

I sat up in excitement, jostling Magpie. He meowed in protest and gave me a glare before settling back down on my lap. I mumbled my apology to him and waited. Nothing more appeared. My ancestor was holding out on me again, dropping one sentence at a time as a tease. I sighed and turned the page expecting more blankness.

The beginning of this journey for you is the end of mine. I do not keep a standard book of shadows. You will not find my stories or woes. You will not find answers to your questions. You will find only what you need when you are deemed receptive.

- Oona Quinn, Sorceress

I exclaimed out loud, nothing that resembled a word. Magpie dug into my thigh with his claws, warning me not to move again and interrupt his slumber. I ignored him. Finally there was more, a hint that offered far more than before. I reread the words, taking care to think through what was written. I couldn't expect the rest of the book to be the same as Oona's mother Helen's. The historian in me was disappointed not to be getting Oona's life story, or bits of it at least. Sandra had told me a few of the tales surrounding her — her power as a witch, her scandalous love life of courting married men but never marrying herself, her tragic death, ruled a suicide which meant she was buried outside of church grounds. I would have loved to hear her account of her life, but it also made sense she wasn't that type of person.

The word "sorceress" caught me. I hadn't heard any of the other witches refer to themselves as such. I would have to ask Sandra what she knew about it.

Sandra. I was sitting here in her empty home with no idea on when she'd be home. Or how changed she might be. I had so much to share with her and so many questions. Tears welled up in my eyes and I let them fall before sniffling up my emotions and refocusing.

I flipped to other pages of the book, but they remained blank. I flipped back and everything was the same as before. I tried what had worked before by trotting out in my head all that had happened. Nothing changed. I tried going back to the deep breaths and concentration. Same words, nothing new.

Frustrated, I slammed the book shut and set it aside. I needed to be receptive in the eyes of a powerful dead witch who called herself a sorceress. What would she mean by that?

I sat thinking and looked out the window at the night that had come on in full. Stars peered out between scattered clouds overhead. Being out of the city and away from lights and sounds was still odd for me but I was growing to love it. Sometimes I missed the hustling energy of so many people and all of their desires spilling out everywhere but when I was honest with myself, those moments of appreciation were rarer than the feeling of being overwhelmed. Being out on the farm suited me. For now, at least.

My legs were in desperate need of a stretch. I looked at my phone for the time and was surprised two hours had passed since I came into the trailer. I carefully picked up Magpie from my lap and placed him down where I had been sitting. He looked at me with disdain before rearranging himself in the warm space I left. I stood and stretched, relishing the feeling. I was still sore in places but my ring, my ancestral ring no less, was healing me at a faster speed, like it had worked on my wrist injury when I first put it on. I looked down at it on my finger. The stone caught the light, making it look like it had winked at me. I wondered if I could give it to Sandra, see if it could heal her. She needed it more than me.

I spun the ring on my finger and tried to ease it off. It spun but wouldn't come off further than third finger joint. I felt that familiar panic of having a ring stuck, the fear of circulation being cut off and all the other feelings that arise in that situation. As quickly as the panic came on, I calmed myself. I had been wearing the ring with no issue for over a month. It wasn't stuck. It was where it should be. I couldn't loan it out, even to family. It was mine. Or more likely, I belonged to the ring.

I casually picked up the journal, ready to head back to get ready for bed when I felt a quick urge to open it again.

The page that held the new words was blank. Already what I had discovered was gone. I flipped back a page to look at the welcome message. The words there were also gone but in their place was something entirely new:

The Classification of Demons

I sat back on the bench, narrowly missing Magpie's paws. I guess I was receptive enough to need the demon information from Oona and I had no idea what if anything I had done to encourage the new page. I wished for magic to be more black and white, like math or something with clear parameters, before dismissing the thought as the letters on the page faded like drying invisible ink. The words stopped fading. I waited but nothing more appeared on the page. I turned it and there was an entry:

Many have attempted to classify all the demons — scholars and Christians with particular fervor. I do not pretend to follow in their steps — I classify demons based on information fellow practitioners have helpfully provided, some at great cost, and my own unfortunate experiences, of which I would prefer to be a novice. The rarity of my own magic and temperament makes me a rather tempting target for many of them. Take caution in all my words and *avoid demons of any sort at all costs. Should one come hunting, Godspeed.*

I waited for more words which did not come forth. Sitting there alone I felt vulnerable, and Sandra's trailer went from cozy to exposed. I closed the journal and headed back to the house where I would have the others closer. I made sure Magpie was set on water and food before stepping out into the dark.

A cold wind blew across the grass as I left the trailer. The chill sliced through the insubstantial sweatshirt I had on. The clouds above me had scattered, leaving larger pieces of star-strung sky above. A light fog curled around the trees, reminding me of the demon's forest in the Other. I hoped it hadn't recharged enough to pull me through again. With that in mind, I hurried toward the house and the warmth of the fire.

Chapter 19

The next few days, we gathered in the mornings to try to work out a plan, both offense and defense. Defense strategies were more plentiful, mostly on bringing my magic knowledge and skills up to speed. I kept waiting for the demon classification information to show itself in the journal, but the page stayed unchanged.

"Maybe it's broken," I said one morning. "Like a computer virus or something."

"Magic artifacts can get corrupted, but I doubt that's the case here. I think your ancestor is just prickly and likes fucking with you," Alex responded absentmindedly as she made a schedule of practice for us — me, really — on the whiteboard.

"Yeah, it usually takes another magic to do that," Sora chimed in. "Using your computer metaphor, it'd be like a magic version of a magnet on a hard drive. Not just time."

"So the verdict is Oona likes fucking with me?" I sighed.

"Yep." Darcy nodded. "If I get to be as powerful as her, I would totally leave a legacy like that."

"My mother's book of shadows has quirks that match her personality traits," Sora said with a touch of sadness. "We used to make up silly languages only the two of us knew and that's how her book of shadows is, shorthand only I know now."

I observed a short moment of silence in consideration to Sora's departed mom. "That's sweet though, Sora," I said afterward. "You get to share something special with her even after she's gone. Oona just seems to be ornery."

"I think Sora's point is that a lot of the witch's personality ends up in the book. So you're getting to know your ancestor and who she was in a way most of us don't get to," Darcy said with a touch of jealousy in her voice. Any book of shadows talk always made Darcy moody. Now that I knew she had run away from her family, I understood her reaction better. Books of shadows passed down in families to the next generation. Was there one in her family of origin that she was locked out of?

"Getting to know her through her silence when she could be helping out is irritating, though," Alex said. "We haven't really gotten much of a plan besides get Reva better trained. That's not going to do much good when the demon comes back to pull you into the Other, or the demon seeker pulls another stunt."

"Maybe she wants you to do your own research on demons," Keena suggested before quickly adding, "Just reading! Not hunting."

"Demon hunting is really dangerous. I used to know some witches who did that," Alex agreed. "*Used to know* is the key phrase here."

"Did they die?" I asked, already knowing the answer.

"Oh yeah. Pretty horribly," Alex said. I was relieved not to hear the details.

"I think Keena is right. You can't just sit around waiting for the book to reveal more." Sora redirected the conversation away from terrible deaths by demons.

"I also think you should call Mikhael and invite him over," Keena said.

"Come on, don't you start again," I responded with exasperation. Alex had been riding me to call Mikhael and invite him over for days now. I had finally told them he was a lightning witch and described the weird electrical magic between us, which led to raised eyebrows and a lot of teasing. The others had dropped it but not Alex. Now Keena was bringing it back and sure enough Alex pounced.

"That is an excellent idea, Keena." She smiled and turned to me. "Reva, we were teasing you at first, but I actually think you owe Mikhael a phone call to say, 'Thanks for pulling my ass out of a wreck.' He's a good guy. You could, I don't know, make a friend, perhaps."

Heat rose to my cheeks. I knew I should call him to say thank you at the very least. And I was curious about the magic between us. But I got weirded out every time I thought of the phrase "magic between us.". That was a rom-com movie phrase, a promise of ridiculous implausible true love happening between two people who shouldn't like each other and who treat others around them like trash all in the name of love.

"A friend would be nice right now. It doesn't feel like we have very many outside of the farm," Sora said sadly. The demand for her baking had dropped suddenly, places like the market in Silverdale suddenly not wanting their usual orders. The demon seeker's message was spreading, and more people were turning against us. At least according to Alex, who still went into town to see Sandra and hunt down clues for how to fight the campaign against us.

What she reported back was depressing. The hospital staff were still mostly supportive and caring for Sandra. Sora had sent all her baking energy into daily treats for them until Alex reported the head nurse Linda, the same delightful woman I had met the night of the wreck, had asked for less.

"She was adamant to not stop bringing stuff, but asked for less because, and I quote, 'my ass is spreading like pancake batter on a warm counter'." Alex had laughed trying to gently let Sora down. Sora had taken it all right, but it had left her with spinning energy that none of us, including Sora, had figured out how to redirect. She spent her days studying cookbooks and old spell books on potions.

Alex's news from town the day before was that there was a rumor going around we were practicing Satanists. I had scoffed at first. Surely satanic panic was a ridiculous scare tactic from the 1980s that no one fell for.

"It actually makes a lot of sense a demon would use satanic panic as a weapon," I had finally conceded.

"Demons invented satanic panic," Alex had said with sureness. All of us agreed.

With that news and the push/encouragement from the others, I finally took Mikhael's card and dialed the number on it. He answered after a few rings.

"Gray's Electrical."

"Hi, Mikhael? This is Reva. We met ... I came over ..." I stumbled over my words before he interrupted and saved me.

"I remember you, Reva. Nice to hear from you. How are you doing?" His voice held concern, which brought unexpected tears to my eyes before I realized he was referring to recovering from the wreck. Of course he didn't know all we were going through.

"I'm better. Recovering well. Thanks." The awkwardness continued. The line was quiet as I struggled with what to say next.

"How's Sandra?" he asked to fill in the void.

"She's ..." I faltered. "Actually, all I know is what Alex tells me. I haven't been to see her."

"Oh." He sounded confused for a second. "I guess you'd want to avoid being on the road after what happened. And with the other shit you're dealing with."

"It's hard." I hated myself. "It's hard" wasn't stellar conversation. I sounded like I was twelve. "I mean, I want to see her but yeah. Every time I leave the farm, trouble follows."

"Yeah, I heard about the bar fight." He sounded amused. "That fool Dawson was talking it up. Would love to hear your side."

"Officer Dickface?" I wasn't sure why I said that. Again, I was twelve.

He laughed out loud. "That's an apt nickname."

"Why don't you ... I mean ... would you like to come over? To the house? As a thank you. I mean, you've done so much." I couldn't stop talking.

"Sure. That sounds nice. I haven't been to the farm before," he interrupted my blathering. "Not too surprising since Sandra isn't my biggest fan."

He sounded chagrined. I had thought he wasn't Sandra's biggest fan, not the other way around. Fortunately, I fought the impulse to say as much. It wasn't that odd, really. Sometimes people get off on the wrong foot and it is never clear who didn't like who first, but the assumptions keep them from working it out.

"Okay, great!" I said stupidly. "I mean about coming for a visit. Not the Sandra part."

Clearly I wasn't out of the woods yet on being awkward.

"I know it's short notice but would today work? I have a big job in Bandon starting tomorrow so ..." He trailed off.

"Yes!" I said with far too much enthusiasm before trying to qualify it. "That would work for me. Sora probably will probably have a batch of cookies or something."

"I haven't met Sora, but I have had the pleasure of experiencing her baking." Mikhael sounded excited at the prospect of cookies. Or maybe of meeting Sora. I squashed down a twinge of silly jealousy. I was trying to make a friend. Nothing more.

We wrapped up the call with an agreed upon time of 4 p.m., three hours away. I let the other witches know. Alex grinned at me and said to have fun since she'd be at the hospital or skulking around Coos Bay (her words). I felt a sudden worry for her I didn't usually feel. I hadn't stopped to think about how often Alex was out in a community that actively hated us.

"Should you be going into town so often?" I asked.

Alex looked at me for a half beat. "We can't let the bastard keep us down. One of us needs to go out, see Sandra and see what's going on. The whole town hasn't turned on us. I have friends here."

I nodded and let it go.

Sora was beside herself with excitement at the prospect of a guest. She started planning a whole 4 p.m. tea meal before turning to me with a look of concern.

"Is that okay? If this is a date ..." She sounded so worried.

"It's not a date," I cut her off. How could I steal the joy of hospitality from Sora? "He's our guest and that sounds lovely."

She beamed and left to make a dried cherry and apricot galette with frangipane, none of which besides the fruit was recognizable to me. I let Keena know next. She smiled at me.

"Sounds lovely. I hope you have a good time."

"You're welcome to join us. Sora's putting on a full English tea spread. Or maybe French. What's a galette?" I asked. She laughed and said she'd come down in that case.

I knocked on Darcy's door and waited. I knocked again. Nevermore squawked inside and I knocked a third time. Finally she pulled open the door and all but glared at me.

"What?" The word was clipped.

It occurred to me I hadn't talked with Darcy since she had learned about Wynona being a space-shifter and Sandra not telling her. I stood there awkwardly like an asshole before deciding to push through.

"Mikhael Gray is coming over this afternoon. Wynona's nephew," I added.

She raised an eyebrow at me but didn't close the door. I felt like a heel for not realizing she was mad at me.

"Sora's putting together a spread. I wanted to invite you to come down. Keena will be there, too." I gave her a tentative smile.

Her face remained blank. "I'll think about it."

Then she closed the door on me. Not rudely or roughly but pointedly. I sighed. I should have come up sooner to talk to her one on one, but I struggled to connect with Darcy. I wasn't sure why. I promised myself I'd try to work it out. At least I had invited her even if she didn't show up. I hoped she did though. As much as part of me wanted to be alone with Mikhael, something I didn't like to admit, another was scared to be. Friend, I reminded myself. I was looking for friends.

A little before 4, I stood on the front porch waiting. Mikhael's pickup came bouncing up the drive a few minutes later. In the daylight, I could see Gray's Electric painted on the side in blue lettering. The Cloud Pack was elsewhere as no furry dog heads were bouncing in the back. He got out and looked up at the house for a second before waving and walking up the steps to greet me.

I reached out my hand again to shake before pulling it back, remembering his reluctance on touch greetings.

"Hi," I said.

"Hi, Reva. Nice to see you in better circumstances," he replied, tucking his hands in his pockets. "Nice spot here. Sandra picked a good piece of land. This old house is impressive, too."

I invited him in and gave him a quick tour of the downstairs. He glanced at the whiteboard in the library, but I didn't bother to explain it despite the fact it had the words "AT WAR" emblazoned on the top in red marker. The altar room was locked, which it never had been before. He smiled and said he didn't need to see everything.

The green room impressed him the most. We walked around while he pointed out all the plants he recognized, which I hadn't bothered to learn.

"I'm not good with plants, though." He shrugged after pointing out a semi-tropical shrub that had healing properties.

"For someone not good with plants you sure know a lot about them. I can only tell you these are green." I laughed. His face stayed serious.

"The electrical touch makes it hard to work with them. I do, but it takes a lot of channeling to block the current, so I can't take as much on as I would like to." His voice was resigned. I hadn't thought about what it would be like to have that current running through like he did.

"So it's always present?"

He nodded. "I have safety gloves for work that protect from electrical currents, which helps but going through life with a barrier to touch like that is —" He cut off, falling silent.

"That sounds really tough." I reached out and put my hand on his arm.

He jumped away quickly as I dropped my hand just as fast. He mumbled an apology.

"No, all my fault. I'm sorry. You were literally just telling me about it." The heat rose to my cheeks.

"I've hurt people before who touched me without my being prepared," he said softly.

"Do you ..." I paused, not sure if I should go on. "Have you noticed we have a magical connection? I don't think I react the same way as others."

Mikhael nodded slowly. "You haven't complained about electric shock like others have. I assume you have a higher tolerance, being a stormweaver."

"I don't think it's tolerance. I don't get an electric sensation. It's —" I blushed again. "Warm. An unusual warmth."

He stared at me, and I felt a wave of desire to touch him more. Friends, just friends I told myself. His amber-colored eyes locked with mine. The same electric feel I had experienced when I first met him came thrumming back between us.

"Hello?" Keena's voice called out behind us. I felt a mix of relief and disappointment as Mikhael turned away from me toward the sound.

"Hi, Keena — we're over here," I called back.

Keen walked around the corner to us, smiling as she greeted Mikhael and introduced herself. She didn't offer to shake hands, which at first I was self-congratulatory about until I remembered Keena's magic was also touch based. She could learn dark secrets of others by simply laying her hands on them. Something the two of them had in common. I quickly stomped down a twinge of jealousy .

"Sora has our tea ready," Keena said, motioning for us to follow. Mikhael looked around the green room one more time as if reluctant to leave. He followed Keena into the kitchen with me trailing behind them.

Sora was waiting in the kitchen, fizzing with excitement like a freshly poured soda. The table was laden with far more than an afternoon snack: two pots of tea (jasmine and assam with rose petals), the galette, which was a rustic tart filled with almond paste and fruit, two kinds of cookies which Sora modestly apologized for having been made yesterday as if any of us cared, open faced smoked salmon sandwiches, and cups of curry-spiced butternut squash soup.

"Wow. Do you roll out the royal treatment for all your guests?" Mikhael asked after introductions. He was looking at the table in amazement. It was over the top even for Sora, more so since she'd been on a hiatus for the past few days. Keena and I were also impressed.

"We don't actually have any guests here," Keena said as Sora gestured for us to take seats so she could pour us a cup of our preferred tea.

"Clearly a damn shame." Mikhael didn't look like he knew where to start.

"It is," Keena agreed.

I nodded as well. It was nice to have someone else in the house and to see Sora light up. Keena seemed perkier, too. Mikhael finally tentatively took a salmon sandwich and a cookie onto his plate and we all followed suit, helping ourselves, which led him to another cookie and a cup of soup.

Sora put a piece of galette on his plate, taking care to not get in the way of his hands.

"We're not really on the top of the people-to-party-with list locally," I said. "Who wants to hang out with Satanists?"

Mikhael shook his head. "I've been hearing rumors. Ridiculous. People are always scared of differences. Magic, skin, language, culture."

I wondered how his childhood was, if he felt like an outsider in his community. Keena and Sora nodded, and I wondered about them as well. Being a magical child was probably rough all around.

"Don't forget gender and sexuality." Darcy's voice came from behind us, startling all four of us. Mikhael tried awkwardly to stand but being seated by me made it hard for him to move the bench back. He half stood, waved, and sat back down as Darcy strolled over and took a seat next to Sora.

"You must be Darcy," Mikhael said politely.

"The one and only. My reputation precedes me again," Darcy said with a grand smile. Only those of us who knew her detected the bitterness behind it all. Keena's brow furrowed and a little of the fizz went out of Sora as she tried to pull the worry from her face in front of our guest.

Mikhael smiled at Darcy. "Nice to meet you."

Darcy looked at him coldly. The easy conversation we'd had rolling stalled as Darcy let Sora pour her a cup of tea and took a single cookie.

"Reva says you're a realmwalker," Mikhael broke the silence.

Darcy glowered for a second. "What else has Reva told you about me?"

I had a moment of understanding flash about why Darcy was mad. One of the reasons anyway. She thought I had outed her as trans. I bit back my irritation. I had hoped she would trust me by now.

"Just that," Mikhael responded smoothly. "I know you came here a few years ago, hurt or something, but not much more than that."

"I don't have a nickname or anything? Surely you've heard some from the town." Darcy pounced again with her words, leaning forward defiantly.

He shook his head. "I only returned to town in the last two years. I was up in Washington for a while. I've only heard Wynona refer to you as the runaway witch."

Darcy sat back. "Runaway witch. That's not the worst out there."

"We would have reached out sooner had we known you were a realmwalker. We haven't had that skill in our tribe for two generations. The Ghost World is a special place. To be able to go there of your own accord instead of through ritual, that must be something else."

"Ghost World?" I asked.

"We call it the Other," Darcy said to Mikhael.

The conversation flowed freely between everyone but mostly Mikhael and Darcy, who shared notes about the Other. Mikhael said he went there once a year when he had the opportunity.

"How do you get there if you don't have a realmwalker to guide you?" I asked, my mind on being pulled into the Other by a demon. I couldn't imagine going into the Other willingly without Darcy after those first visits to the fog forest.

"There are substances and rituals that put one in the right frame of mind to enter it," Darcy said.

Mikhael nodded. "It's better when you have a guide like a realmwalker, though. Safer."

"I've heard cryptids can pull you there as well," Darcy said. I thought of the Evernia stag. And my childhood visions.

Mikhael nodded. "We have traditions with spirit guides. Usually the cryptid guide only gets you partially there. The rest is up to you, which is why it can go awry so easily without a realmwalker."

Was the stag pulling me into the Other? And what about my childhood visions, the blue chipmunk? Maybe I was always being pulled to the edge of the Other. Not a comforting thought for me.

The conversation faded out in a natural way as first Darcy and then Keena excused themselves. Mikhael said he had a bit of a drive to get home so he better get going. Much to his delight, Sora packed up a whole stack of leftovers for him to take. We walked out to his car together.

"I meant to say thank you earlier," I said as we stood in the fading light by his truck. "Thank you for being there for Sandra and me. I'm not sure how long we were on the side of the road but if you hadn't found us ..."

"I have a confession to make on that," Mikhael said, looking down at his feet. "Wynona asked me to follow you home. I think she felt something amiss. I refused at first. I have been thinking what would have happened if I hadn't argued with her and just done what she asked."

I stared at him and went through the scenarios in my mind before shaking my head. "It happened fast, and they were determined. You could have ended up being run off the road, too. And then who would have called 911?"

He looked up from the ground and our eyes met. "You're a good person, Reva."

I shook my head. "No, just realistic. You were there when we needed you. I don't even know what happened after we went off the road. I came to next to the van."

"The medics think you crawled out. If you had been thrown from it, you probably would have suffered more injuries. You don't remember?"

"No. But I haven't really tried."

He nodded in understanding. I wanted to hug him but figured that would be too forward and make him uncomfortable.

"Can I call you again?" I asked instead. "I really enjoyed hanging out. All of us did."

He smiled wide. "I'd like that."

The rest of the evening was quiet, but the house had an upbeat energy coursing through it. We all convinced Sora we could eat the leftovers from the visit for dinner. There was only a little teasing from the other witches over warmed-up soup and sandwiches.

"Mikhael is nice," Sora said.

"He sure seems to like you, Reva." Darcy smirked at me. I had been relieved she joined us. Maybe I could start to repair our rift over a slice of galette.

"Sparks fly between you two," Keena chimed in with a laugh. "Maybe literally!"

"Stop. We're friends." My cheeks warmed.

"Sure. For now." Sora jumped into the mix.

We were laughing together when Keena's cell phone rang. She glanced at it, ready to reject the call but frowned instead and answered.

"Hello?" Her face turned serious as she listened. "Alex, slow down. Where are you?"

I couldn't make out the words on the other end, but a franticness came through in the sounds. Keena snapped her fingers at us and made a gesture that she needed something to write with and on. Sora flew across the room and dug out a notepad and pen she used for ingredient lists and notes. Keena wrote information down.

"Okay. Hang tight, Alex. We'll be there as soon as we can." She hung up the phone and turned to us. "Alex is trapped in an abandoned warehouse with an angry mob outside."

"What?!"

"We need to go get her out. She thinks we can use an access road and sneak up without them seeing. If we create enough of a distraction."

"Why don't we call the police?" I asked. It seemed like a trap.

Keena looked at me sharply. "You think the police are going to help? That with people like Dawson on the force that we can trust she won't end up being carted off to a dark cell? We don't know how many of the police are on our side. If any."

I opened my mouth for a second and then closed it. I had to agree with Keena. Every day Alex told us about people she had been friendly with who were now cold. And Dawson, for all his incompetence and the scorn I had seen thrown his way, still had a badge. If he was there, he could be the one responding to the call.

"All of us in the Civic?" Darcy asked.

Our car options had dwindled with the van being totaled. Sora was working through the insurance process, but it was slow. And Alex had taken her truck to town.

"What choice do we have? I'm not sure what we're going to do as a distraction, but likely Alex has an idea. Her fire magic makes the most sense. Darcy, can you navigate from the front? Sora, you're shorter so if you're okay in the backseat —"

"What about me?" I asked.

They all turned to me and paused before Keena said gently, "Reva, you need to stay here."

"But I could provide the distraction. With a storm. It worked before."

Keena shook her head. "It would be very effective, but we can't put you in that much risk. Alex was clear on the phone. You stay here."

"But —" Impotent anger stirred in my core, the sort where I knew it was useless but I didn't want to give it up. "I could help."

"You're protected on this land. You aren't out there," Sora said softly.

"But neither are any of you!" My voice rose. Keena had stood and walked out into the hall. We all followed. They started putting on coats and getting flashlights.

"You have said more than once, Reva. You are the one they are hunting," Darcy said, an edge to her voice.

"But look at what lengths they're going through to get to me. They hurt Sandra. They've cornered Alex. I don't want anything to happen to you all." Desperation crept into my voice. I didn't want to face a mob, but I also didn't want to be left alone, wondering if my friends were going to come home.

"We have to go now. We can't argue about this. Alex has a plan." Keena grabbed the car keys and motioned for everyone to get out. Everyone but me.

"It's a trap!" I said. Keena was already out the door with Darcy behind her. I followed them out onto the porch. Sora paused and looked at me. Conflict rippled across her face.

"Do you want me to wait with you?" She said. I could hear in her voice that she had misgivings about the plan.

"Yes! What if something happens to you all? If there's two of us —" I stopped. I had no plan. Would Sora staying do anything other than make me feel better?

Keena stomped back up the porch steps. "We need Sora. What if one of us gets hurt? You have to —"

I turned away from them and ran into the house, slamming the front door behind me. I listened to them talking to each other in low voices I couldn't understand, the sound of car doors slamming shut. A car engine started, tires crunching on gravel and then they were gone. I was alone.

Chapter 20

I went into the warm green room for a while, sitting at the same table where Keena and I had first met. Kiz and Tuna meowed on the other side of the door, but I ignored them as I sat with all my complex and awful feelings: fear for the witches, anger at being left behind, guilt that I was the reason they were going through it all, frustration that I couldn't stop what was happening.

I stared out the window at the darkness outside. I could see Sandra and Alex's trailers, empty and unlit. As I was looking out, fog crept in low in the fields beyond. An involuntary shudder ran through me. It was just fog, I told myself. It was not moving faster than normal fog. Was it?

The warm humidity in the room started to feel stifling. The fog was getting thicker outside. I heard Flame bark. It sounded like a warning. I pulled myself up and left the room.

Tuna and Kiz swarmed around the door. I went to block them with my foot from trying to get into the green room, but they weren't interested. They meowed and trotted down the hall to the library. Midori was standing by the kitchen door watching them, alert. Goosebumps rippled down my arms. Something was wrong.

I followed the cats into the library, afraid of what I might find. On the main table sat the Quinn book of shadows. I thought I had left it upstairs. Even more alarming, it was open. The book never stayed open. I had once or twice left it open and walked away to get a cup of coffee or water only to find it closed and locked upon my return five minutes later. I walked up to the table and looked at it.

The book was open to the "Classification of Demons." I sighed and went to shut it, when I noticed additional words had appeared.

Lesser demons can be vanquished through the usual rituals: sage and salt, protection wards and distraction spell work. Demons of the more voracious appetites can be banished with a circle of twelve seasoned sorceresses. Those with great powers or magical alignment can do so with fewer but at greater risk.

It would be nice, I thought, if some of those rituals and spells appeared in the book. I kept reading.

There is one type of demon that is to be avoided at any cost. Such demons are opportunistic predators looking for ultimate power: andras demons. Named for a Christian demon ranked in hell, andras demons hunt two types of prey: those who hold power to corrupt and consume, and those with a weakness of spirit. As with humans, no one demon follows the same rules, but the general traits of andras demons: Sow discord, build unruly armies compelled to hurt and kill, often turning brothers on fathers, mothers on daughters, siphoning off magic powers from witches through disturbances of spirit.

Andras demons seek one or two prey at a time and use their victims to sow the discord they feed on. Those strong of will and virtue are not swayed easily. If weakness is in the heart, the violence in one's soul, that is when the andras demon takes hold like an illness. Only by invitation can they enter but beware the ease at which an invitation can be given. For each entry to your soul, the demon will take root until there is nothing left of you.

It stopped there. I flipped the pages, but nothing more appeared. Fury at my tight-lipped ancestor rose in me for a moment. Clearly the message was that our enemy was this type of demon. It checked all the boxes. What good was this information right now? How did it help me? Or Alex? Or anyone else?

A knock on the door startled me. Tuna gave a low growl, the type she usually reserved for other animals creeping into her territory. A warning. I looked down at Kiz. His tail was bushy like a bottlebrush and his ears were back.

Another knock came. I hadn't heard any car pull up. Had I? I went to the window to pull back the green velvet drapes. Right as I reached my hand to the curtains, a sharp pain struck my ankle.

"Ow!" I glanced down in surprise. Tuna had bit me. She looked up at me with ears back and yowled. The knock came again, this time reverberating through the house. I walked toward the hall and peered out.

There was a dark person shape on the other side of the stained glass in the door, but I couldn't make out any features. The person knocked again.

I started toward the door, a growing fear deep in my core spreading like spilled paint on tile. Kiz shot out in front, tangling with my legs and tripping me. I caught myself on the door jamb and stayed upright, barely. A deep voice came from the other side of the door. A voice I knew all too well.

"Let me in, Reva."

I backed up against the door jamb and stared at the door. It couldn't be. I was imagining things, my paranoia and concern breaking my fragile mind.

"Reva. I missed you." Anthony's voice was muffled but unmistakable.

"No." My voice came out in a whisper.

"You knew I was going to come back for you. You're my favorite."

My legs unlocked and I ran into the library to the window. It couldn't be Anthony. Someone was playing a trick on me. I tore open the curtains and looked out.

When the light poured through the window onto the porch, the man walked over. Tall, dark curly hair, handsome face with a James Dean pout. Anthony.

He came up to the window and looked at me, smiling. He was wearing faded jeans and his beat-up leather aviator jacket, the one I had bought him for his birthday. The fog swirled heavy behind him.

"Did you miss me?" His voice was hard to hear through the window. He smiled at me, little lines around his eyes crinkling. Just like I remembered, the lines that had made him seem vulnerable. The ones I had loved.

Tuna jumped up on the table behind me and began to hiss and spit. Kiz followed suit. They had never liked him but then I heard a third yowl in the mix and looked back. Midori had jumped up with my cats, arching her back. Her big green eyes were taken over by the black of her pupils. All the cats were staring at the window.

I stopped myself from turning back around to look at Anthony. Something was wrong, more wrong than my deadbeat ex-boyfriend I thought I had drowned in a storm showing up on my doorstep. The jacket. It was my favorite of his, but it wasn't his favorite. He had left it at my apartment, and it had ended up in a garbage bag covered in condiments.

The tapping of knuckles on glass came from behind me. I started to turn around but stopped again. That wasn't Anthony. The tapping sound continued.

"You're not Anthony," I said softly.

"But I am. I've always been Anthony." The voice came through clearly this time. It no longer sounded like Anthony, not entirely. "Let me in, Reva."

I ran from the room without looking back. I stopped in the hall, so afraid. The three cats followed me and huddled around my ankles, tails still puffed up. The knocking started again. I looked at the door. The dark figure was there again. Tendrils of fog seeped under the door.

"Let me in." The voice echoed through the house, no longer pretending to be human. I pressed my hands over my ears, a futile desperate gesture. Why was the demon on the porch? The wards, the promised protection of the land wasn't working. Tears rolled down my cheeks.

Knocking started on the window in the library, at the door, all over the outside of the house. It sounded like an angry hoard of people banging on the house.

"Go away!" I screamed. My legs gave out and I collapsed in the middle of the hallway. Tuna and Kiz crawled into my lap, Midori curled up around my back. They purred, a low steady rhythm of cat humming. The banging continued all around until the house was shaking like an earthquake had struck. I screamed again but couldn't form any words. The cats dug their claws into my legs.

The house continued to shake. I heard a ferocious growling from the front porch. The shaking stopped as more growls started. A long howl like a coyote echoed through the night outside. More howls joined in, closer. The cats jumped off my lap and stood in a line in front of me, backs arched like Halloween cats. Everything went quiet and still except for low growls from Tuna.

A tremendous frenzy of growling and barking erupted from the porch. A high-pitched shriek went up, an unearthly noise like I had never heard before.

"Reva, help me." Anthony's voice came through, ragged and hoarse. He sounded like he was at death's door. He sounded exactly how I had imagined in my worst guilt-ridden nightmares.

I pulled myself up, stepped over the cats and walked toward the door. The cats ran at my legs, coming from behind, from the sides. I tripped, cursing them, and fearing I'd hurt them. I stopped and dove into the library. The cats followed hot on my heels but stopped trying to trip me. I went to the window and looked out.

A blur of dogs was on the porch. Or maybe coyotes. I couldn't tell. They were focused on attacking a curled-up figure in front of the door. I recognized his hair, the dark curls matted now with blood. The jacket was gone, and his muscled arms were covered in bites with blood oozing out. I screamed again. No matter how awful a person Anthony had been to me, could I stand here and watch him die in such a terrible way? I couldn't. I couldn't take the chance and have him die.

The door slammed behind me. Midori sat in front of the closed door, her big green eyes looking at me defiantly. Tuna and Kiz trotted over and sat next to her giving me the same look. I guessed Midori could close doors as well as open them.

I looked back to the porch and the scene had changed. Anthony was nowhere to be seen. Fog swirled where he had been curled up. Two dogs were barking in a frenzy. Flame and Bear. The fog dissipated, blew off the porch and up out of view.

I sagged against the window and closed my eyes. How in a few seconds had I forgotten it hadn't been Anthony on the porch? I had felt so sure for those few seconds seeing him, the demon forgotten. My mind felt frayed around the edges, like a torn rag. I looked out at the porch again. Flame and Bear were gone but there were still smudges of blood. Demons didn't have blood. Did they? Or was it the demon seeker? But everything I had read on demon seekers in the short span of time since finding out about them was that they were physically human. A demon seeker couldn't shift into fog. Could they?

I heard barking in the distance, coming from the back door. The cats began to meow urgently in a chorus. I pulled myself off the window frame where I had been leaning and walked to the kitchen, the cats trailing behind me. Flame was barking at the back door, the dog I rarely heard bark. Bear whined. I started toward the door to let them in and froze. What if this was another trap? Was it safe to open the door?

Midori ran to the door and jumped up, hooking her paws on the doorknob. She hung for a second trying to turn it and jumped up again to repeat the process. I stared in fascination until a sharp nip from Tuna on my ankle shook me out of it.

"Okay, okay!" I said as went to the door. Midori ran off as I tentatively pulled it open a crack. A heavy weight flung itself from the outside and the door opened. Flame came barreling through. Bear limped in after, favoring his back right leg. They both went and lay down in front of the fire, tongues lolled out and panting fast.

I bent down and took a look at Bear's back leg. A large gash of about four inches ran diagonally across the upper part of the leg. Dark blood was matted with his fur but looked to be clotting. I couldn't tell how deep it was. He probably needed stitches.

"Oh, Bear. You good boy, you." Tears welled up in my eyes. Bear and Flame had saved me. Tuna gave a pointed murmur behind me. "Right, Tuna. You all saved me. Thank you."

I wished for the witches to return right now but when I looked at the clock, only about ninety minutes had passed. They couldn't have driven out and back in that short amount of time, let alone rescued Alex. I sat for a moment and sighed. I couldn't leave Bear to suffer.

I turned at a noise of metal hitting the floor. Midori was up on a high shelf, delicately batting at tins of herbs Sora kept there. Now I understood why she kept most of her herbs in the tins. Jars of glass or ceramic wouldn't hold up to Midori's meddling.

I walked over and picked up the tin. There on a large label in Sora's neat writing was: Wound Salve. In small letters below were clear instructions. I glanced up at Midori in time to catch the next tin as it came sailing over the edge of the shelf. I caught it in my other hand, almost dropping it. Midori meowed from her perch.

"Okay, point taken," I said, setting the tins on the counter. I got to work to prepare the salve and bandage up my furry savior.

Chapter 21

The adrenaline wore off after I managed to cobble together a makeshift salve and bandage for Bear, who vacillated between whining in pain and trying to lick my face as I worked on him. Midori continued to be irritatingly useful by batting wrong ingredients out of my hand and meowing loudly when the water was boiling. It was like Sora in cat form, but Sora was nicer. Midori had her own personality.

After I managed to fix up Bear, I fed him and Flame a plate of raw hamburger and the cats each got canned tuna. Fancy canned tuna in water in separate dishes spaced out in opposite corners of the room so no one got greedy. Not that it stopped Tuna from coming over and trying to eat out of Kiz's dish. She was most displeased when I picked her up and made her sit on my lap in front of the fire. Her purring under my petting hand had a distinct pissed-off quality.

The tiredness hit me while I was sitting there. It felt familiar, like the beginning of the exhaustion from the demon encounters in the Other. I put Tuna down and stumbled to the fridge, finding a jar of Sora's hot chocolate. I drank straight from it, the cold chocolate milk pouring down my throat. It didn't have the same amount of caffeine as Darcy's iced coffees but hopefully it would help. I couldn't imagine going upstairs, either physically climbing the steps or being alone up there with my lingering fear. What would happen if the demon came back? I preferred to stay in front of the fire with all the animals who had helped me, but I couldn't stay upright and awake. I managed to make it to the library and collapsed on the worn leather couch. Just a few minutes of rest, I promised myself. That was all I needed.

I awoke to a stiff neck and someone shaking me. My head hurt and my mouth felt like it had been stuffed with cotton balls. I was getting really tired of waking up with magic hangovers.

"Reva." Keena was standing over me, gently shaking me by the shoulders. She had dirt streaked on her face and her hair was wet, the usual loose waves of curls hanging in her face. "Are you okay? We called out your name after we got home but you didn't answer. Is that blood on your shirt? And — chocolate?"

She pointed at my mouth, which I self-consciously wiped with the back of my hand. A large smear of the chocolate came off. I looked down at my sweatshirt, spotted with dried blood from when I had cleaned Bear's wound, a process I would rather never repeat. I didn't have the stomach for blood.

"Where's everyone? Is Alex okay?" I asked, my voice strained and croaky. Like I had spent the evening yelling at a concert. Which aside from the concert part, I supposed I had.

"We got her out. It was —" Keena looked exhausted. I sat up and made space for her to sit next to me on the couch. She sat gingerly with a grateful sigh. "It was rough but we're here."

"You want me to get you something? Some hot chocolate or tea?" I had never seen Keena so tired. Not tired. Drained. She looked drained, like I imagined someone would look after a run-in with a vampire.

"No. Sora has taken over the kitchen to work on healing Alex. Darcy is playing the role of her helper." She smiled wanly, then frowned. "I should be in there helping. But I can't."

I patted her on the knee but stopped when she winced. "Sorry. Don't be hard on yourself, you can't help if you don't have the capacity. You look like shit, Keena."

She laughed, a short bark. "I did a piece of magic that is incredibly dangerous. But it worked. So it was worth it."

"Don't you need something to start replenishing your energy? Or healing magic?" I felt bone tired but better than Keena looked. I was thankful I had drunk that cold chocolate from the fridge but Keena probably needed it more than I did.

She shook her head. "Alex is in worse shape. She has priority. Then me."

"Maybe I can help? I bumbled through some healing work this evening." I spoke with a touch of pride that evaporated on my lips when I remembered it was Keena's own dog I had been helping. And she didn't look ready for that news.

She looked at me sharply. "What? Why were you doing healing work? What happened?"

I froze for a second and considered lying to her. "There was a visit from the demon. I —"

"What?!" She sat up alarmingly fast and grimaced in pain. "Here? The demon came here?"

I told her an abbreviated version of what happened, leaving off that it had been Anthony at the door. I didn't want to tell her but finally got to the end.

"Flame and Bear attacked it. They saved me. But Bear got a hurt. A cut on his leg," I added hastily. "I think he'll be okay. It didn't look deep."

Keena pushed herself up, teetering on her feet before sitting down just as suddenly. "Help me up. We need to get to the kitchen."

I flung Keena's arm around my shoulders and helped her up. My own legs felt like gelatin but hopefully better set than

Keena, who wobbled under me as we walked. She was breathing heavily, so I paused.

"Get moving. I'll push through it." Her words were clipped with pain. We walked slowly through the library, all the coziness of it now presenting obstacles for our unwieldy twosome. I banged my shin on a side table leg and cursed. Keena stopped to let me get a grip but sagged against me. I winced through the momentary pain and kept going. Any loss of momentum would take us down.

We got all the way to the kitchen door before Keena collapsed. I heard voices on the other side of the door. Sora mostly — barking out orders with the efficiency of a general. Maybe she and Midori were more similar than I had thought. I didn't know what was going on. Rather than calling out for help , I kicked the kitchen door in, more forcefully than I meant to. It came swinging back and hit me as I carried Keena through it.

Sora and Darcy turned from the table where Alex lay unmoving. Darcy frowned and made a movement to come towards us but stopped. I had never seen Sora look so furious.

"What the hell, Reva? Keena needed to stay in the library. We'll get to her next." Sora exhaled and pointed to one of the benches pushed far from the table against a wall. I struggled to the bench, half dragging Keena with me. I helped her sit and lean against the wall.

"Bring me Bear," she whispered and closed her eyes. I turned back to the room.

Sora was bent over Alex again, ignoring me now. Her chest rose and fell as she lay on the table, so I knew she wasn't dead but I had no idea how bad she was hurt. Darcy was watching Sora and had both her hands around Alex's ankles. I didn't know how to move around them and didn't want to interrupt them.

I moved as quietly as I could around the table to see if the dogs were by the fire. Flame sat there intently watching her master. Bear was lying on his side where I had left him, snoring softly.

"Bear," I whispered as quietly as I could. He didn't budge. "Bear."

"Reva. Is there a reason you're interrupting us?" Sora said severely. I had never seen this side of Sora, intensely focused and angry in an icy-cold way.

"Bear was attacked earlier tonight by a demon." I went with a short but concise version of the evening's events.

"What?" Alex spoke, her voice like gravel against a chalkboard. I was relieved to hear from her. Aside from the quality, she sounded like herself.

"Stop speaking," Darcy directed Alex. "Reva, what are you talking about?"

I gave her and Sora the same abbreviated version I gave Keena. Sora didn't stop her ministrations while I was telling the story but when I ended, her head hung down for a second.

"Fuck!" She exclaimed, making us all jump, except Alex who let a small smile creep up on her face. She was probably happy to have someone express what she herself was thinking.

"This has been a spectacularly crappy night," Darcy sighed and then addressed Sora. "What do you want to do?"

"I don't —" Sora paused and looked over at me. "Are we in any immediate danger?"

"No. It's gone. As far as I know," I said. "Nothing else happened for hours after."

Darcy frowned with worry. "I think we have to stay focused on Alex and Keena. We can talk more about how a demon got through our wards later."

"How long has Bear been hurt? Physical wound? We don't have a lot of time to get a salve on a wound like that." Sora shifted gears, going back to helping Alex.

"Oh, I put a salve on him." Sora didn't turn around, but shoulders went up around her ears in puzzlement. "Midori helped me."

"The cat helped you?" Alex piped up skeptically from the table.

"For the love of all that is good and green, shut up!" Sora scolded Alex.

I waited in the hanging silence before going on, feeling defensive. "She didn't measure out ingredients or anything. She just knocked the right tins off the shelves. Your instructions on the tins were really clear, Sora."

Midori took that moment to appear from under the table. I hadn't realized she was waiting there. She rubbed up against Sora's ankles and meowed. Normally I would assume she wanted something a normal cat would want: food, pets, a chance to kill small birds. Now I figured she was looking for praise, though her desire to have that praise be in the form of food, pets, or a small live bird probably still stood.

"Good kitty," Sora murmured. Midori meowed again and skulked back under the table. One "good kitty" wasn't going to cut it for her. "Reva, that's an immense relief. With two of us not able to do healing work, we're a struggling. Don't take Bear over to her, though. She'll try to heal him, and she can't spare the energy."

"I can hear you," Keena croaked from across the room. "I won't use my energy. I just need to know how bad he is. Bear!"

Upon hearing his mistress call his name, Bear lifted his head out of his slumber with perked up ears. He scrambled up clumsily to his feet, giving a short whine of pain when he put too much weight on his hurt back leg. Flame snapped at him, a warning to sit his ass back down, but Bear was undeterred. He hobbled over to Keena, flinging himself at her feet and resting his head against her leg.

"How's my good boy?" Keena whispered to him and put her hand on his head. A complex mix of emotions flitted over her face before she finally let a small, relieved smile creep over. "The salve is helping. It feels like he'll be alright. Thank you, Reva."

"Least I could do. He and Flame came to the rescue," I said as I sat next to her. She leaned her head against my shoulder. I wrapped my arm around her and let her lean in more. Her exhaustion came off her in waves. It was her magic energy I was feeling. It was something I'd never experienced before. Slowly it dawned on me I was probably feeling her magic through my own empathetic magic skill. I wondered if tuning further to her magic would allow me to heal her. I concentrated on the pulse I was feeling from her, closing my eyes.

Suddenly Keena was standing before me. Fear and tears shone in her eyes. She was saying something I couldn't make out, but the pleading and begging were apparent. Her hair was short and choppy, like it had been hacked off by scissors. A man was shouting incoherently but one word kept coming through: whore. A blur of motion, metal flashing in light and a knife was sweeping through the air. It hit Keena's arms as she held them in front of herself for protection, blood everywhere.

I sat up, startled. I was back in the kitchen. Keena shifted off me and looked at me with an odd look.

"What just happened, Reva?" she asked though it sounded like she was asking only to confirm her suspicion.

"I felt your magic and thought maybe I could pick up your healing skill to help you. I got your emotional divining instead," I said, remorse immediately flooding through me. "I'm so sorry."

She frowned at me, but her tiredness kept her from doing more than saying, "Don't do that without my permission."

I nodded as she shifted off me and sat up. I wanted to continue to explain, to ask for forgiveness, to say now she knew how it felt, but I stoppered it all up in my head. No need for that sort of self-serving now. Or maybe ever. Keena hadn't wanted to know my worst moment but had needed to in the moment to heal me after my storm at the parade. I hadn't wanted to see hers either but had been doing so from a place of healing as well. We were even.

Sora and Darcy wrapped up the healing and helped Alex to sit up on the table. I hadn't gotten a full good look at her until that moment. Her left eye was bruised, her lip was swollen and cut, and she was favoring her left arm. Darcy helped her off the table and over to where I was sitting.

"Alex, what happened?" I asked.

"You should see the other guys." Alex grinned at me through the obvious pain she was in.

"Now is not the time for stories. Reva, I need you to help Darcy get Keena over here," Sora commanded. Darcy and I did as she asked, catching each other's eyes long enough to convey our surprise and appreciation at this new Sora.

The healing process continued. I made coffee when Sora started to drag. Darcy gratefully accepted a cup. Sora did as well but not before making sure I wasn't going to give any to Alex. I glanced over at Alex, who was asleep upright on the bench, and agreed. The clock said it was 3 a.m. As soon as I saw it, I regretted looking because exhaustion swept through me. How was I still awake?

Another hour passed and then we were scrambling to find an air mattress and bedding to set up for Alex and Keena. Neither could make it to their own beds. We set them up in a makeshift bed in the library, though the process of getting them to said bed was a challenge. Alex insisted she could walk on her own and almost fell on her face before Darcy, who was trailing her closely, caught her. Keena had to be carried between Darcy and me. Eventually we got the two of them settled with their dogs curled up next to them.

"I should take a look at Bear," Sora said wearily.

"Keena took a look and so did I. Reva set him up pretty well. It can wait until morning," Darcy said.

"It is already morning." I pointed out the window where the sky was lightening to gray. I looked out at the porch and shuddered remembering the demon, the Anthony look-alike. I hastily shut the drapes, blocking out the memory and the rising sun.

"Point taken. Come on, you." Darcy gestured to Sora. "It's time for bed. We can't help anyone if we're dead on our feet."

We all trooped upstairs with agreements on setting alarms at intervals to take turns checking on Keena and Alex. I walked into my room and found Tuna and Kiz curled up in the middle of my bed. I gently moved them before crawling in; they rearranged themselves around me, not ready to be awake despite the fact it was their usual time to demand food. I lay there waiting for sleep to come over me, wondering what the hell we were going to do.

Chapter 22

I slept through the day, waking in the late afternoon from a disconcerting dream of Anthony and the girl from the boat. In the dream, I had sent both of them to the bottom of the bay in the storm, where the demon lay waiting for them. I woke feeling guilt even though it was just a dream. I dragged myself out of bed and to the window to see the sun lower in the sky than I wanted. I wasn't ready for another night to fall, not with how vulnerable I felt. Would the demon reappear?

The cats had stopped being patient with me and were meowing, rushing diagonally in front of me as I headed downstairs. I ignored them to peek into the library to check on Alex and Keena. In the dim room, I could see the outline of one of them, chest rising and falling deep sleep. I quietly closed the door and went into the kitchen.

Sora was sitting at the table with Alex across from her, facing away from me. Alex turned when I walked in. I almost gasped in shock at the sight of her face. The black eye had progressed to a violent reddish purple and the cut on her lip had scabbed over to almost black. She smiled at me as I walked in.

"Good morning, sleepyhead. Sounds like we have some catching up to do," she croaked, her voice scratchy like she had a cold. Or spent a lot of time screaming. Or both.

"Glad to see you up. I guess Keena's still asleep," I said as I walked over and got a glass of water from the tap. There was a plate of leftover galette and cookies on the table, but I didn't feel hungry. It was hard to believe Mikhael's visit had been the previous afternoon.

"Keena did amazing and dangerous work yesterday. She deserves all the sleep she wants," Sora said fervently. Alex nodded in agreement.

"Sounds like you had an eventful night as well, Reva. We better get to trading notes," Alex said. Sora frowned at her.

"Shouldn't you save your voice?" she scolded.

"You tell the story, Sora. I'll add anything missed."

"You start. I haven't heard it from the beginning, what led you to the warehouse." Sora smiled. Alex nodded and started filling us in.

She had been out in Coos Bay visiting Sandra. Afterwards, she had chased down a tip from someone at a bar about Satanic rituals being performed in an old warehouse past the railroad and into the industrial outskirts. Alex found the warehouse and climbed up some stacked pallets to break in via an unlocked window. Inside, she climbed down metal shelving under the window.

"You're lucky you didn't get hurt just getting inside!" Sora exclaimed.

Inside it was the usual abandoned warehouse filled with piles of unidentifiable junk. There was a second floor. Before heading up, she noticed the main doors were unlocked.

"I should have known then," Alex said, shaking her head.

She wasn't sure about alarms, so she locked the door. She would go out the way she came in, after checking out the second floor. There were a few small offices and one conference room.

In the conference room, the large dust-covered table was pushed up against a wall and a huge pentagram was spray painted on the floor. Then Alex turned around and there on an old dirty whiteboard was more spray paint. It said "Gotcha, Witch".

"Not very imaginative," Alex laughed. "But they aren't the brightest of the bunch we're dealing with."

"Except for the demon," I said.

"And the demon seeker," Sora added. A look crossed Alex's face like she wanted to argue but instead she continued.

At the sound of engines, Alex looked out the window and saw multiple headlights rushing to the warehouse. She ran down to the doors but knew she couldn't make it out in time. She had parked her truck down the road out of sight just in case. Running to it in time was out of the question.

"So stupid, in hindsight."

"Don't be silly, Alex. At that point if you'd gotten into your truck, they'd have been on your tail." Sora crossed her arms in front of her.

"And maybe driven you off the road, too," I added. It sounded like a much more remote area and no Mikhael was going to come find her. Alex looked at both of us and shrugged. Maybe we were right. Maybe not.

Instead of running, she found a long metal bar and slid it through the warehouse door handles that prevented the door from opening, happy they weren't doorknobs. She dragged large heavy containers in front to double it up. Then she moved the metal shelving in front of the side door to block it and so no one else could get in the same way she had through the window.

"I didn't think I was trapping myself in there at that point. I just knew those obvious ways in had to be closed."

The vehicles all pulled up at that point so Alex ran up the stairs, grateful she had her cell phone.

"That's when I called Keena. I tried to convey as much as I could before I had to get off the phone."

"You gave very clear instructions. Darcy had no trouble following them."

Alex stayed out of sight and looked out the window, staying low. Below she saw a hair-raising scene: people in white hoods with crude eye holes, lighting torches for each other. They worked in the glow of their head lights while others tried to open the doors of the warehouse.

"When they didn't try that hard to get in, I knew it was a lure. For you all." Alex dropped her eyes to the table and stared for a bit, her face blank. Sora and I waited. "I tried to call but no one picked up. I left voicemails to try to get you all to stay away."

"We got them but only after we had turned down the road to the warehouse," Sora said, concern and care imbued in her voice. "We saw the glow of the torches. We couldn't leave you to them."

Tears pooled in Alex's eyes. She wiped them and gestured to Sora. "Your turn. Now the story is yours."

Sora picked up the thread, describing how they were sitting in the car on the road to the warehouse listening to messages. Keena had killed the headlights and they paused there unsure of what to do next until Darcy came up with a possible solution. She knew of a back road, if it was still there — it had been years since she had been on it. That road would take them onto the other side of the warehouse so they could get closer without being detected. Hopefully.

The road turned out to be a set of overgrown tracks through a field that they drove by twice before finding, feeling the seconds tick by with increasing fear for Alex. They were able to drive it up until it dead-ended in a thicket of willows. Keena had turned the car around so they were pointed out for an easier escape.

"I wouldn't have thought of that. Very impressive," Alex croaked.

I thought of the visions from Keena's past I had seen, wondering about her full story. Maybe someday she'd tell me.

Sora, Keena, and Darcy had crept through the dense thicket, Darcy leading because according to Sora, she had keener night sight. They got to the edge of the thicket and found they were a couple of yards away from the warehouse, coming up on the side of it where the smaller door was located. They saw the circle of hooded men with torches, mostly watching the main doors. Keena had drawn in a sharp breath and turned away.

"It was hard to come up with a plan on how to get Alex out. Fortunately we had cell coverage."

Keena and Alex texted back and forth, Keena staying deep in the thicket to keep the glow of the phone from being seen. Sora and Darcy waited, watching.

"It was odd. They seemed to be waiting for something. Us? We didn't know but they weren't storming the building like we expected. It gave us time but was also troubling."

Finally Keena had returned with a plan. It wasn't going to be easy or safe, and was going to take a lot of magic, but it was all they had. The men were getting agitated, murmuring with each other at increasing volume. Keena laid the plan out to Sora and Darcy. Just as they were getting into position, a man stepped forward out of the group.

"The demon seeker. I never saw his face, but he was definitely the leader, and he had an evil aura."

"You can see auras?" I asked, sorry to interrupt but unable to control my curiosity.

Sora nodded. "It's considered 'outdated' magic by most people. The craze of aura readings by regular people didn't help. Telepathy and channeling are subject to the same prejudice."

"Reva, stop interrupting. Sora, back to the story," Alex commanded before adding. "Please."

Sora returned to the story. The demon seeker stepped forward and turned to the crowd with a flourishing gesture of his torch.

"Typical high dramatics for a bunch of Nazis." Alex rolled her eyes. "I watched it from the upstairs window, waiting for the cue from Keena. The upstairs offices were on the end of the building by the thicket, right above the side door.

The demon seeker began to speak, a standard white supremacist speech according to both Sora and Alex.

"You know the same old shit — this is our country, needing the place to be safe. All the dog whistles set for the ears of those who want to hear it." Alex sneered at the memory of it.

"It was awful. We couldn't catch all of it, thankfully. When they started chanting, though ..." Sora shuddered visibly. I thought of my three friends hiding in the thicket, all people that group would want to harm, to claim didn't have a right to live, and shuddered myself.

The hooded crowd chanted at the end of the speech — "Burn the Witch!" Before they worked themselves into full frenzy and began what all the witches guessed would be breaking into the building or burning it, Keena gave the command and the witches put their plan into action.

Keena went into a trance, according to Sora.

"It was scary, her eyes rolled back into her head so we could only see the whites in the glow of the torches. And then she convulsed."

Darcy held her as she did that. Sora heard shouts from the men. There on the other side of the building, all the way at the other end, appeared Keena. She smiled and shouted at the men, her voice singing through the night: "Catch me if you can."

"A projection. Mirror magic, a pretty rare skill," Sora clarified. The real Keena was still convulsing in Darcy's arms. But the frenzied crowd had no idea. They shouted in excitement.

"Fuckers. They thought they got to kill not just a witch but a black witch." Alex went somehow paler than usual with rage.

Mirror Keena disappeared into the dark after a teasing smile and all the men ran after her. Alex took that moment to race down the stairs and out the door. In the moment she had to move the metal shelving enough to get out, the demon seeker got wise to their plan. He was at the back of the pack of torches moving through the night toward their phantom victim and heard the scraping of the metal. Maybe. Or he was smart enough to recognize the magic.

Alex shot out the door, heading to the thicket. Sora helped Darcy drape Keena's now still body over Darcy's shoulder, balancing the weight so Darcy could move her to the car. Sora was going to follow to help move the branches out of the way when she heard the demon seeker yell out.

"No words, just a growling shriek. It didn't sound human," Sora said. She had turned back and screamed a warning to Alex who was running as hard as she could toward the thicket.

"I heard it, too," Alex said. She felt her legs knocked out from under her and she went down about a foot from the thicket. The demon seeker was running full force after sending the spell that had knocked her down.

"I've never seen magic like that before," Sora said, shaking her head. "It was like he had an invisible bowling ball he rolled at Alex."

"More like a dodge ball made of snakes. I felt all these stinging bites around my ankles and calves."

The demon seeker was on top of Alex before she could get up. He pulled her head up from the ground by her hair and slammed her head into the earth. He pulled her head up again to repeat the action and Alex had mouthed "run" to Sora.

"I don't remember that," Alex said. "But it sounds like me. I was going into fight survival mode but it's really hard to get out of that position with a grown man on your back."

Sora had screamed and the demon seeker had looked up, his face still obscured by the awful white hood, but a wicked demon grin cut through the blank space where the mouth should be. He kneed Alex in the lower back two times and drove her head down again.

"I also went into fight mode," Sora said fiercely. "I'm trained in potions, healing, and plants, not war. Not like Alex with her warrior magic. I didn't know what to do but a thought floated up in my panic. Plants have defenses."

Sora called on all the plants around her for help. The thicket of willows bent toward the demon seeker and then sprang violently at his face, going straight for the black eye holes of the hood. He howled and lurched back, giving Alex enough of an edge to buck him off and drag herself up and into the thicket, getting hit with the branches.

"The willows were our heroes, but the real saviors were the blackberry vines." Sora beamed remembering them. Thick blackberry vines shot out from the sides of the thicket, covered in thorns, and curled around the demon seeker's ankles. He yelled in pain and frustration but was trapped in place.

"We turned and ran. The thicket absorbed some of the spell he threw at us but not all of it. Alex pushed me in front of her and took the force of his magic." Tears were running down Sora's cheeks and she had to pause.

"You're a stronger healer than I am, Sora. The warrior takes the hit." Alex reached over and put her hand over Sora's. "Though you have warrior skills, too. Those blackberry vines were genius."

We all were quiet for a bit, absorbing the story before I had to ask, "So how did you get out of there?"

Sora had managed to keep Alex upright and Alex had managed to keep her feet moving to get to the back of the Honda. Darcy had opened the back hatch, and Sora and Alex collapsed inside.

Darcy punched the gas as soon as Sora and Alex were in the car.

"Apparently Darcy can drive like a motherfucker. Not sure where she learned those skills but if I ever do a bank heist, she's my first choice for a getaway driver." Alex grinned.

"She didn't even wait for us to close the back hatch, so it was a terrifying car ride out of that dirt track," Sora said.

Alex admitted she passed out shortly after getting in the car. Sora watched the thicket behind them go up in flames, heard the demon seeker screaming in rage. The crowd must have finally realized the Keena they were chasing wasn't real and they could be heard in the distance, the sound of engines starting. Darcy drove them home through a series of back roads, somehow managing to navigate at high speeds with no headlights.

"The headlights would have been visible to anyone trying to follow." Darcy's voice came from behind us at the kitchen door. She had dark shadows under her eyes, her hair was swept back in a bun, and she was in a simple black dress but still managed to look chic.

"How long were you listening there?" Sora asked as Darcy came in and sat next to her.

"Long enough to get the part of the story I wasn't there for." She smiled. "Killer blackberries, huh?"

Sora smiled shyly but with pride before getting up to make tea for us all, a healing herbal that Alex made a face at but agreed to drink.

We were drinking tea when Keena came into the kitchen. She looked rough, sunken eyes and drawn features as if she'd lost weight in her face. I wondered briefly how I looked but a reflection in the windows gave me a glimpse: uncombed hair, puffy eyes. We were all worse for the wear after the previous night.

"So, Reva. Now tell us what happened here. Because clearly this was a coordinated attack," Alex said. Her cup of tea sat half drunk in front of her. I took a sip of mine, enjoying the taste of lemon, honey, lavender, and some other floral component. I told them the demon had shown up at the door.

"Demons shouldn't be able to get on our land. Certainly not close enough to knock on the door," Keena said. Her voice was raspy, but it was good to see her up. I hadn't even realized how hard both she and Alex had taken it until their story but was glad they both were okay.

"I learned something before it showed up, from the Quinn book of shadows. It's an andras demon. I think." I spun my cup nervously in front of me. I had been afraid to tell them, though rationally there was no reason for the fear. It was something deeper, a nagging feeling around the edges that refused to take shape.

"Andras demon? Are you sure?" Keena looked alarmed. Alex had her lips in a thin line, a gesture I recognized as her disapproval.

I explained the book passage, how it had been an introduction to demon classification but that was the only classification I was shown. They all quieted at that.

"That is how a book of shadows like yours works. It wouldn't show you that randomly. Not based on your experiences to date," Sora said thoughtfully.

"But how did the demon get in? Our wards should work on andras demons." Alex slammed her hand on the table in frustration and winced. Sora had worked her healing magic, but recovery wasn't instant.

"Tell us what happened. From the beginning," Darcy demanded.

I took a breath and told them the story, from the moment they left the house to when they returned. When I tried to tell about the demon looking like Anthony, I couldn't get the words out. It was too embarrassing, though they already knew about Anthony. I skipped that detail and continued my story.

Upon hearing about the heroics of Flame and Bear in detail, Alex pulled herself up off the bench gingerly and limped to the freezer. She pulled out two giant wrapped oblong packages.

"Bones. For two very good dogs," she said before sitting back down.

"I gave Midori, Tuna, and Kiz their own special cans of tuna when I woke up," Sora admitted.

"I gave them some last night, too." I laughed. "And hamburger for the dogs."

"Well deserved for all," Keena said, bending down to pet Bear, who had limped over to her and was now panting happily at her feet. "There's something I don't understand though, Reva."

"What?" I asked, still thinking about all the treats the cats had scored. Sneaky creatures.

"You said you almost opened the door a few times. If you knew it was the demon, what would compel you to do that?" She was suddenly watching me carefully. The others looked at me with curiosity, but Alex caught on to what Keena was asking.

"You're leaving something out, Reva. What is it?" Alex had no qualms going right to the question.

"I —" I froze, not sure what to do. Something inside me clicked into place. I had no reason to hide the information but something inside wanted me to. And I was beginning to think that little voice wasn't actually me. Which scared me more than anything.

"It sounded like Anthony. It looked like Anthony." I broke down, a garbled sob coming out after. "He begged for my help."

I couldn't look at any of them. We sat in silence for a few moments while I wiped at the stream of tears coming down my face.

"I think we know how the demon got through the wards," Darcy said in the quiet. I looked up at her, waiting for the inevitable conclusion. "You invited the demon into your life when you invited Anthony in."

"The demon had a foothold in. Through you." Keena nodded. She looked at me with compassionate eyes I didn't deserve.

I felt better and worse at the same time, hearing it all said out loud. Better that I wasn't crazy or wrong, and the nagging on the edges had stopped. Worse because, well, what could be worse than what I was about to say?

"Not through me," I corrected her. "Inside of me." There was a piece of the demon in me. And I had been ignoring it all along.

Chapter 23

"What do you mean, *inside you?*" Sora asked after a spell of silence.

"It — I'm not sure how to explain it but I feel certain," I fumbled, looking down. "It's like there's this little curl of evil inside me. I don't notice it and I can't find it, but sometimes it pops up on the edge. Like something in my peripheral vision I can't quite make out that disappears when I take a closer look."

I stopped my rambling and looked around the table. Sora was nodding thoughtfully but with a furrowed brow telling me she didn't know what I was talking about. Keena's face also held confusion and worry, her hands clasped in front of her mouth. Alex looked angry, which I was beginning to understand came with additional emotions but was always her starting point. Darcy's eyes were filled with compassion and a few tears. At least I hoped it was compassion, not pity.

"Sounds like bullshit," Alex finally said.

"Alex!" Keena exclaimed.

"It does. It sounds like Reva's guilt and any number of emotions. I've never heard of a piece of a demon inside someone. Not outside of fairy tales. Not in this world."

"It's not in this world, though," Darcy cut in. She looked pale. "It does happen. I've seen it. In the Other."

We all paused and turned to her. She shook her head.

"I don't know much about it. I just know the foothold happens in the Other. I've read of realmwalkers who have had this happen. Like a burr or a seed, it attaches to the soul in the Other. And then, as Reva described, lives there mostly unnoticed."

"For how long?" Sora asked.

"Unnoticed until when?" I asked at the same time.

Darcy shifted uncomfortably. "Possibly years. It waits until the demon comes to collect. It's like a magical tracking device."

Alex blew a sigh out loudly. "That explains a lot. What happened to the realmwalkers you read about?"

"I —" Darcy faltered, a miserable look coming over her face. "They became entrapped by the demon or died. Often both."

"Fun," I said sarcastically while dread filled my throat. I felt like throwing up.

"That must have happened when you first got here? The first trip to the Other," Keena mused.

I shook my head. "No. I think it happened years ago. My first depressive bout when I was a teenager. It's when I first met the demon."

After the revelation of my tie to the demon, no one knew what to say for a while. The exhaustion that was so apparent in all of us hit again and we struggled through a meal of leftovers, trying to come up with solutions or ideas or anything that might help.

"That means it can come back. At any time. It has decided to collect on me," I said despondently while spooning salmon spread on a cracker.

"Yes, but not any time soon." Alex made a sweeping gesture across the table at our weary faces. "It took a beating from the dogs, let alone the energy to manifest itself like that on our doorstep. We have a little time."

"We're going to need that time to heal and recover," Sora pointed out.

"All of us," I said. "Including you."

Sora waved my concern away. "I'm fine."

"After that business with the vines and willows, I'm surprised you could come back here and heal not one, but two witches. How do you do it?"

She shrugged it off . "Youth?"

"You're only what, three years younger than me?" I pointed out. She shrugged again.

"Stop being so modest, Sora. You're a goddamn force. Don't let anyone, including yourself, tell you otherwise." Alex pointed her spoon at Sora, flinging butternut soup on those of us around her. Darcy frowned and delicately sponged at a drop from her sleeve.

"Force or not, I think there's a reality we need to face." Sora looked at each of us. "We can't do this alone. We can't take on an andras demon and an army of white supremacists headed by a demon seeker tied to said demon."

"An andras demon that has been cuddling up inside of Reva, no less, our least experienced witch. No offense." Alex was blunt, nodding in my direction. I was too tired to be offended. Or too aware of how right she was.

"Could we ask the other witches?" I mused. They looked at one another in confusion. "The other witches here on the farm."

"No." The one word from Darcy emphatic and louder than usual. Alex snorted at the same time.

Keena shook her head. "Reva, you may have fond memories of those ladies, but they aren't ..." She paused, not sure how to say the next part.

"They have skills and knowledge but more in healing, herbs, and that sort of thing," Sora chimed in.

"But —" I stopped. I didn't know the other women well and hadn't seen them much outside of the awkward visit I had made when I first got there. And my lessons in magic in high school had mostly come from Sandra, though my memories of the content remained fuzzy.

Sora continued, "Sandra is the most powerful of them. She was always the head of the magic parts. They took their lead from her. They're nice ladies —"

Darcy interrupted with a pointed throat clear. I couldn't blame her after how they had treated her. I felt a momentary surge of guilt that I had all but forgotten that.

"They're old-fashioned farming hippies who dabble in magic. They are witches, but not like us," Alex finished.

"Oh." I sat back, stunned but not surprised. I knew there was a separation between us and them on the farm but hadn't given it much thought beyond the conversation with Sandra about it. I hadn't realized there was a bit of a magic hierarchy going on as well.

"You know who might help us?" Keena spoke up, ready to change the subject.

Everyone looked at Keena expectantly. She continued, "The tribe. Maybe not all of them but certainly we could ask Mikhael and Wynona."

Alex nodded, warming up to the idea. "They have the juice to help us in the fight. Not sure they'll want to stick their necks out for us though, invite a demon to notice them."

"I think it's worth asking," Darcy said, her demeanor improved since the conversation about the other women on the farm had moved on.

I sighed. I didn't want to ask for help this early in knowing either Mikhael or Wynona, though for different reasons. With Wynona, entangling her in my own personal mess would be asking something of her I couldn't repay, and in a way, repeating the history between her and Sandra. It wasn't a logical thought since the situations were not the same, but it was a feeling burrowed under my skin I couldn't ignore.

With Mikhael, that was because I liked him. I had been questioning my feelings since I met him and there was a lot to confuse me, but I wanted a chance to see where a friendship with him might go. Without him coming to my rescue a second time. I wanted to get to know the guy without the pressure of a demon fight.

I opened my mouth to speak up and closed it as I looked at my friends. A few months ago, I didn't have any friends. Not like these women. And looking at them, I saw the bruises on Alex's forehead, the wanness of Sora's cheeks, Keena sitting at a slight hunch, and worry etched between Darcy's eyes. I wanted to protect them. But the reasons they were sitting there recovering were all because of me. I had to do something to get them out of the line of fire.

"Sure. I'll text Mikhael," I said but a different idea was forming in my head. One I couldn't tell anyone about.

Everyone went to sleep early, needing the recharge time more than usual. I lay in my bed tossing and turning. The idea I had was bad. I knew that but I didn't see any other way out. Not without possibly hurting another person. Or worse. My hands were still stained by the death of the young woman from the boat, and Sandra's injuries. And maybe Anthony, though him appearing as a demon on the porch made me question what he actually was. I didn't know anymore, and nothing provided answers. I couldn't stay trapped on the farm. Especially if the wards couldn't prevent the demon from waltzing up to the door.

I fell into a restless sleep, dozing off into bad dreams and waking up. After a few hours of this, I got up and pulled on sweats and an old sweater and made my way downstairs. The whole house was asleep. Tuna and Kiz slept at the foot of my bed, warm piles of dozing fur, probably relieved the tossing and turning human was leaving. Keena was back in her room and Alex had limped out to her own trailer. The air mattress was still on the floor of the library, a deflating reminder of the previous night. I went into the green room.

The air was warm and humid inside, a relief to the creepy cold of the house at 3 a.m. I had glanced at the clock when I got up and regretted it instantly. 3 a.m. The witching hour. I was a witch though, so I shouldn't feel as off about it as I suddenly did. I crept through the plants, leaves trailing against my hands, and found the table I had first met Keena at, where she had read my tea leaves. The table from which I had been pulled into the Other, pulled in to where the demon had been waiting for me. It felt like so long ago, not two months ago.

That visit to the Other had seemed like the first time, but I had clearly had this demon hunting me earlier. I sat and rehashed the whole ordeal with Anthony in my mind. I hadn't let myself do that much. There had been the confession to the witches, but I hadn't spent much time on my own thinking about it. And to complete my plan, I needed to. I had to look at every angle.

Anthony had of course been a mistake. But he had been a mistake I was looking for, if I was honest. Did the demon seek me out or did I seek the demon out? I didn't know for sure, and I wished it didn't matter but clearly it did. Thinking about Anthony made me feel unclean and unfinished in an odd way that was hard to formulate into words, feelings drifting through me to be stamped down.

One memory I hadn't pulled in was that dark one from when I was in high school, the one that had set me off of the craft for years and planted the seed for the demon. If thinking of Anthony made me feel like I had a film of sticky grease all over my skin, the memory from high school made me feel like there were beads of black grease coursing through my bloodstream.

I was sitting in the dark when I noticed a movement outside the fogged-up windows. I froze in fear. It was too soon for the demon to return. Unless it was getting stronger as we got weaker. The movement came again. An animal, I decided. It was just an animal. To prove it to myself, I got up and walked to the big wall of windows, using my shirt sleeve to wipe away the condensation.

An eye blinked back at me. I jumped back in surprise. The eye turned and I saw another one. Something tapped on the window. My heart was racing as my mind slowly pieced all the different images together: the Evernia stag.

He tapped on the window again and made nodding gestures with his head before walking away. I gathered he wanted me to follow him. I hesitated. It was dark, cold and the middle of the night. It seemed foolish to follow the stag. I should stay here, in the warmth of the house.

The ring on my finger warmed, a strange and disconcerting sensation since it was starting from the same temperature as my hand. It was moving to the territory of burning when I sighed and started toward the kitchen. I guess my ancestors were telling me to go after the stag.

I bundled up in a fleece jacket left by the door, probably Sora's, and pulled on my running sneakers from the since abandoned exercise routines with Alex. I paused at the back door, rethinking my craziness, and the ring began to heat again.

"Alright, alright," I muttered and opened the door to step out into the night.

The air was cold and damp. Immediately I wished for another layer and as I stepped onto the grass, wished for boots. I almost turned back but the light from the kitchen caught the eyes of the stag, turning them to two yellow glows. I shut the door and followed the Evernia across the fields.

The deer was headed to the forest. The two sentinel trees loomed dark against the cloudy night sky as we walked closer. I hesitated there, at the edge of the forest. Inside it was dark, darker than I could imagine with no flashlight or even moonlight to guide me. My imagination went wild with all the scary things in the woods, starting with regular predators and moving on to monsters before logic helpfully pointed out that tripping and falling in the dark was more likely and just as dangerous.

The Evernia paused before snorting and pawing at the ground. Enough, he seemed to say before walking into the darkness. I took a deep breath and followed, hoping I wasn't making a huge mistake.

The darkness of a forest in the middle of the night was unlike anything I had ever experienced. I could see dark shapes as I walked slowly, slivers of sky through the canopy, but down on the ground I couldn't see my hand in front of my face when I held it up, trying to keep from walking into obstacles. My knee hit something solid in front of me and I fell forward onto a downed log, the soft moss keeping me from scraping up my hands. I bit back a curse and a whimper as my knee throbbed.

A soft glow of green light caught my eye off to the right — bioluminescent mushrooms on the forest floor. They were in a pattern, specifically around the trail I had been following. The Evernia stood in the middle waiting for me to catch up.

"I don't have your night vision," I whispered to him. My voice felt loud, and it was only in breaking the silence that I realized how quiet it was all around me. I imagined all sorts of noises from frog choruses to occasional hooting owls would be a part of the night forest but all I could hear was the slight bending of the trees under occasional puffs of wind. Water dripped silently from the moss above onto my shoulders. I flinched when a drop hit my cheek..

The Evernia walked ahead of me, never allowing me to get closer than a few feet from it. I couldn't help but feel like he was annoyed by my lack of night walking coordination but that was probably my imagination. The mushrooms helped, kept me on the path at least, though I stumbled on tree roots I couldn't see. I was relatively calm though, which was a surprise to me.

A branch snapped off to my right and my heart leapt into my throat. Both the stag and I stopped short. So much for calm. We waited, tension thrumming through my limbs, but nothing happened. Another animal perhaps. We walked on slowly but the calm I had felt was gone.

After a few moments of walking, the mushrooms disappeared and the canopy opened up overhead. We had come to a clearing. The Evernia walked around the edge, sticking close to the trees. I tried to follow, but it made a harumphing noise and darted into the trees. I stood at the edge of the clearing, wondering what to do next. I looked behind me, but the mushrooms had gone dim. I didn't know how I was going to find my way back.

A light wind rustled through the trees, reminding me the lack of layers I was wearing. I shivered and wrapped my arms around myself. Surely the Evernia wouldn't lead me out here for no reason? Or worse, a trap? Seconds ticked by.

How foolish I was. I had followed a deer into the woods in the middle of the night. I wasn't even sure what time it was anymore. I glanced up at the sky, the night clouds swirling overhead.

Swirling? I looked up again. The clouds had a strange orange tinge to them and were moving faster than the wind could account for. The longer I watched, the more it seemed like they were moving in a spiral, right above the clearing. I walked out a few steps to get a better view. The clouds shifted, changing in color and swirling faster. I kept going until I was in the middle of the clearing. The clouds were a vortex above me now, deepening to a reddish purple.

I waited for fear to overcome me, to feel dread or panic. Instead, I felt a calm focus sharpen in my mind. This was what I was here for, the clouds above me in the sky. The ring on my finger brightened and a current of energy crept out of the center and up toward the sky. Instinctively, I raised that hand up so it was closer. The energy became a jittery red beam of light. It reminded me of the sprite shadows from the Other.

The red light shot up to the clouds. They glowed red like a reflection from a traffic light. Then the light vanished, and the clouds went dark. The temperature shifted, as if I had walked into a sudden fog but the air stayed clear.

The swirl of the clouds overhead slowed. They called to me, in a language that wasn't sound or even sight-based. It was a language of touch and temperature. I raised my hand again to the sky, drawn up into a fist. But the shape felt wrong and the clouds withdrew. I unclenched my fist and opened my palm up to the sky, waiting, looking up.

A streak of red lightning ran across the sky. Thunder rumbled low and loud above me. I raised my other hand up, palm open. The air shifted again. Fat drops of rain began to pour down. I felt like a kid in a sprinkler, the thrill of water beating down all around me. I smiled and laughed out loud. Lightning forked out above me, like a tree branch. The storm responded with a thunderclap. I felt another pull, the electric charge filling the air. My arms were beginning to ache but rather than drop them, I stretched up further onto my tiptoes. The lightning ran across the sky a third time. It was playing with me. A faint electric current crossed my palm. I closed my hand around it gently and slowly lowered my arms. I felt a tug from the sky and a flash of bright purple shot down at me.

I shrieked and jumped back, dropping my arms. The lightning dissipated into the air above me, leaving a lingering feeling of disappointment in the air. Or maybe it was in me. I couldn't tell. The rain slowed and petered out. I looked up, an apology forming in the back of my throat, but I didn't know how to apologize to a storm.

The clouds began to break up and scatter. I felt bereft at their departure. I wanted to cry to them to come back but it was too late.

I looked down at my damp clothes, my hair clinging to my wet face. Just a foolish witch in a clearing unable to fulfill her own magic, I thought. A shiver went through me. I was both cold and alone, standing in the middle of a forest at night with no clear idea on how to get back.

The air changed again around me. I looked up hopefully at the sky, but the clouds were gone. There was a creeping mist around the tops of the trees, pale against the black trees as it swept down. I looked out into the dark forest around the clearing and saw glowing orange eyes. Horror flooded my core.

The orange eyes pulsed in a pattern like hazard beacons. They weren't eyes, I realized with only a little relief. The mushrooms that had glowed green were now orange. I felt a creeping sense of actual eyes watching behind me. I ran toward the mushrooms, hoping they would provide a path to safety.

Behind me a wail rose, a familiar unearthly howl of sorrow and rage. The banshees. A second wail joined in, and then a third. I ran faster, stumbling over rocks but not falling. I had to get away. I was across the clearing and on the edge of the forest when I made the mistake of looking back.

Three figures had emerged from the woods behind me and were at the edge of the clearing. In that brief second of terror, I saw their skeletal faces, no eyes just black holes, and their reaching pointed hands like dead tree branches.

A strangled scream escaped my mouth as I tripped over a tree root, going face down into the dirt. I sensed their delight at my fall and felt them rushing toward me. I tried to get up, but their wails drowned out my thoughts, my senses. It was like being stuck in a small room with a stereo turned up on blast and all I could do was try to cover my ears uselessly. An unbearable heat curled around my finger and rushed up my arm as I clenched my eyes tight. The banshees were coming for me and nothing I could do would stop them.

The noise stopped and I jolted upright suddenly, tilting off balance before careening down to the ground. How could I fall if I was already on the ground? I looked around, dark shapes becoming familiar. I was sitting in the dark in the green room, next to the chair I had been sitting in when the Evernia stag had shown up outside. I was home. Not in the forest at night.

My hand hurt, particularly the finger with the ruby ring. I tentatively touched the gem with a finger. It was warm like a cooling pan on a stove. I pulled my finger away quickly, thinking about how to pull the ring off. I gently tugged at it but that increased the pain, so I stopped.

I sat there on the floor for a few seconds as I tried to piece together what had happened. A bad dream was the easiest explanation: I fell asleep and dreamed it all up. But that didn't explain the ring and the lingering pain. I stood and immediately sat in the chair as a wave of dizziness came over me. Then it hit me. I had been in the Other.

Questions and fear flooded my mind. How had I gone into the Other without knowing? The Evernia seemed to be the key, but I had never felt a negative sense from it. Was I kidding myself? How had I gotten back? How had the banshees known I was there?

I closed my eyes. After a few seconds, I was able to drag myself upright and stumble into the kitchen. Leaning on the fridge door, I stared inside like a bored teenager waiting for the perfect snack to walk out and onto a plate. Our fridge was filled with a few neatly labeled jars of leftovers like salmon spread and butternut soup, as well as eggs and slightly wilted vegetables. None of which was going to work for my quick sugar and fat needs.

I sighed and shut the fridge, glancing over at the stove. The stove top espresso maker was sitting there. I didn't want to make coffee. I wasn't sure how much more time I had as a wave of exhaustion hit. I picked up the coffee maker and shook it lightly, feeling liquid sloshing inside. I grabbed a mug out of the cupboard and poured in a meager half cup of cold dark liquid. I dumped in tablespoons of sugar, stirring frantically in hopes it would dissolve. My legs wobbled under me as another spell of bone tiredness hit. I gave up and chugged the coffee, gagging at the cold bitterness followed by the sandy sugar dregs.

Finished, I pushed myself over to the fridge and took out a container of half and half. I took a deep breath before taking a swig right from the carton. The fat coated my mouth, and I fought the urge to heave up everything. I shoved the cream back in the fridge and sat heavily on a bench in front of the fireplace.

My eyelids shuddered closed a few times and my body began to shiver. I gripped the edge of the bench and rode through an intense series of body spasms. There wasn't pain but it also wasn't pleasurable. It was like the beginning stages of a charley-horse, right before it becomes excruciating. And all over, not isolated in a calf or foot.

Slowly the symptoms subsided, and I was left feeling drained. I wasn't sure if that's what normally happens after being pulled suddenly out of the Other. The one time with Darcy that had happened, I had gone to bed so soon after that I may have missed it. But I doubted it. I wasn't sure what had caused the extreme reaction — the banshees or the residual burn from the ring that had pulled me out — but either made sense. The banshees for obvious reasons: while they hadn't touched me, their wailing had been closer than ever, and they were known for the power of their keening. No need to touch an enemy if you can herald death with your cries. The ring though, that had been taxing magic to pull me out of the Other. It had hurt both there and in this world. After what Darcy had told me about the strange ways injuries in the Other transmitted to this world, it might explain the reaction.

I looked at the coals glowing in the fireplace and tried to rest my mind for a moment. Maybe figuring out why didn't matter right now. I had bigger problems, namely how to deal with a demon and the spawn following it. I had thought I had more time to sort through my half-baked plan but being pulled unknowingly into the Other had changed that. I wasn't safe anywhere. And everywhere I was, someone I cared about was unsafe too. I had to do this alone.

The first hitch in my plan was how to leave without being noticed when I had no car. I watched the darkness outside fade as dawn approached. I was exhausted and wanted nothing more than to pour myself into the bed I had eschewed earlier. But once the others woke, I wouldn't be able to leave. I had considered trying to convince them I needed to visit Sandra but after the past few days, I didn't think that would be allowed. I was contemplating a combination of walking and hitchhiking, a dubious idea bound to fail, when I looked over at a calendar hanging on the wall. I walked over to it for a closer look.

A photo of yellow daffodils announced the month as March, which surprised me. February had passed in a blur. Sora originally used the calendar for tracking her baked-good delivery dates, a quaint habit given her age and the ubiquity of cell phones. Since the waning of the demand, Alex had started using it for tracking visits to Sandra. There were names in her scrawled handwriting. I had forgotten Sandra's old hippie commune sisters were taking shifts as well. I breathed out a little of my guilt. Each day had a good list of support: "Alex – morning", "Lily – afternoon", "Juniper – evening read". My eyes lingered on the day I guessed was today. There it showed "Sunray – morning." Sunray had always been an extremely early riser, hence her name. I remembered her chipper quips about having already been up for hours when I was forced as a teenager to get up at the ungodly hour of 7 a.m. for school.

The plan fell into place. Sunray wouldn't hesitate to give me a ride into town. I had to act fast, though. I looked down at the gray sweats and the moth-eaten sweater I was wearing and ultimately decided to forgo changing, as much as I wanted to. I couldn't risk waking anyone up, even the cats. Tuna and Kiz. The thought of not seeing them again caught in my throat. I shoved the thought hard into the back recesses of my mind and crept out the front door.

Chapter 24

I found Sunray outside her cob house, her hand on the driver's door of her truck.

"Good morning," I said in a loud whisper.

Sunray turned with a welcoming smile. "Well, hey, Reva! Are you morning people now?"

"Not really. I was hoping to catch a ride with you to visit Sandra."

"You're welcome to join me. Lily will be sorry she missed you, but she's still asleep."

"I'm sorry to miss her, too," I fibbed. Lily would have insisted on giving me a full breakfast before we left. "I'll catch her another time."

"You want a cup of coffee for the road?" Sunray asked, holding up a muddy-purple ceramic to-go mug.

"No, I can get coffee at the hospital." I stopped myself from looking over my shoulder at the house to make sure none of the other witches had worked out I was gone yet.

"Suit yourself. Coffee there is awful," Sunray said before getting into the driver's seat. I scrambled into the passenger side, grateful for the lack of argument about the coffee.

We drove in silence for a while until eventually she spoke.

"It's good you're coming to see Sandra. She's been asking after you."

I swallowed a big heaping of guilt with the breath I took before giving what I assumed was a watery smile. "I'm looking forward to seeing her."

"Are you? It'll be a bit rough. She's healing and better but it's still hard to see her like this."

I nodded, not knowing what to say.

"We've missed Sandra," Sunray said. "This accident put a lot of past shit into a different perspective."

I realized a beat later Sunray was talking about the split at the farm between the two groups. I started to comment but closed my mouth as she kept going.

"I can't speak for everyone, but Lily and I have done a lot of talking about it all. We weren't understanding of Sandra for too long, of what she was trying to build. She didn't make it easy, of course. Stubborn old broad."

"What do you mean?" I asked, fiddling with a peeling piece of vinyl on the pickup truck door.

Sunray paused to take a big breath and sip of coffee before continuing.

"Did Sandra tell you about the fight? Among the commune sisters and her?"

"Sort of. She said you all wanted more privacy and she wanted to make sure the legacy of the commune was passed down to another generation." I left out the gossip from the other witches. And Darcy. I didn't know where Sunray stood with her and a guilty part of me didn't want to find out if she was among the women who didn't trust Darcy. I wanted to hold on to the Sunray I knew who fed me raspberries threaded on rosemary twigs as a kid.

Sunray scoffed. I looked over and she had a disappointed frown on her face.

"God love her, but she can be a pain. Always glossing over the conflict as if that ever turns down the heat. Heat she usually started." Sunray glanced over at me. "What else did you hear?"

"Uh. Um." I stalled, not knowing where to take the conversation. "That you all didn't like Darcy because she's trans."

Sunray nodded. "Yeah. That's been unfortunate. There are factions of us lesbians who think vaginas make a woman. Silly that we spend so much time trying to be free of gender roles ourselves but impose them on others."

I let out an audible sigh of relief. Sunray laughed bitterly.

"I can't cop to being in the right always on this but damn. Darcy was so young when Sandra brought her in. I can't fault anyone for being who they are nor Sandra for helping. But that was just extra heat on the already boiling pot."

"What do you mean?" I had thought Darcy coming to the commune was the catalyst but there was clearly more to the story.

Sunray was quiet for a moment. I looked out the window watching the green fields and trees pass by.

"I love your aunt. She has so much she shares with the world that I'm grateful for. But she isn't perfect."

"None of us are," I replied.

"True." Sunray paused again.

"I've had my own issues with Sandra," I filled in, not wanting Sunray to stop. I remembered the fight Sandra and I were having right before the car wreck and winced.

"I haven't forgotten about all that," Sunray said. She was talking about when I had cut Sandra off, the depression and high school. "That's a good example of ways Sandra can be difficult. Do you still take your medication?"

I looked over, surprised. Sandra didn't talk about my depression. The other witches were more upfront about it but let me lead on when to discuss it or not. No one had asked about my meds in weeks.

"I do," I said slowly while briefly thinking about how all my prescriptions were back at the house. Future problem for future me. "Why?"

"It broke my heart watching you go down that dark hole in high school and not get the help you needed. We were all relieved when Olivia took you to the doctor. She was pushed off the farm after that. By Sandra."

I opened my mouth, but nothing came out. I had known the woman who had taken me to the doctor all those years ago wasn't still on the farm, but I had assumed it was of her own accord.

"Magic, healing with herbs, the ways of the witch — we're all on board with that stuff. But you have to be careful to not turn your back on all else, on science. It all works together, solving different problems. Sandra doesn't agree, though. She picks and chooses what suits her, and since she's always been more powerful than the rest of us, what she says goes. Or used to."

Sunray took a sip of coffee before continuing. I glanced yearningly at the cup. I would have to find coffee in town. I could feel the effects of my trip to the Other around the edges of my mind, like a mild hangover. I hoped someplace would be open, other than the hospital.

"Alex was the first witch Sandra brought in from the outside. We were all sharing the house then, living in little trailers while we built our own small homes nearby but eating communal meals at the table, putting the house together. It was a good time. We were so excited. You know Lily practically designed the greenery room? It breaks her heart to not see it regularly. I hope it's faring well."

"It is. It's thriving," I chimed in, wanting to set her mind at ease without interrupting her.

"That's good to hear. Lily will be pleased. I bet it's that Sora, isn't it? She's quite the talent," Sunray mused before she picked back up. "Anyway, where was I? Right. Alex. What a whirlwind of energy she brought. And her fire magic, far and above stronger than Sandra's. We were relieved honestly when they broke up. They didn't always bring out the best in each other."

"Wait — what?" I was surprised at how loud my voice sounded. Sunray looked over at me and grinned, a mix of sheepish and gleeful.

"You didn't know that? About Sandra and Alex?" She laughed. "We were all shocked they became friends. Better friends than lovers, actually."

"I don't know what to say." I wondered who else Sandra had dated. I had always suspected she was into women. Hard not to think that when someone lives on a women-only commune. But she had never once told me about a partner. Not in all the time I had known her. What else did I not know?

"Sandra has always had a taste for powerful witches as partners. Not that it ever works. Like Wynona. Oof, she got burned by Sandra. I know they're back in touch, but I can't imagine it's an easy friendship." It was like Sunray could read my mind. I hadn't realized Sunray knew Wynona, though it made sense she would. Sunray had known Sandra for decades.

"With Alex, she got a taste of power. What would it be like if we weren't all just some hippie witches who like to ferment things and call it magic?" Sunray chuckled but there was an edge to it, her last sentence sounding like someone else's voice, someone else's insult. "We were supportive when she brought in Sora after her parents died. Sora's such a joyful person, talented beyond what she understands. I think sometimes Sandra holds her back without meaning to. She's sure Sora will be a great healer and has focused her learning on that, but she's young. She needs to find things on her own.

"And then Darcy. Sure, some felt anyone with the wrong genitals didn't belong on the farm. But most of us, we saw a very vulnerable person who reminded us of you."

I sat back against the bench seat of the truck, harder than I meant as the full scope of Sunray's words hit me. When I had left for Seattle all those years ago, I hadn't thought of all the other women who had been a part of raising me all those years. Who had been in my corner whether I knew it or not. And then I thought of Darcy. My jealousy toward her. Of Sandra's overprotectiveness toward her. Maybe I could connect it all and make more sense of it but with my lack of sleep, I became overwhelmed. Tears rolled down my face and I let out a sob followed by another until I was shaking and crying.

"Oh, honey. There, there." Sunray reached out and patted my knee. Normally I would have dismissed all the cliches in her comfort but right then, it was what I needed. We drove in silence the rest of the way as I hiccupped my breakdown to a close.

My eyes were dry but probably still red and puffy as we pulled into the hospital parking lot. Another surge of guilt hit me as I tried to plan how I was going to ditch Sunray and get out of the hospital. Without seeing Sandra.

I didn't want to leave without saying goodbye, but I couldn't risk it. I was already guilty of so many things including her being in the hospital that I figured adding more to the pile was fine. I also didn't want to risk running into Alex, who often came in the morning to visit Sandra. I paused to consider the new knowledge of their history together. I hadn't known Sandra as well as I had thought.

"She'll be discharged in the next day or so," Sunray said as she opened the door of her truck and got out. I reluctantly followed her as she walked to the hospital entrance.

"Already?" I said to fill in the space.

"Honey, it's been over two weeks." Sunray stopped and frowned at me. "She deserves to be home where she can get sleep without someone coming in every hour to check her vital signs and asking if she's had a bowel movement. She's ready."

"Right. Of course. Time has been a blur lately," I sighed . And it had. Days and nights were bleeding together, events seemed like yesterday and eons ago.

"Come on. I know this is hard." Sunray patted me on the shoulder. "You haven't had a great track run with hospitals this year, have you?"

I thought back to the Seattle hospital, a place I had been blocking out of my head for weeks now. The gray of the sky outside, the gray of the walls, the hum of fluorescents, the beeps of machines around me and through the walls. I thought of everything physical to avoid remembering the emptiness I had felt inside but it always came back around.

"No. I —" I stopped in my tracks and looked at the doors a few yards away. "I need a minute. Do you mind if I catch up with you?"

Sunray looked at me with a piercing gaze for a few seconds before nodding and turning away. I felt as transparent as wet tracing paper, as if she could see my plan written on my forehead. Which was odd since I didn't fully know my plan.

"We'll be in room 34 when you're ready. Don't forget to check in with the nursing station for the visitor pass," Sunray said before walking off with her mug of coffee. I leaned against the truck and watched her disappear through the automatic doors. I waited a few seconds more and moved quickly through the cars in the parking lot, dodging the glowing circles from the streetlights that had not gone off yet. The overcast sky kept the rising sun shrouded in gray. I crept across the road we had driven in on and through another parking lot toward a line of tall pines on the edge of the hospital grounds, looking to avoid being on roads or sidewalks for now.

On the other side of the trees was a quiet neighborhood of gravel roads and small unassuming houses. I wandered for ten minutes past houses to paved streets before a sense of despondency enveloped me. What was I doing? I was in sweatpants and an old sweater trudging around Coos Bay as if I knew where I was going.

I reached for my phone to map a way to the nearest bus station. It wasn't in my pocket. I must have left it in my room. I had my wallet at least but the lack of phone was disconcerting.

Who does that? I was exhausted from the unexpected visit to the Other and general lack of sleep for days. I settled on that excuse to keep myself from spiraling as nothing good would come of that. At least no one could track me, a bleakly humorous thought.

I turned and started walking downhill, a direction I figured would lead to the big bay the city sat along. That at least was a landmark to help orient me. And hopefully I could find a cup of coffee. It was early, not yet 7 a.m., but I tried to maintain hope. After coffee, I would look for the bus depot and take the first route out to anywhere. I thought about Kiz and Tuna curled up on my bed and a pang hit me. How could I leave them? But they would be safer with the other witches than with me. I would take this sliver of demon lurking inside me and get away from those I loved so it couldn't reach them. Not through me. It had almost taken Sandra. I couldn't risk anyone else.

A distant figure was walking up the hill toward me on the opposite side of the street. Just someone out for a morning jog, I thought as the hair on my arms stood up under my sweater. I wasn't dressed warmly enough for a March morning, trying to explain away the chills running across my lower back. The figure crossed the street. I turned quickly to my right onto another gravel street, hoping it went through. I got to the corner and looked back. No one was there. I considered waiting, to prove to myself I was being paranoid, but I kept going, turning left and heading back downhill. I needed to get out of these quiet neighborhoods.

As I resumed walking, I thought I saw the flicker of curtains as I passed houses. Window blinds being peaked through. I wished the sun would come out now as I walked through the gray dimness. A bank of fog appeared on the street below me, like a cloud had dropped from the sky in defeat. I steeled myself to keep going, to push through, when I saw another figure in the mist. And a second one. Both walking toward me. I looked behind me. The fog was a wall of white there too, and as I stared in horror, a third figure appeared.

I ran in a blind panic to my right, up someone's driveway and into a small backyard. No lights came on in the house as I ran across the slippery grass, thankful for the workouts Alex had been making me do. I crashed through the shrubs at the end of that backyard, branches scratching my cheeks, and into another yard. I tripped over the tire of a child's prone bicycle, righting myself without crashing to the ground and kept going past another house. As I passed the front of the house, lights went on inside. I sped up and flew down the driveway into the street.

A horn blared. Headlights blazed suddenly and then I was on the other side and running up a slope of grass. I glanced back. A car was stopped in the street and a person was shouting. I didn't stop to find out what they were saying. The slope leveled out at the top where a wall of shrubs stood. I broke my way through them only to hit a tall chain link fence.

I clung to the fence panting, clutching my side. I hadn't run that hard and fast in years. I heard voices down the hill. I tried to pull myself up over the fence but the pain in my side from the sprint made it impossible. I didn't have the upper body strength to climb it right then. I quickly picked my way along the fence staying in the bushes, hoping they continued and wouldn't leave me exposed.

The fence ended after a few yards, continuing up to the right. A small forest continued past the fence. I slowed to a quick walk and moved into the darkness of the trees. The fog was thick here and as I walked carefully and quietly, trying not to trip on tree roots, my face caught little spider webs. Another well of panic built up in my chest as I wiped away the sticky silk from the webs I was destroying. Was I going crazy? Or was I being chased? I had good reason to think I was being chased. The truck that ran us off the road. The mob that had surrounded Alex. I sped up, weaving faster through the trees.

I heard nothing behind, but I kept going until the trees thinned and I came out into a clearing. Fog clung to the edges of everything, obscuring the distance. I could make out a play structure in red and blue across the clearing. I breathed a small sigh of relief. I was in a park. No one was chasing me. I was being paranoid. I took a step forward, heading into the clearing.

A figure stepped out from behind the play structure. I stopped. Just someone on a walk, I told myself. Heat wrapped around one of my fingers. I looked down. My ring pulsed red. A warning. Another figure emerged and then a third. I couldn't see faces or much of a form, just figures in the mist. The image of the banshees popped into my head. The ring glowed again.

Panic bled into my limbs, threatening to freeze me to the stop. The figures didn't move. Surely I wasn't in the Other again. I looked around. Trees and fog, nothing else. But those three shapes in the fog weren't morning joggers. I was certain of that, finally trusting my intuition.

Did they see me? I waited, hoping I was out of sight in the trees and fog. I felt a sudden urge to pull the fog close to me, like a cloak. The ring went cold, the familiar sensation of moisture like raindrops on my palm. . The fog closed in around me slowly and unlike in the Other, it made me feel safe. I turned to leave.

A haunted cry went up from behind me. No. I wasn't in the Other. I couldn't be. I turned around slowly, afraid to look. The three figures were there but shrunken now. Another piercing wail went up from one as it moved forward. A deep welling of fear shot down to my feet. The figure bobbed and twisted and another followed. A third cry and the figure turned, the fog dissipating.

A peacock. They were all peacocks, calling to their flock in the early morning. I breathed out a sigh. I was losing my mind. I choked back a laugh. Just peacocks.

Three heads swiveled toward me. Their eyes glowed eerily. Did peacocks have glowing eyes? Blue glowing eyes? They watched me intently, suddenly still. Like predators waiting to strike.

I slowly stepped back and into the trees as they continued to stare. I turned and swiftly but quietly trotted away. The fog moved with me, clearing enough in front of me that I could see my way around rhododendrons and huge ferns but creating a white wall behind me. I stopped after I felt I had crossed enough distance and listened. No sound of leaves crunching underfoot. Nothing appeared to be following me.

A cry rose up to my right, the haunting call of a peacock. I took another few steps. Another call to my right. Was that one closer? I picked up the pace. Another wail, this time behind me. Closer than before. I ran, as fast as my shaking legs could carry me.

Chapter 25

My chest burned as I ran. Thin branches whipped into my face. I tripped over a tree root, managing to right myself but twisting my ankle in the process. The pain forced me to slow down. I was at the edge of the park, still heading downhill. An image of trying to run uphill with mutant peacocks chasing me ran through my head. I would have been doomed.

I couldn't hear anything behind me as I slowed to a painful limp. Walk it out, walk it out, I thought as I pressed forward through the fog and reluctantly out of the trees. I felt exposed as I crossed a street, feeling sure a glare of headlights would burn suddenly through the fog and mow me down. I made it across with no issue. Everything was quiet, no noise of roadways or people waking, as if the fog was shutting out all sound. That didn't make me feel any better.

On the other side of the street was a short grassy slope and another chain link fence. I reached it and peered through the metal x-pattern. Boxy white cars lined up in rows in the parking lot beyond the fence. They were familiar but for a second, I couldn't place them. Mail trucks. I was at a post office.

The banality of it set my mind at ease. A post office. Where people in uniforms worked and sorted letters and packages. Sold stamps. It sounded safe. Or safer than being out in the fog with weird birds and lurking figures. I followed the fence to my right until I found a big gate that was open, leading into the parking lot.

I walked in cautiously, the pain in my ankle subsiding, though not enough to run. I didn't want to run anymore. My throat was raw from the exertion and my skin felt clammy as the sweat dried. I needed to get somewhere warmer and take a minute to rest. I walked past the ghostly boxy cars and toward the loading bays with roll up doors like mini-garages all in a row. A set of stairs off to the side climbed up to a cement outcrop and a set of double doors. Warm yellow light glowed through the barred glass windows of each of the doors. I wished desperately for the doors to be unlocked.

I pushed on the door. It didn't budge. Locked. I leaned forward and hung my head against the door in frustration. Below my head were short door handles. I pulled tentatively on the right handle and the door swung open. Shaking my head at my stupidity, I walked in.

A wide hallway with beige walls and beige linoleum spread out before me. I walked down it to another set of doors and through to a silent sorting room. It was somehow quieter inside than outside. I had expected the sounds of envelopes being shuffled, of metal equipment engaged, the voices of co-workers bantering about working for the weekend. There was a strange absence of smell as well, just a hint of something burnt. Old office coffee maybe. I walked on through a series of short hallways and unlocked doors, simultaneously hoping to see someone and dreading it. Where was everyone? Maybe it was Sunday. I had lost track of what day of the week it was. But why would the backdoor be unlocked?

I was peering into the window of a dark office when I heard a distant swishing sound. The same sound of the back doors opening. People! I started to backtrack when my ring warmed. I looked down at its red glow. I swallowed my panic as best I could and walked quickly down the hallway, hoping it would take me out, trying to be as quiet as possible and cringing as my sneakers squeaked on the linoleum. I pushed through a set of doors into a long, wide room. Rows of post office boxes lined the long wall in front of me. There were no doors. And no windows. A bank of fluorescent lights buzzed above me. I backed out of the door, about to retrace my steps when I heard the footsteps. Multiple people. I assumed they were people. I heard faint voices.

"She's here. I'm sure of it."

"This way. I can smell witch."

My fear reared up and I had to take a deep breath to not break into a panic blind run. I retreated into the post office box room. Maybe I could hide. I fumbled with the door handles as my hands shook, looking for a lock. My fingers found the handle lock buttons and gratefully pushed them in. I switched the lights off, plunging into almost pitch black save the light from the windows in the door. I moved deep into the room to the left, as far from the light as possible.

The room seemed so much longer in the dark. My feet caught on an industrial runner rug and I flailed, my arms pumping like a cartoon until I righted myself. I moved to the wall of post office boxes, running my right hand along them for stability. My ankle twinged, reminding me it couldn't take much more. I needed to get off my feet, but that wasn't an option.

I could hear movement and voices getting closer in the hallway. I froze, hoping I was invisible in the dark and far enough from the rectangles of light from the door. I kept going, as quietly as possible. I knew I was trapped but if I could get to the dark corner, maybe that would buy me some time. Time to do what besides wish I had made different choices, I didn't know, but time seemed precious.

My right hand landed on the next post office box. A sudden low glow on it caught my attention. As I turned to examine it, my ring grew cold and damp on my left hand. There in small script was the number 11 glowing in a soft orange. I cupped my hand around it, trying to hide the glow from anyone who might peer inside the door as I looked closer at it. Why would there be a glowing number on a post office box?

The key from the Evernia. Wynona had said it was a key to a post office box. It had to be for this weird glowing 11. If only I had brought it! My ring tightened on my finger to the point of discomfort and glowed red. I shoved it in my pocket to try to hide the glow. My fingers brushed against cold metal and closed around a small key. I had the key with me. How was that even remotely possible? But I had been to the Other, guided by the Evernia.

I heard voices in the immediate hallway, shadows darkening the door windows.

"She's got to be in here!"

"There's nowhere else she could've gone."

"She could have left."

"Nah, I still feel that witch around here."

The sound of the door handles jiggling. The cry of male voices that it was locked and a follow-up plan of finding something to smash the windows. I didn't have time for magic post office boxes. Though maybe that's all I had time for. Maybe there was a gun inside of it. Or a weapon I knew how to use. I pulled the key from my pocket and jabbed in the dark until it slipped into the keyhole. It made a satisfying click just as I heard noise from the hallway.

"I see movement! She's in there!" Shouts came from outside the door. I turned my head to see looming figures backlit by the hallway lights. I watched in horror as one of the figures lifted something and hit the glass. The thump was dull, and the glass didn't break but the sound sent terror racing through my limbs.

"Stop being a dumbass and put that down. Smith is bringing the key."

I didn't have much time. I pulled on the little key to open the post office box door. It didn't budge, like it was stuck. Or really heavy, which couldn't be the case. I backed up from where I had been leaning, ready to pull.

"We're coming to get you, witchy!" The voice yelled through the door. It sounded familiar.

"Shut up, Dawson!"

Great, Officer Dickface was here. Please let me open this, I prayed. And please let there be something useful inside. I feared it'd be a journal, something fascinating I would love but pointless in my current predicament.

I pulled and something heavy and metal hit my foot. I bit back a yelp of pain and then one of surprise. In the dim light I could see that rather than the tiny opening I was expecting there was a door. An entire door. The fronts of all the little boxes were connected into a secret door. A cold fog trickled out around my feet from the other side, and it seemed even darker in there than where I was. Was I going to go from bad to worse by going through this magic door?

The jingling of keys and a few shouts of victory from the hallway made my decision. If Dawson was there, so was the demon seeker. I would take my chances on the other side of the door. I pulled the key out and slipped around the door just as I heard the other doors opening behind me and the shift in air of people pouring into the room. I felt frantically for a doorknob on the other side to shut them out, finally finding a small moon-shaped crevice that pulled it shut, sending me into complete darkness.

It was quiet on the other side of the door. And pitch black. I waited, trying to hear if they were on the other side trying to open the door before realizing I was being an idiot. I needed to put as much distance between the mob and me as possible. Though I couldn't help feeling that by going through the door, I was already far away. From everything.

I put my arms out and found smooth walls, cold to the touch, on both sides. I was in a long skinny room. Or hallway, hopefully. There was only one way to go, forward. I knelt down quickly and touched the floor, hoping to get some sort of clue there. It felt like cement or stone, cold and a little damp. I got up and cautiously moved forward, feeling my way along the walls, all while waiting to hear the sound of anything from the other side and hoping the floor didn't give way to a giant hole before me. Silence filled the cold air around me.

I walked and hit a dead end. The familiar feeling of panic overwhelmed me. I was in a big coffin, a tomb. My own tomb. I reached out to the walls on my left and felt air. The hallway turned to the left, that was all. I kept going and it turned to the right. This time, there was a faint bit of light at the end of the hallway, thin lines around what I hoped would be an unlocked door.

I got to the end and found small wooden door, a little less than my height. It felt worn and smooth like it had been used for hundreds of years. There was no door handle. I sucked in my breath and hoped for the best as I pushed. The door wasn't heavy, but it opened reluctantly, as if it hadn't been used in a long time. The hinges creaked softly, the first noise in a long time besides my own breathing and footfalls.

The light blinded me for a second before I stepped out. I was in a strange shell of a building. It was a large room with big arches lining the front of it. Furniture lay in discarded heaps and strange metal shelves made up of little squares lay all helter-skelter. Moss covered everything and ferns were growing from the stone wall I had exited from. The strange metal shelves were old post office boxes, little metal doors dangling from a few. The big arches in front were open, though as I carefully walked forward, I saw the remains of panes of glass where there had once been windows.

Mist curled around the edges of the big, abandoned room. A thick fog obscured any view out of the archways. I cautiously moved forward, a dull crunch under my feet as I walked. The floor was littered with letters, hundreds and hundreds of envelopes turning brown around the edges and crumbling to dust like fallen leaves. I bent over to get a closer look at one. Though there was writing on the front of it, the ink was smeared so badly as to be illegible. It was strange that the letters were simultaneously damp looking but sounded like leaves. I glanced up and saw that instead of a roof, it was a large cave with stalactites hanging. The whole place felt otherworldly.

Otherworldly. I paused and almost cursed out loud. I was back in the Other. Which was disconcerting on so many levels. Would I meet the banshees again? Or worse, the demon. And then the real horror hit. Where was my body in the real world? Had the demon seeker found me unconscious in that post office back in Coos Bay? I felt prickling goosebumps at the thought. I had to hope the portal wasn't all in my head. It had felt real. Before I shut the door, I had heard a shout about not letting me get away. I fought the urge to panic but was failing miserably. A fat tear rolled down my cheek as I collapsed on the floor.

I sat on the dead letters and cried for a while, all sobs and snot. How I wished I was a pretty crier as I wiped my nose with my sweater. This was the second time today I had broken down. It wasn't a good track record. Unlike the cry in Sunray's car, this didn't leave me feeling lighter the way a good cry can.

At some point I had no tears left or energy to keep crying. I sat there numbly, wishing for a tissue or a whole box as my nose continued to drip. I looked down at the letters I was sitting on, wondering if I could use them to blow my nose. My eyes scanned the different colored illegible scrawls in different handwriting, some with little stamps desperately clinging to the envelope. I made out a word. North. And what looked like "pole." I stopped. North Pole? I reached out tentatively, recalling Darcy's admonishment not to touch anything in the Other before deciding not to worry about that. My body, wherever it was, had bigger issues than pink eye from a paper cut in the Other.

The letter felt fragile and damp in my fingers. I held it gingerly and looked at the front. It was addressed to Mr. Claus of the North Pole with a small aging snowflake stamp. I flipped it over. There was no return address on it. I let it flutter to the ground and picked up a handful underneath it. Two more for Santa, one for the Easter Bunny, one too old and smudged to read and one addressed to "My Beloved" with the address line saying "Hell?" None of the letters had return addresses. Some had stamps, some didn't.

I spent a few more minutes looking through the letters. All were made out to make-believe entities like Santa Claus or were being sent to places beyond, such as heaven or hell. I was in some sort of dead letter room. I started to sort them into piles by type before recognizing that I was just distracting myself from my real problem. Sorting letters in the Other wasn't going to make this raging caffeine withdrawal headache go away.

Wait a minute. I stood and stretched. My muscles were stiff and painful from the bursts of running, the exhaustion from the Other, and the overall wear and tear from the past weeks. I didn't remember such a clear physical presence from my body when I was in the Other. There were sensations, the overwhelming cold I had felt from the demon and the potential pain from the wrong plant. But most of the day-to-day physical hadn't translated Had it? Having only been a few times and only once intentionally, I was second-guessing myself.

I walked around the large room, noticing piles of boxes flung about and moldering slowly, and made my way to the big arch windows. The fog was so thick I could see nothing. It was like a big breathing wall. I reached out my right hand and felt a weird sensation, like static. It was familiar. I reached out my left hand, watching for my ring to react. It glowed a warm purple, something I had never seen from it before. I moved my hand in the fog back and forth. It was like passing over a curtain charged with static electricity. Then I placed it. It felt like the time Darcy had taken me into the Other.

I dropped my hand back and looked out. I wasn't in the Other, but I didn't know where I was, some sort of border perhaps. I wished Darcy was here. Maybe she would know. I wished Keena, Sora, and Alex were also here. I sighed. I had been sort of successful in my plan to run away but was now faced with how pointless it was. Here I was trapped in a no man's land of dead letters sandwiched between a demon seeker's mob and the Other. The Other where the demon resided. Maybe I should just spend the rest of my life here sorting letters with no destination.

My stomach growled and I was suddenly aware of how much I needed a glass of water, how I had skipped breakfast. And my fantasies of being the postmaster dried up. I had tried to run away from my problems, but I was always going to end up here. Not here in the abandoned dead letter room but here having to face my demons. Literally.

I turned from the window staring out into the Other. The room that had seemed so vast was smaller than I had thought. Still large but I could sweep my eyes through and take it in. The back wall was the same mottled pale brown as the ceiling, streaked with deep golden brown from centuries of water running down. The ferns glowed green against it, tucked into crevices and hanging down. The door I had come through almost disappeared into it all. That was my choice, the Other with a demon or the real world with demon seeker mobs. The hairs on the back of my neck stood up as I felt a strange tug deep inside me, pulling me to the Other. I turned and looked into the fog. The Other was calling, telling me the choice.

I snapped my head back around. No. That wasn't the Other. That was the demon, that little piece lodged inside me that was trying to lure me to it. My stomach growled again, a reminder I was in a physical body that needed taken care of. The Other would take more out of me. I was weak, too weak to battle a demon in a realm I didn't understand.

Then I saw it. Off to the right of the door, dug deeper into the rock and almost hidden by a denser patch of ferns dripping over it, was another doorway. I walked away from the Other, the pull increasing for a moment as if I was walking against a strong wind before dissipating. I stepped carefully around piles of damp boxes and trod as lightly as I could on the letters, feeling bad for stomping on the discarded dreams they represented.

The doorway was set back into the rock about a foot. A pile of boxes was in front of it, almost as if stacked to block anyone from using it. I had to restack a few out of the way to get closer, trying not to get distracted by the boxes themselves, which were as intriguing as the letters. Maybe more so since they had items inside.

When I was able to get up to it, the door was shorter and more gnarled than the other door. In some ways, it looked like the tree it was made from more than a door: streaked with orange and white lichen patches, a rough bark-like texture ran over it begging to put splinters in my fingers and. There didn't appear to be a door handle. I pushed. The door resisted like it was welded shut. Or grown shut more likely. I pushed harder. Nothing. A surge of anger pulsed through me, and I pushed as hard as I could, my feet sliding on the smooth damp floor suddenly. The boxes behind me stopped me from sliding onto my face.

I paused, brushing my hands on my sweats to try to remove the bits of wood and lichen clinging to them. The frustration tried to creep back up, but I pushed it down. It wasn't helping me, and I didn't need to use up my limited energy on being mad. I took a few deep breaths like Darcy and Keena had taught me and reexamined the door. I lightly ran my hands over the wood, seeking carefully with my fingertips for a hidden handle. My fingers found a burl, raised up off the wood more than usual. I slid my fingers around it and found there was a space underneath it. I unsuccessfully banished the thought of spiders and delicately reached my fingertips into the crevice.

It felt smooth, cold, and damp. My fingers probed deeper until they found a small, raised bump that reminded me of a smaller version of the burl. I pressed on it. A deep click sounded in the hall, echoing off the curved roof. The door slowly opened inward to darkness.

I peered into the black void before me. I weighed my options. I already knew it was a terrible idea to go back into the Other in the state I was in. Maybe the other door was an option to go back through, hoping those hunting me on the other side had moved on. I didn't want to risk it, though. If they were smart and as numerous as I feared, it would be easy to leave someone there to guard it. The best option was the unknown, as unsettled as that felt. I looked at my ring. Nothing. I had to make this decision on my own. I took a deep breath and stepped into the dark.

Chapter 26

I fought the urge to turn around as the door slammed shut behind me. I didn't know if the door would open for me again on this side but unlike in the last passage, I felt more confident that going back was safe. Well, as safe as any border land to another dimension could be. I reached out to find the edges of the wall and walked forward. The walls were gnarled and crumbly, something like cool damp sand giving way under my fingertips. I tripped over something on the ground, catching myself on the walls. A little shower of the sand fell onto my forearms. I tentatively bent down and touched the ground in front of me. Like the walls, it felt damp and sandy with hard organic shapes snaking around.

Roots, I thought. It felt like I was walking through the roots of a tree underground. I probably was. I continued my journey, much slower than the last trip as I continued to trip on unexpected roots and occasional rocks. It would be nice if my ring would glow now, I thought miserably as my foot caught again, aggravating my tender ankle. I was glad I could walk without limping, but one more wrench on a root and I might twist it to an unwalkable state. I'd be stuck underground with no one to help, not even a clue as to how to find me. I took a deep breath, held it for a few counts, and slowly though a bit raggedly breathed out. I could not panic. The ring stayed dark.

I lost sense of the time passing. It could have been ten minutes. It could have been an hour. I kept steadily moving forward and trying to not let my mind stay on any buried-alive fears that kept popping up. Later, I told myself. I could melt into a panicked puddle later.

Right as the last of my calm was evaporating, I reached a bend. The palest of light came through holes in the wall as I turned right.

A door, I hoped. Please be a door.

I moved in front of it and pushed hard. The door swung open so easily I almost did a face plant. Cool, fresh air hit my face. It was dark but it was outside. The smell of pines and rotting leaves filled my nostrils. Towering tree trunks soared above me. The sky was the deep teal of the sky at dusk, the stars yet to reveal themselves.

My relief at being above ground faded like the last of the light. Where was I? Was I in the Other? I whipped my head around, searching for mist, for some sign I was in the nightmare forest of the banshees. I checked in with my body. I was still hungry and incredibly thirsty. I could feel the cold of the night air, but it wasn't the bone chilling cold from the Other. My fingers felt gritty had dark streaks of dirt from the underground tunnel. I looked behind me at the dark passage. I was in the middle of a forest at night. Should I wait in the tunnel until the morning?

My stomach gurgled. I didn't want to wait. I didn't know if waiting was smart, but it felt like the wrong choice. I stepped forward, noticing the faint twinge in my ankle. A loud creaking began behind me. I turned to watch roots crisscrossing the doorway like a mass of snakes until it was just a tall, scarred notch in the bark of a great cedar.

I immediately regretted the loss of the option to wait until morning. I had desperately wanted out of the tunnel but now I wanted back in. I rushed forward, tracing my hands over the notch trying to find a way to open it back up. The key! I pulled it out and held it up to the door. As with the post office box, it glowed a faint green and a small keyhole appeared in the middle of the bark. I put it in and turned. The roots uncrossed, opening up. A breath of relief rushed out of me. Going back was still an option.

I turned and stepped away, listening to the door re-knit itself behind me. The knowledge of having a choice, to stay in the safety of the passage, gave me the strength to go forward. I looked around for something to mark my way. I stooped over to see if there were any pebbles I could create a trail with, but the darkness combined with the thick underbrush all around me ruled that out. How did Hansel and Gretel manage it with breadcrumbs? I stood and started to walk. I had somehow found the hidden post office door. I had found my way out of the dead letter cave. I had to keep having faith it would work. Somehow.

It only took a few minutes after the light faded to complete darkness for me to feel lost. I had tried to walk in a straight line, but the damp underbrush and the trees made that impossible. Looking over my shoulder, I couldn't see the door tree at all. I had a vague notion of where it was, but my certainty was waning. I kept walking until I reached a small clearing.

I stopped on the edge of the tree line. The moon wasn't out yet but the open sky above the clearing provided more light. The clearing looked familiar. Like the one in the Other the Evernia stag had led me to. Uneasiness threaded down me for a second. That was the Other. This was my world. My stomach growled to prove my point.

A dark shape suddenly appeared in the middle of the clearing, followed by another one. Green eyes glowed briefly as one of the shapes shot toward me. A growl came as the second shape ran forward hot after the other. Fear coursed through me, but I was frozen. Run, I yelled in my mind, RUN!

A short bark brought me out of my fear. I thought I recognized it.

"Bear?" I said tentatively, hopefully. "Flame?"

Bear barked happily at the recognition, reaching me swiftly. He jumped up on my thighs, doggy nails digging in. Flame followed right on his heels and nipped at them. With an indignant yip, Bear dropped down to wiggle his whole bottom while I bent and stroked his head. Flame stood behind Bear and watched.

"What are you two doing out here?" I asked while Bear took it upon himself to leap up and lick my cheek. I reached out a tentative hand to Flame who I had never petted, never touched. Flame stepped forward, sniffed, and let out a low, short half bark. Bear turned as if an errant soldier and reluctantly trotted over to Flame who immediately turned and strode to the left across the clearing. Bear followed with a slight limp in his back leg from his demon run-in. He turned back to me, running over and then back to Flame as if to say, "Come on!" I quickly took off after Flame who didn't turn back once. I knew the two would lead me home.

Home. I was such a fool. Thinking I should leave the only place that truly felt like home. I had left the memories of Seattle behind, no longer wistful for my life in the city. Well, sometimes I wished for a truly great restaurant to go out to, but now I couldn't imagine going without Sora to see her enthusiasm with the food. Or Darcy to turn heads with her fashionable presence. Or Keena who would keep warm conversation flowing. And Alex who would grumble but keep us all laughing with her jokes. Sandra would need to be there, promising to leave early and then cajoling us into one last round. My eyes teared up at the thought. I wanted to see all of them again, right now.

As we crossed the clearing, I recognized the thin path I had followed with the Evernia the night before. An odd thought since it was night again, but I didn't feel like a whole day had passed. Nor was I sure I had followed the Evernia on this exact path or if it was a duplicate in the Other. A sense of unease settled along my spine as I followed the dogs. I would have missed the path on my own, but I hoped Bear and Flame wouldn't morph before my eyes into banshees, dashing my hopes of home to pieces.

Flame stopped and looked back at me for a second, her golden colored eyes obscured in the dark, but the message was clear. Keep it together, Reva. We walked on.

As we got closer, I heard a familiar but indistinct sound in the distance. Or sounds. Shouting? I picked up the pace. Through the trees, I saw a strange glow. Not the usual faint warm glow of the farmhouse. This was a brighter glow. Also familiar. Orange? I began to run, the dogs at my heels as I flew to the edge of the forest. I stopped between the two sentinel cedars and let my mind catch up to the sight unfolding before me.

A mob of white hooded figures surrounded the farmhouse, shouting and raging. I heard the word "witch" and "send her out". Behind the house was the source of the orange glow. Sandra's trailer was ablaze, flames roaring out of the broken windows. The cedar fence ringing it hadn't caught fully due to the recent rain, but it was losing the battle. Behind that, dark smoke rose from Alex's trailer. More figures in white were dancing in front of the trailers as if they were at a merry bonfire, just needing hot dogs on sticks to make it a party.

My knees buckled as I caught myself and leaned against one of the cedars, frozen again. Where were my fellow witches? I was relieved the farmhouse wasn't on fire, though I didn't dare to imagine anyone would still be in the burning trailers. The mob seemed to be focused on the house and for some reason, not able to approach it.

I glanced over at the other side of the farm. The houses of the other commune members were dark but appeared to be intact. Where were all of them? And why wasn't the mob attacking their houses? And how did the mob get in? Perhaps the wards were down.

As I watched, I saw movement in the windows. A firework like a bottle rocket flew out and into the crowd, bursting into red hot coals that rained down on the mob as they ducked and screamed. Alex. I hadn't seen her magic at work before, but it had her signature all over it. The back door opened, and a woman ran at full speed out of it across the fields in front of me. The members of the mob who were close chased her, others following until a mass of them were running. Keena. My heart leapt into my throat. Why was Keena racing out of the house like this? Was she mad? She was nearing the edge of the trees across the field.

I opened my mouth to yell out to her when I felt a sharp nip on my shin. I let out a surprised yelp and turned around. Bear was behind me, looking incredibly guilty. He shifted his eyes to Keena as she ran. I watched as Keena evaporated, leaving a thin white trail of smoke or mist.

I remembered from Alex's story this was Keena's gift, the projected prey illusion. The mob that had chased her began yelling and turning in circles trying to find out where she went. A few ran into the trees, sure she had escaped into them. Cries of terror erupted from the forest where they had run. More ran in after them and similar cries came. One or two who had just entered came struggling out, pulling vines off them as if they were poison. Which maybe they were. Sora's handiwork.

I fell back into the trees and crept to a different vantage point where I could see the front porch. The crowd was thickest here, practically obscuring the front steps which no one had walked up. They milled around pushing at the air in a confused way. I guessed some sort of magic was preventing them, probably Darcy's. A few kept trying to hold their torches to the porch railing to light it like the trailers but the fire went out like cheap birthday candles, only whispers of smoke left. I could hear the mood of the crowd shifting to frustration.

As I watched, a large white truck came up the drive. It was driving fast, bouncing in the muddy ruts like someone was on a joyride, splattering the white clad crowd as it came to an abrupt stop in front of the house. A momentary quiet descended on the crowd. The door to the driver's side opened and a figure jumped out onto the ground. A loud cheer erupted, and the crowd parted to reveal the demon seeker walking around the front grille of the truck straight up to the porch.

Dawson popped his head out the passenger side of the truck and yelled with his hand in the air. A loud crack ripped out of his hand. The crowd ducked. The idiot had fired a gun. The demon seeker turned around momentarily and glared. Dawson lowered the gun and look apologetic before getting out of the truck to join the group now moving to the front steps.

I knew the demon seeker was able to breach the protective shield. He had the power of the demon on his side, the demon who had come through our wards and onto our porch. All because of me. I wanted to run, to hide from this angry mob I knew was after me. I wanted to storm down and unleash absolute rage on these people who dared to threaten my friends and burn my home. So instead, I froze and watched the demon seeker push through the shield and put his foot on the front step as the crowd roared in approval.

The door to the house opened and Alex stepped out. The demon seeker paused. I couldn't hear the words as they started to talk. There was no shouting, but I could see the tension held in both of their bodies. Dawson was dancing on both feet like a kid waiting to use the bathroom, the gun dangling in his hands. The crowd waited as well, occasional murmurs going up as they reacted to the words I couldn't hear.

It happened so fast I couldn't process it. A shot rang out. Alex fell back. The demon seeker spun around, yelling in anger. The crowd surged forward ignoring him. I watched Flame shoot out from the woods, knowing her mission to avenge her mistress was futile but not caring. Bear went barking out after Flame.

And then I was running, searing pain shooting through my ankle but I didn't care. My ring glowed hot on my hand, and the air coalesced around me, thick and hot. A howl tore out of my throat and with it a gust of wind so strong the white hoods flew off the heads of the startled crowd.

Shouts of alarm went up through the crowd and they turned to me. I didn't see where the dogs had gone. I didn't see anything. Raw fury poured out of my soul and into the air, collecting into thick storm clouds. The air became stagnant like right before a thunderstorm, the temperature rising unusually for a March night. Not that any of this registered with me. I was back on the dock in Seattle, calling forward a storm. This time though, I knew I was in charge, and I wasn't just raw hurt. I was rage. Murderous.

The demon seeker watched me as his crowd parted. Dawson raised his hand with the gun toward me, but I screamed again, a gust of wind so strong he struggled against it. One of the white hoods flew into his face. He fell to the ground, the gun going off randomly twice. A cry rang out through the crowd as someone was hit. Those closest to Dawson fell on top to pry the gun from his grasp.

The demon seeker didn't even notice. He smiled, the wide unnatural grin stretching his mouth through his cheeks. He strode toward me; the wind didn't break his stride. Every gust I sent his way, he laughed and raised his arms out as if I was showering him with confetti. We stopped within two feet of each other, sizing each other up. The rest of the fray fell away as we locked eyes.

Anthony's eyes looked out at me. It couldn't be. This generic unmemorable man had Anthony's eyes. I blinked and Anthony was standing in front of me, grinning. The wind died down as I went still. I could hear yelling behind him, the sound of my name, the sounds of car doors and motors. All of it was nothing as I stood in front of the man I had loved. Who had broken me.

"I was always here, Reva," Anthony's voice said. It was his voice. It couldn't be him though. He gave me one of his off-center grins. The asymmetry of it had always made it sexy. I could smell him, sweet musk, whiskey, and cigarettes. The smoky smell was stronger than usual.

Wait. I flinched. The smoke smell wasn't Anthony. That was the smell of a burning home. The burnt plastic smell wafted over, releasing me from the spell. I blinked, hoping the demon seeker would come back but it was still Anthony.

"I'm sorry for how things ended." He had the gall to look contrite and cast his eyes down. "It was necessary for you to learn who you really are."

"Cut the bullshit. You're not Anthony." I wanted to sound tough, but I heard the waver in my voice as I spit the words out.

"Oh, but I am. I always was." He grinned at me, a mix now of the demon seeker and Anthony. The grin turning up the corners across the stubble on his cheeks. "I can be anyone you want, Reva."

And then standing in front of me was my mother, down to her signature dyed burgundy hair and overplucked eyebrows.

"Sweetheart," Ginny purred and opened her arms for a hug.

"No." I turned away. My mother would never call me sweetheart. That was a nickname I had heard one of my friends called by her mother, a friend I had for all of four months before Ginny had uprooted us again.

"Reva." Sandra's voice. I turned back to see Sandra standing in front of me, glowing with health and her eyes pooled with tears. I choked back a sob.

"It's alright, Reva. Hug?" Sandra held out her arms. She sounded just like Sandra. I felt the pull of that hug, all the forgiveness I needed from her all in that simple gesture. That was something Sandra would offer.

A searing pain shot up my hand and into my arm. I looked down at my ring, glowing red hot. I stepped back.

"You're not Sandra." Tears poured down my cheeks.

"I can be anyone you want, Reva." Demon Sandra replied. And then before my eyes, Sandra fell away to Mikhael. He looked at me with big gray eyes and smiled.

"Reva!" I heard Mikhael's voice, but it didn't come from the creature in front of me. I tore my eyes off and saw him standing next to a prone Dawson. A crowd of people were standing with him, Wynona by his side. The white-power crowd had scattered, a few on the ground next to a person crying and holding their thigh. More of the newcomers were up on the porch, gathering up Alex. Darcy and Keena were with them. I didn't see Sora, but I suddenly felt she was close. They were all close. And the newcomers were the tribe. Mikhael and Wynona had come to help despite not owing us anything. Less than anything.

"Reva." The creature in front of me pulled me back. And this time, I saw it clearly. I saw the demon from my visions. From the Other. There was no face, just empty hunger in a dark void. It reached out and I felt it, the cold that went through bone. And the feeling, depression magnified a thousand times. A hundred thousand times. The lack of emotion. Of anything.

The wail of banshees went up around me. And then it spoke. In its real voice.

Succumb.

Give in.

I was never going to escape. I felt the pull, it was buried in me. The demon standing in front of me was one the manifestations of what had already taken root in my soul. Soon I would have no choice. I would follow it into the abyss. It would be worse than death. Worse than anything I could ever imagine.

I felt desperately inside myself for something, anything to try to fight it. And there, buried deep was the spark. I had felt it before. It had saved me before. But only temporarily. It had to be more than a spark this time. At whatever cost that meant.

I raised my fist to the sky. The spark traveled up and shot up into the clouds above me. Only I could see it. The demon in front of me only felt my power build, a power it hungered for. I could feel the clouds swirling above me, the air changing but I continued to stare into the dark void in front of me. My ring glowed but this time it was purple. The demon hesitated, but I didn't. I stepped forward and brought my arms around it. A wave of victory rolled through it. It had won. And it had. I gave myself freely to the demon and felt it merge with me, give me all of it as it took all from me. In that split second, I felt it. The power, the what-if. I could have ruled the world if I wanted to give up my soul.

Then the lightning I had called down hit, right through the clouds and down to us in our demon embrace. I felt the sear, unbelievable pain and hot white light shattering as the demon screamed before everything went black.

Chapter 27

Pain was the first sensation, pain all over. Then it was the absence of sensations, all darkness and silence. I drifted in and out of consciousness. I guessed I wasn't dead but at times I wished for it. They tell me that was the first three days.

The pain stayed but the silence and darkness faded. The noise returned first, electronic beeps and voices. I didn't want to make out what they were saying at first, but bits and pieces came through.

"She should be dead."

"Absolute miracle."

Sometimes all I felt was pressure in my throat, like a creature was sitting in it, and a sensation of wanting to breathe but having it taken away right as I would try to draw in air. And thirst, an incredible thirst that never seemed to be quenched. Later I found out it was a breathing tube, removed after a few days when I was still unconscious.

The word *scars* came through in the flotsam of noise around me, fascination or revulsion of scars depending on the person.

I didn't recognize the voices when my hearing returned at first. Then I did.

"Hi Reva. Hang in there, honey." Keena's soft words.

"You're healing amazingly well, Reva." Sora's optimism cutting through the haze of pain.

"Stay with us, Reva." Darcy's honeyed voice, thick with emotion.

"We love you," Sandra said over and over. How I missed her voice, all that time I had hidden from her in guilt. But here she was for me.

The one voice missing was Alex. I thought of Alex falling back on the porch. Where was Alex? Had we lost her? Then the voices would increase, sounding agitated and I would go back to sleep.

My vision returned slowly, first blurry light and shapes, but slowly I could see more. Sandra sleeping next to my bed in the night. A glimpse of Keena at the foot of the hospital bed. A swish of black velvet as Darcy left through a door. Sora pouring water for someone. Still no Alex.

The doctors kept remarking on my strange recovery as if I was not present. And in a way, I wasn't. Senses were returning but my voice wasn't. But it wasn't just physical, from the soreness left by the breathing tube. I didn't know what to say. If I opened my mouth and spoke, I was afraid of all that would pour out. All the questions. And even worse, I was afraid of the answers.

I opened my eyes one early morning as a nurse was monitoring me. Sandra slept on a chair beside me, gently snoring.

"Good morning, Reva," the nurse said cheerily and with no softness. Sandra's snoring cut short as she woke. She groggily rubbed her eyes.

"You shouldn't be sleeping in this chair, Sandra," the nurse chided as she finished with some chart notes. "You're still recovering yourself. That can't be good for your hip."

"Oh, don't start, Becky. I don't want to leave her side. Not until she wakes up," Sandra replied grumpily.

"She looks to be awake now." Becky the nurse flicked her pen at me and smiled before continuing her scold to Sandra. "You won't be any use to her if you don't take care of you."

Sandra ignored her and looked at me, recognizing an alertness in me that must have been missing in the past few days. Weeks? Time didn't make any sense to me.

"Good morning, Reva," she said softly, looking at me with hopeful eyes.

"Hi," I croaked out. My voice was raspy and my throat was raw.

"Welcome back." Sandra smiled widely. "We almost lost you."

Over the next few weeks, I learned bits and pieces of the story. I knew I would have to ask about the demon, but I didn't want to know. Not yet. Since no one talked about another lightning strike victim, it seemed the demon seeker and demon had vanished into smoke. I had more immediate things on my mind. The first news I demanded was what had happened to Alex.

"She was shot in the shoulder. It was touch and go at first but she's recovering," Sandra told me that morning. "We're lucky the tribe was there. Four of them are EMTs who triaged all the injuries and provided treatment before the ambulances came."

In addition to Alex, Dawson had shot a person in the crowd. Shot in the thigh, the man had survived as well only due to the Coos tribe's help. I wondered if being saved by the Coos people after being shot by a fellow white supremacist at a mob gathering would change the man's political views. I feared the answer wouldn't be as easy as I hoped.

"Alex is returning to her spitfire self," Keena said later that day. Just as with Sandra, the witches were taking turns visiting but this time with two of us in the hospital. Dark circles under

Keena's eyes worried me. She didn't look like she was sleeping but she waved me off when I tried to bring up my concern. I still couldn't talk much.

"Some of the nurses absolutely hate Alex. The others love her. Those are the ones she flirts with, the minx." Darcy's laugh was infectious. I laughed with her until I started to cough and a flair of pain surged through what felt like all my nerves. Which was probably exactly what happened.

"You'd be dead if not for the EMTs reviving you on the scene," one doctor told me. "Lightning strike victims are so rare in these parts, it is amazing they had an inkling of what to do. You should buy a lottery ticket."

"Mikhael saved you. He started your heart after you sacrificed yourself in the lightning," Sora told me after the doctor left. She looked at me with huge eyes. "Which is just the most romantic thing ever. Literally started your heart."

I groaned. "Easy, Sora. I'm still healing in so many ways."

"But pretty quickly. The doctors are amazed. And without your ring."

My ruby ring had been taken off me at the hospital, but Sandra and Darcy had secured it with the help of Linda. She worked as an ER nurse so shouldn't have had sway, but all the hospital nurses respected her, either out of appreciation or fear. She even came to visit me.

"Show me your Lichtenberg scars! They are all the talk of the hospital," Linda demanded after the usual chitchat, shushing Sandra as she tried to stop her.

"My what?" I looked at her perplexed.

"Have you not done a rundown of your own body? Honey, no! Sandra, have you all not helped her see them? You don't want her to see them on her own and flip out, do you?"

"Linda, she hasn't been able to see *anything* until a day ago," Sandra said fiercely.

"A day ago — that's too long! Okay honey, you should brace yourself for this."

Along my left arm was a strange fern-like pattern of raised red flesh. It continued up my neck and down my chest, branching out like tree limbs. Or lightning strikes. It was intricate and only slightly painful to the touch, like a burn with a slight electric shock at the end. Mild compared to the pain in the rest of my nerves.

"You know these are supposed to disappear after about forty-eight hours but yours have stayed," Linda told me. "Can you imagine what a tattoo shop would charge for this?"

I laughed but Sandra shot up out of her chair.

"Linda!" Sandra said, an appalled look quickly being replaced by a wince.

"Easy there, honey." Linda quickly shifted over to Sandra and helped her sit back down. "You know you can't move like that."

Sandra grimaced as she settled back into the chair. She looked over at me and seeing the look on my face, her face softened.

"It's not that bad."

"You have to use your cane." Linda tapped on a plastic stick next to Sandra. I hadn't seen it before. "I know you are getting a witchy one more suited to you, all carved hexes on wood —"

"Pentagrams. Not hexes."

"Whatever, you always said you wanted to embrace your crone years and slide into death with a well-used body. That means adjusting to how you can use it," Linda stated. A loud irritated voice came on the hospital intercom paging Linda. She bolted out the door with a quick wave.

"You have a cane? From the accident?" I asked after Linda left, my guilt floating to the surface again.

"Yes." Sandra looked at me. "You know that wasn't your fault, Reva."

"I know," I said while thinking otherwise.

"You don't. You've taken on the burden of what happened as if you were responsible. As if you drove the truck that ran us off the road. As if you courted that demon and invited it in."

"Didn't I?" I said quietly. And I did believe that. I had opened up somehow to let that piece of the demon in.

"No." Sandra's voice was firm, almost hard. "You were stalked and hunted by a powerful evil. Since you were born. It knew before any of us did. Before you did. You didn't invite it in. You were trapped, you were tricked. It found weaknesses and weaseled its way in."

I let that sink in. Logically, I knew all that was true. I wasn't ready yet to embrace it as true on all levels. Maybe I never would be.

"If anyone should be guilty, it's me." Sandra dropped her eyes as she talked. "I didn't do right by you when you had your first depressive episode. I know that. I didn't at the time, I was foolish. But I know that now. I think that was when the demon first took a foothold. I should have helped you. I should have been the one to drive you to get help all those years ago. I'm forever in debt to Olivia for that but I can't erase my failings."

We sat in silence for a while. I ran her words over and over in my head. Years ago, I would have relished those words. The "I was wrong" and the "I'm sorry". Now, I didn't feel triumph. Only sadness that she was carrying that guilt.

"You can't erase it, that's true," I said tentatively. "But you can accept it and let it go. I have."

Sandra reached out and put her hand in mine. We sat in silence for a while, letting the tears rolling down our cheeks fill in the unspoken words.

"Wake up! You ready for push-ups yet?" Two weeks later, Alex burst through my hospital door. I had moved from intensive care to a regular room. I was ready to check out, but the doctors had been concerned with some aspects of my recovery — the Lichtenberg scars that no longer hurt but seemed to be permanent, and nerve pain flairs that came on in the evenings. The scars didn't bother me, but the nerve pain could take my breath away. Literally.

Alex was somehow paler than usual, but she was grinning, her right arm and shoulder in a huge cast. Keena was behind her, asking her to slow down.

"Slow down? Why would I slow down after I've looked death in the eye?" Alex plopped herself down in a chair, wincing as she leaned back. Keena brought a small pillow she was carrying and gently pushed Alex forward and slid it behind her left shoulder.

"Stop playing nurse, Keena. I'm fine."

"You're not. Do you want to be able to use your right arm again?"

"I could handle being one armed."

Keena rolled her eyes and smiled at me.

"So, Reva. How are you doing?" Alex looked at me after she settled into the chair. "Did you hear that Dawson is going to prison?"

"We don't know that yet," Keena interrupted. "The trial isn't even set yet. And he's out on bail."

"Officer Dickface was charged with assault with a deadly weapon, attempted manslaughter, attempted arson, and trespassing. All while off duty but using his police weapon. He's going down." Alex grinned with a fury in her eyes. I knew Alex well enough to know she would have preferred to seek out her own justice.

"We'll see. The justice system isn't known for holding police officers accountable." Keena frowned as she pulled up a chair. I suspected Keena would have preferred Alex was able to seek out justice as well, aside from the consequences.

Everyone else had been tiptoeing around what had happened that night. And that day when I had tried to run away. I had come to terms with my actions, and running away was the best way to describe it. Like a willful child, I had not thought through the impact of my actions on those I loved. Sitting in a hospital bed had given me time to work through some hard truths I had been avoiding.

"What about everybody else?" I asked, stalling on the harder questions.

"The angry mob?" Alex asked. She tried to shrug and grimaced in pain. "They scattered before the police showed up. Except for the poor bastard who was shot with friendly fire. There were so many of them there. The police have done nothing on that. I know who a lot of them are, though."

We all sat in silence, letting the frustration and hint of revenge seep in before Keena continued the thread.

"We were so worried about you, Reva. What happened to you that day?"

I took in a deep breath and filled them in with my story: leaving with Sunray, which they knew about since Sunray had been the one to alert them to my being gone; the chase to the post office; and the dead letter room.

"A dead letter room?" Keena said. "On the edge of the Other? Tell me more." She leaned in, fascinated as I dredged up all the details I could recall. When I finished, she grinned. "Darcy is going to want to hear about this!"

"We looked all over town for you," Alex said, not hiding her irritation. "We thought you were gone, either tied up in some dark Nazi basement with those shitheads or on a bus out of town."

"We were hoping it was out of town," Keena said softly. "For your sake."

I could hear in Keena's voice the hurt that I would up and leave them. But I saw an understanding in her eyes, that she knew how I ended up making the decision to run. I suspected she knew from personal experience. And that realization made me feel even guiltier for having caused them so much worry.

"Then the mob stormed the farm, and we knew you weren't with them. But at that point we were fighting for our lives and home." Alex didn't mince words or try to cover it up. The mob had come through the wards with the help of the demon seeker. The demon had learned enough by coming through earlier when it had showed up as Anthony on the doorstep, enough to pass on how to disarm them.

"What about the others, Sunray and everyone? Their homes were dark and untouched."

"Sunray and Lily hid in their house, putting all the lights out. Sunray was the one who called Wynona. Didn't know they even had each other's cell numbers. The others though —" Alex clamped her mouth hard, unable to finish.

"We think they were in on it. Particularly since the mob didn't go after their houses," Keena said. "They were all hiding out with Lonnie down at the store when it happened. A group of old biddies who never leave their cob houses suddenly all needed to have an outing. Suspicious."

"Sandra is furious," Alex said. "She's been looking into ways to dissolve the commune and see if those bitches can be kicked out."

"They may leave on their own," Keena said optimistically. Alex shook her head, clearly not expecting that.

"How long was the fight happening before I got there?"

"Long enough to burn a trailer or two," Alex said grimly but breezily, as if it wasn't her own home that had burned. "We were all in the house when we felt the wards go down, sort of like a cold breeze of static electricity. Sandra was clever in how she set them up."

"Darcy got the shield up quickly when we heard the cars coming up the drive. We didn't know there were others closer, on the edge of the property, so they were able to set fire to the trailers."

"Was Magpie in there?" I thought of Sandra's black and white cat, hoping for the best news.

"No. Fortunately. Sunray and Lily had brought him to theirs to get ready for Sandra's release from the hospital the next day. She was going to be staying with them. The timing was pure luck." Alex blew her breath out in a big gust. "Flame and Bear jumped the fence, or we would have lost them."

"They found me in the forest, led me home. Wait, Bear jumped the fence?" I imagined short Bear leaping over a burning fence. With a healing back leg, no less.

"It's the rottweiler in him," Keena said proudly.

The two continued telling me the details of the fight. Alex told the story of how she tried to talk with the demon seeker.

"He was looking for you, of course. I tried to tell him so were we. He wasn't really listening to me, but it was buying us time. Then that asshat Dawson shot me."

The bullet had wreaked havoc on Alex's shoulder. It had missed the artery, or she would have died, according to the doctors. And may have anyway without the help of the tribe.

"If they hadn't been there —"Tears pooled in Keena's eyes. "We would have lost Alex. And you."

"Though without you pulling that crazy stunt, everything would have gone wrong," Alex said after a spell.

"Was there a body?" I said, thinking of the demon seeker. Of Anthony.

"There wasn't," Keena said, knowing exactly who I was talking about. "It was just you in the end with the lightning. It's good news in some ways. None of us wanted to answer questions about a dead demon seeker. And none of the mob are talking. Not the fellow who was shot, who claimed he had wandered up to our house drunk. Definitely not Dawson. It's like they were under a spell that broke."

"Did anyone see the moment the lightning struck?" I asked. Who was the demon seeker? Was it Anthony? I couldn't conjure up the face of the demon seeker in my mind. That there was no dead body was not surprising to me, as there had been no questions from police about it or gossip trickling in about a lightning strike death. Disconcerting but not surprising.

"No one can really remember. You weren't that close to the house, and it happened so fast. It is a miracle you didn't receive more damage," Keena said.

"Your heart still stopped. You aren't invincible," Alex pointed out. "I guess Sora already told you what Mikhael did."

I nodded. I was hoping Mikhael would come and visit me so I could say thank you. But I also strangely understood his need to keep a distance. We barely knew each other. And I was clearly a mess and a half.

"Is it dead? The demon?" I asked. The one question I wanted to know more than anything. Was I free? Was I safe? I wanted an answer as concrete as a headstone on the demon's grave.

Keena looked at me with concern and shook her head. "You can't kill a demon. I do think you banished the hell out of that one, though. Do you still feel it?"

I had thought about searching for the piece of demon inside me but hadn't wanted to delve in, to press on it like a tender scab. But with my friends watching, I felt safe. I looked for the hard tendril that had taken root deep down internally and found nothing.

"It's gone." I smiled softly.

"You just had to die to get rid of it." Alex grinned.

"Unfortunately, that's probably not a joke. You probably did have to actually die for it to leave," Keena said sagely.

They continued to talk, about demons and narrow escapes. And more positive topics. Rebuilding and new connections. I sat back and listened. I had miles to go in my own healing. Not just from the lightning, which would forever be etched in my skin and nerves. Within myself, to learn to forgive and to embrace who I was. A stormweaver. A witch. And part of this coven of amazing women.

The End

About the Author

Beth Gibbs loves bringing the magic of the American West to life in her fiction. She writes about strong women, witches and spirits who face battles while living outside the norms. In all of her work, food plays a big role, due to her own love of culinary creations, and because a character going through rough times still needs to enjoy life. Beth lives in Portland, Oregon with her husband and loves to go on adventures, from local hikes  to road trips to walks all over the world. She has a background in fine arts and human resources and comes from a family of storytellers.

Ackowledgements

Though writing is considered a solitary pursuit, I'm never really alone when I write. First there almost always a small gray cat named Fofo sleeping by my side. And second there's always my community there in spirit saying "Keep going!" and "Don't delete that. Just keep writing," all the voices of support shutting down my own inner critic. And now I get to say thank you to all those who provide me the encouragement needed to thrive as a writer.

Huge thank you to the talented writers in my writing group: Lynne Allan, Stephanie Argy and Franny French. You are my first readers, my mentors and my cheering section. Without you and your honest supportive feedback, this book wouldn't exist.

A debt of gratitude to Not a Pipe Publishing: to Benjamin Gorman for hearing my nervous pitch and saying "I'm excited to read this!" and then saying "I'm excited to publish this!" To Karen Eisenbrey for editing the book to make it the best version of itself it could be. To Michaela Thorn for creating the stunning cover and bringing the image to life just through a few notes.

Unending thanks to my family and friends for their support: M.E. Gibbs, amazing sibling and pitch extraordinaire, for geeking out on writing with me and sharing all their advice. Amber Gibbs, fabulous sister for reading this book in the earlier stages and giving feedback. To my parents, Valerie and Bob Gibbs, for all their support and encouragement from the very beginning. To my friends, Rebecca Kane and Robin Song, for their constant cheering to chase this dream and modeling the pursuit of the creative life.

A very special appreciation to my departed grandfather, David Irwin, the first writer I ever knew and a master storyteller with a wicked sense of humor. I'm proud to carry on the family tradition.

And last but far from least, to my husband Dave for all the ways you support me, from giving me the gift of time to write, to reading the first hundred pages one morning while I slept and demanding the rest so you could know what happened. Thank you.